The AUCTION Series

MICHELLE WINDSOR

The WINNING Bid

The Auction Series Book One

MICHELLE WINDSOR

THE AUCTION SERIES: BOOK ONE

The WINNING Bid

MICHELLE WINDSOR

For my mom, who always believed I could do this, and for Doug, who let me.

Foreword

I wanted to state for readers that I do not consider this a 'BDMS' story, or a story of erotica. It's often classified as that by other readers, so I feel a need to clarify.

This is a love story. There are elements of Dom/Submissive behavior, however, as I do not live this lifestyle, I know without a doubt, what's expressed in this book may not be a true representation. I did do a ton of research online, and understand that this particular lifestyle is very different from what I've written, so please forgive an author for taking certain liberties in the story. I tell you this, the reader, so I don't set unrealistic expectations before you dive in. This is truly a work of fiction.

I hope you enjoy getting to know Drew and Scarlett as much as I enjoyed writing them!

xo Michelle

CHAPTER

One

NAKED AND NERVOUS, Hannah wondered if she was making the right decision. She knew what to expect but still shivered as she stood in line waiting for the auction to begin. It was too late to turn back now. The auction would begin in moments. There were six other women and two men standing with her, but unlike her, they were flushed and heated with anticipation. Two of the girls were practically panting.

Domme Maria, owner of Baton Timide, strutted down the line, loudly clapping her hands to draw the attention of each submissive. "All right, my little slaves, submission begins now!"

She opened the door and held it wide as each individual stepped through onto the adjoining stage, assuming their submissive position as trained. Hannah's heart hammered in her chest as each second brought her closer to her turn. Standing in the doorway twenty seconds later, Domme Maria hustled her onstage with a slap to her ass.

She darted across the stage and knelt as expected: hands open flat on her spread thighs, head and eyes down. The heat of the spotlight instantly warmed her nude body. She had never been on such blatant display before and was surprised at the surge of excitement that ran through her. Murmurs and exclamations of appreciation from the crowd rolled through her like thunder before a storm. She desperately wanted to lift her head and see the people in the room. It was her first time attending an auction and was curious to see if the room was filled with men, or if women were present too. She wondered if the men would be handsome, or if they would be older and more lecherous. Unable to resist, she tilted her head up just a pinch and peeked through her lashes to try to capture a brief glimpse of the crowd. Her eyes immediately locked on a dark-haired gentleman staring right at her. Her cheeks heated in embarrassment, and she quickly lowered her head and eyes, praying that no one else had noticed.

Only Master-level Dominant members of the exclusive club, Baton Timide, were allowed to participate in submissive auctions. They had to be a VIP member as well, which basically just meant they had to be filthy rich. She was a new submissive—a fact she hoped would push her bidding price higher. Dominants loved to break in a new submissive and would pay dearly for the privilege.

Auctioned submissives made twenty-five percent of the winning bid. The house took seventy-five percent. The minimum starting bid was fifteen thousand dollars, so she figured she could, at the very least, walk away with almost four thousand dollars for a few days' work—four thousand dollars closer to her dream, to purchase her own floral shop. The owner of the current shop she worked in was retiring and had agreed to sell it to her at an amazing price. The only caveat: the thirty-thousand-dollar down payment to secure the loan was due in three months. With no savings, no rich family and no fairy godmother waiting in the wings, this auction was her only hope.

Behind Hannah, Domme Maria closed the door the girls had just come through. She strutted past the lined subs, her black leather boots halting at center stage as she turned toward the gathered bidders. She was quite an intimidating force, with dark hair that gleamed like silk, a face that was almost porcelain white, and lips painted a blood red to accent her crisp blue eyes. Hannah could only guess how the club members perceived the Domme, but after training with her, the stunning woman could bring Hannah to her knees with a single glance.

"Welcome, ladies and gentlemen. It is my great pleasure, and hopefully yours, to bring you nine submissives to select from this evening."

Domme Marie smiled, turned and waved her hand toward the line of kneeling subjects. Shifting, she strolled to the first person in the row. She stroked the girl's long, flaxen hair like she was a new pet before ordering the sub to rise. Like Vanna White displaying a new puzzle, she presented the girl with a flourish. "Let me introduce you to Lahna, one of our more experienced submissives. She has no hard limits and quite thoroughly enjoys a bit of pain."

Validating her declaration, Domme Maria took the black leather riding crop in her hand and smacked Lahna across her breasts, leaving a bright red welt. Moaning, Lahna's head fell back, her eyes closing in distinct pleasure. Hannah was shocked by the sight. She'd expected to be showcased, but not to be so blatantly excited by it. And Lahna wasn't the only one affected. Peeking under her lashes and out across the people in the room again, Hannah saw one gentleman adjust himself as he moved closer to the display area.

While Domme Maria continued the introductions, Hannah discreetly continued her investigation of the room, her attention falling on the gentleman she'd locked eyes with earlier. Shifting her view upward, she realized he was staring at her again. Instead of diverting her gaze, she lifted her chin a fraction higher to boldly meet his eyes. He was breathtakingly handsome. His dark hair was smoothed back from his face but long enough to hit the collar on the black suit jacket he wore. A thin coating of stubble didn't distract from his chiseled chin, or the full lips currently set in a straight line. But it was his eyes that mesmerized her. They were dark, almond shaped and framed with a set of thick, full lashes. He was too far away for Hannah to be sure what color the irises were. As she continued to stare, the corner of his eyes crinkled as if he was stifling a laugh, and a slow grin spread across his face. Hannah's eyes flew wide before shifting her attention back to the floor under her knees. His grin was that of a feral hunter, and she just might be his prey.

Domme Maria continued down the row of submissives, displaying and touting each one's specialties and hard limits, until suddenly she was behind Hannah. The Domme stroked Hannah's long, wavy hair with a soft touch until suddenly grasping it firmly, yanking her head back.

Hannah's chest thrust forward as a small yelp of surprise escaped her.

"This very lovely lady is Scarlett, and this is her first time at one of our auctions." Domme Maria looked down, bending to brush a kiss across Hannah's lips before releasing her hair to gesture for her to stand.

As Hannah rose to her full height, Domme Maria surveyed the bidders and, with a sly smile, continued, "And oh yes, she tastes as delicious as she looks. She is a bit like a scared kitten though, with many hard limits, and will require a Master with patience to show her the pleasure in breaking some of those limits."

She stopped and scanned the room again before continuing, "and believe me, as I have personally trained her, there is a tigress waiting to emerge." Domme Maria skimmed her hand down Hannah's—no, *Scarlett's* body, stopping to cup her firm breast before pinching her nipple sharply, and then sashayed on to the next submissive.

Hannah dropped immediately into the submissive position again, looking down and taking a deep breath to try to calm her pounding heart. She was shocked to realize it was beating with excitement, not fear. And shock at the warm feeling between her legs when Domme Maria had pinched her nipple.

Realization struck. *This is definitely something I can do.* She could perform this role. *Here*, she was Scarlett, not Hannah. She could be whomever she chose to be, without any shame. Any doubts and fears she'd had evaporated, and excitement began to course through her instead.

Hannah knew she had made the correct choice for an alternate identity. When asked what name she'd wanted to be called, she had chosen Scarlett. Hannah was a closet romantic, and even though she had no illusions about finding her Rhett and living happily ever after, she loved what the name stood for. Scarlett O'Hara had been fearless, breaking boundaries for the things she loved and believed in. Hannah was here for the same reasons.

Domme Maria finished introducing the last submissive and retook center stage. "Ladies and gentleman, at this time, if you would like to personally inspect any of the submissives for auction, please do so, but keep in mind the rules of engagement prior to purchase. You may look, speak and touch—with the permission of the submissive only—but nothing more. You have exactly one hour before bidding begins." With that, Domme Maria strode off the stage and down to greet the bidders in the room.

There were only a dozen bidders at the auction, so the inspection period really didn't require a great length of time. But an hour of anticipation, on your knees, in submissive form, could seem like ten. Hannah kept her head down, trying to busy her mind and remain still and patient.

DREW TOOK a sip of his gin martini while casually appraising each submissive walking through the door. He was happy to see Jenna take a place onstage. He'd purchased the submissive at two previous auctions and had hoped she would be present again. The last three weeks had been hell, and he really needed this weekend to relieve some much needed stress. And he really wanted to do that

12

without any of the practicalities that a new submissive required.

Having already made up his mind about his bid for the evening, he was about to turn away and take a seat in the back of the room when the next woman walking across the stage caught his attention. Her head was down, her long, straw-colored hair hiding her features, yet he knew he'd never seen her before at an auction, or at any of the club events. She was someone he would have remembered.

Even without seeing her face, he knew she would be beautiful. She was petite. Not skin and bones, but perfect curves of honey-colored skin. Her breasts—tipped with small, dark pink nipples, already peaked and ready—would fit nicely into his hands. *Or better yet*, he thought, *in my mouth*. Her hips flared only slightly, but they weren't boyish, and her ass arched with a soft, yielding roundness.

As she stopped on the stage and knelt, she peeked up quickly, and in that instant, their eyes met. She immediately looked down again, cheeks flushing, palms flat on her spread thighs. Her hands trembled slightly, and he comprehended then that she must be a new submissive. He also realized his plans to purchase Jenna for the weekend had just gone out the window, practicalities be damned.

His undivided attention was focused on Domme Maria as the unknown blonde was introduced. *Her name is Scarlett.* And seeing her face now, albeit from a distance, confirmed that she was in fact beautiful. She gasped in surprise when Maria pulled her head back, but then softened when the Domme's lips met hers in a gentle kiss. When Maria tweaked Scarlett's nipple, her nervous energy disappeared. Her breath quickened and her body flushed a light pink, revealing her excitement. She may be a new submissive, but her behavior indicated she was made to be dominated. He had to have her.

He listened as Domme Maria finished the introductions and offered the submissives up for inspection. From the back of the room, Drew remained in his chair, lazily sipping his gin, as he waited to see what happened. He needed to appear aloof so as not to pique the interest or the challenging nature of some of the other Dominants in the room. In particular, he watched one of the other club members, Deacon Roberts. He was well known for his preference of new submissives. There was no doubt that Roberts would throw his hat in the ring for a chance at Scarlett.

Just as expected, within ten minutes of the submissive intros being completed, Roberts made his way to the stage and stopped directly in front of Scarlett. Drew got up, casually walking through the room to where refreshments were being served, which was several feet from the stage. He nibbled on a random appetizer while eavesdropping on the exchange between Benson and the new submissive.

HANNAH'S NECK was starting to feel a bit sore from keeping her head down. She was tempted to reach up and rub the back of it, but of course knew better. She remained still and waited patiently for whatever happened next, as trained. A pair of brown wing-tip shoes stopped in front of her, their owner looming over her. She wondered if it was the man she had locked eyes with. Or if she was being honest, hoped. If she was going to spend a weekend at someone's beck and call, why shouldn't that someone look mighty fine as well? A strong voice interrupted her thoughts and snapped her back to attention.

"Please rise, Scarlett. I'd like to inspect you." Hannah drew up from her knees, standing straight but continuing to look down, as taught. This wasn't her mystery man after all. *He* had worn a black suit, while this gentleman's suit was a darker tan. The man's breath ghosted over her skin, he was so close, and she caught a faint trace of whiskey on his breath. He finally spoke, ordering her to raise her head and look straight ahead. She did as she was told and was finally able to get a better look at him from her peripheral vision. He was five or six inches taller than she was and had dark blonde hair with darker blue eyes. About thirty-five or forty, he seemed to have a fairly good build. She stifled a sigh of relief. At least he wasn't hideous.

"Scarlett, may I touch you?" As had been explained to her in training, bidders were encouraged to check potential purchases for firmness of breast, or state of grooming, or smoothness of skin. She knew to consent immediately or risk not being bid on.

"Yes, Sir."

He nodded, then added under his breath, "Well, aren't you a good little submissive. So eager. So ready to please." He stroked a finger down the side of her neck and then back up toward her face. Hooking his finger into her mouth, he pulled it open harshly. "Oh yes, I think these lips would fit quite nicely around my cock."

Hannah's eyes widened in surprise, and she had to force herself not to retreat as the man stepped closer. He trailed his finger down to the juncture between her legs, then prodded her clit before pushing in just a little bit. "And this? I think I'll enjoy stuffing my cock in here even more."

Hannah tensed as the man spoke even more softly into her ear, "Oh yes, breaking you will be so much fun," and turned and walked off the stage. She stood, shocked, still staring ahead, as he barked one more order. "Kneel, Scarlett!" And she did, complying immediately.

DREW COULDN'T HEAR the exchange between Roberts and the new submissive, but he saw the fear in her eyes. He watched her body go rigid at his touch, and knew that Roberts had most likely crossed a line. Inside, rage soared, a possessiveness and a need to protect this girl overtaking him. It was a feeling he hadn't experienced before. But no matter its origin, he had to stay his course and remain calm so Roberts wouldn't notice his interest in Scarlett.

Drew decided not to go up and investigate her for fear of triggering Roberts' competitive nature. But he did want to get a closer look at this new submissive. So instead, he walked up on the stage, stopped in front of Jenna and asked her to rise. Jenna's posture straightened in obvious happiness, and he was hit with a moment of regret, knowing she would be disappointed when he did not bid on her.

"Jenna, you may look at me." Jenna lifted her head and smiled. She really was quite lovely. She was taller than average and possessed the body and grace of a dancer. Her short pixie cut suited her dark hair and exotic, angled features.

"How have you been, Jenna? You look lovely as always."

Her eyes sparkled with desire, and she responded breathily, "I am very well, Master. It is very nice to see you again. Have you been well, Sir?"

Drew looked down, shook his head and smiled. "Now Jenna, are you supposed to ask a Master a question?"

Jenna cast her eyes downward. "I'm sorry, Master. I meant no disrespect."

Drew couldn't help but notice Scarlett's head tilt slightly in their direction. A surge of satisfaction ran through him at the realization that she was listening to his conversation with Jenna. Just as quickly, another wave of guilt washed over him. No doubt Jenna would feel betrayed after his current attention didn't lead to a weekend together.

Drew smiled warmly and almost apologetically before taking Jenna's hand, kissing her knuckles kindly. "Kneel, Jenna, and be well."

Jenna kneeled immediately as he turned and walked back the way he'd come. He stopped, just for a moment, to look down at Scarlett. His hand rose to stroke her hair, but he stopped himself, drawing it quickly back to his side before continuing down off the stage.

Domme Maria made an announcement shortly thereafter: bidding was now open. Each Dominant could submit a starting bid for any given submissive. Once all bids were submitted, if a submissive garnered only one bid, Maria would text that bidder to let them know they'd won. If multiple bidders bid on a single submissive, Maria would text them all a request for a higher bid. No one would know who bid on which submissive. Each bidder was allowed a maximum of three bids on any one submissive. The highest bid after three rounds won.

Drew waited until every other Dominant had met with Maria before approaching her.

She smiled sweetly, if not seductively. "Master Drew, it is always a pleasure when you are in my house. Can I hope that you'll be placing a bid tonight?"

Drew took Maria's hand, swept his lips across her knuckles and graced her with one of his most charming smiles. She always felt so cold to him. "The pleasure is all mine, Madame. And yes, I will be placing a bid this evening."

He presented her a slip of paper with his bid for Scarlett: $25,000. Maria took the ticket and then nodded at him with a raised eyebrow.

"Well, this is a bit of a surprise. Not your usual taste." A sly smile curved her lips. "This should make for a very interesting night. Your girl has two other bids. Good luck."

"Thank you, Madame. May the best man win, right?"

Drew turned but not before Maria added one final word. "You mean may the best *Dom* win."

Drew went to the bar and asked for another gin martini. He usually had only one drink at these affairs, but to his surprise, he found himself a bit anxious, knowing Scarlett had two other bidders. Certainly Roberts was one of the bidders, but who could the other be? No one else had approached or inspected her. He slowly swept his eyes across the room to see if anyone's body language gave them away. He stopped on Roberts, who looked up at him and nodded. Drew nodded back and continued his search of the room. His phone buzzed with a text message: "High bid is currently $25K. Please submit new bid if so desired."

Well, at least he was the highest bidder so far. Now was the tricky part, what to bid next? As rich as Drew, Roberts was the only other Dom in the room who could compete. And like Drew, Roberts usually went after what he wanted, damn the cost. Drew decided to bid conservatively and submitted $30K.

Several minutes went by, and his phone buzzed with another text message: "High bid is currently $30.5K. Please submit a new bid if so desired." Drew scratched at the stubble on his chin and looked around the room. His gaze stopped on Maria, who was smiling broadly. She loved a good duel if nothing else. She nodded at him, just slightly, so as not to bring attention to herself from the other Dom's bidding. The other bidders were bidding conservatively. Time to take the opposite strategy and go large. He wanted this submissive, and he was going to make sure the other bidders knew it. It was the final bid, and he did not want to lose. He sent a text back with $50K. And waited.

After what seemed like an eternity but was really only four minutes, Drew's phone buzzed with another text: "Congratulations. You have won the bid. Your submissive will be delivered to your bungalow in thirty minutes. Please provide payment before your departure." Drew heaved a sigh of relief, then felt a surge of victory as he sat back and finished his martini.

CHAPTER
Two

AFTER THE BIDDING BEGAN, each submissive was escorted from the stage and into a comfortable sitting area. Each sub was provided a robe and a glass of water. Hannah practically gulped hers down. Between her nerves and being on display like an animal at the zoo, she was desperately parched. One of Maria's attendants, Lexie, came into the room and took a seat with everyone.

"For our more experienced submissives, you know what happens next." Lexie looked at Lahna, Jenna and the other experienced subs and nodded. "But for the new submissives, Scarlett and Helena, let me just review what will happen next."

Lexie switched her focus to Hannah and Helena and began. "In about fifteen minutes, one of the attendants will bring you to the residence you will be occupying this weekend. When you arrive, you are to go into the living room. Remove your robe, and then kneel in the submissive position until your Master arrives."

Hannah's heart pounded in anticipation, finally grasping how real the decision she'd made to sell herself had just become.

"Now, this is the hard part—the waiting, the not knowing who your Master will be for the weekend. Please try not to be too nervous. Remember everything you've learned in your training sessions. Your Master should ask you for a safe word almost immediately. Don't be afraid to use it if you need to, but also remember, once the safe word is used, the weekend is over, and the amount of money you make will be prorated for the amount of time your services were actually provided."

Would the man that had so *intimately* inspected her be her Master? Because she believed using the safe word would probably be required. All of the Doms had been provided their submissives' soft and hard limits, she still had to wonder just how far she would be willing to go to earn the money she needed. There was something about the blonde that just screamed a need for control, and she was afraid he might use a lot of pain to get it.

Lexie took a breath, looked at everyone and said, "You have one job: be submissive. From 8:00 p.m. this evening until 5:00 p.m. Sunday evening. Any questions?"

Surprisingly, Lahna, who had scared Hannah a bit after the demonstration onstage, leaned forward and took her hand. "Don't worry, Scarlett. You'll be fine. Just remember what you learned, don't question your Master, and you may even enjoy yourself." She squeezed Hannah's hand before letting go.

"Thank you." Hannah was truly touched. Finding any kind of solidarity was not anything she'd expected within a group of submissives. "I really appreciate hearing that. I have to admit, I'm more nervous than I thought I would be."

Lexie rose then, and at the same time, nine attendants arrived to take each sub to their weekend residences.

Hannah's attendant introduced herself as Rose. Wearing a gauzy white dress that floated around her, she was extremely soft-spoken and only seemed to speak when absolutely necessary. She had shoulder-length, strawberry-blonde hair and the softest, palest complexion Hannah had ever seen. She led Hannah to a golf cart and started off on one of the paths to the many private residences nestled throughout Baton Timide's property.

The sky was starting to darken earlier now, a reminder that summer was ending and transcending into fall. Only an hour outside of New York City, the estate was like another world. Given the dense forest that surrounded them, it was hard to believe a concrete jungle was mere miles away. Between the night air and the very light robe Hannah was wearing, she started to shiver.

"I'm sorry. Are you cold Scarlett?" Rose inquired quietly from her side of the cart.

Hannah nodded to indicate she was, "A little bit."

"We won't be but another moment." Rose looked over at her with an apologetic look on her face, "We haven't brought the heavier robes out yet. I'll remind Domme Maria that it may be time."

"Thank you Rose."

As promised, Rose pulled up in front of a bungalow within a matter of minutes. She led Hannah to the front door and opened it. "You are aware of your next instruction?" Rose asked quietly.

"Yes, I am to disrobe and wait in my submissive pose until my Master arrives."

"Very good. I will take my leave now. Have a good evening." And with that, Rose walked out of the bungalow and shut the door gently behind her.

Hannah wanted to explore the bungalow, even though she had been given a tour of one previously. It was different, knowing this is where she would stay all weekend. Where she would experience . . . well, she wasn't sure what she would experience. Time would answer that question. But she knew she had to comply with the directions given or face punishment. Domme Maria had advised all the submissives that there were cameras throughout the house to monitor behavior. Hannah was quite sure taking a tour would not fall into the good behavior department.

As instructed, she went into the bedroom and left her robe on a hook in the dressing room. There were hangers upon hangers of different outfits: dresses, suits, costumes. She ached to run her fingers through them but turned away, shut the door and went into the living room. She positioned herself beside the couch, faced the door and knelt as required.

As Hannah waited, her thoughts turned again to the identity of her new Master. Even if the scary blonde was her Master, she was there to do whatever made her Dom happy, which should thus result in him treating her well. She had no doubt that she could perform sexually. She liked sex and was actually looking forward to being more submissive. Her everyday life was so regimented and required so much control all of the time. It would be nice to not have to think and just let someone else be in charge. But the few sexual partners she'd had in the past had always involved a relationship. Not knowing who she would be with, or what this person would be like, was a bit frightening. Some Dominants thrived on punishment and humiliation. She silently prayed for a kind Dominant while reminding herself that this weekend was the only solution to obtaining the money she needed without actually selling herself on a street corner. Hopefully this sacrifice could provide the security she needed.

Hannah was beginning to wonder if her Master was ever going to arrive. She had been down on her knees for at least forty-five minutes and was beginning to lose the feeling in her legs. Plus, she was cold. She hadn't had enough time to warm up in the bungalow before having to strip naked again. She was also starting to get hungry, her stomach letting out a small growl at the thought of food. And thirsty too, now that she was thinking about it. Listening to the clock tick, she tried to keep her thoughts focused on keeping her position.

Footsteps on the porch sent her heart racing, erasing all other concerns from her mind. She made sure her legs were spread apart appropriately, that her hands were palm up on her thighs and let her gaze slip to the floor. *Please, god, let this work out okay.* The door clicked open and then shut again quietly. She wanted to look up so badly to see who her Master would be, but she dared not break a rule so soon.

Instead of footsteps coming into the living room, she heard a jacket being removed and placed on what may have been a chair. It was amazing what your brain could decipher by sound alone when required. Then the footsteps headed toward the kitchen. The refrigerator was opened, and something was removed. Then a glass was taken down from a cupboard, and a drawer was rifled through. A pop, and then liquid was poured not once, but twice. Then footsteps again, but this time walking toward her. They stopped in front of her, and two glasses were set down on a table before he moved and sat on the couch closest to her. It was then that she noticed the shoes in front of her weren't brown. They were black—and definitely not wing tips. She almost sighed in relief, but . . .

Who did *buy me, then?*

DREW TOOK his time arriving at the bungalow. He had finished his drink at the clubhouse and then decided to walk to the residence. He'd wanted time to think about the direction he was going to take with this submissive. It was clear from the auction display that she was new, and she was also nervous. But when she'd met his stare and hadn't backed down, he'd also known there was a strength in her that would need a little bit of bending and molding. More than anything, he really wanted to *look* at her.

The short eye contact they'd had wasn't enough for him to really assess her. He'd hated not going up and speaking with her at the auction, but his strategy had worked. He was quite sure that if Roberts had known who his opponent was, Drew would have ended up paying sixty thousand instead of fifty. Not that the money mattered. He made that much in interest every hour. One of the perks to being a billionaire that he didn't mind enjoying.

He walked quickly up the steps of the bungalow and entered. She was waiting for him, kneeling submissively, in the living room. Just seeing her like that, and knowing it was for him, instantly fueled his lust. Instead of going to her, he removed his jacket and then walked to the kitchen to retrieve a bottle of water. She had been waiting for some time and was probably thirsty, if not hungry. If he was being truly honest with himself, he also needed a moment to gather his frayed control before speaking with her.

He took two glasses from the cupboard, filled each with the water he had opened and then made his way back into the living room. He placed the glasses down on a side table, stopping to gaze down at her a moment before sitting down on the couch. Much to Drew's enjoyment, she never broke her submissive position. She evidently already wanted to please him and she didn't even know who he was yet. He leaned forward to caress the long, wavy tresses away from Scarlett's face, pushing them over her shoulders and down her back. She shivered, and he wanted to do what he could to make her feel safe and unafraid.

"Scarlett, rise and stand before me, please." Drew spoke softly so as not to scare her.

She rose immediately and stood before him, blonde hair cascading almost to her lower back, some falling forward to conceal her breasts. And he had been correct—her face was as beautiful as her body. She had a heart-shaped face with a bit of a long chin that was balanced by her lips, a soft pink and full. A petite nose—not quite a button, but it could only be described as cute, small, straight. It was her eyes that captivated him though. They were the color of caramel, the lightest shade of brown, almost golden. They were surrounded by thick lashes, unusual for a fair-haired woman. He guessed her to be twenty-four, possibly twenty-five. He stood and placed a finger under her chin, tilting her face upward so he could see her eyes more closely. They had chocolate flecks in them. In the right light, he was sure those flecks shimmered.

She said nothing as she kept her eyes glued to his, and he admired her for it. She would be a good sub. He remained silent and swept her hair back over her shoulders. He backed up and looked at her now, really looked at her. Onstage, she'd been beautiful; up close, she was a knockout. Her breasts really were perfection. He loved the small nipples peaking under his examination. He wanted to touch her, but not yet. He wanted her to feel comfortable first, and she was shaking with nerves.

He cupped her face, again tilting it to him, and said, "You don't need to be afraid of me, Scarlett. I will not hurt you. I hope to bring you more joy and fulfillment over this weekend than you have ever had with a man before."

"Sir, I'm not afraid of you. I'm cold," Hannah murmured. It was the first time he had heard her voice, and it was like the most beautiful notes of music were being played. Stifling his reaction to that melody, he responded to her needs instead.

"I apologize. Please tell me immediately if you are ever uncomfortable." Drew turned, walked into the bedroom and came out with a fur blanket that had been on the end of the bed. He wrapped it around her, then motioned toward the couch. "Please, sit down."

HANNAH SAT and pulled the blanket closer around herself. The fur was luxuriously soft against her skin, and she was already beginning to warm. She was still in a bit of shock from discovering the very man she had made eye contact with at the auction had purchased her.

She watched as he moved to the thermostat on the wall to turn up the heat. "Thank you, Master."

He turned and smiled pleasantly at her while returning to the couch, sitting next to her.

"You may call me Drew or you may address me as Sir. I only request that you reply appropriately when addressed." He shifted and reached for one of the water glasses he had brought into the room, then handed it to her. "It's seltzer water with lime. Very light and refreshing."

"Thank you, Sir." She took the glass from him and sipped it. It was delicious, and anything in her stomach right now felt wonderful.

He brought the second glass to his lips. She noticed how his lips arched around the rim of the glass as the liquid met his mouth. The short stubble outlining his chin and mouth was in stark contrast to the elegance of the glass he held.

As he sipped, he looked over the glass at her, his eyes intense. She could see now that his eyes were actually a very dark blue. Was he Irish? No, then they would have been green. Perhaps Greek? When his dark brows furrowed in thought, it gave him an edge, a gravity beyond his years. He was, what, thirty-five? He pulled the drink away from his mouth and placed it on the table.

"Let's start with some preliminaries. We must pick a safe word, although I hope we never have to use it. My goal as your Master is to make you feel safe and bring you contentment, which in turn will make me happy."

Hannah nodded. "Yes, Sir. Do you have a word you would like me to use?"

Drew shrugged. "We can use the standard 'yellow' if you are at a point where I make you nervous, but you must choose the actual word. Choose a word that you won't use in everyday conversation but one that will be at the tip of your tongue if needed."

Without any further thought, Hannah blurted out, "Ghost."

Drew nodded in acceptance. "If you ever feel unsafe or scared or like you're going to break, use this word. But only in those instances. In normal circumstances, we would have more time and I would learn what your boundaries are, but in the course of three days, this obviously isn't possible."

Hannah nodded and sipped more of the water. Between the blanket and the heat blowing through the vents, she was slowly thawing out.

"Domme Maria gave me the list of your hard limits. I have no issue with any of them and understand the need for most of them, although I would like to discuss the option of possibly altering one or two of them though, once you have gained more trust in me. Is that something you are open to?"

"Which limits would you like to change, Sir?"

Drew reached for his water and took a sip before responding. "Well, I'd like you to reconsider swallowing."

Hannah blushed and, taking several large gulps, finished off the rest of the water in her glass.

Drew chuckled at her reaction and then continued, "I'm sorry. I know this is an awkward discussion to have, but much better to have it now than later. When we are in the act and your warm mouth is sucking my cock, I will not want to stop. I will want to enjoy that moment. Do you understand?"

Hannah blushed crimson at his bluntness, a bit mortified at having to actually discuss her aversion to giving a blow job. "Yes, Sir, I understand. I would like to give you this pleasure, but I'm afraid I'll throw it back up on you. It's just never been my thing. I'm sorry."

Drew laughed. "All right, well, let's chalk that up to a maybe. Perhaps I can get you to change your mind. I also want to define what entails excessive pain methods for you."

Hannah nodded again, now going a bit pale as she wondered how far over her own personal boundaries she may actually have to go. In training, it had seemed so easy to safe word out. But in the here and now . . . "Okay. What do you want to know?"

Drew rose off the couch, took Hannah's glass and started walking into the kitchen. "Let me get you another glass of water, and we can finish discussing."

Drew was back within a moment and handed her a refilled glass before settling back down on the couch. "Okay, pain. Can I use clamps? Nipples and on your clit?"

Hannah nodded in response, gulping almost audibly. "Yes, as long as they aren't weighted or too tight."

"Okay, very good. What about cuffs? I know you agreed to be restrained, but are you opposed to metal, zip ties, ropes?"

Hannah couldn't believe she was discussing this, even though Domme Maria had explained this would occur. And really, it was a good Dom who did discuss these things. "Cuffs are okay. I prefer not to use metal. I have to go back to the real world on Monday and don't want to have to explain any marks. Rope is okay. Zip ties are possible, again, as long as they don't leave any marks."

"Okay, perfect. That's enough for now. I'm not sure how much torture I can fit into a single weekend anyway," Drew said with a wink.

Hannah's eyes were wide as she nodded in acknowledgement, not sure if she was hiding her apprehension very well. She must not have been doing a good job, because Drew took one of her hands in his, holding it reassuringly.

"I will do nothing to hurt you." He smiled wryly. "Well, at least nothing you don't want me to do. I will listen to what you want, and I know what your limits are. Don't be afraid. That's the last thing I want you to feel about me. Understood?"

Her relief must have been palpable as she smiled because Drew leaned over and kissed her gently on the cheek, as if to seal his promise to her. He stood up then and looked down at her questioningly.

"Are you warmer now? And when was the last time you ate? Because I'm starving."

Hannah nodded to indicate she was much warmer, and her stomach growled loudly as if it, too, was responding to

Drew's question. They both looked at her stomach and laughed.

"Okay, why don't you get dressed while I make us something to eat in the kitchen? Some Doms prefer their subs stay naked at all times when present. I am not one of them. I prefer a woman in lingerie. Silky, lacy, sexy. When we are here, in this house, I want you dressed as such."

Hannah stood and wrapped the blanket around her, more now for security than warmth. "Yes, Sir."

She knew she was lucky to have been purchased by a Dominant who seemed to be gentle and caring. If the other man had purchased her instead, her evening probably would have taken a much different turn. She hoped her first impression of him proved correct.

CHAPTER
Three

HANNAH WALKED into the bedroom and pulled open the drawer of the wardrobe. She gasped at the beautiful colors and fabrics that were revealed. Mostly silks, but some lace, but all in beautiful jewel tones of sapphire, emerald, ruby and onyx. There were more undergarments in the drawer than she could wear in two weeks, let alone two days.

She had no idea what Drew's preferences were, but black was always a classic. There was a gorgeous pair of silk boy-shorts, cut high in the back and trimmed with lace. She pulled those on and found the matching bra. The material of the bra was of the sheerest silk, again trimmed in lace that matched the panties. The demi-cups pushed her breasts up, almost spilling her nipples over the top of the lace. She felt incredibly sexy, sexier than she'd ever felt naked. There were garters and hose and beautiful, high-heeled shoes, but she decided to keep things simple and forgo those accessories for the time being.

Hannah walked into the kitchen to find Drew at the counter, his back to her, chopping something on a wooden block. He stilled and then turned as she entered. She stopped and waited for his next command.

He had removed his tie and released the top few buttons on his dress shirt, revealing dark, curly hair on his chest. His shirtsleeves were rolled up, and he had fastened a makeshift apron around his waist by tucking a dish towel into his belt. He still wore his dress slacks and shoes, but he looked completely at ease in the kitchen. A wicked smile spread across his face as his gaze traveled over the length of her body.

"Scarlett, you look amazing. If I didn't know you were so hungry, I'd throw you up on that counter right now and have my way with you."

Wiping his hands on the towel at his waist, he walked slowly around her and then stopped directly in front of her. He grasped her behind the neck and pulled her to his mouth for a kiss. Soft at first, he swept his tongue against her lips, urging her to open them, and then caressed the inside of her mouth, entwining his tongue with hers.

She could taste the bit of lime that had flavored their water, but the connection was anything but refreshing; it was searingly hot. As the kiss became more urgent, Drew pulled her up against his body, his hand no longer gentle on her neck but sliding firmly to her backside, pressing her into his hardened length.

Hannah moaned as she wrapped one hand around his waist, clutching onto his shirt back, while the other fisted in his hair, trying to deepen the kiss consuming her. Their chemistry was electric, like a bolt of lightning had struck them both. Drew broke away from her mouth slowly, trailing a line of wet kisses down her throat, stopping at the base of her neck, nipping lightly before she felt him pull away from her.

Hannah regarded Drew with hooded eyes, curious why he stopped. Drew grasped her chin, lightly kissed her lips and then pointed to a stool at the counter. "Sit. I need to feed you, and then we can finish that kiss." Hannah looked at the stool, looked at him and then did as he asked.

Drew walked back to the counter and returned to cutting a tomato. "Grilled chicken salad okay?" Drew looked over his shoulder at her.

She nodded her approval, but kept silent. He stopped chopping and turned around again.

He looked at her with hard eyes and, his tone short, asked, "Don't you mean, 'Yes, Sir'?"

Hannah flushed red, nodded again and forced out a weak, "Yes, Sir."

"I need you to respond to me verbally, Scarlett. Is that understood?"

"Yes, Sir," Hannah responded quickly, chastising herself for forgetting the most basic of command responses within an hour of being a submissive.

"Good. There will be no misunderstandings this way." He finished chopping all the chicken and vegetables and swept them into a bowl. "Do you have a preference on salad dressing? I was going to use a balsamic, if that's okay?"

"Balsamic is fine, Sir."

Drew poured a small amount of dressing into the salad, grabbed a fork, pulled up a stool and sat in front of her. He was so close that her knees were inside of his spread legs.

He punched the fork into the bowl, spearing a piece of chicken and some lettuce before bringing the fork up to her mouth.

"What are you doing?" Hannah asked as she leaned back away from the fork.

Drew frowned in obvious frustration. "I'm going to feed you."

"Why? I can feed myself." Hannah knew she shouldn't question a Dom, but it seemed silly to have someone feed her like a two-year-old.

"Because I want to. It gives me pleasure to take care of your needs." Drew looked down and, after letting out a long breath, said in a sterner tone, "And if you question me again, I will punish you. Do you understand?"

Hannah nodded and replied meekly, "Yes, Sir."

"Good. Now open up and eat."

Drew raised the fork to her lips, and this time she complied, taking it into her mouth. He slowly slid the fork out, his eyes never leaving hers as he speared more of the salad and again held the fork to her mouth.

His eyes still locked on hers, a warmth gathered low in Hannah's belly as it became apparent that feeding her was a much more intimate act than she'd realized. While she chewed, he fed himself bites of the salad, using the same fork. They remained silent throughout, eyes always on each other.

Drew put the fork down after several more bites and brought a glass of ice water to her lips, tilting it until the chilly water slid into her mouth and down her throat. Every action he performed had an undertone of sexuality, of what was sure to come. He fed her several more bites until she shook her head to indicate she was done.

"Had enough?" Drew asked, raising his brow.

"Yes, Sir."

"More water?"

"Yes, Sir."

Drew raised the glass to her mouth again. Ice cubes gathered against her lips, creating a damn, causing some of the cold water to spill over the glass, down her neck and onto her breasts. Hannah pulled away quickly, bringing her hands up to her chest to try and stop the spill.

"Stop." Drew stood up quickly, causing Hannah to jump and look up at him timidly under her long lashes.

"I'm sorry, Sir. It was a natural reaction to try and stop the spill."

He blew out a slow exhale and then spoke in a firm tone. "Go in the bedroom, kneel beside the bed, and wait."

Hannah looked up at him again apologetically and whispered, "Yes, Sir," before walking quickly into the bedroom and kneeling in position as ordered.

She was thoroughly embarrassed, her body flushing a bright pink as her heart beat more quickly in her chest. Drew was beautiful, and so far, gentle, and did nothing but offer kindness, but she couldn't seem to follow the simplest of orders to please him. She'd had training—she knew better.

It was that kiss. That hot, wet, *'please throw me up on that counter and fuck me'* kiss that had her head rattled. After that kiss, and the way he'd stared longingly at her mouth with every bite he fed her, her body hummed with desire. Who could think straight feeling that way? Not her, that was evident. She needed to gather some control over these desires, or his frustration with her was sure to either lead to some type of punishment, or worse, disinterest.

DREW CONTINUED to pace in the kitchen after cleaning up the salad dishes. He knew a maid was available to perform the task, but he needed something to keep his mind busy as he got his emotions under control.

Confusion swirled inside of him. He wanted to take Scarlett over his knee and turn her bottom a light shade of crimson, but he also knew she was a new submissive and didn't want to scare her. Trying to control his needs, his desire to do the right thing, wasn't something that came naturally to him.

What was it about this girl that made him so soft, so yielding against her disobedience? He needed to punish her if he was to teach her to be a good sub and what his expectations were, but damn, the thought of doing anything that might frighten or scare her away made him hesitate.

Besides, weren't these girls supposed to be already trained? Why did he feel so beholden to treat this girl with kid gloves? The last three weeks had been hell for him, and he had been looking forward to fucking his way back to being halfway sane again. Instead, she was making him crazier. He had barely been able to stop himself from throwing her up on the counter and driving himself into her during that kiss, and if he didn't do something to regain some of his control, it would never happen.

"Fuck it." Drew grabbed a large pitcher from the cabinet, filled it with ice and water and walked quickly into the bedroom.

Scarlett was kneeling in position at the corner of the bed, her head down. "Get up, Scarlett."

Scarlett stood up quickly but kept her head down.

"Look at me."

Scarlett complied as he placed the pitcher down on the bedside table next to her.

He stepped closer, grasped her chin lightly and bent down so his face was within inches of hers. "You will do what I ask, when I ask for it, however I ask for it. And you will not question me. Is that understood?"

Scarlett tried to nod, but he held her chin firmly as a reminder to answer him verbally. She refused to meet his gaze but replied, "Yes, Sir."

"Good girl. Now I want you to reach above your head and grasp the bedpost behind you."

Drew didn't move an inch as Scarlett obeyed, the position arching her back, pushing her breasts out, brushing her nipples up against him.

"This is about you learning to obey my commands. Whether you like it or not. Your job is to do what pleases me. Do you understand?"

She responded quietly, "Yes, Sir."

"Good. Remember that."

Drew let go of her chin, took a step away from her and pulled his shirt over his head, exposing his broad, sculpted chest. He worked out almost daily to maintain a fit frame, and the result was a well-defined set of abdominals and a trim waistline. His arms flexed as he grasped the shirt and threw it in a chair across the room. Her eyes raked over his naked torso and darkened in what appeared to be desire. Seeing her reaction brought on a wave of his own desire that further hardened his cock.

Drew grabbed the pitcher and stopped a few inches before her. He leaned into her and whispered in her ear, "I can see how hot this is making you. Let me help cool you off."

He raised the pitcher over her chest, tilted it and slowly let the cold water and ice spill over and onto her chest. She gasped in shock at the cold water, sputtering as it splashed up, hit her mouth and ran in small waves down her body.

She let go of the post in an attempt to wipe the water from her face, but Drew spoke in a commanding tone before she could. "No, Scarlett. Do not let go of that post."

He continued to pour the entire pitcher of water over her chest, causing her already sheer bra to become completely transparent, her chest heaving as she drew in deep gasps in reaction to the cold.

He panted with need, watching Scarlett cling to the bedpost as she groaned and twisted from the shock of the cold water and ice. He dropped the empty container onto the carpeted floor and grasped her roughly at her sides, bent his head, and pulled one of her nipples into his mouth. He brought one hand to the other breast, pinching the already hard nipple, before sliding the wet fabric of the bra under her breast, freeing it.

His mouth was an inferno as it moved over her cold, wet nipple, sucking and nipping, while he peeled the fabric down below the other breast, baring it as well. Using both hands, he pushed her breasts together, sucking on both nipples. Scarlett still held onto the post with a firm grip, not letting go, moaning in pleasure as he continued to relish her breasts.

Drew moved his body up against her, wrapping his arm around her back, yanking her into his hard length. Scarlett reacted by rubbing up and down on him, pressing her core tighter to him.

He pushed her back suddenly and looked down. "No, Scarlett. No relief for you. This is all about what I want. When you please me and learn to obey me, that's when you get your reward."

HANNAH'S EYES widened in disbelief, even though she knew what he was doing. This was torture in its finest form. Her punishment. And she would and could play this game. She had to think about the money at the end of the weekend and what that money would ultimately do for her.

She would obey, even if it meant she would be aching for release if he kept this up. "Yes, Sir."

"Good." He lifted a hand and used a finger to make a twirling motion. "Turn around. I want you bent over with your hands back on that post."

Hannah complied and immediately felt Drew against her backside. He ran his hands down her hair, then draped it down over one shoulder, leaving her back bare. He bent over her then, his lower body flush with hers. His soft lips peppered kisses down her back, stopping only when he got to her panties. He hooked his fingers into each side and pulled them down around her ankles, guiding her to step out of them. His breath caressed up her legs as he slowly worked his way back up her body, before placing a hand on her lower back, pushing it down flatter.

"Open your legs more, and hold the bedpost lower. And don't let go."

Hannah obeyed immediately. "Yes, Sir."

Her entire backside was exposed in this position, but instead of feeling embarrassed, she felt wanton. She curved her back even further as Drew continued his advance up her body, anxious to feel him between her legs now.

He was running his tongue up the inside of her thigh, the stubble of his chin lightly scraping against the tender skin as he got closer to her apex and the growing heat pooling there. She couldn't contain the groan that escaped her as his tongue flicked against her clit in a swiping motion.

He let out a small growl, the vibration stimulating her further. She threw her head back, groaning in frustration, wishing he would fuck her already. Instead, he licked her again and then sucked just the tip of her clit, biting it gently before letting go. She was so close to exploding but didn't want to disobey Drew or worse, disappoint him.

She panted desperately, "Sir, I'm going to come if you keep doing that."

Drew stood up, then leaned over her back, his lips at her ear. "Will you obey me now, little one? Do you feel now just how much pleasure I can bring you?"

Hannah whimpered, "Yes, Sir. God, yes. I'll be better."

Drew pulled away taking a couple steps back. His shoes hit the floor with a thunk, then his pants. She was panting with desire for him. She looked over her shoulder and watched as he stroked his hardened cock. His eyes fixed on hers as he stepped forward again, lining himself flush against her body. He reached down between her legs and stroked her slick pussy with his cock. She pushed herself back against him and down on his cock.

"Tsk, tsk. Remember, Scarlett, this is about what I need right now."

She gasped in surprise as a hard smack suddenly landed on her ass, and stopped her pushing back onto Drew's cock. His very hard, very generous length continued to rub back and forth against her pussy. *How in the world does he expect me not to come when he keeps doing that?*

"Are you ready?" Drew pushed down on the center of her lower back with one hand, causing her ass to arch even higher, as he slid his cock into her pussy in one quick thrust. He stayed seated for a moment before grasping her shoulder with his other hand and then began to glide back and forth in a steady motion.

Hannah couldn't help herself—she moaned loudly and pushed back to meet him thrust for thrust. The hand at her shoulder tightened, and the other moved to her waist as Drew surged into her harder and deeper. She was so close. She could feel the build of her orgasm as she grasped tighter onto the bedpost.

"You may *not* come, Scarlett," Drew gritted between clenched teeth as he continued to slam into her.

"Oh god, Drew, please. I don't think I can stop. Please," she begged.

Drew let go of his grip on her waist and smacked her ass again, this time harder. "No! You may not come!"

She shrieked from the smack and then held her breath and tried to think of anything else but the build of her impending climax.

Drew clutched both his hands on her waist now and thrust three more times, hard and deep, before groaning in relief. His hot seed coated her insides with his final push. He held onto her tightly for a moment, his cock jerking slightly at the last of his release, before slowly sliding out of her.

Hannah moaned in frustration as he stepped away, leaving her feeling empty and cool all at once, and without an ounce of relief. Her pussy was hot and wet and pulsing. Not to mention her ass was tingling where Drew had smacked her. *He's going to leave me feeling like this? Goddamn bastard.*

Drew pulled her into an upright position, turning her in his arms. He nuzzled the nape of her neck and whispered, "Thank you for that. It was amazing." He trailed the softest kisses up her neck until he reached her mouth, fusing his lips against hers in passion. She was surprised by his sudden tenderness and felt herself soften and mold into him and his kiss. How could he go from one extreme to another so quickly?

He pulled back and pushed the hair away from her face, looking down at her. "Do you need anything? Some water?"

She raised her eyebrows in disbelief and laughed. "Seriously? I think I've had enough water for now."

46

Drew chuffed and pulled her back into his embrace. "Ah yes. I guess so."

He hugged her quickly and then, taking her hand, led her to the adjoining bathroom. "Let's get you cleaned up then, shall we? Do you prefer a bath or a shower?"

"That depends . . . Are you joining me?" she asked coyly.

Drew smiled. "You know what? I think I will join you."

"Then I prefer a bath." Hannah's cheeks growing warm at the admission.

Drew bent down and kissed the tip of her nose. "Your wish is my command. Why don't you go find us something to change into after our bath while I start the water?"

"Okay. Do you have something specific you'd like me to wear, Sir?" Hannah fluttered her lashes and looked up at him with her most innocent and demure look, hoping to draw another laugh from him.

He took the bait and grinned. "Oh, I see you're finally getting the hang of this. I suppose I'll have to keep that last punishment in mind in case you forget."

She blushed, but smiled and responded, "I won't forget again, Sir. I promise."

Drew leaned over the very deep, very large oval tub and started running the water to fill it. "I'd prefer you to sleep naked so I can feel you against me whenever I want." Drew raked his gaze down her still-nude body, causing her to blush again at his brazenness.

Feeling emboldened by Drew's approval of her body, Hannah replied in a quiet voice, "I can do naked. If it means being up against you again."

She thought she saw a spark of desire in Drew's eyes before he turned and started walking back toward the bedroom. "I'll go get us something to drink while the water is running. There are usually several types of bath salts and bubbles under the sink if you'd like to pick something out and add it to the tub."

"Okay, thank you, Sir."

She used the toilet and cleaned herself up a bit. It was strange to think of having sex with a relative stranger without having a discussion about protection. When she'd become an employee of the club, her blood had been tested for sexually transmitted diseases. She'd also had to agree to birth control and regular testing to confirm she stayed clean.

She found a bottle of ginger-scented bubble bath and added it to the running water. Once the tub was about half full, she decided to climb in and wait for Drew to return.

Before stepping in, she wound her long hair up into a bun and knotted it at the top of her head. The tub was so deep that it had an actual step around half the inside perimeter to use.

She slowly lowered herself into the hot, bubbly water. The heat felt so good against her skin, a stark contrast from the ice-water shower she'd just endured, causing her to sigh in pleasure. When the warm water hit her core, it stung a moment from the aggressive fucking she'd just received, but after a moment in the water, she felt nothing but soothed. Hannah scooted herself up against the far side of the tub wall, leaned back and let herself relax.

Still naked, Drew walked in a moment later, carrying two glasses of white wine, and set them on the ledge of the tub. She couldn't help but admire him, her eyes taking in his entire body.

"I thought this might be refreshing in the tub. How's the water?"

Hannah reached across the tub to take a glass of the wine. "It's divine. Are you coming in?"

In response, Drew stepped into the tub, grabbed the other glass and settled himself down across from her. His legs were long and instead of moving them to the side, he entwined them with hers.

"What scent did you choose for the bubbles? I love it."

"It's ginger. I was so happy when I saw it. It's one of my absolute favorite scents. I'm glad you like it as well."

Drew nodded. "I do."

There was silence between them then, but Drew didn't take his eyes off of her. "You're quite beautiful, Scarlett."

Hannah blushed at the compliment. "Thank you. You're quite beautiful too. But I'm sure you're aware of that already."

Drew smiled. "Yes, well, I suppose I've been called handsome. Tall, dark and mysterious. Rich always helps, of course." He looked down into the water and then back up at her. "But I don't think I've been called beautiful."

She took another sip of her wine and frowned slightly. "Well, I think you're beautiful. I don't think I've ever seen or been with a man as beautiful as you. I really don't think I want you to put your clothes back on this weekend."

Drew threw his head back and laughed. "Well, you're in luck, because I don't think I want you to put your clothes back on all weekend either."

She smiled broadly, raising her eyebrows in a teasing fashion. "I guess that takes some of the mystery out of what I'll be doing while I'm here."

He grinned back. "Tell me more about yourself. Are you a new submissive or just new to Baton Timide?"

She gazed into the water before answering. She had been warned by Domme Maria to only expose what she really needed to about herself and to try to not get overly personal with the Doms. Hannah didn't want to cross that line of course, but she also knew they needed some personal engagement between each other. She just wanted to make sure it wasn't too much.

"This is my first time. At Baton Timide or anywhere. Is it that obvious?" she asked nervously.

"No." He paused. "Well, maybe a little."

He sipped his wine, slowly brushing his legs up and down hers, and shrugged. "We've only just started out, but it seemed like you were a bit nervous up on the stage at the auction, so I assumed you were new, and then of course Domme Maria confirmed you were at least new to the club."

Hannah looked down at the water as she answered timidly, "Yes, I was definitely nervous. Then excited, and then nervous again when I wondered who had bid on me."

She glanced up at him then, meeting his eyes before continuing, "And then excited again when I discovered it was you."

He put his wineglass down on the edge of the tub and sat upright. "Come here, come closer to me. Let me wash your back."

She untangled her legs from his and scooted closer. He took her wineglass and put it on the edge of the tub next to his. He grabbed a washcloth, squirted some body wash on it and started to rub slow, small circles over her back. She sighed, her body relaxing totally. When her entire back had been washed and rinsed, he pulled her between his legs, her back now resting against his chest.

She wiggled for a moment and then stopped. "Your chest hair feels ticklish against my back."

"I'd offer to shave it for you, but seeing how we're only spending the weekend together . . ."

"No, don't shave it. I like it. It's sexy when it peeks through your shirt."

Drew smiled at her admission and began to wash her front. He started at her neck, continued across her breasts, down her stomach, ending between her legs. As his fingers brushed lightly over her clit, she gasped, her legs spreading wide for him.

Drew let the washcloth drop into the water, and continued to caress her. Using both hands, he massaged each breast. Hannah moaned and pushed them higher into his hands. Her nipples elongated as he pinched and tweaked them.

His cock hardened against her backside as she rocked back into his length. He hissed and snaked one of his hands down her stomach, into the water and over her pussy, finding her sensitive nub. She cried out as her body hitched out of the water from his touch.

"Do you like that, little one?" Drew whispered in her ear and began licking and sucking down the length of her neck.

She leaned her head back and to the side to give him better access as she sighed out a husky, "Yes." Her entire body was pulsing with desire, aching to feel his touch on her everywhere and anywhere.

He whispered in her ear again, "Turn around and sit on me. It's your turn now."

Hannah rose up so quickly that water sloshed over the sides and knocked one of the wine glasses into the tub as she turned around.

Drew chuckled and held her by the waist as she lowered herself back into the water, over him. "Anxious, are we?"

She locked her eyes with his, bringing her head down to his, her lips to his, and breathed, "Yes," before kissing him deeply, tasting the wine on his lips.

He tugged her closer with a hand at her nape, thrusting his tongue in her mouth, stealing her breath away. With the other hand, he held his cock and guided it into her as she sunk herself onto him. As she became fully seated, a groan rolled out of her mouth and into his.

He was big, not just in length but in girth as well, and sitting on him like this filled her differently than when he took her from behind. She felt so full as the throbbing of her pussy clenched around his cock, getting used to its size.

Drew pulled away from her mouth, kissing a trail to her ear before commanding, "Ride me, Scarlett. It's all about you now." And then he continued kissing down her neck, lightly nipping her along the way, fueling her desire even further.

Hannah's head fell against his as she began to rock back and forth, riding his cock, holding onto his shoulders to help her move. Her clit was grinding along his shaft every time she slid forward, weakening any chance of her keeping control.

"Drew, I'm going to come," she huffed as she continued to ride him, head still against his. She increased her speed, throwing her head back, her long hair falling out of its makeshift bun and grazing the top of her arched ass, water sloshing over the edge of the tub.

DREW STARTED to move with her, pumping his cock into Scarlett harder, urging her to go faster. The sight of her on top of him, head thrown back, moaning in pleasure, was one of the sexiest things he had ever seen.

He fisted her loose hair in his hand and pushed Scarlett down harder on his cock while he thrust up. He felt the moment she exploded as her pussy tightened around him, imprisoning him in warmth. He loosened his grip on her and nuzzled his nose into her hair. She smelled like fresh flowers in the spring.

"So beautiful." He sighed, then kissed her lips. She began to rise and lift herself off him, but he drew her back onto his still-hard cock and held her in his arms. "Stay like this for a minute. I just want to feel you."

Scarlett relaxed back onto him and trailed soft kisses down his neck before resting her head there. He wrapped his arms around her waist, pulling her tighter for a moment before loosening his hold.

She lifted her head up off his shoulder and turned her face to his. He met her gaze and then kissed her gently on the mouth. Leaning away, he traced a finger down her cheek and over her lips. She flicked her tongue out and used it to guide his finger into her mouth. Closing her lips around it, she sucked hard, staring down at him between her lashes. Drew sucked in his breath as he rocked his hips, pushing his cock a little deeper inside her.

He rested his forehead against hers and, in a strained voice, whispered, "What are you trying to do to me, Scarlett?"

He pulled his finger out of her mouth with a pop and replaced it with his tongue. As the kiss became more heated, a need to possess her further swept through him.

Drew dragged his lips from hers and grasped the edge of the tub with one hand. "Wrap your legs around me and hold on."

Holding on to the edge of the tub, he pushed and stood up, Scarlett wrapped around him tightly. He folded both arms around her after he stepped out of the tub and walked into the shower, turning it on quickly.

Freezing-cold water rained down, causing Scarlett to gasp and clutch him tighter. Drew wasted no time pushing her up against the shower wall and driving into her with lust.

Scarlett's arms cinched more tightly around him as she met him thrust for thrust. Moans of pleasure escaped her mouth each time he drove his cock into her, making him even harder. He braced one hand up against the shower wall so he could push even deeper into her.

She clung to him and panted out between thrusts, "Drew, I'm going to come again."

Hearing his name come moaning from her lips caused his balls to tighten and his own release to reach its peak. "Then come, let me feel you again."

With Scarlett clutching his shoulders and her legs wrapped tightly around his waist, he thrust his hips into her mercilessly, hand still braced on the wall. Her muscles began to tighten around him as her orgasm crested. He lowered his head to her shoulder and bit hard as they both yelled out their release.

He lowered Scarlett's legs to the floor but continued to hold her close. He leaned over her and, bringing his lips to hers, brushed them over them. He traced his nose softly across her cheek and whispered into her ear, "You are amazing." Her cheeks rose in a smile before she kissed him back warmly.

They gradually separated as he turned to adjust the water to a warmer temperature. Without saying a word, he took a washcloth and, applying soap, tenderly washed and rinsed her off before doing the same to himself. He shut the water off, stepped out, grabbed a towel and wrapped it around her small frame.

Scarlett looked at herself in the mirror, running her fingers over the bite mark he had left on her shoulder. Her eyes met his in the mirror questioningly. "You bit me?"

He'd forgotten he'd even done that. It wasn't something he ever remembered doing before, but with her, when he came, something had possessed him. A need to mark her as his. He wasn't even sure how to explain it.

He stepped closer and grazed his fingers lightly over the bite mark. "I'm sorry. Does it hurt?"

She shook her head in response. "Not really. I was just surprised."

Little did she know that he was too. He pulled some antiseptic ointment out of one of the drawers. "Let me put some of this on it. It will help quicken the healing."

He didn't want to apologize again, because deep down,

as hard as it was for him to admit it, he liked seeing his mark on her. *Jesus, am I turning into some kind of animal?*

After applying the ointment, he kissed the top of her head and turned her toward the bedroom. "Go ahead and climb into bed. I'll just clean up a bit in here and join you."

"We'll sleep in the same bed then?"

In her training, Scarlett had probably been made aware that a Dom generally didn't sleep in the same bed as their submissive. And normally, that was the case with him as well. But since he'd first seen her on that stage this evening, he'd felt an inexplicable urge to be near her.

"Yes, I'd like that, if you would?"

"Yes, I'd like that too." She reached up on her tiptoes and kissed him before walking away. He watched as she left the bathroom, still wrapped in her towel, hair loose and damp down her back.

He rinsed the tub and gathered the wineglasses. As he entered the bedroom, his heart stopped at the sight before him: Scarlett, eyes closed, her long, golden hair spread out around her face on the pillow, her cheeks flushed, her lips pink and soft as she slept.

She took his breath away. He had only spent a few hours with her, and already it felt like more. It wasn't just that she was beautiful. He'd been with many beautiful women, and all had been eager to please him.

Perhaps it was her innocence? He wasn't sure. He continued to stare down at her while contemplating. Was there such a thing as love at first sight? He shook his head at the absurdity of his own thoughts. He definitely didn't live in a land of fairy tales, but he couldn't deny the possessive feelings he was having.

He put the wineglasses down on the bedside table, turned out the lights, climbed in beside her and pulled her into his arms. She muttered something unintelligible in her sleep and then settled down. She was like a newborn kitten cuddled up against him. He listened to the soft, steady cadence of her breathing, and felt the satin of her skin against his, and soon was sound asleep as well.

CHAPTER
Four

DREW WOKE around six and was surprised to find himself wrapped around Scarlett. It was an intimacy he hadn't experienced since his divorce four years ago. Waking up in bed with his wife and spending mornings with her had been one of the happier parts of his marriage. Until the day he'd come home early from a business trip to find her in that same bed with another man.

She blamed it on him, of course. Saying he'd betrayed her first when she realized his business was like a mistress and would always come first. Perhaps she'd been right. Owning and running a billion-dollar hotel chain required much of his time, but she'd known that when she'd married him. He had always invited her to attend all of his business trips with him, but after only a few trips, she'd begun refusing, claiming she had her own schedule to keep.

After the divorce, he'd been introduced to the club by a friend. He'd become instantly intrigued and found that the club allowed him to maintain a level of control over relationships that real life didn't allow.

He wouldn't or couldn't even claim to be a full-time dominant. He enjoyed the control and light punishment his role encompassed, but it was something he only maintained in the bedroom—and as a convenience to help maintain order in his world. He had no time to deal with the complications that came with feelings or commitment. Or at least, that's what he had thought before he'd laid eyes on Scarlett last night.

He disentangled himself as gently as he could from Scarlett and sat up on the edge of the bed. He looked over his shoulder at her sleeping form and wondered again what the fuck she was doing to him. Her hands were resting together in prayer formation against her face, her thick eyelashes brushing against her cheekbones, her full lips parted slightly as she breathed. It was very tempting to climb back in that bed and wake her in a way he was sure would be satisfying to both of them, but he needed a little space.

He rose and tip-toed to the walk-in master closet that housed his clothes. He dressed quickly, pulling on jogging clothes before exiting the house, grabbing his iPod on the way. It was still dark out, so he stood on the porch for a moment to let his eyes adjust to the light.

September had arrived, but the early morning air was chillier than he had anticipated. He contemplated going back inside to grab a sweatshirt but didn't want to risk waking Scarlett. He would warm up once he started running.

He popped his ear buds in and selected his favorite playlist for a run: Bon Jovi's *Slippery When Wet*. His older brother had given him the CD when he was younger, proclaiming it was the best album ever written. Drew didn't know if he would go that far, but it was a classic, and the familiar songs always relaxed him while running. The songs also had some great memories associated with them, so it remained a permanent fixture on his iPod.

His eyes adjusted to the light as he followed the sidewalk out to the road. He started jogging at a slow pace until his muscles warmed up and then worked his way up to a steady gait through the first song on the album, "Let it Rock."

Each breath he took left his body in a puff of white fog, and he could feel the echo of each foot hitting the pavement. By the third song on the album, "Livin' on a Prayer," he had reached his stride, and his muscles stretched a bit as he increased to a run. He tried to run five or six miles every morning. Not only for the health benefits, but to keep his head clear. This morning though, he had only one thought on his mind, and that was Scarlett.

His mind raced, trying to determine how to handle her when he returned to the bungalow. Maybe it would be best to become truly dominant for the rest of the weekend and dispense with any of the casual pleasantries they had so thoroughly enjoyed last night. It would eliminate any of the personal details and emotions she seemed to be invoking within him thus far.

He still had to decide whether or not he wanted her to accompany him to the fundraiser he was scheduled to attend that evening. Normally he wouldn't leave the club during a weekend stay, but it was for his brother's organization, and he'd promised Benny he would be there.

Drew was running at a hard pace now, covering almost a

mile every seven minutes or so. He'd lost track of how long he'd been running and was surprised to look at his watch and discover he'd been at it almost an hour. He slowed down to a light jog and cut across the woods to bring him closer to the bungalow without having to backtrack.

It was lighter now that the sun had risen and the temperature had warmed, so the shade from the trees was welcome. When he came out of the other side of the woods, he realized he was only about a mile from the bungalow and decided to walk the rest of the way to cool his muscles down.

Inside the bungalow, all the lights were still off and the house was silent. Scarlett must still be sleeping. He walked into the second bedroom and into its accompanying bathroom and stripped out of his workout clothes.

He turned on the shower and stepped in to wash off the sweat from his run. As the water ran over him, rinsing him clean, he was reminded of the shower he and Scarlett had taken the night before. He recalled how good she'd felt wrapped around his body, him buried deep inside her as she moaned his name. The memory stirred his blood and hardened his cock.

He shut the water off, stepped out of the stall and grabbed a towel off the rack. He quickly dried himself off and, staying naked, walked into the master bedroom, where Scarlett was still sleeping. Here, now, he needed to treat Scarlett as his submissive if he had any hope of walking away from her at the end of this weekend.

He stood beside the bed, naked, his cock growing harder at the sight of her, and jostled the bed with his knee. "Scarlett, wake up."

HANNAH FELT the bed shake and rolled over, slowly opening her eyes. She blinked a few times, trying to wake herself up. She rose up on her elbows to find Drew standing over her, naked.

Before she even had time to form a thought, he spoke roughly to her. "Get on your hands and knees, facing me."

She paused, momentarily shocked by his tone and request.

He lunged forward, grabbing a handful of her hair painfully as he bent toward her and seethed into her ear, "What did I tell you about repeating myself?"

As he let go and straightened to his full height, she quickly scooted onto her hands and knees and faced him. He was tall, so his cock, hard and jutting, was right in her face. She looked up at him, unsure of what he wanted her to do next.

"Open your mouth."

Now she knew. But still she hesitated. Before she could react, a hard smack rained down on her ass. She instinctively lowered her ass away from his smack while looking sheepishly up at him.

"I told you I would punish you if you hesitated again." He stared down, his eyes hard and dilated with lust. "Open your mouth. *Now*."

This time, she didn't hesitate. Her mouth opened instantly. In the same instant, Drew took a step forward and, gripping his cock, led it to her mouth. She closed her lips around it, raising her hands up off the bed to grasp him.

"No," he commanded. "Hands on the bed."

Hands midway to his shaft, she froze. He, however, didn't hesitate and smacked her ass again, not once but three times, and they weren't gentle. The quick gasp she took in surprise sucked his cock deeper into her mouth, and he hissed in response. She returned her hands to the bed, her eyes still raised in question.

"I am going to fuck your mouth, Scarlett. And since I can't have the pleasure of coming in your mouth, when I'm ready, I'm also going to fuck your beautiful pussy."

He took a fistful of her hair in one hand and, pulling it, used it to guide her mouth back and forth over his cock in a slow, agonizing rhythm.

She should feel humiliated by this, but instead, adrenaline coursed through her body, going straight to her core, which quickly dampened from the excitement. She wrapped her lips tighter around Drew's cock as he slowly entered her mouth. She sucked on him hard, bringing him deep into her throat, and then pressed her tongue against the bottom of his hardened ridge. When he pulled almost entirely out of her mouth, she swirled her tongue around the tip and then sucked again, bringing him back deep inside. His head was thrown back, his mouth open in an O as he let out a low, guttural moan.

His grip on her hair tightened with each thrust as he began pushing his cock in harder and faster. Just as her jaw started to ache and she worried he might come, he pulled away and used the grip on her hair to yank her head all the way back, forcing her to look up at him.

"Now, turn around, Scarlett. I want your elbows on the mattress and your ass in the air."

When he released her hair, she instantly turned, fell onto her elbows and thrust her ass up. His finger grazed her wet pussy, and she jerked in response.

"Look how wet you are." He hummed appreciatively as he ran his finger up and down her pussy. "You like sucking my cock?"

"Yes." Hannah flinched as she felt a hard smack on her ass. *Shit! That hurt.* She had to remember to answer immediately.

"Yes? Yes, what?" He growled.

"Yes, Sir. Yes, I like sucking your cock, Sir." She spoke quickly, but softly.

He rubbed her ass where he had smacked it, just beyond where the ache in her pussy was now throbbing with need.

"Good girl. I liked you sucking my cock. Next time maybe you'll reconsider taking everything my cock has to offer."

She wasn't sure what to say, but she didn't want to get spanked again. To be safe, she responded, "Yes, Sir."

"Now I'm going to fuck you." Drew began stroking her pussy again with his finger, running it up and down her clit, spreading her juices, staying a breath away from her sensitive nub. "And you will not come."

At that statement, Drew guided his cock to her entrance and drove into her in one thrust, her body jerking forward. And he kept thrusting into her. She had to push herself down harder into the bed on her elbows and shove her ass back to keep up with the punishing movements.

His cock, rock hard, was hitting her in just the right

place every time he pushed into her and she wasn't sure if she was going to be able to hold back from having an orgasm. As if he could read her mind, Drew grabbed a fistful of her hair and, dragging her head back so she could see his face, said through gritted teeth, "Do not come."

"Yes, S-sir," she stammered.

Drew released her hair, grabbed her hips roughly with both hands and slammed into her even harder. She moaned in pleasure, in frustration, in fear, before he thrust one final time, grunting loudly as he came. She could feel his release explode inside her and she had to bite down on her lip, hard, and concentrate with every ounce of her being to keep her orgasm at bay.

Drew's harsh breathing decreased as he softened inside her. As he slid out of her, he released the firm hold he'd had on her hips and then took a step away. His seed slid out of her and down the inside of her leg. She didn't dare move an inch without his consent for fear of another spanking.

"You can relax." Drew spoke quietly, but with authority from behind her.

She responded immediately with a faint, "Yes, Sir," and then rolled onto her side, pulling the covers up over her body. Drew stood looking down at her for several moments before shaking his head and walking away.

"Scarlett, please shower and dress. When you're done, meet me in the kitchen. I'd like breakfast." As he reached the doorway, he turned back with one final command. "Do not touch yourself or offer yourself any relief."

She lay in the bed for just a moment after he left and then quickly got up. She was a mix of emotions. Frustration being at the top of the list. The throbbing at her core needed attention, and knowing she couldn't provide it—and not knowing when she would actually get some relief—did nothing but inflame her. She knew she had no right to be angry. This is what Drew had paid for. She was his to do with as he pleased.

She turned the shower on, keeping the water more cold than hot in an attempt to quench some of the heat coursing through her. She stepped in and let the water run over her body before pulling her hands through her long hair, getting it wet enough to wash. As she shampooed and conditioned her hair, her thoughts went back to Drew's behavior from last night and how it contrasted with his behavior this morning.

Perhaps he'd wanted to ease her nerves last night, but today, it was game on? Last night seemed to be more than that, but how would she know? This was her first time, and one of the most important things Domme Maria had instilled in all the trainees was to keep their emotions in check. This was a job and nothing more and she needed to remember that. No matter how well Drew could fuck.

She finished her shower quickly, stepped out of the stall and dried off. She found some lotions in the vanity and, picking one blindly, applied it liberally to her body, spending a little extra time on her smarting bottom.

She stepped into the bedroom and opened the drawers, viewing the many lingerie sets, trying to determine which one Drew would like. Since she was going to be cooking, practical would be smart. Boy shorts were a more appropriate choice, than say, a thong. She slipped on a beautifully colored lilac set that would be perfect.

She wasn't quite sure what to do with her hair. Blow-drying it would take another fifteen minutes and she didn't want to chance angering Drew if he was already sitting in the kitchen, waiting for her. Perhaps the easiest thing would be to brush it and then wind it up in a messy bun on top of her head. She needed it out of her way anyway for cooking. Hoping Drew would be happy with her presentation, she made her way out to the kitchen.

Drew was sitting at the kitchen table, hair still wet and disheveled from his shower, holding a cup of coffee and a paper spread out before him. He wore a pair of faded jeans and a white T-shirt. She couldn't help think, for just a fleeting second, that it felt like a normal morning in any other relationship. Except for her scantily dressed form, and her stinging bottom of course.

FUCK. Fuck. Fuck. He was so fucked. All he'd wanted to do when she'd rolled off her knees and under the covers was to crawl in there and cradle her in his arms. He'd wanted to stroke her hair, cover her in kisses and then taste her sweet pussy, giving her the satisfaction she'd so willingly given him.

He'd never felt this way about any of the subs he'd had before. He'd gone in there to get some of his control back, to fully dominate her, to impose order on the emotions she was triggering.

What the fuck is she doing to me? Because that definitely didn't go as planned. Drew turned the shower on as cold as he could make it and stepped inside, hoping it would shock some fucking sense back into him.

After showering, (again), dressed and barefoot, he made his way into the kitchen to fix a pot of coffee. He could still hear the shower running in the other bedroom and wondered if he should check to make sure she was okay. *No.* He'd better give himself a bit more space before seeing her again.

The coffee finished brewing, so he poured himself a cup and sat at the table to read the paper that must have been dropped off at some point.

Several moments later, the patter of her footsteps drew his attention as Scarlett entered the room. She was wearing some delectable lace in a purple color that was doing nothing to tamp down the desire he was already struggling with. He focused his eyes back on his paper, trying to remain aloof, and gestured to the counter.

"There's coffee made if you would like a cup."

"Thank you, Sir." She stood rooted in place for a moment before walking over with soft, quick steps to the counter and pouring herself a cup of coffee. He'd left the cream and sugar on the counter, and she added a bit of each to her cup.

"Sir, would you like more coffee?" She raised the pot in question.

He glanced up briefly before looking back down at his paper. "Yes, and a little cream, please."

He was trying very hard to pretend the paper had his full attention but he wasn't sure she was buying it. She walked over, filled his cup and then added a bit of cream.

"Thank you." He took a sip. Without looking up at her,

he said, "I'd like an egg-white omelet with tomatoes and cheese, please."

Scarlett stood with the pot suspended midair, hesitating yet again, something obviously on her mind. If only he knew what.

Drew raised an eyebrow and instead of asking her what she was thinking responded casually, "Really, Scarlett? Is it that hard to follow an order?"

"No, Sir. Sorry, Sir. Do you want toast or any meat with your eggs?" She quickly replaced the pot and walked over to the fridge to gather the ingredients needed for his breakfast.

"No toast, no meat." Drew turned the page of the paper he was supposedly reading and continued to ignore her as she went about making his breakfast.

Jesus Christ, her ass looked fucking edible in that lace. What he really wanted to do was throw her up on the table and eat *her* for breakfast. He silently cursed himself for being such a cold prick, but he needed to get a grip on his emotions.

Scarlett's body language and ever-expressive face screamed frustration. As he continued the pretense of reading the paper, he covertly watched as she reached for a pan out of one of the lower cupboards.

He couldn't help but notice that she bent at the waist and pointed her delectable ass right in his line of vision. Watching her try to push up her breasts while nonchalantly beat the eggs for his omelet had him raising the paper up to cover his smile. When he lowered the paper again, she stuck her ass out, making sure it swayed each time she adjusted the omelet in the pan.

Drew shifted in his seat, trying to gain some control

over his growing erection, and knew Scarlett was teasing him. Every action she performed resulted in some kind of ass or breast thrust. And damn if it wasn't working. He was ready to bend her over the counter, rip that lace off and fuck that ass until she learned who was boss. But then she really would be the winner of this little game she was playing, and there was no way he was letting that happen. After this display, he had much bigger plans for that ass, and it would be on his terms, not hers.

Scarlett placed his breakfast before him—bending deeply, of course. "Can I get you anything else, Sir?"

He chuckled at her seductive efforts. "No, thank you. Please make yourself something to eat though."

"I'm not really much of a breakfast eater, Sir."

He looked at her sternly. "You will eat breakfast when you are with me. I have plans for you this morning, and you will need the nourishment."

She flushed at the meaning of his words and then answered, "Yes, Sir."

He turned his attention toward his omelet as she walked to the fridge and took more items out. A few minutes later, he looked up from his breakfast and frowned at Scarlett standing motionless in the center of the room. "What's wrong?"

"Sir, am I allowed to sit with you?"

He was taken aback by her need to ask the question. "Of course." He got up and pulled out a chair for her, then helped her to sit.

"Thank you, Sir. May I eat, or will you be feeding me again?"

Drew tilted his head at her question, surprised at how

quickly her behavior had altered. "You may feed yourself, Scarlett. Thank you for asking."

He continued to watch her and realized she was looking for some kind of praise for her actions. She wanted to please him. She wanted to know that he was pleased. She was more submissive by nature than even she may have known. This alone pleased him more than any ass thrust she'd given him.

HANNAH BEGAN EATING. *Why am I doing this again?* She was worrying a little bit too much about what Drew thought of her. As a submissive, her goal was to try and physically please him, but she was alarmed to discover that she was actually starting to really care about how or what he was feeling.

When she made him laugh, her heart soared in elation. And the way he'd held her as they'd slept last night had felt more intimate than some relationships she'd had with past lovers. Her feelings were starting to confuse her.

Although the sex was pretty damn amazing, this was all about the bottom line. She was fooling herself if she thought she was going to run away with the rich playboy at the end of this weekend. Buying the shop—*her* shop—was going to give her the independence and security she hadn't felt in years. That was why she was here. This wasn't just about her.

Only one of her friends knew what she was actually doing this weekend. She'd had to confide in at least one person. Her best friend Tammy not only understood but would be there to catch her if she fell. She had tried to get a bridge loan from the bank to cover the down payment for the shop, but she couldn't meet all of their strict requirements. And what normal person has an extra thirty grand around for someone to borrow?

She looked up from her yogurt to find Drew staring intently at her. She knew why she was here, but what about him? What went on in that moody mind of his, and what made a man like him purchase sex? He was amazingly good-looking and obviously had money, so it would probably be safe to assume he had his choice of women.

Drew raised an eyebrow as she continued to stare at him. "What's on your mind?"

She blushed crimson at being called out on her bold appraisal. "Um, just wondering what we'll be doing today, Sir?"

Drew rose and circled behind her, removing the clip holding her hair up. He ran his fingers through her still-damp hair, trying to straighten it down her back. "I like your hair down. Please leave it this way unless I instruct otherwise."

"Yes, Sir. I was only trying to save time by not drying it so I threw it up instead," she defended.

He still stood behind her, slowly caressing his fingers through her hair. She loved the feel of his touch. She wanted to lean back into it but was nervous at his sudden sternness again. "I appreciate that you were trying to be efficient. Down from now on though."

She nodded. "Yes, Sir."

He moved beside her again, looking down at her. She

didn't know how to read him yet and wasn't sure what the look in his eye meant. "I want you down in the playroom in position in five minutes. Do you know where it's located?"

She nodded. "Yes, Sir, I know where it is."

"Good. Five minutes." Drew turned and started walking out of the room, then stopped. "And, Scarlett?"

"Yes?"

"Be naked."

CHAPTER
Five

HANNAH SQUEAKED OUT A, "YES, SIR!" before quickly getting up from her chair and following him out of the kitchen.

He turned left into the second bedroom, and she turned right, opposite the entryway, going through a doorway that led down to the playroom. Her training session had occurred in a similar bungalow, and she knew that a play-room was housed in the basement of each residence on the property.

Her heart started beating heavily as she descended the stairs down to the playroom. The room was warm, in both temperature and color. The floor was made up of honey-colored hardwood, and beautifully colored Oriental rugs were scattered throughout the room. The playroom was large, encompassing in one room what the entire first-floor space shared with five rooms.

In the farthest corner of the room, an enormous bed was covered in a rich, blue velvet sheets. Of course the bed had four high posts, one at each corner, but unlike other bedposts, these had ornate rings attached for tethering. The headboard also had several rings across its front for similar purposes.

Directly in the center of the room lay a table, a bit higher than a standard table, but as long and wide. But this table had a layer of brown leather padding and was studded with rings at certain points. In the opposite corner of the room from the bed, a large wooden cross dominated the wall: a St. Andrew's Cross.

The ceiling was crisscrossed by a suspension system that could be used for various swings, attachments or straps. The room also had a spanking bench, several other stools and smaller wooden chairs. An elegant brown leather couch sat against a wall next to the bed.

Straps, belts, floggers, canes and other tools for implementing pain and punishment decorated an entire sidewall, hanging for a Doms use. Near the stairway, a wooden cabinet with drawers and doors of different sizes housed other "tools" of the trade.

Hannah removed the lace garments she was wearing and placed them neatly on top of the cabinet. She moved to one of the Oriental rugs strategically placed near the bottom of the stairs and kneeled in her submissive position. She blew air slowly of her mouth, trying to calm her rapid breathing over the anticipation she was feeling.

In this place, a Master could truly have his every desire, but the cost could be at the expense of her breaking point. And she had no idea what or where that point was. At least her first real experience with a Dominant would be at Drew's hands. She already felt she could trust him, that he wouldn't hurt her. On the heels of that thought, the door above opened, and footsteps descended the stairs.

Blood rushed through her as adrenaline spiked and her body flushed a dark pink. Surely Drew would hear, if not see, her pulse beating so rapidly. His bare feet appeared in front of her, and then his hand was on her head, sliding under her chin to raise it. She turned her gaze up to meet his, lust evident in his dark eyes.

"Are you nervous, Scarlett?" he asked quietly.

"Yes, Sir. A little." Her voice was barely above a whisper.

"Good." He let go of her chin but still stood above her. "You should be. After all, it is your first time." He paused, leaning a tad closer to her, his face a few inches from hers now, his voice almost a growl. "But, tell me, are you afraid?"

She shook her head while continuing to look up at Drew. "No, Sir. I'm not afraid of you."

One corner of his mouth ticked up. "Good. I don't want you to ever be afraid of me. I won't hurt you. Do you remember your safe word?"

He isn't going to hurt me, but he wants to make sure I remember my safe word? Hannah gulped before replying, "Yellow if I'm scared, ghost if I want you to stop."

He bent further and feathered a kiss against her lips before whispering against them, "Good girl. Don't worry, you won't need them. If I have my way, the only thing you'll be screaming is my name."

A small gasp of surprise escaped her mouth as he quickly rose and approached the cabinet near the stairs. He opened several drawers, pulling various things out, placing them next to her underwear on top of the cabinet before returning to her.

Something was in his hand—what was it? As if he had read her thoughts, he flashed her the elastic he was holding before walking behind her.

He ran his hands slowly down her still-damp hair and gathered it in a ponytail at the base of her head. Her constrained hair bobbed up and down as he bound it with the elastic.

"As much as I love your hair loose and free down your naked back, I'm going to pull it back while we are in here. I don't want it to get caught in anything."

"Yes, Sir."

Drew's hand ran lightly over the long mane of the tail, his fingertips grazing her naked back with each downward stroke. "Do you know what you remind me of, Scarlett?"

"No, Sir."

"A little kitten." His fingers stroked over the top of her ass, as he continued. "A bit fierce and petulant when it's not under its mother's paw. A kitten will bite and tease its mother's tail, or run away from its mother's call. But as soon as the kitten is hungry or is back under its mother's paw, it is sweet and complying. Do you know what I'm referring to, Scarlett?"

She shook her head again. "No, Sir, I don't understand."

He grasped Hannah's ponytail and, pulling it gently, motioned for her to rise. He took her hand and led her to the padded table in the center of the room. "Stay here."

He kept speaking as he walked back to the cabinet and pulled several more items from one of the drawers. "This morning, making my breakfast, shaking and pointing your delectable ass at me. Teasing me." He looked over his shoulder at her with a pointed stare. "Playing with me like a little kitten."

She turned crimson at the mention of her actions less than a half hour earlier. She was definitely going to be punished. "But, Sir—"

Drew lifted his hand abruptly. "Did I say you could speak?"

"No, Sir. I'm sorry, Sir." She looked down at the floor quickly, her gaze not meeting his.

"I'm quite sure you are sorry now, my little kitten."

He gathered all the items he had removed and walked slowly back to her side. He placed them on the table, in clear view, as if to give her an idea of what was about to happen. One by one, he lined up four silk straps in a deep blue color, a vibrator, a tube of lubricant and a medium-sized butt plug.

Her eyes widened in shock before flying up to meet Drew's. He was looking down at her with a wicked grin on his face, a feral look in his eyes.

"And, Scarlett, do you know why little kittens tease like this?"

He stood directly in front of her now and removed his T-shirt, revealing his sculpted chest. Her eyes trailed down his body and she clenched her fists tightly to keep her fingers from raking through the downy hair that covered his muscular chest.

She stammered, "S-s-sir?"

Making her feel like his prey, Drew walked slowly around her in a circle, then leaned in close, lips brushing up against her ear. "Because they want attention."

His hand stroked down her arm until he reached her

hand, pulling her tenderly to the front of the padded table. He guided her up, sliding her back about a foot before pushing her torso down flat.

Her heart beat wildly as he grabbed each of her ankles and pulled them to the edge, and she let out a short, startled cry. He took one of the blue silk ribbons and began winding it around her right ankle.

His fingertips felt like hot bolts of electricity each time he grazed her skin, the heat slowly trailing up her legs and throughout her body. He was barely touching her, and already her desire for him was building to a burn.

"Was there something that warranted my attention this morning, little kitten, that I didn't respond to?"

Drew took the ends of the blue silk he'd wrapped around her ankle and secured them to one of the rings at the corner of the table. The silk felt tight as he pulled it taut, but soft and pliant, so she wasn't as scared as she'd expected at being constrained.

She knew exactly why she had teased him, but she wasn't going to admit it to him. "Sir, I was simply trying to make you breakfast."

He clucked his tongue in disapproval as he took another one of the silk ties and began wrapping it around her left ankle.

"Oh, Scarlett. Shame on you. Do you really think you can fool me? I'll give you one more chance, and if you don't answer honestly, after I'm done with you here, we'll visit the spanking bench."

She blew out an exasperated breath and shakily responded, "Sir, I didn't like being treated like the help. You're hot, then cold, and it's confusing. I guess I was trying to act the part I thought you wanted." Her cheeks flamed in embarrassment, and Drew stopped tying the binding he had been working on.

DREW RAN his hand through his hair in frustration. He wasn't disguising his conflicted feelings as well as he'd thought. He rounded the table so that he could better see her face and took one of her hands in his.

"Since the moment I saw you walk onto that stage last night, something about you captivated me. I don't usually take baths or sleep with my subs. You—and what you're making me feel—are what's confusing, Scarlett. I'm in unexplored territory here."

He watched Scarlett's emotions run across her face as he spoke, a barely audible, "Oh," coming from her lips.

He dropped her hand, moved back to the end of the table and picked up another silk strap. He grabbed both her thighs and yanked her down the table until her ass rested at the edge, her knees bent.

Taking the silk, he began weaving it between the front and back of her leg, so that it remained bent and couldn't be straightened. His movements were quick and succinct, though jerky with suppressed anger.

"Yes, 'Oh.' So, I'm going to do what I know how to do, and that's fuck you." He finished tying the silk on the first leg and began weaving another restraint around the second.

Surprised that Scarlett was remaining quiet for once, he hoped he hadn't scared her with his confession, but there was also a piece of him that wondered what she was feeling. *Am I the only one who thinks this feels different?*

Drew completed the tie and stood directly in front of her spread legs. He ran his hands slowly up each inner thigh until they met at the juncture of her legs. Using both thumbs, he grazed back and forth over her clit, shocked to find that she was already soaking wet. He moaned as his cock got even stiffer.

"You're so wet already. Aren't you even a little bit afraid?"

Her pink tongue darted out, running over her lips, wetting them. "Yes, but I'm excited too."

He shook his head and chuckled. "What am I going to do with you, my little kitten? So curious, so ready to play."

He continued to stroke her with only his thumbs, spreading her juices over her entire core, then stopped. Keeping his eyes on her, he walked slowly around the table and slid one thumb into his mouth, sucking hard. As he sucked, his eyes closed, the taste like a bite of the most delectable dessert.

Coming up beside her, he opened his eyes, placed his other thumb against her mouth and pushed. Scarlett sucked hard, pulling his finger all the way into her mouth, moaning as her tongue swirled around it.

His knees grew weak at the sight of her sucking his thumb before he pulled it out of her mouth, bent down and claimed her mouth with his own. He might explode at her luscious taste.

Pulling away from the kiss before he could get carried away, Drew straightened and walked back to the cabinet. He was back in seconds with more silk ties in hand. Scarlett was breathing heavily and her eyes were sparkling with excitement.

"Raise your hands above your head and cross your arms in an X."

She did as he requested, her chest pushing forward, exposing her body further to him, her eyes following his movements. She was shaking, though he knew instinctively that it was from anticipation and not trepidation.

He took one wrist and then the other, silently lacing the silk around each in an intricate pattern before securing the binding to a ring.

He stepped back and let his eyes rove over her entire body. "Do you know how unbelievably sexy you look, open and waiting for me?"

"Sir, I'm here to please you."

He let out a huff of laughter in response. "Oh yes! See how the kitten behaves under its mother's paw?"

He traced a finger around one already-taut nipple. "Since you very much wanted my attention on your extremely lovely ass earlier, I think it only fair that I comply now."

Her head snapped up off the table, and for the first time since her arrival, he saw a glint of fear in her eyes.

"Oh, yes, I see I have your full attention now."

He pinched her nipple hard, then bent quickly to take it in his mouth and suckle even harder. She arched off the table in response, groaning at his intensity. She was pulling at her bindings, her fingers splayed out in an attempt to try and touch him, pleading out her frustration at being stuck. He let go of her nipple and walked back down to the end of the table.

"I know you don't have anal play as a hard limit, but I also know it was listed as a possible soft limit. Has anyone ever taken your ass before?" He began caressing the inside of her thighs just shy of her apex, watching as she tried and failed to writhe away from his touch, her bindings holding her in place.

"No, Sir. Not completely. I tried once, but..." Her face was flushed in apparent embarrassment as her sentence trailed off.

"But what?" he pushed.

Her face lightened, and she quickly clenched her eyes shut before opening them to answer him.

"It hurt. So I— We stopped." She was embarrassed by her admission.

He moved his fingers a little closer to her core, applying a bit more pressure now to try and distract her from feeling that way. Her hips surged forward in a short motion, and her knees opened wider.

"If done properly, there should be very little pain, usually just in the beginning, but then it's quite enjoyable. Some women even begin to prefer it over vaginal sex. I'd like very much to show you how enjoyable it can be."

Her core was glistening with wetness, revealing her obvious arousal, but she confirmed it when she nodded, biting her lip before replying with a soft, "Okay, Sir."

He honestly didn't think he could get any harder, but just hearing Scarlett assent to taking her virgin ass caused his cock to swell and strain against the zipper of his jeans.

Needing the relief, he unbuttoned his fly, pulled the zipper down and quickly stripped himself naked. He grabbed his thick shaft at the very base and squeezed hard to try and quell the desire to sink into her right then. When the urge dissipated slightly, he grabbed one of the shorter wooden chairs and placed it at the foot of the table.

He positioned himself between Scarlett's spread legs and didn't bother hiding the hungry look in his eyes. Without saying a word, he leaned over, resting his hands at the base of her neck. His fingers were splayed wide as he caressed her throat, slowly moving down until his hands were on her breasts. Her nipples were already hard and tight, so when his fingers grasped each nipple and tugged roughly, her back lunged off the table, causing her head to fall back as a loud moan of pleasure to escape her mouth.

His groin grew wet as it pressed against her core, her hips thrusting against him craving relief. He took a small step back, continuing the trail downward with his hands until they landed just above her swollen lips. Again, she pushed herself forward, still searching for some kind of release, mewling a tortured, "Drew, please . . ."

He leaned down, spread her labia wide and blew softly on her clit. Her hips bucked off the table and her moans of pleasure grew louder. "It's my turn to tease you now, my little kitten."

He blew softly again, but this time followed it up by running his tongue over her pussy and lapping at the juices that were flowing from her. While he continued to lick her from front to back, he used one finger to spread her juices down toward her soft, puckered hole. At the first touch of his finger around her hole, she clenched, but as he continued licking her pussy, she gradually relaxed. Then he pushed his finger in quickly up to his middle knuckle. She clenched tightly again and froze.

He raised his head slightly to comfort her. "It's okay. Just breathe out and feel what I'm doing to the rest of your body. I need to stretch you enough to take me."

She rocked her head back and forth as he drowned her in sensation, groaning out an assent. He used his other hand to rub her clit while giving her some direction. "Scarlett, I'm going to push my finger all the way in. I want you to take a deep breath in, and when you breathe out, push down on my finger as I push in."

She did as he asked, and a second later, a small cry escaped her as his finger pushed all the way in. "Good girl. You okay?"

"Yes, yes. I'm okay. Please don't stop," she panted.

He bent back down between her legs and sucked hard on her clit as he began to plunge his finger slowly in and out of her ass. When she started to move with him, into the motion instead of against it, he used the juices flowing freely from her pussy to slip a second finger into her ass. This time, there was very little resistance from her.

She threw her head back and moaned, then hissed. "It burns."

He stilled. "Do you want me to stop?"

She shook her head and rocked her ass against his hand, pushing his fingers deeper. "It feels good too. Just go slow."

His cock jerked at her concession, and he growled in satisfaction. He took his other hand and squeezed a small amount of lubricant where his fingers were inserted. He continued to move two fingers in and out of her ass; she pushed back against him harder now.

"Drew, please, I'm ready for more."

"Shhh, okay Scarlett. You're almost ready." He sucked in

his breath at how easily she was opening up to him and begging for more. He began scissoring his fingers to spread her hole wider. He had intended on only inserting the butt plug for now and taking her ass that night, but he was certain neither of them could wait.

He slowly pulled his fingers out and grabbed the lubricant he had left next to her hip. He squeezed a generous portion up into her hole and then more into his hand, rubbing it over his rock-hard length. She watched him, wide eyes locked on his cock.

"Don't worry, it will fit. I'll go really slow. Just tell me if I'm hurting you too much, and I'll stop."

"Are you sure?" Her eyes were still locked on his shaft, which was swollen and hard.

"I'm sure."

He grabbed her hips, pulled her to the very edge of the table and lined his cock up with her ass. He held his cock in one hand and slowly started inserting his length into her ass. His cock was throbbing as it started to slide into her hole. She tensed again and tightened like a vise around the tip. He grabbed the vibrator off the table and, turning it on, rubbed it up against the sensitive lips of her pussy and pressed it to her clit.

Her entire body jerked and tightened around him before slowly relaxing. "*Oh! Drew!* What are you doing?"

He pushed into her ass a little deeper and didn't know if he was going to be able to fit his whole cock in before he exploded. "Just feel the vibration against your skin. It will help you through the pain."

He brushed the vibrator back and forth over her pussy as he continued his slow progression into her ass. It was so fucking tight squeezing his cock, but he could feel her relax and open up as the vibrator starting bringing her closer to orgasm.

Scarlett was panting and grasping the silk ties binding her wrists as she tried to push her ass harder onto his cock. He took the opportunity to thrust the rest of the way in. She yelled out and he stilled for a moment while her body adjusted to his girth. When he felt her relax again, he slid back about an inch, then back in, and then out again.

She started to move with him as moans of pleasure continued to fall from her lips. He dropped the vibrator on the floor, grasped both of her hips with his hands and began to thrust in and out of her hard and quick, his balls slapping the bottom of her ass. His cock swelled even larger as she pushed her hips to meet his, and he knew he wouldn't last much longer.

They were both coated in sweat, eyes closed, moaning loudly. He released one hip and used his fingers to pinch her clit, causing Scarlett to scream his name, fingers clenched tightly around silk, body stretched taught, her muscles clenching around his cock so hard that he exploded, spilling his release deep inside her.

He fell forward onto her, pressing his forehead to hers, and just breathed for a minute. When he had caught his breath, he kissed her and whispered, "Wow."

She smiled shyly and closed her eyes in satisfaction, her head rolling to the side. Drew straightened up and slowly slid out of her, feeling her wince as he came free.

"Sorry, did that hurt?"

"A little, but it was worth it." Her cheeks flushed a light pink as her gaze fell away. "It was pretty amazing overall."

He moved to the end of the table and started unfastening all the ties securing her. In minutes, he had her in his arms and was carrying her over to the huge bed. He tenderly placed her down and began rubbing the circulation back into her arms and legs. When he got to her shoulders, he ran his finger over the bite mark he had made the night before. A wave of possessiveness washed over him. He bent down and pressed his lips to the bite before trailing his tongue up her neck to find her mouth and capture it in a kiss. He broke away and looked into her eyes.

"You did incredible. You were incredible." He stood up abruptly. "I'll be right back."

He returned with a glass of water, some orange pills and a small bowl. He placed the bowl on the floor next to the bed and handed Scarlett the water and pills. "It's ibuprofen. It will help with some of the residual pain." He pulled a washcloth out of the bowl. At her questioning look, he responded, "Just warm water. I cleaned up in the bathroom, but I wanted to take care of you as well."

As Drew finished washing Scarlett, he watched her. She was flush from the exertion they had both endured. Her eyes were shining brightly and were framed by blonde wisps of hair that had escaped from her ponytail.

His heart swelled at her beauty and at the innocence she had just entrusted to him. He leaned down and kissed her, holding her face in his hands as he did. She kissed him back, snaking a hand around his neck and feathering her fingers through his hair.

He slowly pulled away but kept his face close to hers. "Are you sure it was okay for you?"

She closed her eyes, blushing, and nodded. "Yes, very much. It was better than I had ever thought it could be."

He leaned down, kissed her forehead and, smiling, caressed her cheek. "I'm glad. But now I'll have to come up with another form of punishment the next time you tease me."

She laughed and rolled her eyes. "Well, if it's as good as this punishment, I'll have to make sure I tease you sooner rather than later."

He sat up and shook his head. "You really are a naughty little kitten."

She grinned contentedly. "If I could purr right now, I would."

"Do you want to lie here for a bit or would you like to go back upstairs?"

"Do you mind if we just lay here for a little bit?"

He lay down, pulled her up against him and wrapped his arms around her.

A FEW HOURS LATER, Hannah jerked awake and sat up, forgetting where she was for a moment. Then she saw the St. Andrew's Cross hanging on the wall across the room. *Nothing like a cold dose of reality to wake you up.*

She looked down to see Drew on his back, sleeping soundly next to her. God he was beautiful. He really did take her breath away. In more ways than one, apparently. At that thought, her hand flew to her mouth as it formed an O in disbelief. She had just had some of the most amazing sex of her life with this man. And she was the one getting paid. It really didn't seem fair, but there it was.

Domme Maria had warned all the trainees repeatedly that the Doms bought them to serve one purpose: the Dom's pleasure. The subs were to please their Masters at any cost, no matter the pain, pride, or lack of compassion from the Dom. She didn't know if it was the norm, but she seemed to be getting just as much pleasure from this experience as Drew. At least, he *seemed* to be getting pleasure from this. But even more than that, he genuinely seemed to want to please her and make her happy as well.

As she watched him sleep, she ran her fingers over his chest and wondered again why a man this beautiful, this rich, needed to buy a woman for the weekend. Perhaps it was just easier for him? But he seemed like such a kind man. One who would willingly give his heart to the right person. Maybe his heart had been broken one too many times. She sighed and pulled her hand away.

"Don't stop," he mumbled sleepily. "That feels nice."

She put her hand back and continued to caress his chest. "I'm sorry if I woke you."

"It's okay. Much nicer way to wake up than my usual alarm clock or my assistant calling me at some ungodly hour."

She sat up on her knees and stretched, her hands over her head. She belatedly realized what the pose had done to her breasts when Drew's gaze fell directly on her chest. She lay back down on the bed and, putting her arms around his neck, drew his head to where his gaze had been. Without a word, he pulled a nipple into his mouth and sucked. Her head rolled back on her shoulders as a soft moan escaped from her.

She wrapped her legs around his waist, pulling him flush against her. Their mouths found each other and joined in a slow, sensual tangle of tongues and moans. Her fingers weaved through his hair as his tongue trailed slowly from her mouth to her ear and then down her neck, where he sucked. Soft whimpers of desire left her lips as he lazily trailed his tongue down to her breasts, laving each nipple into hard points before continuing south.

She might die from the pleasure his tongue was bringing her. Every nerve in her skin was heightened by his gentle strokes, leaving her mind in a state of bliss and her body beyond aroused. She'd never had a lover be so gentle, so thorough, so completely in tune with her needs and desires.

As his tongue drew closer to her core, she brushed over her nipples, then pinched them, trying to balance the gentleness with some pain. Moaning in desperation, she pleaded, "Drew, I want you in me."

His fingers covered hers, encouraging her to pinch her nipples harder. At the same time, he dragged his tongue across her clit, causing her to moan loudly and buck up against his mouth. He continued to slowly lick and suck her core, still pinching at her nipples, her body on fire.

When she thought she wouldn't be able to stand another moment, he rose, slid back up over her body and pushed into her while claiming her mouth in a kiss. Her hands clutched around his back, nails biting deep into his skin as he pushed deeper and deeper.

Her muscles began to tighten as she felt the familiar build toward her climax, when he suddenly stopped. He kissed her softly then and pulled out. She opened her eyes wide in question but then understood as Drew held tightly to her and rolled over so that she now straddled him. Without a word, he guided her soft core back onto his erect cock.

She started to rock back and forth, her clit sliding against the roughness of him. Her head tilted back and she groaned as he surged harder, her core beginning to tingle again. His arms snaked under hers and pulled her tighter against him, grasping her head in his hands, as he bit out a command through gritted teeth. "Come now, baby! Come with me!"

She could only whimper, "Yes, yes, yes," as she came, meeting each of Drew's thrusts, holding onto him with every ounce of strength she had left. She clenched her eyes tight as her body exploded in a flash of fireworks, sparks flying free, floating away into oblivion.

DREW HELD Scarlett in his arms, feeling her release and then her complete surrender as he came apart inside of her. He rolled her onto her side, holding her gently, not wanting to separate himself from her yet. As if she could read his mind, she adjusted her body and melted into him, releasing a deep, satisfied breath.

He lay there, holding her for several minutes, before sliding out of her. He pulled her hand into his and held it against his lips, kissing her knuckles lightly. "Thank you for the best morning I've had in a while."

"I could say the same to you," she whispered, squeezing his hand in return.

His heart thundered in his chest as he realized he may have just wandered into dangerous territory. He was supposed to be fucking away his worries this weekend, but what he'd just done with Scarlett went beyond fucking for him. Every time he tried to draw a line with her, he seemed to cross it. And what was worse was that this was her first time; she likely didn't realize that this wasn't normal behavior from him or any Dom.

Her stomach grumbled as she lay flush against him, and then she giggled.

"Hungry?"

"I won't even try to deny it this time!"

He dropped her hand and sat up, looking down at her reclining form, smiling. "That's what good sex will do to you."

He stood and extended his hand to help her from the bed. As they walked to the stairs, he gathered their clothing and carried it up with them.

Once they were back in the main house, he stopped at the phone in the entryway. "What would you like to eat? I think I'll just call in the chef to make us something for lunch."

Scarlett tilted her head in thought. "Would you think I'm crazy if I told you that a grilled cheese and tomato soup sound heavenly to me right now?"

He smiled broadly. "That actually sounds delicious. I can't remember the last time I had a grilled cheese. I'm sure it was probably years ago and made by my mother."

"It's a staple at my house. We love them." Scarlett smiled back at him.

His brow furrowed for a moment, causing Scarlett a moment of pause. "Are you okay?"

He recovered quickly and smiled. "Yes. I'm fine. You go ahead and shower. I'll call the kitchen and order for us, then shower in the spare to give you a bit of space."

She bowed slightly, grinning. "Why, thank you, kind Sir. Any requests on attire?"

"Surprise me." He watched as Scarlett's naked ass disappeared into the bedroom. He tilted his head. *Who the hell was "we"?*

CHAPTER
Six

"DAMN IT, Scott, you knew I was off-limits this weekend! Is it impossible for you to handle this one thing?"

Drew paced the length of the kitchen, feet landing hard with each step, as Scarlett silently sat on one of the stools at the bar where two covered trays waited. Jesus, she was wearing navy blue silk—the same color he'd tied her up in.

He gave her an apologetic look and then held up a finger to indicate he would be a moment. Scott was clamoring on about a complication with one of the hotels being built. He could really care less at this point but knew his father would and knew it had to be dealt with.

"Fine, fine. Give me fifteen minutes and I'll call you back. I need to deal with something else right now." He clicked end on the phone screen and raked his hands through his hair in frustration before turning back to Scarlett.

"Time to deal with me now?" she quipped and then instantly regretted it as his expression morphed from frustration to anger. That was exactly something his ex-wife would have said to him, and the last thing he wanted to hear from Scarlett.

"Scarlett, not now." He walked over to the bar, removing the cover from both trays before sitting down beside her.

"Let's eat. I only have fifteen minutes."

He pushed one of the trays closer to her and noticed her head was down, an apologetic look on her face. She turned toward him timidly. "I'm sorry. It wasn't my place to speak to you that way."

He shook his head, frustrated at having to explain himself, and placed his spoon down on the counter. "No, I'm sorry. Everyone knows I'm off-limits this weekend, but something came up that can't wait, and I need to deal with it."

He brushed a lock of hair away from her face, hooking it behind her ear. He took his finger and, placing it under her chin, lifted her head up. "Look at me, Scarlett."

She raised her eyes, meeting his intent stare.

"My job demands a lot from me." He sighed, wondering how much he should share with her before continuing. "I was married once. She left me because she said my job always came first. I'm trying really hard to separate my personal time from my business, but there are always situations that can't be avoided."

He dropped his hand, placing it back on the counter but continued to look her in the eye.

She was looking at him with surprise on her face. "Drew, I'm sorry. I didn't realize. I mean, I didn't mean to infer—"

He put his hand up to interrupt her. "Stop. How could you? You just hit a nerve. You're actually the first person in a long time to make me want to forget about my job. No more apologies. Let's just eat lunch."

He leaned forward and brushed his lips against hers, lightly at first but then becoming more intense as both of her hands came up to his face and pulled him in closer. He pulled away after a moment, breaking the kiss with a few smaller ones, and then leaned back.

"I'm really sorry, Drew."

He nodded and then turned back to their lunches.

"We should eat before this gets any colder."

He dipped a corner of his sandwich into his soup and took a generous bite, groaning loudly. "I forgot how amazing these are!"

She laughed and took a bite of her sandwich. "See? I told you!"

When they had both finished their soups and sand-wiches, Scarlett got up to put the dirty dishes in the sink. He got up and followed behind her, startling her when she turned around.

"What are you doing?"

Instead of responding, he stepped forward, forcing her to take a step back and bump up against the sink. He placed both hands beside her on the counter, leaning down to whisper into her ear, "I love you in that color. I can't wait to tie you up in it again."

He ran his nose down her cheek until his lips met hers in a sensuous kiss. She wrapped her arms around his neck, clutching his hair in her fingers, deepening the connection. He groaned loudly and then pulled apart from her.

"Every time I'm in this kitchen, I want to throw you up on this counter and have my way with you."

"So do it. I'm not stopping you." She reached out to pull him back to her, but he put his hands up and walked backward, smiling.

"I've never hated my job more than I do right now, but I have to go make these calls or I'm afraid I'll be pulled away even longer. "

She pushed her lower lip out, pouting, and ran her hands seductively up her body, over her breasts, then leaned back into the counter. "Okay, well, I'll be ready whenever you are."

He raised his eyebrows. "Are you teasing me again, naughty little kitten?"

She shook her head. "Nope. Just making you a promise."

He clucked his tongue as he turned and walked away. "Oh, I'm going to hold you to that promise, beautiful."

HANNAH COULDN'T HELP the huge smile that spread across her face as Drew walked away. He wanted her. He really wanted her. She was doing this submissive thing right. It was going better than she had thought it would.

Still smiling, she walked into the bedroom. She decided she would go outside and spend some time by the pool. The sun was out and maybe she could catch some extended summer sun.

She opened the wardrobe to look for a bathing suit. She found a simple black bikini and pulled it on. The top had ample coverage, but when she turned around and looked in the mirror, more of her ass was showing than was covered. *Hmm, not half bad,* she thought, deciding to keep it on.

She walked into the living room and opened the French doors that led out to the pool. One of the advantages to staying in a bungalow was that each one had its very own private pool and hot tub. The back yard was completely surrounded by an eight-foot oak fence but was beautifully landscaped with flowers and bushes to create an almost tropical feel.

After grabbing some sunscreen and a towel from a cabinet against the house, she made her way over to one of the lounge chairs.

It was a gorgeous day without a cloud in the sky. If only she'd thought to bring her phone out so she could listen to some music, but she was too comfortable to get up and go back in the house. Instead, her head filled with thoughts of Drew and the time they had spent together so far. As this was her first auction experience—well, her first submissive experience, if she was being honest—she had no idea if the way Drew was being with her was expected.

Domme Maria had given the impression that her time as a submissive would be much more taxing in nature. But thus far, Drew had demanded very little of her, and this seemed more like a weekend spent with a lover than a Dominant.

The sexual chemistry between them was instant and electric, and in no way was she "performing." She was truly enjoying his company and had to admit the sex was amazing. She wasn't going to fool herself into thinking all outcomes with a Dominant would be this easy or natural. She had gotten lucky.

After a half hour in the hot sun, she knew she was in danger of melting if she didn't get into the pool. She dove in gracefully and swam a few laps before stopping in the shallow end. She used the stairs to climb out of the pool and walk back to her chair. She could see Drew pacing in the living room, talking to someone on his phone. It certainly didn't seem like he was going to be done anytime soon.

Before lying back down, she looked around nervously and wondered if she could get away with sunning topless. The perimeter fence seemed to completely obscure any possibility of anyone outside the yard from seeing her. Safe enough then. She untied her top, dropping it next to her chair before lying on her stomach and stretching her hands overhead. She lay there, listening to the gentle breeze and birds chirping, and slowly drifted to sleep.

Hannah felt something tug on her wrists and slowly opened her eyes. She was met with Drew's smoldering glare as he kneeled down at the head of her chair. She glanced at her hands and was startled to see that they'd been bound to the top slat of the chair with her bikini top.

"Good afternoon, Sleeping Beauty," Drew drawled before rising to his full height.

She was still on her stomach and had to lean her head all the way back to keep her eyes on his. She glanced down at her hands quickly, tugging, and then back up at him. "What are you doing?"

"The question is what were *you* doing?" He walked toward the foot of the chair. She tried to track him with her eyes but found it difficult due to her bindings.

"I'm not sure what you mean. I've just been lying by the pool."

Instead of answering, he grasped the waist of her bathing suit on each side of her hips and dragged them down and off her. His hand traced back up her leg and then rested on her ass. He started rubbing her cheeks in a slow, circular motion. He finally spoke, and it wasn't gentle.

"Don't you mean you've just been lying by this pool without your top on? Where anyone could have entered and seen you?"

She was surprised he was so angry. "But, Sir, there is a fence. It seemed safe to me."

Drew scoffed in disagreement. "You think it's safe? I decide what's safe for you. And where it's safe for you. And most of all, I decide when you take your clothes off."

She was trying to form another response when his hand stopped caressing her ass and suddenly came down in a hard smack. She yelped in surprise, ceasing any further argument that had been on her lips.

His hand rose again, and she prepared herself for another smack. She wasn't disappointed. This one was harder than the last. She felt him sit and slide her legs up and over his lap.

"Do you know why I'm spanking you, Scarlett?" His voice was harsh, his breathing heavy. He was excited by this. And that excited her.

"Yes, Sir. Only you are allowed to see me this way," she replied huskily, already anticipating the next smack against her ass.

"That's right. And to make sure you remember, you'll get ten more slaps. I want you counting out loud."

He brought his hand up and down again ten more times, each time a little harder than the last, waiting for her to count between each one. After the tenth smack, he rubbed her ass lightly, his breathing heavy. His lips kissed one side of her buttocks, and then his fingers rubbed over her pussy. She was soaking wet, and he sucked in a breath when he felt it.

Then he chuckled, still caressing her swollen nub. "You liked that?"

There was no way she could say otherwise. Her core was pulsating from the vibrations of his spanking and she wanted nothing more than to climax. "Yes."

As if he could read her mind, he stuck two fingers inside her and started pumping them back and forth. She spread her legs wider, pushing herself back into his hand as she whimpered in ecstasy.

He grabbed onto her hip with his other hand, steadying her. "You want me deeper, Scarlett?"

"Oh god," she breathed out, "please, Drew, yes."

DREW COULD FEEL his cock getting hard but pushed down his desire. He pushed his fingers deeper into Scarlett, and as her muscles started to clench, he pulled out and slid her off his lap, standing up. Her head spun around to look at him, shock on her face.

"What are you doing? Why did you stop?"

He kneeled down beside her so that his face was even with hers. Then he slowly inserted the two fingers that had just been inside Scarlett into his mouth and sucked.

"Mmm, you taste so good." He felt wicked as she stared

at him, mouth open, eyes wide in disbelief. "Don't take your clothes off again where someone could see you."

He reached up then and quickly untied the bikini top, rubbing her arms to bring circulation back into them.

"You are evil, Drew. Pure and simple." She sat up, glaring at him.

"Believe me, this hurts me almost as much as you." He looked down at the prominent bulge in his jeans.

"I can help you with that if you want," she offered suggestively.

"Maybe later. I think my cock needs a break, even if it doesn't realize it."

He lay down behind her on the lounge chair, drawing her back to his front, wrapping his arms around her. He nuzzled her hair, inhaling deeply, savoring the smell of the oil and sun on her, but also the light floral scent that always seemed to be on her skin.

"You smell good," he rumbled into her ear and tugged her in closer.

Hannah smiled but didn't reply. She was enjoying being in his embrace and the simplicity of the moment. She ran her fingers up and down the length of his arm, grazing the downy hair that covered it. When she touched his hand, he pulled her fingers into his, entwining them, and held her there. They stayed like that for a long time before Drew finally kissed her head, released her and sat up.

She lifted herself off him and turned to face him. He stroked her cheek lovingly and then leaned forward, capturing her lips in a gentle kiss. He pulled slowly away, never breaking eye contact with her. She was starting to feel nervous, as this seemed entirely too intimate for what her purpose was supposed to be. She broke his gaze by looking down at her hands and cleared her throat, unsure of what to do next. Luckily, he broke the silence.

"I have a surprise for you."

She raised her head in apprehension, not sure if she could take any more surprises. "Really? Good or bad?"

Drew laughed. "It's a good one. I think."

He stood up, dragging her with him. He grabbed the towel on the chair and wrapped it around her, pulling her close. He leaned down and whispered into her ear, "Do you want to go to a party?"

She looked up at him, her eyes crinkling as her cheeks rose. "What kind of party?"

"The kind where you get to dress up like a princess."

"Then yes!" She jumped up and down in place like a little child, unable to contain her glee.

"Good. Because I have a whole team of people inside, at your beck and call to help you get ready."

She stopped jumping and looked at Drew, eyebrows drawn up, her hand covering her mouth. "Oh my god, Drew. Were they inside while you were spanking me?"

His reply was casual and dismissive. "Yes, but believe me, it's nothing they haven't seen or heard before."

Her face turned a bright crimson. "I have to go in there now knowing that they probably either saw or heard everything you just did to me?" She covered her face with her hands, groaning, "I'm so embarrassed."

Drew grasped her gently around the neck, pulling her face close to his, and practically growled, "Are you saying you're embarrassed to be with me? Because I'm pretty sure any one of the people in the next room would be more than happy to take your place."

She balked at his suggestion and the callousness of his statement. She couldn't keep up with his hot and cold behavior. Less than ten minutes ago, he'd been holding her hand in an act of surprising intimacy, and now he was suddenly reminding her she was simply a paid servant.

She fell back into submissive mode. "No, Sir. I'm only embarrassed that someone may have been watching us."

Drew pulled her in closer and whispered in her ear, "I don't care who is watching. As long as I'm the one that's with you." He kissed her roughly and let go of her neck.

He started walking away toward the house. "Come. Let's go meet your entourage." And just like that, any anger he expressed was gone.

Am I a dog now? Cause that's what that last command felt like. Hannah shook her head in confusion but quickly followed so she wouldn't provoke another outburst of anger.

CHAPTER
Seven

WALKING INTO THE HOUSE, Hannah hugged the towel tightly to her chest to ensure it didn't slip and reveal any more surprises to the staff waiting inside. Drew stopped at the opened door, waiting for her to pass through. Surprisingly, there was no one in sight.

"Where are they?" she whispered as she stepped further into the living room.

Drew closed the door behind her and once again pulled her close before speaking. "Do you really think I would risk anyone else seeing you naked?"

She wasn't sure how to reply, so she remained quiet, her eyes on his feet. He placed his finger under her chin, lifting it. "I had the staff set up and wait for you in the master suite. I don't want to share you with anyone, Scarlett. You are mine and only mine. Understood?"

"At least until tomorrow," she replied quietly, knowing she might just be adding fuel to a simmering fire.

As if burned, he dropped his hand suddenly and took a

step back. He took a deep breath as he looked up at the ceiling, eyes closed. He blew the breath back out slowly and, returning his gaze to her, nodded.

"Well, until tomorrow then." He turned sharply away from her and started walking to the bedroom. "Come."

She wanted to scream in frustration over the mixed signals he was sending her but instead just stayed quiet and did as he commanded.

When she came around the corner to the doorway of the bedroom, she could hear chatter that immediately stopped when they saw Drew. He stopped just beyond the entrance to the room and motioned for her to enter before addressing the staff.

"You have two hours." And then he pivoted and walked away. She watched him leave, surprised at the way he'd addressed them and at the lack of any to her. She sighed and then turned her head back to the staff.

"Oh my god! Just look at you!" She finally took in the staff Drew had left her with. A young Asian man, dressed in shiny black pants and an even shinier silver button-down shirt, came forward and circled her, arms waving above his head as he went. "Drew said you were beautiful, but this is just too much!

"Karla! Laura! Are you seeing this?" he exclaimed loudly to the two other women in the room.

A small, wavy-haired brunette took one of Hannah's hands—which were still clutching her towel—and led her further into the room. "Yes, Marco. We see her. But please, stop! You're scaring the poor thing! Just look at her!"

Turning to the other woman in the room, the brunette

continued, "Karla, you are so lucky! Look at all this beautiful hair you get to work with!"

Karla, now that Hannah knew what her name was, had long blonde hair, similar to her own, running like strands of silk down her entire back. Jealous did not even begin to describe the envy Hannah felt at its beauty.

The woman looked a bit bored with Marco and the brunette's whole excited routine and just nodded her head before drawling, "Yes, well, we only have two hours, so we better get to work."

"Oh, Karla, you're such a little grouch!" Marco shot an exasperated look at the blonde and then herded Hannah and the other women into the large attached dressing room.

"First things first!" Marco continued in a rush. "We have to show you your dress and make sure it fits."

Hannah gasped at the creation hanging from the center of the room. "Oh my god," she whispered. "Is that for me?"

Marco slapped her playfully on the arm and replied gleefully, "Of course it's for you! Do you love it?"

"It's absolutely gorgeous." She padded closer in excitement.

In the front, the dress was held up by a single strap embroidered with diamonds that wound up and over the shoulder. More diamonds spilled down the left side waist and wrapped around to join four straps that angled diagonally across the back, joining the shoulder strap.

The sheer silk fabric was pitch black starting at the shoulder but spilled down in an ombré effect, turning to a deep, royal blue at the floor-length hem of the full skirt. Under the top layer of silk, a fitted, black satin sheath was attached.

Of course he would choose royal blue. It seemed to be his color of choice. She ran her hand over the luxurious fabric and marveled at its softness. She turned to the three others in the room, who had been standing quietly while she admired the dress. "I feel like freaking Cinderella!"

She started hopping up and down, clapping her hands in excitement. Marco rushed over, grasping both of her hands in his. "Well then, let's try it on, Cinderella, and see if it fits!"

"Yes, please!" She could not contain her astonishment at wearing this splendor of a dress and smiled from ear to ear as Marco removed it from the hanger so she could try it on.

"Drop that towel, darling. The dress isn't going to fit over it."

She looked down at the towel and then up at Marco, the spanking she had just endured fresh in her mind and still stinging her buttocks. "Oh, I don't think I had better do that in front of you. I don't think Drew would like that."

"Listen, darling, I'm about as interested in seeing you naked as I would be my grandmother." Marco waved one of his hands in disagreement. "You just don't have what I'm looking for. Get my drift?"

"Oh!" She deciphered his meaning and blushed at his candor. So, without further ado, she dropped the towel and let Marco help her into the dress.

After zipping up the side, he strolled around her, hmming and umming under his breath while shifting some of the fabric, placing a few pins strategically to adjust the dress on her before finally exclaiming, "It's almost perfect. You would think I had made this dress for you!"

She beamed at him. "It feels comfortable. Do you want me to walk around at all? It seems a bit long."

"That's because you don't have the shoes on yet, darling! But yes, do a little walk around for me please so I can see it move on you."

She paraded back and forth across the dressing room, twirling at each turn, watching as the bottom of the skirt swished out each time.

"Okay, you're good. Let's get you out of it now. I just have to make a few little adjustments."

Marco helped her unzip the dress and step out of it. She quickly grabbed the towel lying on the floor and wrapped it around her.

"Not so quick!" Laura—the curly-haired brunette—was snapping orders at her now. "You need to shower and wash your hair. But be quick please, we have so little time."

"Okay, I'll be extra quick." Hannah scurried out of the dressing room and made her way to the shower as ordered.

Fifteen minutes later, she was covered in her robe and sitting at the dressing table as Karla brushed her hair and Laura removed her current polish from her finger and toenails. "Mr. Sapphire wants your hair up, but I think we need to add a little framing around your face, so I will blow your front out a bit straighter and curl your hair in the back, okay?"

"Who's Mr. Sapphire?" Hannah asked curiously. Both girls stopped what they were doing and looked at her strangely.

Laura replied in a confused tone, "Andrew Sapphire. You know, that gorgeous drink of water that brought you in here?"

"Of course!" She laughed nervously, trying to cover up

her mistake. "I'm so used to calling him Drew that I totally spaced out!"

Both girls looked at her like she had two heads and resumed their work.

His name is Andrew Sapphire? How could I have fucked someone four—or was it five?—times in the last twenty-four hours and not know his full name? But then, I guess he doesn't know my real name either. And now all the blue makes sense . . .

Hannah twisted her hands together as the reality of her situation hit her. She was so caught up in the moments and the way he had been making her feel that she'd forgotten that this was just a job. She needed to get herself back in line, and quickly, before her heart completely took over.

The next hour and a half flew by as Karla curled and primped and pinned her hair into the most amazing hairstyle she had ever worn. The stylist had created large, curly waves, then swept them to the side of her head in a large bun and pinned them up loosely so that a few locks of hair dangled down. The front was swept over to the same side and pulled into a side bun, again with a few longer, curled strands left out to frame her face.

Her makeup was heavier than she normally wore, but it still looked minimal on her, only enhancing her features. Laura had outlined Hannah's upper lid in a popular cat-eye style and then softened it with a darker blue shadow, highlighted by a swipe of silver.

Soft, pink cheeks and lips brought it all together. Laura had also discreetly applied some cover-up over the fading bite mark on her shoulder without so much as a word about it. Hannah's fingers and toes were now covered with a silver nail polish that she normally would have thought a bit too bold but matched the diamonds embroidered on her dress perfectly.

Before Marco would allow her to step into the dress, Laura and Karla worked to strap on the most amazing shoes that had ever been on her feet.

The base of each shoe was silver, elevated by a thin, four-inch stiletto heel. A single, inch-wide silver strap crossed the top of the shoe, embroidered with the same diamonds on the dress. The back of the shoe connected to another inch-wide silver strap, similarly embroidered, that wrapped around her ankle and tied in the back with a silver ribbon. It appeared as though she was wearing diamond cuffs on her ankles. Had Cinderella felt this wondrous about the shoes she'd worn to the ball?

At last, Marco allowed her to step into the now-altered dress, and zipped her up. Her personal beauty team of three all stepped back and simply gazed at her without saying a word.

"What?" Hannah exclaimed. "You're all making me nervous!"

Marco, as usual, was the first to speak. "Oh, darling, it's just that you are so unbelievably stunning. Just a vision."

Laura nodded in agreement, eyes wide in wonder. Karla just nodded, a satisfied, if not smug, smile on her lips.

"Are you sure?" Hannah asked, unconvinced, working her hands nervously over the skirt of the dress.

"I'm sure." Drew's rich voice sounded from behind, and she spun around, almost losing her balance on her four-inch stilettos.

"Out. Now." Drew's gaze was fixed on her, but he made it clear that Marco and the ladies were done.

Marco clapped his hands. "Come, girls, grab your things! It's time to go."

Like little mice, they quickly gathered their tools and scurried out of the room. As Marco walked by, he pecked Hannah on the cheek and beamed with pride. The front door slammed behind them as they left.

Drew was still staring at her, having not moved a step or spoken another word. He was wearing a traditional tuxedo, but instead of a standard black bow tie, he wore a dark, royal-blue silk tie in a Windsor knot.

"Do I look okay, Sir?"

He took a step forward and then circled around her, examining her like a lion assessing its prey. "Something is missing."

"Is there? I think Marco did everything you requested." She inhaled deeply, savoring the scent Drew left in his wake. It was crisp and light, but carried with it a subtle cedar-and-musk undertone. It immediately aroused her senses and made her want to run her hand up his neck so that she could bring him closer and nuzzle him.

He walked over to a drawer on the far side of the closet and opened it. He reached inside and pulled out two light teal suede boxes. And not just any blue—they were Tiffany blue. She practically swooned just seeing the boxes.

"That's because this is something only I can do." He beckoned for her to follow him to the full-length mirror against the opposite wall of the dressing room. He set the boxes down on a table and turned toward her.

"Do you know what a submissive collar is?" he asked her quietly, his hand still lying over the boxes on the table.

"Yes, Sir."

When a Dom and a sub entered into an exclusive relationship, one that involved a commitment almost as strong as a marriage, the sub was very often collared, demonstrating ownership to everyone else. "But . . ."

"But what, Scarlett?" He still spoke quietly.

"But I am only yours for another day. There shouldn't bet be any reason to collar me." Her hand rose involuntarily to her neck, her fingers running around its base absently.

"Oh, but that's where you're wrong. I very much want to collar you. Even if it is just for another twenty-four hours."

He moved behind her, resting his hands on either side of her shoulders. "Look at yourself. Can you see what I see?"

She looked at her reflection in the mirror. She did look beautiful. More so than she had been before. But it was the clothes, the hair, and the makeup. This wasn't really her. "I suppose I see myself, but made up to be what you want me to be."

He shook his head in disagreement. "Oh, Scarlett, you are exactly who you should be, and that is just you." He met her eyes in the mirror. "Yes, you're beautiful, but it's your grace, your charm and your wit that will grab anyone's attention. I intend to make sure everyone knows you belong to me, and only me."

With that, he reached down to open the larger of the two boxes sitting on the table.

She gasped at what lay inside. It was the most exquisite diamond necklace she had ever seen. Eight rows of diamonds circled in a lace-like collar.

"Do you like it?" He looked at her in the mirror as he pulled it out of the box and unclasped it.

"Like it? Drew, it's amazing." She raised her hand to stop him from putting it on. "Are you sure?"

"About collaring you?"

She looked at him, trying to assess if this was a trivial moment for him, but as always, his face remained neutral.

He turned her around, raising the intensity of the moment, and looked in her eyes while he answered. "I'm sure. Are you?"

"I-I don't know." She tilted her head. "I know I shouldn't ask this, but I'm just going to anyway. Is this something you do to all your submissives?"

His eyes narrowed in thought at her question before he broke his gaze and turned her back toward the mirror. His hands brought the choker around the front of her, and then his fingers trailed over the diamonds before fastening it.

She looked up, meeting his eyes in the mirror, and could see desire coursing through them, darker than she'd ever them before.

"No. I've never put a collar on someone before."

Her heart hammered in her chest at what this implied. Even though some of his behavior toward her had seemed too intimate, this act definitely confirmed he was feeling more for her than he should.

He chuckled low as he opened the other box. "Don't worry, Scarlett, it's just for the weekend. I promise I'll take it off later."

Although the comment was meant to offer her some relief, it didn't. She tried to push back her confusion and questions until a later time. She didn't want to spoil this moment, whatever it was. Even though she didn't want to admit it to herself, deep down, she was secretly thrilled that he was claiming her.

She liked Drew, more than she probably should, and wanted to stay in this fairy-tale bubble for a little while longer before having to think about the real world again.

"There's more?" she spluttered, watching as he opened the second box. It was overwhelming.

"Only one more thing." Out of the second box, which was smaller and squarer in shape, he pulled a matching, smaller cuff and secured it around her left wrist.

"Now you're complete." He looked at her again in the mirror, eyes smoldering. "You look absolutely ravishing. There should be no doubt in anyone's mind who you belong to."

"I'm yours," she whispered, not breaking his gaze.

He grasped her chin, tilting her mouth back to his, and kissed her fiercely and quickly. "Fuck yes. Hearing you say that makes me so hard."

She was practically panting and really didn't care anymore about going to some ball. She reached her hand back to feel his erection, rubbing it through the material of his pants. He chuckled and grabbed her wrist, ceasing the motion.

"As much as I'd like to ravish you right here, we need to go so we won't be late." He kissed her softly on the forehead and shifted his grip from around her wrist to her hand instead. He led her out of the dressing room and through the bedroom.

"One second please; I just need to grab my clutch."

Earlier, Marco had given her a small, black satin clutch with just a few scattered diamond stones embroidered on the edging. Laura had given her an extra lipstick and powder compact for touch-ups throughout the night. Those were the only items in the clutch.

"You shouldn't need a thing. I'll be taking care of everything."

"It's just lipstick and powder. You know, for touch-ups and such." She smiled at him.

"Very good." He extended his arm to her, which she took, and led her out of the house to a waiting car.

"Are we driving?" she inquired as he helped her into the front seat of the sleek black car.

"Yes. I'm driving."

He shut the door before she could ask any more questions, walked around to the driver's side and seated himself in the car. He started it, backing out of the driveway, and then slowly proceeded through the compound. When he got to the large wrought-iron gates, he slowed to a stop and rolled down the window.

The guard seemed to recognize him immediately. "Oh hello, Mr. Sapphire." He tipped his hat at him before walking to a switch to activate it, allowing the gates to swing open wide. "You're clear to leave."

"Thank you, Jones." Drew nodded as he rolled up the window and then zipped through the gates and out of the compound.

CHAPTER
Eight

DREW PULLED onto the main road, shifting the car into a higher gear, and accelerated, scenery starting to slide quickly past the windows of the car.

"Drew, why are we leaving the estate?" Scarlett asked. "I didn't think we were allowed off the grounds."

"Don't worry. I got permission from Domme Maria." He looked over at her with a mischievous grin on his face. "You don't think I would break the rules do you?"

"Did it occur to you to ask *me* if I wanted to be taken off of the grounds?"

He was surprised by the indignant tone in her voice and glanced over to see if he could read her face. If anything, he was taken aback that she would be angry.

"Why are you upset about us leaving the estate? You do know that I would never do anything to harm you, correct?"

She shook her head, responding, "I'm upset that you didn't think to ask me. It's great that you asked Domme Maria, but this should have been my choice."

Drew swerved the car over to the side of the road, putting it into park. "Scarlett, I'll ask you again: do you really think I would do anything to hurt you? Take you somewhere that would bring you harm? Have I treated you badly over the last two days?"

She took his hands in hers, squeezing them briefly. "Of course I don't think you would hurt me. I would have never let you do what you did to me today if I didn't trust you."

"Then what is it?" Frustration edged his response.

"It should have been my choice to leave the grounds. Not something you should have assumed I would want to do. I don't know where we are going. How do I explain you if I run into someone I know?"

He stared at her blankly. It hadn't really occurred to him to ask her, or that she might know someone. That was an assumption he shouldn't have made. Especially given the fact that he knew nothing about her.

He found himself in new territory once again; he actually felt remorse. He moved his hands over hers now, holding them lightly. The bracelet looked stunning on her wrist.

"I apologize then. I assumed when I told you we'd be going to a party that you understood it wasn't on the estate. I should have explained further. Would you still like to go?"

"May I ask where we are going first?" Scarlett inquired in a soft tone from her side of the car.

"It's a charity ball. In the city. Normally, I wouldn't have attempted to attend something of this nature on a weekend I'm at the bungalow, but the cause is very dear to my heart."

"Then yes, I'd like to go with you to the ball." She was quiet for a moment and then giggled, taking her hand from his, covering her mouth as her cheeks flushed pink. "I feel like I just got asked to the prom!"

He turned back in his seat, smiling broadly, relief washing over him that she no longer seemed angry, and steered the car back out onto the road to continue their journey. "We can pretend if you want. I never went to my prom."

"What?" Her voice held a note of surprise. "How is that possible? You're like perfect prom-king material."

He scoffed before responding, "My father only saw me as the heir to his business, so going to dances and parties were beneath my station. He made sure I only had time for schoolwork, and if I wasn't doing that, I was working for him."

"That's sad."

He shrugged. "It is what it is. It wasn't all bad. I traveled all over the world. Believe me, I had my share of fun when my father wasn't watching."

"You said the charity was close to your heart? Can I ask what the ball is for?"

Drew looked over at her, eyebrow raised, not immune to her attempt at moving the subject away from his father. He smiled inwardly at her ability to recognize a difficult topic for him.

"It's a charity for disabled veterans and their families. Do you know how many vets come back from the Middle East and get no help at all? It's a shame. Or even worse, soldiers are killed and not enough is done to support any family they leave behind."

HANNAH JOLTED IN SURPRISE. *What a small world it is.* "Do you know someone who was there?"

Drew took his gaze off the road to look at her. "Yes."

"I'm sorry. I truly am." *I know more about this than he can possibly imagine.*

"Thank you." He shrugged. "I'm lucky, I suppose. My brother came home. Even if it took us a long time to actually get him back."

She sat in silence for a few moments, looking out the window at the trees flying by, lost in her own thoughts. The lights of Manhattan were looming ahead, and she wondered again about the party.

"How will you introduce me tonight? I mean, in case we see someone I know or someone you know."

He let out a little huff of laughter. "Oh, I'm quite sure we'll see some people I know, and I'm sure they'll be asking about you. I haven't brought anyone to a function with me since my divorce."

"What?" She couldn't contain the shock in her voice. *He hasn't brought anyone else since his divorce? Sweet Jesus, this is getting complicated.*

"Don't worry. Very few people know about my alternate lifestyle. I'll simply introduce you as my date."

"And they'll just accept that?" *Sure they will.*

He chuckled and shook his head. "Probably not. But that's all they'll be getting. Are you really worried you'll see people here you know? The tickets were twenty-five hundred a place setting, Scarlett."

Instead of being offended, she just raised an eyebrow at him. "Snobby much? Besides, you just might be surprised."

His brow raised in response. "Touché." There was a moment of tension between them before he continued. "Besides, neither one of us has to worry about anyone recognizing us."

She eyed him curiously. "Why is that?"

"It's a masquerade ball." A devilish grin spread across his face. "We'll have masks on the entire time. We can even make up names for ourselves if we want."

She laughed at that. "My name *is* made up, Drew."

"Ah, yes. I guess that makes it even easier then, doesn't it?" he acknowledged in kind.

"I suppose so," she said. "But that means we have to come up with something for you now, doesn't it?"

"I already thought of the perfect name."

"Oh, I can't wait. Please, tell me how I should address you this evening—besides Master, of course."

He responded in a forced Southern accent, "Why Miss Scarlett, I'm surprised you even have to ask."

She immediately caught the reference. Was he really going to pick the name Rhett? Could he possibly know why she had picked the name Scarlett as her alternate identity? The mounting coincidences left her mind reeling.

Hiding her bewilderment, she simply responded in her best Southern drawl. "Why Mr. Butler, I do declare, this might actually be a fun evening after all!"

They both laughed and finally, the heavy mood that had started their evening seemed to evaporate.

"I've never been to a masquerade party before. Have you?"

"Yes, several actually." He glanced at her and winked. "But this is the first one I've actually looked forward to in quite some time. I think perhaps the company helps."

"Why thank you, kind Sir." She blushed as she replied, warmed by the fact that he seemed to want to be with her as much as she wanted to be with him.

"That's actually the reason Domme Maria allowed me to bring you off of the estate this evening. She knew your identity would be safe. Do you feel better about attending now?" he asked.

"It's not that I ever minded going. I just would have liked to be asked. That's all."

"Well, I'm grateful you said yes." He motioned out the window. "We're here."

He pulled the car into the long circular drive of a hotel and waited in a line of cars for the valet. As the valet approached, Drew stepped out of the car and grabbed something from the backseat. He took a ticket from the young man, then walked around to her side of the car, opening the door and holding out one hand to assist her.

She rose up gracefully before him. With her heels on, she was much taller than normal and could almost look him in the eyes now. Well, maybe his lips. But that wasn't such a bad view either. Before she could help herself, she leaned forward and pressed a kiss to them.

"I'm sorry we fought in the car," she said as she pulled away from him. "I didn't mean to make you angry."

He smiled back at her, his eyes crinkling. "You do seem to do that a lot, don't you?"

He leaned down to kiss her this time and then whispered in her ear, "But you also seem to have a way of making me forget all about it moments later."

"Here, turn around; I have to put your mask on before we go inside."

"Wait, can I see it first?" she asked eagerly.

"Of course. I forgot you hadn't seen it. Marco had these made for us as well."

He held out the mask for her perusal. It was breathtaking. Black silk had been woven together to create beautiful swirls around the eyeholes, swooping up over the eyes like feathers. The same diamonds that were sewn onto her dress has also been scattered over the mask. The ties were made of delicate black lace woven tightly together to allow them to be tied more easily.

"Oh, Drew, it's so pretty. Will you put it on?" She looked up at him adoringly as she handed the mask back to him.

"With pleasure." He carefully placed it on her face, lining up the eyes properly before wrapping the lace straps around her head and tying it in place.

"Is it comfortable?"

"Yes, it feels perfect. Do you need help with yours?"

But he was already tying his mask into place. His was a much simpler mask, made of a solid black piece of silk cut into a standard eye-mask shape. The blue of his eyes stood in such contrast to the black of the mask, making him look even more handsome than she thought possible.

He held his arm out to her, his terrible Southern accent appearing again. "All right, Miss Scarlett, if you're quite ready, I'll escort you in."

She settled her arm into the crook of his, leaning into

him as they walked. She enjoyed feeling the warmth that always seemed to radiate from him. In moments, they were being ushered into a huge ballroom within the hotel. Its grandeur was something to behold.

Large, round tables lined the perimeter of the room. Each table was covered in sapphire-colored tablecloths, and held eight place settings, silverware gleaming and crystal sparkling. The floral centerpieces on the tables consisted of beautiful white orchids that scented the entire ballroom. The center of the room was kept clear and surrounded a dance floor, and the front of the room held a stage on which an orchestra played.

She gazed around at the opulence in wonder and couldn't believe that she was actually attending this event. The room was quite loud, as most of the guests were arriving, so Drew had to lean down close to her ear to be heard. "Would you like something to drink?"

She smiled back and nodded. "Champagne, please."

"Come this way." He kept her arm in the crook of his and guided her to a table almost at the front of the stage. Two place cards read "Mr. & Mrs. Rhett Butler." He pulled out her chair for her as she stared at him, open-mouthed. Apparently her attending, and each of them with a made-up name, had been a foregone conclusion.

"Stay here, I'll be right back with drinks." He winked at her through his mask and was gone.

She watched in awe as so many beautiful people moved around, chatting and drinking and finding their seats. She tried to count the tables in the room, doing the math at twenty-five hundred a head to see just how much this shindig was bringing in.

She didn't think she could ever get used to living in a world where money flowed this freely. What she could do with the five thousand dollars Drew had paid for these seats . . .

He was suddenly back, a champagne flute in each hand. Other people were now starting to arrive at their table, but she wasn't sure how she was expected to interact with them. Drew sat down beside her, placing her drink in front of her. As if he could sense her nervousness, he leaned over and whispered into her ear, "Just be yourself."

She wasn't quite sure what that meant. "Herself" was Hannah. To him, she was Scarlett. Instead, she just plastered a smile on her face and made small talk with the woman seated to her left about the flowers and her dress.

When she looked up, the entire table was full. Drew seemed to know the gentleman sitting across from him and was deep in conversation. *Hmm, so much for being incognito.*

A waiter walked by with a tray of champagne, so she waved him over and exchanged her empty glass for a full one. It was so delicious she could hardly help it if the first one went down so easily.

Drew's hand rested on her thigh, and then his fingers were slowly inching the fabric of her dress up her leg. When it was high enough, his hand slid onto her bare thigh and rested there, grazing his digits back and forth.

She glanced around the table nervously, hoping no one could see her raised skirt. Just how far north was his hand going to go? As if he could read her mind, his hand started trailing farther up her leg, Drew still deep in conversation with the man across the table as though nothing was happening.

Before things could go much further, she dropped her free hand discreetly under the table and placed it over his, clutching it in warning. As a rebuttal, he pinched the inside of her leg, quick and hard. She cried out in surprise. *What the hell!* The guests closest to her turned their heads toward her.

Drew turned as well and, wearing the slightest of grins, asked, "Are you all right, darling?"

She laughed shakily and addressed the guests at the table. "Sorry, I accidentally stepped on my own foot under the table."

She picked up her champagne and, tipping the glass back, finished it off in a few gulps. Drew's hand was continuing its journey north, and she knew now that trying to stop him was useless. She raised her hand again to signal the waiter for another glass, who delivered it immediately.

His lips were suddenly at her ear, murmuring. "I wouldn't have that third glass of champagne, Scarlett. You haven't eaten in quite some time and I wouldn't want you to lose control."

His innuendo was more than clear. Just because she could, eyes locked onto his, she picked up the glass of champagne and took a big sip.

He raised his eyebrows and tipped his head at her brazen rebuttal, his fingers still moving up her leg until they were at the apex of her thighs. Only a scrap of material covered it as Marco had insisted she could only wear the thong he'd provided to avoid visible panty lines. Drew's finger ran over her pussy before she felt just the slightest bit of pressure on her clit.

She instantly tried to shut her legs, but Drew leaned into

her as if to kiss her, instead growling in her ear, "Spread those legs, Scarlett. Now."

She turned her head to him, eyes wide, silently trying to appeal to his senses, but he was having none of it. He worked his hand further between her legs, laying his palm flat against her mound, and then continued rubbing his middle and forefinger up and down against her clit. The movement instantly brought heat to her core, and her nipples tightened under the silk lining of her dress.

She again brought her hand discreetly under the table, placing it on Drew's forearm, and tried to stop him before anyone else noticed what he was doing.

He leaned over and whispered in her ear, "Your pussy is hot to the touch. Are you sure you want me to stop?"

She turned her head to him and was barely able to whimper, "*Please.*"

He grinned wickedly at her. "Please what? Is that a yes or a no?"

"Please stop or you'll make me come right here," she ground out, lips smiling, teeth gritted.

"Oh, what I wouldn't do to see that." His blue eyes were gleaming under his mask, matching the devilish look on his face, but he complied with her request and slowly slid his hand from between her legs and out of her skirt.

Instead of placing his hand back on the table though, he brought his fingers to his nose and inhaled deeply. He watched as her eyes widened in shock.

"Have I told you how delicious you smell?"

He was leaning close to her and talking low enough that no one could hear their conversation. She nodded hotly, any part of her face not hidden by her mask no doubt flushed a deep pink.

"I cannot wait to taste you later." And then he actually popped his fingers into his mouth, sucking on them as he slowly withdrew them, his gaze locked on hers.

A chuckle escaped him as she leaned away and gulped down more champagne, her eyes darting around the table.

"Am I interrupting?" A deep voice questioned from behind them as a large hand clasped onto Drew's shoulder.

A wide smile stretched across Drew's face as he stood up and embraced the man in a tight hug. "Benny! You're here! How did you find me?"

Hannah quickly appraised the new arrival. He was about the same height as Drew but bulkier, packed with a lot of muscle. He was wearing a tuxedo very similar to Drew's but with a standard black bow tie and no mask. His blue eyes reminded her of Drew's, but Ben's equally dark hair was cut much closer to the scalp. Brothers then, had to be. But, unlike his brother, when she looked into Benny's eyes, she saw something in them she recognized: grief, anger, exhaustion.

"Please, you're my brother. You don't think I know you, even with a mask on? And don't call me Benny. You know I hate that."

"I know, that's why I do it." Drew grinned and turned toward her. "Ben, meet Scarlett, my date."

She stood and faced Drew's brother, extending her hand. Instead of shaking it, he grasped it gently, leaning in close, kissing her on the cheek. "Scarlett. Very nice to meet you."

He turned toward Drew, head tilted toward Scarlett. "This is a nice surprise." And then focused his attention back to her. "I hope he's being nice to you. We were beginning to wonder if he remembered how to date."

She raised an eyebrow at him, wondering just how much about his brother he actually knew, but mustered a polite laugh. "Of course, nothing but a gentleman. It's very nice to meet you."

Upon closer inspection, she noticed he was also holding a cane—part of his ensemble?

"Didn't Drew tell you?" He asked when he noticed where she was looking.

"Tell me what?" Her head tilted.

He raised his left pant leg, exposing a titanium rod fitted into his dress shoe. "I'm a gimp."

She was startled by his bluntness. "I'm sorry. I didn't realize."

"Ben, stop embarrassing her," Drew admonished, then to her, "He likes to make people feel as uncomfortable about it as he does."

Instead of being uncomfortable though, she saw red. "You were in the Middle East, right? Drew did mention that." Venom laced her tone.

"Yes, for three years. Until this." He banged the cane against his metal leg, his anger and frustration over his situation evident.

"Be glad you came home at all." She seethed, her blood boiling. "Some people don't. Think about that instead of feeling sorry for yourself."

Both men drew back in surprise at her harsh response.

"You think I—" Ben started to retort angrily, but Drew interjected, "Okay, why don't we go get you a drink, Ben?"

Drew started ushering Ben toward the bar but not

before turning back and glaring at her in confusion. "Stay here."

Her pulse was beating fiercely, but she did as he requested and sat back down in her seat. She took a sip of her champagne to calm herself, wishing she had something stronger to drink.

A few minutes of quiet fuming later, the music suddenly stopped, the lights throughout the room dimmed, and the crowd quieted. Only the lights illuminating the stage in front of her remained bright.

Drew walked across the stage to the podium in the center. *What is he doing up there?* Once, center stage, he adjusted the microphone and began to speak. She realized he had taken his mask off.

"Ladies and gentleman, I want to welcome you all to the second annual GetVetsSet Charity Masquerade Ball. As many of you know, this is a cause that is extremely personal to me. My brother, Benjamin Sapphire, was an infantryman in the army, supporting our country's efforts in Baghdad, when the vehicle he was in struck an IED. Two men, Ben's brothers in arms, died as a result, and Ben lost his left leg below the knee."

Drew took a deep breath, looked down at the podium for a moment and then cleared his throat before continuing.

"Over time, and with a lot of help from many doctors and nurses, Ben's external injuries were treated and healed. But there were internal injuries that we didn't know how to fix, ones we couldn't see, but that every soldier coming home, injured or not, experiences. Not until my brother almost took his own life did he get the help and support he needed."

Her breath caught in her throat. She'd misjudged Ben and his attitude at his injury and felt regret at the way she had spoken to him. She turned her focus back to Drew, understanding fully the struggle he must have felt over his brother's plight.

There was a long pause before he continued, "Twenty-two. Twenty-two seems like a comparatively small number, right?"

Drew looked out over the crowd, shaking his head in disgust as the passion in his voice increased.

"Well, that's the number of soldiers that commit suicide every day. Twenty-two mothers, fathers, wives, brothers, sisters, sons and daughters that have to struggle with the death of their loved one. When you add that up, it's a staggering loss. One that we hope our organization, GetVetsSet, will help to eliminate entirely."

A loud round of applause echoed throughout the ballroom. She stared in awe at Drew and this side of him that she had no idea how to reconcile with the rest. They had far more in common than either of them could possibly be aware of. Drew waved at the crowd to quiet them again.

"At GetVetsSet, we have created programs to help veterans regain their mental, physical and emotional well-being. And tonight, each one of you, through your generous donations, have helped us raise just over one million dollars. This will allow us to continue building programs and support our veterans. I'll personally be matching that donation with another million. Thank you so much. Please give yourself a big round of applause and enjoy the rest of your evening. You've earned it!"

The room broke out in a loud roar of applause and cheer

as Drew made his way offstage, down a set of stairs. It was then that she saw Ben standing at the bottom of them. Drew pulled him into a tight embrace, holding him for a long moment and speaking something into his ear before letting go and walking away.

Hannah was forced to look away when plates full of food appeared before her, and she lost track of Drew in the crowd milling at the foot of the stage. She didn't want to start without him and searched the stage area, then the bar for him, but didn't see him. She'd just turned back in her seat and was taking a sip of her champagne when she felt a tap on her shoulder. Ben. She stood instantly, wanting to apologize for her earlier actions.

"Ben, I'm sorry if I spoke rudely to you before. It's just that—" Hannah started, but he stopped her with a raised hand.

"Forget about it. I don't know your story and you don't know mine."

He ran a hand through his short hair, baring a tattoo that edged from under his shirtsleeve onto the top of his hand: a black rose with a gold oak leaf. The familiarity of it sent goose bumps across her arms. If she raised his sleeve, the words "Never Forget" would be scripted above the rose.

She looked at him curiously, dragging her gaze away from the tattoo. "I'd like to hear your story sometime."

He scoffed. "Yeah, maybe another time. Right now, Drew wants you to meet him on the terrace." Ben pointed toward a set of curtained glass doors to the side of the stage and then walked away, using his cane as support, not waiting for her response. She made her way to the terrace doors, stepped through and closed them behind her.

DREW STOOD QUIETLY in the shadows as he watched Scarlett make her way across the terrace. A light breeze swirled around her, the skirt of her dress flowing behind her as she seemed to glide over the marble stones.

He wondered about the sharp reaction she'd had toward Ben and what had triggered it. There must be a story there to evoke such a response from her.

"Drew?" Scarlett called his name and stopped walking. He watched her turn in a circle, appreciating the way she moved her body, before he stepped out of the shadows and came up behind her.

"Hey." She startled in surprise as he wrapped his arms around her waist and nuzzled her neck, inhaling her floral scent.

"You scared me!" She exclaimed. "I didn't know where you were."

"I was watching you." He tightened his embrace before whispering in her ear, "I like how you move."

Her cheeks rose up in a smile. Instead of replying, she twisted in his arms to face him, eyes framed by the silk and diamonds on her mask, and brought her lips up to his in a hungry kiss. He swept his tongue across her bottom lip before sliding it into her mouth, the kiss becoming more urgent as their breaths became one with each other. He guided her backward, never breaking their kiss, until he felt her bump up against the railing surrounding the terrace.

Tearing his lips from hers, he planted hot kisses down

the length of her neck until he reached the swell of her breast, now heaving with her panting breaths. He slid the silk of her dress off one breast, exposing her nipple, and then ran his tongue over it, watching it peak as the cold air hit its wetness.

Scarlett sighed loudly, and his cock grew harder, straining against his trousers. He skimmed his hand down the length of her body until he reached her thigh, and then, grasping her firmly, brought her leg up and wrapped it around him, pressing his raging erection up against her core.

"Ohhh, Drew . . ." Scarlett breathed as he continued to rock himself against her.

He pushed her skirt up and over his leg, clearing the thin barrier between them, and then pushed the flimsy fabric of her panties out of the way before sliding his finger over her pussy.

"Oh my god, baby, you're soaking wet." His voice came out rough as he fought to control the urge to bend her over the railing and fuck her senseless.

"That's because you keep teasing me." Scarlett was looking at him, her eyes bright with desire, her response laced in want.

He leered back at her, almost feral. "I can't help it. You're doing something to me. You've cast some kind of spell on me."

He rocked himself into her again and then abruptly dropped her leg, smoothing her skirt back down. As much as he wanted to fuck her right here and now, anyone could walk onto the terrace at any moment. He didn't want to risk exposing her like that. He leaned forward and kissed her deeply, then took a step back from her.

"Do you want to get out of here?"

"But we haven't even eaten or danced yet."

He kissed her lightly on the lips again. "I'll feed you. And if you want to dance, we can do that too. I just want to be with you. I don't want to share you with everyone here. I've done what I needed to do here."

A slow smile spread across her face as she answered timidly, "Okay."

He took her hand then and, entwining his fingers with hers, led her back to the terrace doors she had entered from.

"I need to grab my clutch. I left it on the table," she said as they made their way through the doors.

"Okay. I'd like to try and find Ben and say good-bye as well. Let's grab your clutch first and try the bar. That's usually where he can be found."

He knew from experience that Benny had either left after his speech or was drowning his aversion to these types of social events in whiskey.

After retrieving her bag, they made their way to the bar, his hand still holding hers. As they approached, Scarlett pulled him to a stop, pointing to the restrooms off to their right.

"Do you mind? I'll only be a minute?"

"Of course not. Go ahead and just meet me at the bar when you're done. I'll wait there for you." He leaned over and kissed her softly on the lips, releasing her hand but not his attention.

"What?" she asked in apparent confusion.

"Nothing." Drew smiled seductively. "I want to watch you walk in that dress again. Is that okay?"

She smiled demurely as she turned and walked away, rolling her hips as she went.

HANNAH QUICKLY TOOK care of business and then made her way to the lounge area of the ladies' room so she could freshen her face up a bit. She loved the mask but was tired of its confines, and it was making her face sweaty, so she untied it. They were leaving and Drew had removed his, so she must be safe. Besides, it's not like anyone could know she was his *paid* date.

She touched up her powder and reapplied her lipstick. Miraculously, her hair seemed to have survived the mask, as well as the little make-out session she and Drew had just indulged in. Karla had definitely done an amazing job on her hair. She took the mask and, folding it delicately in half, placed it in her clutch.

As she walked up to the bar, she scanned the area for Drew and found him near the end. Instead of speaking with Ben, he seemed to have found the attention of a rather busty, if not attractive, redhead in a tight black dress. Jealousy instantly flared, surprising her, igniting her bold approach.

"Hello, Darling." She sidled up against Drew, wrapping her arm around his waist and her hand on his chest before placing a kiss on his cheek.

She turned to the redhead, extending her hand. "I'm

Scarlett. Drew's date."

The woman scanned her up and down, a look of distaste stretched over her features. Drew chuckled under his breath, which only raised Hannah's hackles further.

Ignoring Hannah's hand, the redhead turned toward Drew, eyebrows raised in obvious disappointment. "You brought a date?"

Hannah felt some relief at the woman's response—and at the confirmation of Drew's earlier confession about not dating. Though . . . he might have previously *slept* with the woman. She certainly wasn't hiding her disappointment well at Drew bringing a date.

"Yes, I brought a date. And we were just leaving." Drew dismissed her politely, and then turned to Hannah. "Come, let's go, apparently Ben has already left." Then, to the redhead, "Have a good night."

Unable to contain her curiosity—because Lord knew she had no right to be jealous, right? Hannah waited until they were away from the bar before pulling Drew to a stop. "Who was that woman?"

An almost satisfied grin broke out across his face before he responded, "Scarlett, are you jealous?"

She was about to respond when a hand reached out and tapped her arm. "It is you! Harold, come see. I told you it was her!"

DREW LOOKED on in surprise as an elderly woman, bathed in jewels, addressed Scarlett with such familiarity.

The stranger beckoned someone Drew could only assume was her husband over to see Scarlett.

"Mrs. Downing! Hello, how are you?" Scarlett bussed the elderly woman on her cheek. "And Mr. Downing, hello! You look so handsome in your tuxedo."

Drew stood back in shock as he realized she was addressing Harold Downing. *The* Harold Downing, who owned one of the wealthiest brokerage houses in the country. Scarlett seemed to be full of surprises.

"My dear, look how beautiful you are this evening!" Mr. Downing had reached Scarlett and was kissing her on the cheek. "How nice to see you out and about and out of the shop."

"Thank you so much. You both look lovely as well." Scarlett glanced at Drew with what could only be described as sheer panic on her face, clearly unsure what to do next.

While he was extremely curious to learn more about this shop Scarlett worked at, he'd better rescue her before she imploded. He extended his hand.

"Mr. Downing, I presume?" And smiled widely. "Andrew Sapphire. Very nice to meet you. I've heard so much about you. It's nice to finally meet the man in the flesh."

He took Drew's hand and shook it vigorously. "Ah, the same could be said about you, young man. Please, call me Harold. Wonderful speech this evening. Hope you're taking good care of this young lady here. She's a very special girl."

Drew looked at Scarlett, who was still vibrating with nerves, and then back at Mr. Downing. Perhaps he could take advantage of this situation and learn a bit more about her . . . "Yes, I agree, quite special. How do you two know each other?"

But much to Drew's disappointment, Mrs. Downing interrupted at that very moment and tried to unobtrusively lead her husband away. "Harold, let's go and leave these two lovebirds to their evening."

"Oh, Alice! Give me a few minutes with the man." He tried to shoo his wife away.

Yes, Drew thought to himself, *give me a few more minutes.* Much to his surprise, Scarlett spoke up, placing her hand on Drew's arm.

"Actually, we were just on our way out. Drew has an emergency that needs his attention."

Her small hand gripped his arm with white knuckles. He was crossing a line with her that he shouldn't be. Instantly, he put his hand over hers in a conciliatory fashion.

"Oh, yes." Harold started nodding. "I know all about those." He turned his attention toward Scarlett then. "I'm sure I'll see you later this week at the shop, dear."

Mrs. Downing turned towards Drew then to wish him a goodnight. "So nice to see our girl out with someone. Hope you're both able to enjoy the rest of your evening."

Drew had to strain to hear Harold's conspiratorial whisper as the man drew closer to Scarlett. "I think I want to do something different this week for Alice." The old man gave Scarlett a wink then and kissed her on the cheek.

"Of course, I look forward to it." She patted him on the hand and then his wife. "Mrs. Downing, it was so nice to see you."

"You know I always love seeing you dear. Have a nice evening." And with that, Mr. Downing took his wife's hand, placing it in the crook of his arm, and led her away.

Drew raised his eyebrows at Scarlett. "The Downings? You know the Downings?"

She started walking toward the exit again. "Don't think you can change the subject on me. I want to know who that woman was."

"Wait a minute. You know one of the wealthiest couples in the country, and I'm not allowed to ask about it?"

She stopped walking and turned to look at him. "No, you don't. You get Scarlett. That's all you get. You don't get anything else from me."

Dumbfounded, he just looked at her, reality slapping him in the face. This woman had only shared a small piece of herself, and everything else was a complete mystery to him.

He had so many questions about her: Why was her reaction to his brother so intense, who was the "we" she'd referred to with such a warm smile on her face at lunch, and why, if she associated with people like the Downings, was she selling herself at auction? That one small piece wasn't going to be enough.

He wanted more.

CHAPTER
Nine

HANNAH STOOD in quiet thought as Drew gave the ticket to the valet driver. Neither of them had said anything to each other after her last comment. She was still in a bit of shock at running into the Downings.

She'd known there would be a slight risk at seeing someone she knew here and had realized, a bit too late, that she should have left her mask on until they'd left. It wasn't that she was ashamed to be with Drew, but she needed to keep her personal life separate from this choice she'd made. Seeing the Downings reminded her how precariously close she'd come to exposing that life.

"You're shivering." Drew came up behind her and placed his jacket over her shoulders, skimming his hands down the length of her arms before stepping away.

"Thank you." His warmth still lingered on the fabric that surrounded her and she pulled it more tightly around herself. She leaned down and inhaled deeply, taking in his scent as it drifted up from the jacket. She loved the comfort that his warmth and scent were bringing her, and hated herself at the same time for it.

The valet drove up with Drew's car, stopping directly beside them. He jumped out and ran around to open the door for her, but Drew was already there.

He held her hand as she sat down, and she wrapped her skirt around her legs before he shut the door. In less than a minute, he was in the car and pulling away from the hotel.

He turned on the radio, settling on something acoustic. She listened for a moment but didn't recognize the artist.

"This is lovely. Who is it?"

"Jason Mraz. Are you familiar with his music?"

She shook her head. "I think I know some of his songs. Not this one though. I like it."

"Yes, just simple. It eases me."

They rode in silence for a few more moments until she realized they weren't heading back in the direction of the estate.

"Where are we going?"

"It's a surprise." He looked over at her, his voice low. "Do you trust me?"

"Are you going to tell me who that redhead was?" She wasn't forgetting about that encounter anytime soon.

"Are you going to tell me about the Downings?" He countered, "cause I'm dying to know."

"Drew, I can't. I'm sorry." She sighed. "I'm not trying to be difficult. Really. But that part of my life isn't part of this life."

Drew was silent for a few moments before responding. "Okay, Scarlett. I understand, but I'm not going to lie; I hate it. I'm usually the one in control, but I feel like you're holding all the cards here."

"No. I'm not. You paid for this part of me. You paid for Scarlett. I'm sorry, but this is all I can give you."

"Maybe that's not enough," he gritted out under his breath.

She turned her head toward him in surprise. "Drew . . ." She faltered, not even sure what to say.

If she was honest with herself, hearing him say he wanted more was a relief. To know she wasn't alone in her confusion about her growing feelings for him. She couldn't deny that she was beginning to feel more for him than she should.

"Don't." He held his hand up and responded before she could try and continue. "It's okay, Scarlett. I'm being unfair to you. Besides, it's only 9:30. I have you, or at least I have Scarlett, for another eighteen hours. Let's just try and enjoy that."

"Okay." She closed her mouth and just listened to the music flowing through the car's speakers. They seemed to be heading east, away from the city.

"Are you going to tell me where we're going yet?"

He smiled. "My house in The Hamptons. Are you okay with that? I can still have you back at the estate by early morning."

"Your house?" she squeaked. "Is that even allowed? I mean, I know the masquerade ball was one thing, but your house?"

He scoffed. "What's the worst that can happen? Domme Maria kicks me out of Timide? It's not the only club in town."

She looked at him in surprise. "You would risk your membership to bring me to your house?"

"I hardly think my membership is in any real danger. We're supposed to be at a ball. As far as anyone knows, that's where we are. Who is to know any differently unless we tell them? Besides, I think the money I spend there would be greatly missed."

"Well it's nice to know my worth, I guess."

"Scarlett, don't." He glanced over at her, longing in his voice. "I want to share this with you. It's one of my favorite places."

What could she say to that? Besides, she was tired of fighting over what she should and shouldn't be feeling, or doing, or caring about. She bent her head down, kissing the palm of his hand. "Okay."

"Okay?" he confirmed in relief.

"Okay." She laughed. "Just tell me it's not too much farther though, cause I'm starving!"

"In that case," he shifted the car into a higher gear and punched the gas, "I'll get us there as fast as I can."

"What kind of car is this anyway?"

He smiled broadly. "It's a Jaguar. An F-Type S Coupe."

She shook her head, grinning. "Boys and their toys."

A LITTLE OVER AN HOUR LATER, Drew pulled off the road onto a long, white stone driveway. As the house came into view, Scarlett gasped, her eyes open wide, awe evident on her face.

He beamed with pride over her delight. He'd recently had it built, and although it had been designed to be modern, he'd striven to balance cutting-edge with warmth and an inviting presence.

It was a large, contemporary home made up of natural wood and large floor-to-ceiling windows. The windows on the lower floor were glowing a rich yellow, and beyond the house, a rolling, manicured lawn met a pristine, sandy beach, waves lapping lightly against its edge.

"Drew, this is gorgeous!"

"Wait till you see the inside."

He jumped out and came around to open her door to help her out of the car. "Careful. It's all gravel here and probably won't be easy to maneuver in your heels."

Scarlett stepped out of the car and tried to balance on the balls of her feet, tiptoeing over the gravel toward the entrance. Before she got three steps, he swept her up in his arms, a quick yelp of surprise escaping from her, and carried her the rest of the way.

"Sorry, this just seemed easier." He dropped a kiss on her nose as he went. She simply smiled in response and then rested her head on his shoulder.

Once inside, he placed her gently down in the entry-way. He took in her perusal of his home, trying to ascertain her opinion. He'd had the inside designed to be light and airy, the walls a soft white, the floors a light-colored hardwood.

Her gaze focused on the floor-to-ceiling windows that spanned the width of the living room, framing a view of the ocean beyond.

"Drew, it's lovely." She turned toward him.

"I'll give you a tour later, but let's go to the kitchen and see if we can find something to eat."

He walked down the hallway into a large open space that contained the kitchen and living room. The kitchen was modern and sleek but had clearly been customized for a man with its natural wood paneling and butcher block. Stainless steel appliances and light fixtures complemented the wood and white marble countertop. Drew started pulling things out of the large fridge and placing them on the butcher block.

"Let's see," he mumbled as he placed each item down. "Brie, grapes, chicken, marinated mushrooms, blueberries, some olives." He turned and looked at her. "Does any of this look good?"

She nodded. "It all looks good! I'm famished!"

He pointed at one of the cabinets. "Okay, why don't you grab some plates while I go down and find a bottle of wine for us?"

"Perfect." Scarlett walked around the counter and opened the cabinet, selecting two plates for them.

He left and walked around the corner and downstairs to a small room that contained his wine cellar. He picked a white and a red and made his way back to the living room.

He came around the corner with the two bottles of wine just as she finished taking her shoes off. A wide grin spread across his face in joy and surprise as he took in the setting she had created for them.

Instead of the kitchen, on the small coffee table in the living room, plates, glasses, silverware, the food and even a couple of candles all were waiting for him.

"I wasn't sure if you wanted red or white, so I grabbed

one of each." He put the bottles down on the counter and moved to one of the drawers for an opener.

"I'd love a glass of the red. Are you okay eating in here?"

"It's absolutely perfect." He beamed back at her, while opening the bottle of red before carrying it over to their make-shift picnic spot. He poured each of them a glass before sitting down.

"I hope you don't mind this little smorgasbord. It's quick and easy and no cooking required."

"Are you kidding?" she responded as she popped a grape in her mouth. "This is so perfect. I love food you can eat with your fingers."

He smiled and watched Scarlett as she pulled a piece of chicken breast off the roaster and put it in her mouth, chewing happily. *She just might be perfect.* The thought struck him like a bolt of lightning, jarring him to his core.

He hadn't felt anything like this, since, well, maybe ever. Dinners with his ex-wife had always been formal affairs. The thought of her sitting cross-legged, in a ball gown no less, blissfully eating chicken with her fingers was a foreign one.

His ex-wife would send a meal back to the kitchen if a stray pea rolled into her starch, berating the service of the restaurant as inadequate and appalling. He took a big gulp of wine to calm the beating of his heart as the reality of his growing feelings became more evident.

"Do you want me to make a plate for you?" Scarlett asked, pulling him out of his scattered thoughts.

He shook his head. "No, no. I'm good. I'm just going to pick like you."

He grabbed the drumstick on the chicken, twisting it off

and taking a bite. For the next few moments they both just ate in silence.

He liked watching Scarlett's expressions change with each bite of food. She closed her eyes in delight with the blueberries and scrunched her nose up while trying some of the saltier olives.

When she brought the wine glass to her lips and took her first sip, she closed her eyes and moaned loudly.

"You like?" he asked, laughing.

"Oh my god. This is so unbelievably good. It's warm and smooth and tastes like peppered blackberries."

He smiled again at how easily she was satisfied. "Have you had enough to eat?"

"Yes, I'm good. Thank you. Do you want me to clean up?" Hannah started to stand so she could clear their mess, but Drew grabbed her hand and stood up beside her.

"Leave it. I thought maybe we could take a walk on the beach."

She looked out the windows at the waves lapping against the shore and nodded, a smile breaking across her face. "I'd love that."

Drew led her from the living room and through a side door in the kitchen out onto a large deck. He stopped and pulled off his shoes and socks, then continued across the deck and down some stairs. At the bottom, he threw a switch mounted on one of the deck posts, and lights appeared before them, trailing down a pathway that led to the beach.

As he took her hand and started walking down the path, the ocean breeze nipped pleasantly at her exposed skin. "Are you cold at all? I can go back in and get you a blanket if so."

She shook her head. "No, I'm okay right now."

The path meandered down a small hill before opening onto the beach. The moon was high and full above them, reflecting off the water's waves. She stopped and marveled at the view in front of her.

"Oh, Drew, this is absolutely gorgeous. No wonder you love it here." She turned to look at him. He was staring out at the waves, a small, content smile on his face.

"Yeah, this is where I come to just be me. It's my quiet place. I love it here."

"Thank you for sharing it with me." She rose up and kissed him softly on the lips.

"Come on. Let's walk a bit." Hand in hand, they strolled down to the water's edge and then followed it down the beach for about a half mile before turning back.

Her dress trailed behind her in the sand. The waves lapped rhythmically against the shoreline. She eventually broke the silence. "Tell me why this is your favorite place."

He smiled down at her as they continued walking. "My parents have a much larger house on the beach, but it's in California. It's so far north that it's almost in Oregon. It's a town called Crescent City. Anyway, we didn't go all that often, as my father was always busy working or traveling, but when we would go . . ."

She looked over to see Drew's eyes closed as he relayed his memories to her. "This place reminds me of those simpler times. Happy times. Ben and I would play all day on that beach. When we were little, it was making sand castles and chasing seagulls or wakeboarding. When we were older, it was surfing and chasing girls."

She laughed with him at the memory. "I can totally see

the two of you in action back then. I bet none of those girls had a chance!"

"Actually, we were the ones that usually ended up with the broken hearts. But, oh what fun we had getting them. It's actually where I met my ex-wife."

She was unable to mask the surprise on her face. "I think that's the first time I've heard you speak fondly of her."

"Hmm." He raised his eyebrows in thought. "I guess so."

He was quiet a few minutes before continuing. "It wasn't always bad between us. We were happy when we were younger. When I didn't have so many of the responsibilities I ended up growing into and could focus more of my attention on her."

"It's okay, Drew, you don't have to explain." She didn't want to make him feel uncomfortable.

"No, it's okay. The demise of our marriage is probably more my fault than hers anyway. We loved each other very much at one time, but I took that for granted when my father demanded more of me, pulling my focus in another direction. She tried. I think she really did. But ultimately, she was just too lonely."

"You sound sad about that."

"Let's just say I've worked hard not to put myself in that position again."

"Is that why you choose this sort of lifestyle now?" Hannah mused.

"This sort of lifestyle? What sort is that, Scarlett?" he asked, not harshly, but curiously.

"I don't know. I guess the kind where you pay for someone to keep you company. No commitment."

"Unfortunately, I wasn't the one with the commitment

issue," he scoffed. "She was. But, again, if I had paid more attention, listened to her, maybe things would have been different. Maybe we were just too young."

She squeezed his hand in response and pulled him to a stop. "I'm sorry. I didn't mean to upset you. I was just trying to understand."

"It's okay. I get it. I'm probably not the easiest guy to understand."

They both turned and continued walking down the beach, angling back toward the house looming in the distance now.

"What about you?" he asked quietly.

"What about me?"

"Were you ever married?"

For a long time, she didn't answer. Drew stopped and pulled her close, looking at her questioningly.

"Scarlett?"

She looked down at the ground, absently noticing the sand that had gathered around the long hem of her dress. She sighed. "You don't get to ask me these kinds of questions. I'm sorry."

"Why can't I ask you these kinds of questions? I just told you all about my marriage. Is it wrong for me to want to get to know you better?" Frustration was evident in his voice and the tightened features of his face.

"What difference does it make? I'm yours for one weekend." She looked down at the ground again before continuing. "But—of course if I was married, I wouldn't be standing here with you right now."

Drew pulled her flush against him, forcing her to lift her face to his. "I don't know why it matters to me, Scarlett, but it does. You make me want things and feel things I haven't felt in a very long time. I want to know you, all of you."

Drew could see the confusion and angst in her face, eyebrows scrunched up in worry. To stop her from responding, he kissed her. Long and sweet and torturously slow to try and make them both forget what he'd just admitted. Or maybe to confirm it.

When he broke them apart, instead of continuing the conversation, he turned, grabbed her hand and pulled her down the beach closer to the house, his long strides challenging her to keep up. "Come on. I think I promised you some dancing."

She laughed. "What?"

He looked back at her and smiled. "Remember? On the terrace, you said we hadn't gotten to eat or dance."

"Yes?"

"Well, I've fed you. Now I need to make sure you get to dance. We can't let that dress go to waste, can we?"

She pointed down at the muddy hem of the dress and cringed. "I'm not sure you're going to want this messy dress sliding all over your beautiful floors."

He stopped, taking in the hem, noticing for the first time that it was indeed quite muddy. He shrugged and smiled. "Oh well. I don't mind if you don't."

She couldn't help but smile back at him. "Well, all right then! Let's go dance!"

They made it back to the house and entered through the doorway off of the kitchen. Drew wiped his feet off before helping Scarlett shake as much of the sand off her dress as she could. He took her hand and led her to the back of the house where the library was located.

"This room is gorgeous! I would never leave it if I lived here."

He radiated pride as he searched through the songs on the digital music player set into one of the shelves. He knew exactly which song he wanted.

"I didn't want a traditional library. I wanted one bright and full of light. I'm glad you like it."

She walked over to the window, pressing her hand flat on the cool surface of the glass, and the moonlight coming through the window silhouetted her frame. As the room filled with the music he'd selected just for her, he grabbed her free hand and pulled her into his arms.

She laughed when she heard what song he had chosen. He spun her around, and they both sang along with the music as they danced.

Scarlett was laughing, swaying her body to the rhythm as she took in his crazy dancing. "Oh my god, Drew! Seriously?"

"What? This is the perfect song for you and those beautiful eyes!" He grasped her hand again and twirled her this way and that, her dress swinging up and around, revealing her up on tiptoes. "I love Van Morrison, and Brown-Eyed Girl is a classic!"

As quickly as the song started, it seemed to end. They both stopped, breathing hard from their silly dancing, grinning wide at each other. The lyrics from the next song crooned much slower than the first.

Drew gathered Scarlett in his arms and started swaying to the music, singing the lyrics to Crazy Love quietly in her ear while they moved. With each turn, Drew's hand, placed low and flat on Hannah's back, pulled her in closer, so that their bodies felt almost like one.

His heart beat heavily under her hand as it lay against his chest, and his breath tickled against her ear as he sang. She didn't dare look up at him, afraid of what might come next in this intimate moment they were sharing.

The song came to an end. He dropped his hold around her waist and took her hand. "Come."

It was all he said before walking out of the room, leaving the next song to play as he led her up a staircase and then down a hallway. At the end of the hallway, he opened a door and pulled her into what must be the master bedroom.

One exterior wall held the same floor-to-ceiling windows as the rooms below, overlooking the ocean. The room was simply furnished. A king-sized bed sat against the back wall, and a natural wood dresser and wardrobe rested against the two other walls. The floors were a light wood, soft and warm on her feet, and a white fur rug lay in the center.

Drew closed the door and turned toward her. Without saying a word, he slid his fingers down her arms, then pulled her hands up and over her head. He held her like that, delicately, with one hand and used the other to pull down the zipper on the side of her dress. Then he released her hands, letting them fall back to her sides, and pushed the single strap holding up her dress slowly off her shoulder, causing the entire dress to slip down and off her body. He slid her thong down her legs until it fell to the floor.

She stood before him, naked, with only the diamond choker and cuff bracelet adorning her body. He stepped back and gazed at her, lust and desire evident in his dark blue eyes.

She stepped forward, out of the dress and panties pooled on the floor, and waited for his next command. It didn't come. Instead, he unbuttoned and removed his shirt as he slowly walked around her, his eyes never leaving her body.

Her nipples grew tight under his gaze, and though he hadn't even touched her, his scorching look caused her body to flare in heat and wetness to pool at her core. Her fingers tingled with the desire to touch him and run them over his lean, muscled body.

As he stopped in front of her again, he unfastened his belt and then the button holding up his trousers, his gaze still locked on her body. In one motion, he bent over and slid off his trousers. When he stood up, his cock jutted hard and long against his stomach.

Still not having said a word, he slowly walked up to her again. This time, he placed his hand flat on her stomach, leaving it there as he walked around to the back of her and then pulled her flush against his front. His other hand snaked up and around her neck to finger the collar of diamonds that encircled it while his head leaned down against hers. She heard him inhale deeply—was he smelling her?—and his lips pressed against her ear.

"You are so fucking gorgeous." And then he spun her around and pressed his lips to hers in a heated kiss.

Her arms wrapped up and around his neck, then further up to grip his hair as their kiss intensified. As his tongue invaded her mouth and his teeth nipped at her lips, he slowly pushed her backward until her legs met the foot of the bed. Instead of pushing her down, he broke the kiss, bent down and picked her up under the legs, cradling her like a child before walking around to the side of the bed and setting her down in the middle of it.

He trailed his hands down the length of her body as he rose and moved back to the end of the bed. He kneeled and, as he bent down, captured her ankle in his hand, raising her leg to meet his lips.

Starting at her ankle, his lips left a scorching trail of heat up the length of her leg as he made his way up her body. When he reached the juncture of her legs, he kissed her there sweetly before continuing up and along her stomach to her breasts. He dragged his tongue across the tip of each nipple and then ever so slowly took one of the peaks into his mouth and sucked.

Hannah's back arched off the bed as his mouth latched onto her, and her hands grasped onto his head, not wanting him to roam further. Drew continued to suck and lave her breast for a few moments before moving to the other. She moaned at the intense pleasure, the slow, sensual pace of his exploration of her body leaving every inch of her on fire.

When his attention to the second breast was complete, he peppered soft, wet kisses over her clavicle and down the inside of her arm. When he reached the diamond cuff on her wrist, his fingers trailed over it, encircling it delicately before raising her hand to his lips, placing a kiss on her palm, all the while gazing passionately into her eyes.

"Drew . . ." she whispered, not knowing how much more of this sensual intensity she could take.

DREW SHIFTED his body fully over Scarlett's, his elbows on either side of her head, and lowered his mouth to hers in a searing kiss. Her hands snaked up and around his neck, fingers wide around his head, trying to pull him in closer, deeper as his tongue invaded her mouth.

He gradually lowered his body until he was seated between her legs. His cock was hard and throbbing as it lay against her wet center. As he continued to kiss her, he used one hand to guide himself into her heat. Their mouths both opened wide as he slid all the way in, their heads thrown back in shared ecstasy. He brought his hands up and cradled each side of Scarlett's face, his eyes locked on hers as he began to rock in and out of her.

Her hands moved down to grasp his ass, fingernails digging in as she urged him to go deeper and harder with each thrust. Sweat dripped off his forehead and landed on her cheek. Each of them moaning in pleasure. Scarlett started to close her eyes and throw her head back, but his grasp tightened around her face. He wanted to see her, to know if she was feeling what he was, to know it wasn't just him.

"No, Scarlett," he breathed. "Eyes open. I want to see you come apart."

Her only response was a low, guttural moan. He increased his thrusts, pushing harder, but not faster. Scarlett's fingernails dug even deeper in his ass as she grasped onto him in response.

Her body climbed toward its release, all of her muscles beginning to tighten around him. He let go of one side of her face to grab her leg below the knee, lifting it, pushing himself even deeper.

"Yes! Yes, like that!" she moaned. "God, don't stop, Drew!"

She tried to thrash her head back and forth, but Drew managed to hold it firmly with one hand, never breaking his gaze from hers. As she came apart, he thrust hard one final time, joining her in oblivion, and watched as her eyes rolled back in her head. He crashed his lips down on hers, tasting everything his desire brought her, and his cock jerked inside her one last time.

He pulled his lips away, both of them gasping as he did, eyes meeting and holding for a moment before he slid away and rolled to his side. He pulled Scarlett with him, nestling her against him as he wrapped his arms around her. His hands were over her heart, and he could feel it beating quickly as it recovered from their lovemaking.

CHAPTER

Ten

HANNAH'S FINGERS grazed back and forth over the dark hair sprinkling Drew's forearm as she tried to understand what had just happened.

That hadn't been just fucking. Where were the rope and spankings and punishments that had been promised? These weren't the actions of a Dominant controlling a submissive for his pleasure. The way he'd just made love to her—and yes, it *had* felt like love—sent her mind racing.

This entire weekend had been anything but what she had expected. She was in disbelief that she had been in Drew's company for only thirty hours. She couldn't deny their connection: it felt as if she had known him forever.

"What are you thinking about?" he murmured into her hair. "I can hear your mind going a million miles a minute."

She didn't dare tell him what she was really thinking. "Nothing, really. Just relaxing."

"Please tell me your real name," he begged softly.

She remained quiet for a moment, unsure of what to say,

not wanting to ruin the intimacy of what they had just shared. "I can't, Drew. You know that."

"Why? Why can't you tell me? What harm would it cause?" Frustration was evident in his voice.

"Because I just . . . I can't. My life outside of this world is my own, and I need to keep it that way."

He sighed. "Then tell me something that I *can* know. I want to know who *you* are, not Scarlett."

She sighed deeply because she understood what he wanted, and there was even a piece of her that wanted to share everything she was with him. But there was a bigger piece, the piece she needed to keep safe from this world, that drove her decisions.

"Okay, I'll make a deal with you. I'll ask you a question that I think is acceptable. If you want, you can ask me the same question back."

"If that's what you're willing to give me, then I'll take it. Go."

"Let's start out with an easy one. How old are you?"

"I'm thirty-four. You?" Drew returned.

"I'm twenty-seven."

"Huh, I would have guessed twenty-three or twenty-four."

"I guess I'll appreciate that in a few years." She laughed, feeling the mood lighten already. "Okay, what's your favorite food?"

"Oh jeez. I like so many things. I guess if I have to pick my absolute favorite, I'll go with the manly answer and say a good steak."

"So typical!" She squeezed his hand. "Favorite movie?"

"Uh-uh. You didn't tell me your favorite food," he countered.

"Oh yeah, sorry. I love pasta. Any kind. I could eat it every day. But then I'd probably weigh an extra fifty pounds, so I treat myself to it once a week. So, favorite movie?"

"I don't know about that one." He thought for a moment. "I guess *The Godfather*?"

"God, Drew, could you be any more of a typical man?" she joked.

"So, then, tell me yours."

"It's *Pride and Prejudice*. But the one with Keira Knightley. There's about ten versions of that movie by now."

"Um yeah, speaking of typical choices— 'Scarlett'?" Drew mused.

"I know, I know. Hmmm, okay, let's step this up a notch," she said. "Okay, who was your best friend growing up?"

"That's easy. Benny. We did everything together. That guy knows more about me than I care to admit. Okay, now you. Who was your best friend?"

"Cathy. We met when I was in third grade. My family had just moved to town and we were seated next to each other. I was terrified. She was so nice to me. The teacher assigned us to do a science project together, and we picked monarch butterflies as our subject. We bonded over chasing them in a field by her house."

"Are you still friends?"

"Yes, I suppose we are. I don't see her much but we keep up through Facebook. God, we grew up together, swimming in streams, writing notes, singing silly songs and of course chasing boys." She laughed at the memories.

"That sounds nice. Where did you grow up?"

"Nope. I get to ask the questions! Not you!" she chastised.

"Okay, okay! Sorry!" He held his hands up in surrender. "Do you want something to drink?"

She sat up and faced him. "That actually sounds great."

"Okay, sit tight. I'll be back." Drew jumped up from the bed and left the room. Relief surged through her. Not because he was gone, but because he seemed to be content with this getting-to-know-you game. As quickly as the relief came, it left again.

She was developing feelings for Drew. It mattered to her what he thought and how he felt. And she knew from his actions and his questions that he was feeling something for her too. *I mean, he brought me on a date.* Something he hadn't done for years. But it was also obvious that his business was his life. Although she had to question how much of it had been forced upon him by his father.

While these thoughts swirled in her mind, she got up and opened a few drawers on the dresser until she came across one filled with T-shirts. She grabbed one and pulled it over her head. It fell halfway down her thighs and looked more like a dress, but it was soft and comfy and, best of all, it smelled like Drew.

"Cute." He was standing in the doorway, holding the bottle of wine from earlier and their glasses.

"I hope you don't mind. I didn't want to put that dress back on. Lovely as it is."

"Not at all. I like seeing you in my shirt. It's kind of sexy, actually." He grinned wickedly as he walked toward her.

"Oh no you don't, mister!" She threw a hand up. "I need a break!"

He stopped in front of her. "I was just going to kiss you." And with that, he bent down and brushed his lips against hers.

"Oh."

"Yes, well, not that I wouldn't ravish you again if you'd let me." He winked at her, then walked past her to set the glasses and wine down on the dresser. He opened the top drawer and pulled out a pair of boxers, slipping them on. Pouring them each a glass of wine, he handed her one and then sat back on the bed.

"Okay, next question."

"Ugh! Really?" she moaned, hoping he had moved on from this subject.

"I'm just getting started. I'll take whatever pieces of you that you're willing to share, even if it has to be like this."

"Okay, okay." She sat on the bed across from him, pulling her legs into a cross-legged position. "When did you lose your virginity?"

He cocked his head. "Oh, going for the good stuff now, eh? You know you have to answer the same question, right?"

"Yeah, yeah. It's okay, it's not very exciting. It was very standard. I was seventeen, and it was to my high school boyfriend after senior prom."

"Oh, that's romantic, not standard." Drew smiled, examining her a little wistfully, as if imagining a younger version of herself. "Okay, I'm afraid mine probably won't surprise you. Or maybe it will. I was seventeen too, and it was with my sister's nanny, Lisa."

"Oh, you have a sister? Where was she tonight?" Hannah

was more surprised at the revelation of a sister then at how he'd lost his virginity.

"Yes." He paused. "Well, no. Not anymore." Drew's eyes filled with sadness. "I had a sister. Ben and I did. A younger sister. Her name was Elizabeth. We called her Lizzie. She died when she was sixteen."

Hannah's hand flew to her mouth as she gasped in surprise. "Drew, I'm so sorry. I wouldn't have asked if I had known."

He shrugged. "How could you have known? It was a long time ago now. Almost fifteen years." He stopped and shook his head. "Wow, when I say it out loud, it's hard to believe how long ago it was."

"Is it okay—I mean; can I ask how? If it's not too hard for you to talk about it?" she asked somberly.

"She was coming home from a dance with some of her friends and their car was hit by a drunk driver. My sister was in the front passenger seat. She and her friend, Mindy, who was driving, were both killed. There were two more girls in the back of the car that ended up okay. Of course, the fucking drunk that hit them didn't have a scratch on him." He shook his head in disgust.

She got up, took his wineglass from his hand, and placed it down with hers as well. She climbed back up on the bed and, not knowing what else to do but needing to do something, took him in her arms and held him. She hugged him hard, wanting him to feel something other than the pain of the memory he'd just shared.

"I'm so sorry. I have a brother and a sister and I can't imagine how I would feel if I lost either of them."

He kissed the top of her head, holding her back before whispering, "Thank you."

Instead of pulling apart, they both lay down on the bed, her back to his front, his arms wrapped around her, holding her close.

"So, you want to ask me anymore of these fun questions?" Drew joked weakly.

"I think I'm afraid to. God knows what kind of stone I'll kick over next if I do!"

"I'm tough. Go ahead and fire away. Besides, it's my only means of learning more about you."

"Always an ulterior motive with you." She shook her head, smiling. "I was actually just wondering if we had to go back to the estate. Will it be noticed if we don't return soon?"

Behind her, Drew shrugged. "I suppose they'll notice eventually. Do you want to go back?"

She sighed deeply, responding wistfully, "I wish I could stay here forever."

His entire body tightened at her confession. "Then stay."

She laughed nervously, not sure where he was going with this. "Yes, I'll just stay here in your little castle and you can take care of me forever."

He released her and sat up. She sat up as well and twisted toward him, looking him in the eye.

"Well, maybe not forever, but for right now, I'd like you to stay."

"Drew, what are talking about?" Her heart raced.

He stroked her face lovingly. "Scarlett, do you think I've ever brought a sub out of the compound, let alone to my house?"

He looked down, shaking his head before continuing. "I don't know what it is. You make me feel something I haven't felt in a long time. Right now, the thought of saying good-bye to you in a few hours already feels wrong. So I'm asking you to stay. I'd like more."

She looked at him, wide-eyed, surprised at his revelation even though she'd suspected he was feeling just as much, if not more, than she was. "Drew, I . . ." She wrung her hands nervously, staring at the diamonds on her wrist.

"I'm scaring you," he stated and then blew out a breath. "I'm scaring myself! I don't say shit like this to anyone."

"It's just that, this isn't my life. Do you understand that? This isn't me. You don't know me. Not really. I'm just being who you want me to be."

"I don't believe that. You can't tell me that what we just shared wasn't you."

"That was just sex." She knew she was lying as she said the words, but she said them anyway.

No matter what she might be starting to feel for Drew, she had to consider what—*who* was waiting for her back in the real world, and that was more important than anything she might want.

He scoffed. "That wasn't *just* sex. And I'm not just talking about the sex. There was a lot more going on there than just sex and you're lying to yourself if you try to pretend otherwise."

"It doesn't matter. This is all I can give you."

He looked at her angrily. "What do you mean it doesn't matter? It doesn't matter that what we have might be some-thing more? Something worth exploring?"

Sadness filled her eyes. "This isn't my life. My life is . . .

Well, my life is complicated. And this"—she gestured between them— "this is just a means to an end for me."

Drew's eyes were blazing now. "So, it's back to the money again? Is that all this is to you? A job? The money?"

She flinched. Tears began to form and fall from the corners of her eyes. "I'm sorry. I am, really. Of course this weekend has been amazing. You've been amazing. So much more than I thought it could be. But yes, this is a job. And yes, I need the money." She wiped the tears off her cheeks before continuing. "This is just the way it has to be for me."

DREW STOOD ABRUPTLY, unable to contain his anger, even as he watched the tears trail down Scarlett's cheeks. "Damn it, it doesn't have to be this way! I'll give you whatever fucking money you need. *Just choose me.*"

He watched in disbelief as she shook her head slowly, tears streaming down her cheeks now. "I can't. There are reasons that are much bigger than me. I just can't. I'm sorry."

He loomed above her, fury, hurt and confusion ripping through him and then resignation as he spoke. "No. You won't. Because you choose not to. You could. If you wanted to."

He stormed across the room and grabbed his glass of wine on the dresser, draining it in one long gulp before throwing it across the room, smashing into a hundred pieces as is crashed into the wall. Scarlett yelped in surprise, then curled into a ball on the bed.

With long, hard strides, he returned to the bed, grabbing her roughly by the hair and yanking her face up to his. "Then if this is just about the money, I might as well get what I paid for. Get up off this bed. Now!"

HANNAH LOOKED AT HIM, eyes wide in fear and disbelief. Her one moment of hesitation had Drew pulling her off the bed by her hair. She pushed herself up and off the bed before he pulled it clean off her head. When she was standing, he grabbed the neckline of the t-shirt and ripped it off her in two pieces.

Her body lunged forward with the motion, causing her to cry out in pain as she crashed into him. He snatched her shoulders and, shoving her down onto the bed, held her there with one strong arm.

"Drew, what are you doing? Please stop," she pleaded, desperation in her voice.

"You don't get to tell me to stop, Scarlett," he hissed in her ear as he bent down to remove his boxers. "I paid for you. I'll do whatever the fuck I want to you. Understood?"

Hannah lay speechless, bewildered, tears running down her face. How had they gotten to this moment so quickly?

Drew loomed over her in anger, his actions about to lead him to a place she knew they wouldn't be able to come back from. She did the only thing she could think of to save herself, to save him.

"Ghost. Ghost. Ghost . . ."

It was barely a whisper, but from the look of shock that

erupted across his face, it had the impact of a scream. He froze, then jumped back as if someone had dumped a bucket of cold water on him, raising a hand to cover his mouth. *"Fuck."*

She curled up into a sitting position as he looked at her, wide-eyed, his face contorted as if in pain. He took a step toward her again, reaching out, but she flinched back. He stopped, staggering as if he'd been struck.

"Scarlett . . ." He scrubbed a hand through his hair, his eyes blinking rapidly. "I'm sorry. I'm so sorry. Please, forgive me."

Before she could respond, he turned and fled the room, bounding down the stairs. She broke out in sobs as a door slammed below, then pulled a blanket from the bed up and around her body.

When Drew didn't return after a half hour, Hannah got up off the bed and went into the bathroom. She looked at her reflection in the mirror; her face was red and puffy from crying and the outline of the bite mark on her shoulder stood out angrily.

She pulled out the pins holding her hair up, letting it fall around her shoulders. She turned the shower on as hot as it would go and stepped in, letting the water run over her.

She scrubbed every inch of her skin, trying to wash away the confusion flowing through her. When she stepped out of the shower, she was surprised to see a clean T-shirt and a pair of sweats sitting on the counter. Drew must have come in while she was showering.

She dried herself off quickly, the towel catching on the diamond choker around her neck. She worked to loosen the snag, and then placing the towel down, she removed the necklace and the bracelet, freeing herself of Drew's invisible hold. She walked into the bedroom and placed them both on the dresser.

After pulling on the sweats and T-shirt and running a brush through her hair, she tentatively made her way downstairs to find Drew. Her heart was hammering in her chest. Would she find the gentle man who'd worshipped her body earlier, or the monster she'd unleashed with her refusals?

Walking into the kitchen, she was startled to find a stranger sitting at the counter, reading a newspaper.

"E-excuse me?" Hannah stammered. "Who are you?"

The man stood up immediately, closing the paper as he did. He was tall and lean, probably in his forties, with close-cropped hair. He was dressed casually in dark jeans and a light grey, button-down shirt. He nodded at her. "Scarlett, I presume?"

"Yes."

"I'm James." He walked up to her while extending his hand in greeting. "Mr. Sapphire asked that I return you to the estate."

She shook his hand absently, confusion still settled on her face. "I'm sorry. Is Drew—I mean, Mr. Sapphire here? I need to speak to him."

James shook his head. "I'm sorry, miss. He's gone."

"Gone?" she echoed.

"Yes, miss." James shifted his feet uncomfortably, clearing his throat before continuing. "Do you have anything you need before we leave?"

She thought about the dress and the shoes. She definitely didn't want or need those again. She saw the clutch still sitting on the counter and, grabbing it, said, "No, let's go."

Her heart felt like lead in her chest. She couldn't believe he'd just left. Without a single word to her. How had this happened? She'd done nothing wrong. She was his submissive. She'd acted as such. But had she?

Should she have allowed herself to be taken out of the comfort and the protection that the estate provided her? In doing so, had she allowed Drew to believe that their relationship was something other than what it was meant to be? What was she supposed to do now? So many questions she had no answers for.

She rode to the estate in silence, a tangle of thoughts spinning in her head. She prayed that Drew's car would be in the driveway when they arrived. Perhaps he'd just needed some time. As they pulled through the gates, the sun was just beginning to rise and lighten the sky, the exact opposite of her own inner horizon.

Pulling into the driveway, her heart sank as she realized Drew's car wasn't there. One of the estate carts was parked along the walkway, though. Who could be here at this hour? James got out of the car, coming around to open the door for her.

"Thank you, James," she said meekly and made her way to the bungalow's front door. As she was reaching for the handle, the door swung open wide, Domme Maria standing in the entryway.

Hannah couldn't disguise her surprise and let out a little gasp. "Oh! Domme Maria, I wasn't expecting you."

"Come in, Scarlett." Domme Maria raised a sleek eyebrow. "I thought you and Drew had gone to a ball? Please tell me that isn't what you wore."

Hannah looked down at Drew's T-shirt and sweats, then

shrugged. She wasn't sure what Domme Maria did or didn't know, so she answered vaguely, "My dress got dirty, so Master Drew gave me this to change into."

"Well, I'm sorry he had to cut your time short. I'm sure you'll be happy to know it will have no effect on the fee owed to you."

Domme Maria started walking further into the house and beckoned for Hannah to follow. "Come."

Hannah followed her into the kitchen, questions reeling through her mind. She'd safe-worded. She shouldn't get her whole fee. What had Drew told Domme Maria? "Did you speak to him?"

"Master Drew? No, my assistant did. He explained that he was called away on a business emergency and had to cut your time short but wanted to make sure I saw to your needs personally. Apparently he felt bad. Who knew?"

"Oh, okay." She wasn't sure what to say. Obviously Drew hadn't told Domme Maria what had actually occurred between the two of them, and she definitely wasn't going to expose the truth.

The Domme looked at her skeptically. "Are you all right, Scarlett?"

"Yes, Ma'am. Just tired." She yawned to support her claim.

A single brow arched high. "If you say so. My gut is telling me it's something else. You can talk to me if you need to."

Domme Maria clicked her fingernails on the counter as if offering Hannah a chance to speak. After a moment of silence though, she continued. "I've brought your clothes here for you to change into. Once you're done, we can go to the office and I'll provide your weekend payment. Then you'll be free to leave."

"Yes, Ma'am," Hannah said softly and started to walk toward the bedroom.

"Scarlett," Domme Maria called, "you did amazing for your first auction. Master Drew paid fifty thousand dollars for you, which means you made twelve thousand five hundred dollars."

Hannah stopped in her tracks and turned, staring at the other woman in shock. "What?"

Domme Maria huffed in disbelief. "Oh you silly girl! You have no idea of your worth, do you?"

Hannah shook her head and walked quickly to the bedroom to change. Domme Maria had no idea just how close to home those words hit.

CHAPTER
Eleven

Two Weeks Later

"HANNAH, there's a messenger here for you!" her assistant called from the front of the shop.

"Can you just sign for it, please? I need to finish this arrangement for the Hoovers."

Robin appeared in the doorway of their workspace. "I tried. She says it has to be delivered in person."

Hannah sighed, exasperated, and wiped her hands on her apron as she made her way to the front of the shop. Surprise hit her when she saw that the messenger was none other than her attendant from Baton Timide.

Rose looked ethereal as always, dressed in a soft, pink dress that flowed over her willowy body. "Rose? What are you doing here?"

The other woman smiled. "Hello, miss. Maria sent me to give this to you." She held out a flat, gift-wrapped package with a card attached. "Given the nature of the gift, she thought it best be delivered in person."

Hannah took the gift, curious. Setting it down on the counter, she opened the envelope first. The card within was a heavy, cream-colored stock with the initials "AMS" embossed in sapphire blue on the front. Her heart immediately started pounding as she opened the card.

Inside was a check for one hundred thousand dollars, a business card for Andrew Matthew Sapphire and a message written in what had to be Drew's handwriting.

Scarlett,

Please take this and use it for whatever purpose brought you to Baton Timide. I know you quit, and I know I drove you to it. What's in the box belongs to you. I can't imagine it on another. I am sorrier than any words could ever express. I miss you. Please call me.

Drew

Hannah's hands shook as she set the card and its contents down on the counter and broke the seal on the wrapping covering the box. She knew in her heart what it was, but as she tore a corner of the paper and saw Tiffany blue beneath, her breathing stopped. It was the diamond choker necklace she had worn to the ball. Her collar.

She looked up at Rose in shock. "I can't take this."

She pushed the box across the counter, then lifted the check and placed it on top of the box as well. "Please, please, just take these back."

Rose placed her hand over Hannah's, squeezing it in understanding. "Of course, miss. Whatever you wish."

Rose gathered the box and check and placed them in the bag on her shoulder. Before leaving, she asked Hannah one final question. "Do you have a message for Mr. Sapphire?"

Hannah shook her head as a single tear fell down her cheek, which she quickly wiped away.

"Is he— I mean— Have you seen him?"

Rose kindly shook her head. "I'm sorry, miss. I haven't."

Rose gave Hannah one last kindhearted look and left the shop, the bell over the door tinkling as she did. Hannah took the note and business card and walked back into the workshop, where Robin was finishing an arrangement.

"What was all that about?" Robin asked.

Hannah shook her head. "Oh, nothing. A misunderstanding. I took care of it." The bell to the door sounded again, notifying them of another customer. "Why don't you go take care of that? I'll just put the finishing touches on this."

"You got it." Robin bounced out of the room.

Hannah walked across the room and placed the note and card under the silk mask that lay discreetly on the shelf above her desk. After Drew had walked away from her two weeks ago, she'd quit Baton Timide, realizing she wasn't the kind of person who could turn her heart off, as much as she had hoped she could be.

She'd deposited the money she had been paid into a savings account, not wanting to see or think about it again. She had done the same with her emotions and feelings for Drew, locking them away deep inside her, and buried herself in her work instead.

Two Days Later

"What do you mean she sent it back?" Drew slammed his fist down on Domme Maria's desk.

"Andrew, you need to calm down, please." Maria spoke coolly. "She doesn't want it. I can't force her to take it."

"Did you include the note I gave you?" His voice was lower, more even this time.

"I did, even though it was against my better judgment."

He ran a hand through his hair, frustration his reigning emotion, and sighed.

"You understand that this is completely inappropriate? A submissive's identity is to remain private unless *she* allows it to be otherwise."

He brought his gaze up to meet Maria's, fire blazing between them. "You think I don't know that? You think I want to feel this way? Act this way?"

"You're a Master Dominant. This is a situation you should have never allowed yourself to be in. I'm not going to lie here. I'm extremely disappointed in your behavior. Plus, I've lost a beautiful submissive."

He scoffed. "That makes two of us." A look of pleading entered his eyes. "Please, I'm begging you. Tell me her name or where I can find her."

"I'd never thought I would see the day you begged me for something, but you need to let her go. She's made her decision and you have to respect that." Maria spoke firmly, but a note of compassion snuck through.

Drew dropped his head into his hands, nodding in defeat. "I know, Maria. I know."

Two Months Later

Drew and Ben made their way out of the restaurant and across the large marble lobby of the hotel. They had just finished lunch and had decided to play hooky for the rest of the afternoon after they grabbed Drew's car from the valet. Ben's cane clicked on the marble floor as they walked but was overshadowed by the laughter they shared.

Ben pointed to the reception desk. "Hey, isn't that your friend Scarlett?"

Drew skidded to a halt as his gaze darted to the desk. *Scarlett.* She was holding an extravagant arrangement of roses and talking to the concierge animatedly. Her long hair was up in a ponytail, and she was dressed in jeans and a T-shirt. She looked just like an ordinary girl.

"I guess hitting the track is out?" Ben grumbled.

Drew pulled his gaze away from Scarlett long enough to respond, "Yeah, sorry, Benny," and then he hurried across the room.

When he reached her, he touched her shoulder to get her attention. "Scarlett?"

She spun around quickly, surprise splashed across her face, the large arrangement of roses slipping from her hands, crashing to the ground, glass shattering, water spilling in a pool at their feet.

"Jesus, Scarlett!" Drew pulled her back safely away from the broken glass. "Are you okay? I'm sorry, I didn't mean to startle you."

She didn't say a thing. Just stood there, staring at him like he might not be real.

Drew barked at the desk clerk, "You there! Can you please get someone to take care of this?"

The clerk picked up the phone, dialing a number while saying, "Yes, sir, Mr. Sapphire."

ALL OF A SUDDEN, a thousand pieces clicked into place for Hannah. "Oh my god!" She shrugged her shoulders as a chuff of disbelief left her. "Of course, Andrew Sapphire. Sapphire Luxury Resorts."

Drew dismissed her revelation with a quick head shake and took her elbow, guiding her away from the front desk and the mess they had created.

Once again, he asked, "Scarlett, are you okay?"

She finally looked at him, shaking her head, and repeated, "Oh my god. You're Andrew fucking Sapphire. You *own* Sapphire Resorts? How did I not put the pieces together before?"

"Stop saying that." He admonished. "My family owns it. Not just me. It's not that big of a deal." His tone dismissive.

"Not that big of a deal? Are you kidding me? You're a gazillionaire!"

"So maybe you should have kept the gifts I sent you then Scarlett. Obviously I can afford them." His voice was gruff.

"Stop calling me Scarlett," she retorted.

He glared right back at her and gritted out, "I'll call you anything you want, but since I don't know your real name, it puts me at a bit of a disadvantage."

The concierge walked over to them then, pointing to the

flowers strewn across the lobby floor. "Excuse me, Hannah dear, what would you like me to tell Mr. Ruffino about the flowers for his wife?"

She looked at Drew, quickly realizing that now he at least knew her first name, and then responded to the concierge. "George, would you be so kind as to call him and explain what happened? I'll pop back to the shop, put together a new arrangement and have it here within an hour."

"Of course. Thank you!"

Drew looked at her like he was seeing her for the first time and then took a step toward her. He swept a stray lock of hair from her face, back behind her ear, then cupped her cheek. "Hannah. It suits you."

For one moment, she forgot where she was and leaned into his touch, but then she took a step back. "Drew, Andrew, Mr. Sapphire, whatever I should call you. I'm sorry. I have to go."

She whirled around and started walking toward the exit. Drew grabbed her arm, stopping her. "Scar-- Hannah, wait! You're just going to leave?"

She turned back, her feet weighed down with grief. "Drew, I have to go. I have a job to do. I'm sorry, but nothing has changed for me."

"Please. Five minutes. Let's talk. Let's figure this out. I've missed you."

The pain and desperation in Drew's eyes broke her heart. Seeing him again caused every emotion she had finally managed to lock down over the last month to come screaming back to the surface.

She so badly wanted to stay, to listen to what he had to

say, to feel what she felt when she was in his arms again. But instead, she kissed him softly on the cheek. "Good-bye, Drew." And then she walked away, leaving him there staring after her.

As soon as Hannah was through the doors, her hand flew to her mouth to capture the heavy breaths panting from her. She ran to the delivery van she'd left in short-term parking and hopped in quickly, shutting the door on all the emotions she was feeling for Drew.

DREW STOOD FROZEN in the lobby for a good three minutes before he made the decision to go after her. He could wait for her to return with the flower delivery, but he was betting that she would send someone else with it.

He strode in the direction of the concierge and, scaring him half to death, barked out, "George!"

The concierge pointed to himself in question. "Me, sir?"

"Yes, you!" Exasperated. "Tell me what you know about Hannah!"

"Hannah with the flowers?" he asked.

"Yes, yes! Hannah with the flowers. What do you know?" Drew wanted answers and he wanted them quickly.

"N-nothing, really," he stammered. "I only know she works at The Secret Garden Boutique. That's it. She prepares special arrangements for some of our guests from time to time."

"Good, that's good. Okay, thank you." Drew clapped him

on the shoulder before striding to the exit. He gave the valet his ticket and, as he was waiting, googled the address to The Secret Garden on his phone. This time she was going to talk to him and he wasn't going to take no for an answer.

Fifteen minutes later, Drew was driving past her shop. It was in a particularly busy part of town, so he had to park a few buildings down and across from the store. After finally finding a spot, he got out and was about to cross the street when he saw Hannah walk out of the shop, a smile spread wide across her face.

His eyes looked in the direction hers were focused before flying wide. A little girl was skipping down the sidewalk, holding the hand of a man wearing military fatigues.

Drew could see that the little girl was the spitting image of Hannah, the same blonde hair, the same brown eyes. When the little girl spotted Hannah, she released the man's hand and began running toward her, shouting, "Mommy! Mommy!"

Hannah bent down, caught her daughter in her arms and brought her up in a hug, kissing her on top of her little head. The man had reached them now too and bent down, placing a kiss on Hannah's cheek in greeting.

Drew watched the scene unfold before his eyes, his breath caught in his throat, his heart thumping wildly. *She's married?* His hand scraped through his hair, his mouth falling open. *She has a child?*

Hannah swung the young girl up on her hip and, as she turned to walk back into the shop, caught movement out of the corner of her eye. Looking up, she saw Drew standing across the street, eyes locked on her in apparent shock.

She met his gaze for one quick second and shook her head, silently mouthing, "No!" and then walked into the shop with her family, the door slamming shut.

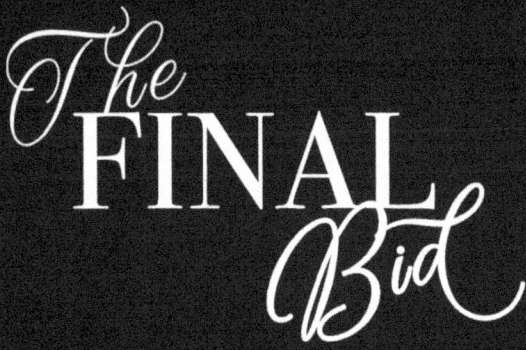

The Auction Series Book Two

MICHELLE WINDSOR

The FINAL Bid

MICHELLE WINDSOR

This is for everyone who ever wanted to write a story and didn't think they could.
I'm living proof that you can.
Go chase those dreams—every single one of them!

Prologue

DREW LEANED against the brick wall of the alley, his breath leaving him in puffy white clouds. Fall temperatures had finally arrived and mornings were dawning chillier each day. He pulled the hood of his sweatshirt tighter over his head and then stuffed his hands into the front pocket to save some of the warmth his body had created during his run. This morning, he'd arrived earlier than usual and had been waiting in the alley across from the flower shop for almost half an hour.

It had been four days since he'd run into her in the lobby of his hotel. Four days since he'd discovered she had a child and a husband. *Is it her husband? Is she even married?* She had specifically stated she wouldn't have been at Baton Timide if she were married. The last four days had been full of gut-twisting agony as he'd wondered.

He shouldn't be here, it was wrong. Still, each morning, here he was, hidden in the shadows like a thief, waiting to steal another glance of her. Scarlett. No. *Hannah.*

There were so many questions he wanted to ask her, but four days ago, when she'd looked straight at him and said "No," she had made it crystal clear she didn't want to see him again.

Yet he was here anyway, waiting and watching. Trying to figure out what to do next but needing to see her in the meantime. As the door in the alley opened, he pushed himself further into the shadows, his heart beating violently in his chest.

Hannah stepped out, and then a second, smaller version of her shuffled out, waiting while her mother locked the door. His eyes remained fixed on Hannah as she took her daughter's hand to guide her out of the alley before buckling her into their van and driving away.

Twenty minutes later, like the previous mornings, the now familiar van pulled back into the alley beside the shop. The brake lights flashed red as the sound of the engine died. The van door opened and closed, and then Hannah emerged between the wall and the van.

Today she wore a black wool coat, a bright pink scarf wrapped around her neck, her nose buried in its warmth as she hurried to the front door of the flower shop. Her loose and wavy hair, the color of gold, flowed down over her back, contrasting starkly with the coat. If he could get close enough, he knew she would smell like flowers.

Drew continued to watch as she unlocked the metal casing covering the door, then slid it up and out of the way. The metal must have been cold because she rubbed her hands together and blew on them. She found another key in the set she held and unlocked the interior door of the shop.

The faint tinkling of the bell carried on the breeze as she shut the door behind her.

He stayed another thirty minutes, waiting to see if this morning would be any different than the last three. It wasn't. Her coworker arrived just before eight a.m., followed by a delivery truck full of flowers a few minutes later. He popped his earbuds back in, pushed play on his iPod, put his head down and began the run back to the hotel before she came out to meet the delivery driver.

CHAPTER

One

"GRACE VICTORIA ROSE, you better have your coat on!" Hannah walked through the kitchen of her apartment and out into the hallway. Sure enough, her daughter was hiding behind the jackets hanging in a line by the front door, instead of putting herself into one.

"Gracie, what in the world are you doing?" Hannah knelt down and gently pulled her daughter out from behind the coats.

"Honey, we're going to be late. Why are you hiding?" Hannah grabbed a small lavender coat off one of the hooks.

"Momma, I don't want to go to school today," Her little voice pouty and sad.

"Sweetie, did you forget what today is?" Hannah swiftly pulled her daughter's coat on, buttoned it up and then stood. "Did you forget someone's birthday?"

Her face scrunched up in thought, and then, just as quickly, a large smile broke across her face. "I remember now! It's Daddy's birthday!"

Hannah bent down again to wrap a dark purple scarf around her daughter's young neck. November had come in like a lion and each morning was colder than the last.

"That's right!" She finished wrapping the scarf and then kissed the tip of Grace's nose. "So, I'll pick you up at eleven, and then you can come help me with the flowers before we go see him, okay?"

The little girl jumped up and down in excitement. "Okay, Momma."

"Okay. We gotta go now, Peanut. Grab your backpack." Hannah pointed to a small pink backpack sitting on a bench next to the front door, then grabbed her purse and keys off one of the wall hooks.

She ushered Grace out the door, through the alley and into the delivery van. After dropping Grace off at the daycare center she attended daily, she drove the short distance back to the flower shop.

As she unlocked the door to The Secret Garden, she was still in a state of disbelief that it would be hers in just a few short days. A month ago, she had told Donna, the current owner, she couldn't come up with the down payment and would have to pass on purchasing the shop.

Then, just three days ago, Donna had called and dropped a bombshell: she'd changed her mind and would like to sell the shop to Hannah in a private sale. She wanted to provide Hannah this opportunity and couldn't see anyone else taking over "her baby." They would work out a monthly payment plan that was beneficial to both of them.

The shop specialized in elegant extravagance and had an extensive clientele that included many of the wealthiest residents in New York. Hannah was thrilled to be able to keep working with her existing clients, but even more excited to finally have something to call her own; something that would allow her to raise her daughter comfortably.

The very best part of the purchase was that she was getting the entire building. That meant the apartment above the shop was now going to be hers as well. She breathed a sigh of relief that things were finally taking a turn for the better.

At that precise thought, her eyes fell on the black silk mask sitting discreetly on the shelf above her desk. On second thought, maybe not everything had worked out as she'd expected.

She still couldn't believe that she had run into Drew Sapphire while making a delivery earlier that week, and, that he was the heir to the Sapphire Luxury Resort chain. She felt incredibly stupid for not putting two and two together before then, but after the way they'd parted, her only desire had been to try and push him to the back of her mind.

She sighed heavily as she removed her scarf and coat, hanging them up in the small closet in the back room. She walked to her desk, picking up the business card that Drew had enclosed in the note he'd sent two months ago, and sat down.

She ran her fingers over the slightly raised sapphire colored font that spelled out his name before bringing the card to her nose. Closing her eyes and inhaling, she swore she could still catch the faintest trace of his scent after all this time. It was a crisp, clean, woodsy aroma that she couldn't seem to escape.

No matter how hard she tried to put her feelings for

Drew in a tightly locked box, every night when she closed her eyes, he was all that she could see. He invaded her dreams, every nerve coming alive with the memory of the way he'd touched her, kissed her, licked her.

She would wake up drenched in sweat, aching for his touch, her body pulsing for him. And every day since she'd seen him, she kept waiting for him to walk through the shop door and confront her.

But each day went by without any trace of him. She couldn't erase the memory of his shocked face when she'd scooped her daughter up into her arms. Her child had finally given him a reason to stop pursuing her. Which is what she'd wanted, after all. At least, that's what she kept telling herself.

"Hannah? Hello? Anyone home in there?" Robin stood in front of her. Hannah hadn't even heard the bells on the door when her assistant had arrived.

Hannah stood up and gave her friend a quick hug good morning. "Robin, hey! Sorry, I was so deep in thought about that arrangement we need to do for the Penn's order that I didn't even hear you come in."

"No worries, sweetie. I brought you a tea from Oslo's."

Robin handed her a white to-go cup, then placed her things on the counter so she could remove her jacket and hang it up.

Hannah took the tea and smiled in gratitude. "Thanks, you're too good to me. Let's go see if Tony's here with the deliveries yet."

FOUR HOURS LATER, with morning orders complete and Grace back at the shop, Hannah glanced at her watch. She needed to leave soon to take Grace to see Jackson. They had to drive out to Brooklyn, and the afternoon traffic would be a challenge.

She walked out of the work room into the front of the shop and found Grace sitting on a stool, working on a bouquet at the counter with Sara, one of the other women that was employed at the shop.

Grace's voice pulled her from her thoughts. "Look what I made for Daddy, Momma!"

Grace proudly held up a large bouquet of white chrysanthemums wrapped in a red felt ribbon. "Sara said we should use these because they are the flower for November and they are perfect for Daddy."

Hannah took the bouquet from her daughter's small hands, held it up to her nose and inhaled deeply. "It's beautiful, Gracie. Daddy will love them."

Hannah looked up and smiled in thanks at Sara. "You okay if I head out now? All the orders have been prepped for the rest of the afternoon deliveries and pickups, and Josh will be back to get those around 1:30."

"Of course," Sara replied while helping Grace down off her stool. "I'll take care of everything and lock up at 5:00. Just call me if you think of anything else."

"I will, thanks." She reached a hand out to Grace. "You ready, Peanut?"

Grace grabbed her mother's hand and followed her into the back room. They both bundled up in their coats and then proceeded back through the shop and out the front door to their van.

The Grand Central Parkway would probably be the best route into Brooklyn this time of day. It was less than twenty miles to their destination, but with traffic, it could easily take them an hour.

Not that the time ever passed slowly when she was in the car with Grace. She was a chatter bug with one tale after another about her morning at Miss Daisy's and how excited she was to go to her Auntie Tammy's on Sunday to play with her cousin Emma. Before Hannah knew it, she was pulling through the gates and putting the van into park. She got out and unbuckled Grace, lifting her out of her seat to place her on the sidewalk before handing her the bouquet.

"Want to go find Daddy? Do you remember where he is?"

"I think so, Momma. Follow me!" Grace turned and ran, Hannah close on her heels.

Grace stopped, turned in a circle, looked to her right and then took off again. "I found him, Momma!"

Hannah walked up behind her daughter, placing both hands on her shoulders, squeezing gently. "Yes you did. You're so smart."

Hannah smiled sadly as her young, sweet, innocent daughter bent down to place the bouquet on the ground next to her father's grave before kissing the white stone. "Happy birthday, Daddy."

As Gracie stood back up, she pointed to the top of the

headstone. "Look, Momma, someone else brought Daddy a flower too."

The single black rose contrasted with the simple ivory of the military headstone. She wondered about who had left it. It wasn't the first time she'd found one on his grave. Her eyes lowered away from the flower as she scanned the simple script on the stone.

JACKSON T ROSE
SGT, US ARMY
NOV 7 1985 - JUN 10 2013
PURPLE HEART
BRONZE STAR
OPERATION IRAQI FREEDOM

IT WAS hard for her to believe that he'd been gone for almost two and a half years now. He would have been thirty years old today. She bent down and ran her fingers over the engraved letters of his name. "Happy birthday, baby. I miss you every day."

"I did it, Jackson." She took a key out of her pocket and placed it in the dirt against the gravestone. "We said by the time you turned thirty we'd have our own place, and I did it."

It was silly to leave the key, but it was her way of letting him know that she had followed through on their dream of owning a home and business.

She stood, brushing the loose dirt off the knees of her

jeans, turning her attention back to her daughter. Grace was weaving through the gravestones, touching each one as she went saying, "Thank you."

Her heart swelled with love and gratitude for the gift of her daughter and the kindness her young soul already possessed.

She called out, "Gracie! You ready to go get some pizza and cake?"

Grace's head swung in her mother's direction, her face lighting up with a smile as she turned and skipped closer. "Can we get ice cream too, Momma?"

Hannah smiled. "Uh, yeah! We can't have cake without ice cream!"

"Yay!" Grace jumped up and down with excitement before zipping her way back to the van, both of them climbing in for the trip back home.

CHAPTER
Two

IT WAS DAY FIVE, and Drew was done with just watching. When Hannah started unlocking the metal casing, he left the cover of the alley and crossed the street. His sneakers were silent on the pavement, making it easy for him to come up behind her with no warning. She slid the metal casing up, unlocked the front door and pulled it open.

He was two steps behind her as he slid through, bells tinkling overhead. Humming distractedly, she still hadn't realized that he was there. The song she was humming stopped him cold. "Into the Mystic." The song they had danced to at his beach house.

"Hannah." His voice was low and gruff. His palms were sweating and his pulse was in overdrive. She shrieked in surprise as she spun around, her eyes growing wide when they landed on him.

"Holy shit, Drew! What the hell are you doing here?" Her hand flew up to her chest, as if to still her heart, her face reddening in anger. "Are you trying to give me a goddamn heart attack?"

He took a step closer, then stopped when she took two steps back. He pushed the hood of his sweatshirt off as he raked his fingers through his hair, lowering his hands to his waist, palms up, to show her he meant no harm.

"I'm sorry. I just—" He shook his head, blinking once before continuing. "Jesus, Hannah. I'd forgotten how beautiful you are."

She stared at him, her features softening as she let out a sigh. "Drew, what are you doing here?"

"I want—" He paused, frowning. "I need to talk to you."

She unwrapped the scarf from her neck and then unbuttoned her coat. She said nothing as she hung them up in the closet. "I'm not really sure there's anything to say."

His eyes followed her as she settled on the opposite side of the work table from him.

"What do you mean there's nothing to say? I saw you with your daughter and husband. Is he your ex-husband? You said you weren't married, but are you? I haven't seen him here since that day." He raked a hand through his disheveled hair again, his eyes darting around her wildly.

Hannah's eyes narrowed. "What do you mean, you haven't seen him here? Have you been watching me?"

He took a deep breath. *Damn it, he'd gone this far, might as well keep going.* "I'm just trying to understand who you are and what the hell happened between us. Because I know for certain, it wasn't like anything I've ever experienced before."

He took a couple steps around the table to get closer to her, but she countered his action, keeping a large space between them. "Don't you think about me at all?"

Her expression remained blank. He drummed his fingers heavily on the table in frustration. "Because I can't stop thinking of you. It's been over two months, and I can't get you out of my system. And believe me, I've tried."

She raised one eyebrow, distaste evident in her tone as she replied. "Girls at Baton Timide helping out with that?"

He scoffed, rolling his eyes. "Try tequila. Lots and lots of it."

He locked his gaze angrily on hers and rounded the table. "You think another woman is the answer to my problem? You think if I go to the club and buy myself someone new, tie them up, and fuck them, that I'll forget the way you felt?" He prowled closer. "That I'll forget how you smell, how you taste?"

Drew had reached her now and grasped her by the shoulders as he whispered in her ear. "That I'll forget how you screamed my name as I drove myself into you?"

Her breathing quickened as he ran his nose from her ear into the soft tresses of her hair, inhaling her scent. He was about to pull away when she turned her head, her lips brushing across his. Before he could stop himself, he put a hand on her cheek and crushed his mouth to hers, sliding his tongue across its seam, forcing her to open up to him.

She hesitated for only a second before her mouth parted on a moan, her tongue meeting his, her hands bunching the material of his sweatshirt.

He dropped his hand from her face to grab her waist, tugging her body close, their kiss growing deeper, more desperate. He lifted her onto the table, her legs wrapping around him, her hips thrusting forward as her core ground against his. With one hand tangled in her hair and their mouths fused together in desire, he used his other hand to palm her ass, thrusting his cock harder against her center.

He hadn't been with anyone since Hannah, and if they kept this up, he was going to explode in a matter of minutes. To slow things down, he tore his lips away from hers and began peppering kisses along her neck.

She whimpered in protest but then groaned softly, her head falling back on her shoulders, her long hair brushing against the table. He cupped her breast and rolled her taut nipple between his fingers, reveling in the sounds coming from her throat. Sounds he hadn't known if he would ever hear again.

She arched her back into his touch, pushing her core more forcefully against his throbbing cock. "Fuck, Hannah," he hissed, leaning down, fusing his lips to hers again.

He reached under her shirt and yanked down the cup covering her breast. He ran his thumb back and forth over the peak of her nipple, elongating it with each stroke.

She broke their kiss with a moan. "Drew . . ."

He moved his mouth against her ear. "I've waited two months to hear you say my name like that again." And then trailed his lips back across to hers, sealing them together once more.

"Oh holy shit! Sorry!" A girl's voice rang out in surprise behind Drew. Hannah's coworker had come in and neither had heard her, or the bell on the door.

Drew quickly pulled himself off Hannah as she simultaneously pushed him away and jumped off the table. He turned in an attempt to hide his still-erect member as she fumbled her clothes back into their proper position behind him.

A very red-faced girl in her young twenties, whom Drew recognized from his morning stakeouts, was standing in the entryway to the back room, her hand held tightly over her eyes. "I'm just going to go out to the coffee shop."

She started backing out of the doorway, her other hand feeling her way behind her. "I'll be back later. Didn't see a thing! I swear!" And then turned and fled out the front door.

Drew took a step toward Hannah, frustrated at his loss of control. "I'm sorry. I didn't mean to put you in that position."

She shook her head as if trying to clear it, shoving her hand out flat in front of her. "No, I'm sorry. I shouldn't have let that happen."

Disappointment bled into his voice. "But it did. And you can't deny that you don't feel something for me. I deserve some answers, Hannah."

"I know you do." She sighed in defeat. "But, Drew, not now. Please, just go. I'm begging you."

He took two steps forward, butting up against her hand, and then stopped. "This isn't over."

'I know' fell from her lips in a whisper before he stormed past her and through the shop, slamming the door behind him.

FOUR HOURS LATER, plus about four miles of pacing in his office, and he wasn't any less frustrated than when he'd left Hannah that morning.

What the fuck was I thinking, confronting her like that? But Jesus, it felt so damn good to have her in my arms again.

A buzzing from the intercom interrupted his thoughts, stopping him in his tracks. He changed direction and pushed the button to respond. "I thought I said no calls, Felicia."

"Sir, it's Hannah. I thought you'd want to take this."

God damn, my assistant is good. "Yes, put her through, please. Thank you."

His heart rate started racing as he sat down at his desk. He blew out a long breath and then picked up the receiver.

"Hannah?" His voice was deep and low, hopefully hiding his nerves.

"Yes, hello, Drew." She did sound nervous, which in a strange way comforted him.

"I wasn't certain if it was really going to be you on the other line."

"Surprised?" She tried to joke.

"Relieved."

There was a moment of silence before Drew continued. "I've been pacing around my office since I left you this morning. I shouldn't have ambushed you like that. I'm sorry. I really just wanted some answers. To understand."

She murmured, "I know. I'm sorry too. This is as confusing to me as it is to you."

"Can we meet? I'd like to talk."

"That's why I'm calling. I'd like to meet with you too. To try and explain."

"Okay, I can be there in twenty minutes," he responded, rising out of his chair.

"No, no. I can't today. I'm working and I have my daughter every evening."

Frustration cut him to the core, his free hand dragging roughly through his hair as he tried to rein in his disappointment. "Okay. When? I'll make myself available any time that works for you."

"I can meet you on Sunday. The shop is closed that day. Will that work?"

"What time?" Sunday felt like fucking forever, but if that's what she had to give, he would take it.

"Is eleven okay?"

"Any time is fine. I can do eleven. Should I meet you at the shop? Pick you up?"

"No, not here. Someplace else."

"Okay. I'll have a car pick you up at ten forty-five and bring you to my place."

A large sigh came through the receiver. "Drew, I can't go out to the Hamptons. It's too far and I don't have that much time."

"No, not my house. I keep a suite at the hotel when I'm in town working."

"Oh, okay, but I don't need a car. I'll get myself there."

"Hannah, just let me send a car." His controlling nature was clearly trying to take charge.

"No. Don't send one or I won't come."

He growled into the phone. Actually growled. "You are so infuriating sometimes. Fine. No car."

"Thank you." There was a pause as she took a breath before continuing. "Which one?"

"Which one what?" Confusion evident in his tone.

"Which hotel is your suite at? There are four Sapphire Resorts in Manhattan."

He would bet his life that she was rolling her eyes. "Ah, yes. Sorry. The one on West Fifty-Ninth. Just let the front desk know when you arrive."

"Okay. I'll see you then."

"Hannah?"

"Yes?"

He wanted to keep her on the phone longer, but didn't want to push her away now that she was almost in his grasp, so he kept it simple. "Thank you for meeting with me."

"Yep." A click sounded, and Drew looked in disbelief at the receiver in his hand as the dull sound of the dial tone came across the line.

She'd hung up on him before he could say goodbye. *Goddamn stubborn woman is going to be the end of me.*

He slammed the receiver back into the cradle and then rolled the chair back from his desk, swiveling toward the window as he grumbled under his breath.

His office was on the thirteenth floor of the hotel, overlooking Central Park. It was mid-afternoon and chilly out, so there wasn't a lot of foot traffic or people waiting for the horse-drawn carriages that lined the street.

A woman emerged from the park, a young girl holding her hand and skipping beside her; both of them had blonde hair. They could have easily been Hannah and her daughter. How many times had they passed right under his window without his ever knowing?

A week ago, he definitely wouldn't have noticed the duo. Had he been better off in that blissful state of ignorance than with the knowledge he had now?

Instead of pondering the question further, he twirled his chair back around to his desk and brought up a chat session on his computer. He pulled up his brother Benny's profile and started typing.

Hey, you there?

Several moments passed without a response, and Drew was about to grab his cell phone to call instead, when a return message popped up.

What's up?

He quickly typed a response.

Wanna go blow off some steam?

It was only a few seconds before another reply came.

Sure, I'll pick you up in ten.

It was only Friday afternoon and Sunday seemed a long way off. Patience wasn't his strong suit, and if he didn't get out of his own head, he might go mad. Benny always knew how to bring him back down to level ground again.

He shut down his laptop, put his phone in his pocket and grabbed his jacket out of the closet before exiting his office. Felicia looked up from her desk as he shut his door.

"Leaving for the day?"

She was a pretty woman, with long, straight auburn hair and big green eyes. She had started working for him about six months ago and had turned out to be one of the best assistants he'd had to date.

"Yes. Do I have anything important on the schedule?"

She quickly brought up his calendar on the computer and, after a glance, looked up at him with a frown. "Your father. Status meeting for the Boston hotel at four."

"Okay, I'll handle that. If he happens to call to confirm, just tell him I can't make it and I'll be in touch." He typed a quick reminder into his phone about calling his dad. "Anything else?"

Felicia shook her head. "No, sir. Nothing that I can't work or move around for you."

"Excellent. You're the best." He smiled and started walking toward the exit. "I'll be with Ben, and I'll have my cell if you need me for any emergencies."

"Very good, sir." Felicia smiled and nodded her head in farewell. "Have a good weekend."

"Thanks, you too."

Drew made his way down the hall to the elevator, taking it to the ground floor to wait for Benny. As he crossed the lobby, he pulled his jacket on over his dark suit, wishing he had thought to change into something more casual. He checked his watch. Did he have time to run up to his suite? But then, there was Benny pulling up in front of the hotel. He shook his head at his brother's typical choice in car, a Dodge Challenger SRT Hellcat in black. A straight-up muscle car.

The doorman tipped his hat as Drew walked through the exit and across the sidewalk to Benny's car. He pulled open the passenger door and slid into the caramel-colored leather seat.

Benny gunned the engine with a grin and sped into traffic as soon as Drew's door was shut.

"Hey, Brother."

"Hey yourself. Thanks for grabbing me."

Ben shrugged. "Sure. What's up? Dad?"

Drew shook his head and blew out a long breath. "Nope. Dad's easy compared to this."

Ben raised an eyebrow. "This have anything to do with Scarlett?"

"Hannah," Drew corrected.

"Who's Hannah?" Ben asked, confused.

"Scarlett," Drew replied.

"What?" Ben's brow now furrowed.

"Scarlett is really Hannah." Drew stated like it should be obvious.

"What the fuck? You're making no sense."

"Tell me about it." Drew shook his head. "I don't want to talk about it."

"Alrighty then." Ben reached over and turned the radio up to drown out some of the silence in the car.

"You said you had something in mind?" Drew shouted over the music.

Ben glanced at his brother as he weaved through traffic and over the bridge into Brooklyn, a big grin spreading across his face. "How do you feel about a little boxing?"

Drew grinned back, a surge of excitement running through him. "Hell, yeah."

"Perfect. I know some guys who will be happy to help you work out some of your shit."

"Why do I get the sense you're looking forward to seeing me get my ass beat?"

Ben reached over, ruffling Drew's perfectly coifed hair. "Cause that's what big brothers are for."

Drew leaned away, punching his brother lightly in the arm. "Yeah, whatever."

"Seriously, these are all good guys. I just gotta make a quick stop at Cypress Hills while we're in Brooklyn. You mind?"

"Nope." Drew looked over at his brother. "Whatever you need."

He had forty-six more fucking hours to kill before seeing Hannah.

CHAPTER
Three

HANNAH ENTERED the lobby of the hotel and walked toward the concierge desk. Her heart was beating hard enough to drown out the clacking of her boot heels on the marble.

She had changed no less than four times before finally deciding on a pair of boyfriend-style jeans (with perfectly ripped patches, of course), a simple black off-the-shoulder T-shirt, an old leather jacket and black ankle booties.

It was an outfit she would normally wear to visit with friends. For this meeting, she wanted to be in her own skin, not in what Drew would want to see.

She smiled as she reached the concierge desk. George, her favorite clerk at this hotel, was on duty this morning. "Good morning, George."

"Hannah! Good morning to you! Are you working on a Sunday?"

She shook her head, her cheeks flushing as she

responded, "No. I actually have an appointment with Drew —er, Mr. Sapphire at eleven. I'm a bit early though."

She glanced down at her watch. She was a whole fifteen minutes early. *Argh, now I look too anxious.*

George smiled warmly and picked up the phone. "Let me call up to see if he's available now. He just came back from a run not too long ago."

She glanced around, taking in the sights and sounds of people making their way through the lobby, wondering where people might be visiting from or where they were heading to.

George came around the desk and touched her lightly on the elbow, guiding her toward a set of elevators.

"If you'll come with me? Mr. Sapphire's on a secure floor, so I'll just need to punch in an access code."

"Of course." She followed George and stood silently as they both waited for the elevator to arrive. He swept his hand out, inviting her to enter the elevator first. He held the door open as he quickly entered a code on a keypad, then pressed PH3 and stepped back out.

"Off you go then, miss." He tipped his head and smiled as the doors slid shut.

Hannah raised a hand in goodbye and got out a quick thank you before the doors shut and the elevator started to rise. Her heart, which had calmed a bit while speaking with George, increased its rate with every floor she climbed.

This was a moment she had hoped never to find herself in, but it would be unfair to herself, and Drew, not to give him some kind of closure to their weekend. She scoffed a bit at that. He was the one that had stormed out on her and left her alone and confused in his house.

The elevator came to a quick stop, a ding indicating her arrival, and the doors slid open. She took a deep breath before stepping out into the foyer of the suite—and right into Drew's steely blue gaze. She stopped abruptly, a small gasp escaping her lips. *Why does he have to look so damn delicious?*

He was leaning against the wall, just a few feet away from the elevator's entrance, wearing faded jeans and a light gray, fitted T-shirt. His toned arms were crossed, as were his bare feet, his hair still wet from a recent shower.

"What happened to your eye?" she asked in concern. She took a few steps closer and reached up, but then stopped short before touching his face.

"Hello, Hannah."

He pushed himself off the wall, watching as her hand slowly sank back down to her side, bending to kiss her softly on the cheek. "You're early." He gave her a quick wink. "Anxious as ever?"

His stubble-lined jaw held that sly grin she had quickly come to know over the weekend they'd spent together. She frowned slightly at his brush-off. "Drew, your eye? What happened? Are you okay?"

"I'm fine. It's nothing. A little reminder that I'm not as good at boxing as I used to be."

He turned and started walking down a short hallway, motioning for her to follow. "Come, let's go sit in the dining room. I ordered some food in case you're hungry."

She walked behind him down a hallway that opened into a large space containing a kitchen, a dining room and a seating area. Three walls were nothing but windows, allowing the bright sunshine of the day to light up the room.

He strolled over to a table filled with several silver-covered platters and pulled out a chair for her, then pointed to her. "Can I take your jacket?"

"Sure, thanks."

She shrugged out of her jacket and handed it to him before sitting down in the seat. He laid it over the arm of a nearby couch and walked back to the table. As he passed her, his fingers skimmed ever so softly over her bare shoulder, and then he sat down in the seat next to her. He stared at her, quiet for several moments.

"What is it?" Hannah looked down at herself, checking to see if something was on her shirt.

He chuckled, his cheeks dimpling as they lifted. "I always forget how beautiful you are. Every damn time I see you, I'm reminded."

Hannah's cheeks heated in embarrassment. "Does your eye hurt?" This time, she did reach up and brush her fingertips over the bruise.

He took her hand in his own, his expression turning serious. "I'm sure it's nothing compared to the pain I must have caused when I left you at the beach house."

Her eyebrows shot up in surprise. She'd been sure he would evade that subject in pursuit of her secrets.

She tilted her head in thought before answering. "Confused, and yes, I suppose hurt. I didn't really want to believe that you would just leave after, well . . . after everything we shared together."

Drew scooted his chair closer, his knee bumping into hers, her hand still clasped in his. "I'm so sorry about that. For losing my temper. For not respecting your privacy. For leaving you. You were trying to meet me in the middle and I had to go and take more from you. I know it wasn't fair."

She looked past Drew and stared blankly out the window behind him as she tried to register his apology. It wasn't what she'd expected from him, and it was throwing her off-balance. *Why did he have to be so goddamn nice?*

"Hannah?" Drew's voice pulled her out of her thoughts. "Are you okay?"

She stood quickly, sliding her hand from Drew's. He stood up just as quickly in response. "Can I use the bathroom please?"

A look of confusion crossed his features. "Um, of course." He pointed toward a hallway off the kitchen. "It's the first door on the right."

"Thanks. Just be a minute."

DREW WATCHED as Hannah escaped down the hallway into the bathroom, shutting the door firmly behind her. He ran a hand through his hair before shaking his head in confusion. *What the fuck was that about?*

Unsure what to do but feeling the need to keep busy, he poured each of them a mimosa, then started removing the covers from all the platters.

He stacked them on the counter and then went back and sat at the table to wait. A moment later, the door of the bathroom clicked open and Hannah's footsteps padded toward him. Would she leave now?

"Are you—"

"I'm sorry—"

They both laughed nervously. He stood. "Are you okay?"

"Yes, yes." She looked down as embarrassment flooded her cheeks. "I needed a minute. I just . . ."

He waited for her to continue, but when she didn't, he placed a finger under her chin, raising it so he could look her in the eyes. "You just what?"

"I just wasn't expecting that." Her voice timid as her cheeks heated.

"That?" Drew scratched the stubble on his chin. "What do you mean?"

She took a step back, breaking their connection. "I wasn't expecting you to apologize. To take any responsibility for your actions that evening. To acknowledge that you hadn't respected my need for some control over my situation."

Astonished, he couldn't help chuckling. "Has no man ever apologized to you before? Your husband?"

She shook her head, a wry smile appearing. "I was wondering when you were going to bring that up."

"Well, you must know seeing you with a man and a child would shock me. Your husband and daughter, I presume?"

He sat down at the table, motioning for her to do the same. He lifted the flute of one mimosa to his mouth, draining it in a single gulp.

Hannah's expression saddened as she took a small sip from the drink sitting in front of her. "Yes, that was my daughter you saw me with. Grace. She's four, almost five now. But that wasn't my husband. It was my brother."

Relief surged through his bloodstream, shooting straight to his heart, flooding it with hope. He forced himself not to break into a grin as he continued questioning her. "Your brother? He's in the military? I noticed he was wearing fatigues."

"He's a recruiter now." She paused, fidgeting with the glass between her fingers before continuing. "Danny—that's my brother—picked Grace up from school for me that day. He helps me a lot."

Drew nodded, but he still needed to know the answer to the most important question. "And your husband?"

A shaky hand lifted the glass to her lips and she took a longer sip this time. "Jackson."

Not a denial. The world suddenly tipped on its axis, and he grabbed onto the edge of the table until the dizziness in his head passed.

He broke out in a cold sweat as the realization hit him that she did have a husband. "Jackson is your husband?" he prodded, needing to know the answer but fearing it all the same.

She nodded and then confirmed his worst fear. "Yes, he was my husband."

Wait, past tense? His pulse quickened at the revelation.

HANNAH KNEW from Drew's body language and the hope gleaming in his eye that he believed she and Jackson had gotten divorced. After all, that was the natural conclusion when one heard someone *was* their husband. If only things were that simple.

"Jackson and Danny were best friends growing up."

Taking a deep breath to steady her nerves, she continued. "Danny's four years older than me, and somewhere around the time I turned fifteen, I fell madly in love with Jackson."

Her eyes crinkled as she recalled those times. She had been a gangly teenager following him around like a puppy, and he had done everything he could to avoid her.

Drew drummed his fingertips restlessly on the tabletop, not so subtly prompting her to continue. She raised a brow as she stared at them pointedly, and his fingers stilled instantly.

"After high school, both boys joined the army. They did basic together and somehow ended up deployed overseas. It was two years before either of them returned home again."

She was quiet for a moment as she recalled that visit. Both men had come home to surprise her for her high school graduation.

No one had known they were coming, but the best gift had been jumping into Jackson's arms, his face filled with surprise upon discovering she was no longer a little girl. When he'd hugged her back, it had been filled with the promise of so much more.

"The boys stayed home for three weeks. Jackson and I spent almost every moment of that time together. By the time he left, we realized we were in love with each other."

She glanced up at Drew to try and gauge his reaction to her proclamation. His face was void of emotion, but his hands were clenched into tight fists on the table. She picked up the pace.

"Of course, both the boys had to go back. Jackson came back twice in the next year, and during the second visit, we eloped. I was only nineteen years old. My parents weren't thrilled, but Jackson and I knew what we wanted."

Hannah's chest rose as she inhaled deeply and then let out a long sigh. "He was gone for almost a year before coming home on leave again."

She'd moved into a little apartment and tried making it into a home for them. She had been so young. And so lonely. Her parents had died six months after her wedding, her sister was busy starting her own family, and her brother, of course, was overseas too.

She hadn't heard from Jackson very often, so it had been hard. When he'd finally gotten leave and stayed with her for a whole month, it had been absolutely perfect. It had been what she'd thought their life was supposed to be like.

"After a month, he had to go back again. But then, about six weeks after he left, I found out I was pregnant."

Hannah looked down and placed a hand over her stomach as she remembered. "He came home two days before I had Grace. He was home for two weeks. He promised me that after that tour, he would come home for good so we could be together as a family."

She looked up and smiled sadly at Drew. He had relaxed his fists, but kept wiping his palms against his thighs every few seconds.

"We didn't see him again for ten months. His Humvee struck an IED. His wounds were minor, though, and not the reason he came home."

She paused, taking a moment before going on. "Several of the men on the truck died and another was transported here back to the states for recovery. He came for their funerals. He was so angry. I almost didn't recognize him. He didn't understand how he could have come out of the accident with barely a scratch when his friends had died."

He'd spent nearly every day at the hospital with his friend. She'd barely seen him. When she had, he wouldn't look her in the eye. She'd known. Without him even telling her, she knew.

She shook her head in anger then, her voice becoming strained as she forced herself to finish. "Before he even told me, I knew he had re-upped for another tour. When I finally confronted him, he told me he had to go back to honor those he had lost. He couldn't stay here. He said he had to make things right."

Her eyes filled with a sadness so deep, Drew's heart stuttered in his chest. "It was as if Grace and I didn't exist for him anymore. I begged and pleaded with him not to go. Tried to tell him that God had given him another chance so he could be here with us. Even my brother, who was home then, tried to reason with him. But it didn't matter. He couldn't see beyond his grief."

She flinched when Drew's hands wrapped around hers. "Hannah, you can stop if you need to. It's enough. It's obvious this is painful for you."

"No, just let me finish. I want you to know. To understand."

His grip loosened, his hands leaving hers as he leaned back in his chair, nodding for her to continue. She rushed her next words, just wanting to get them out and over with. It still wasn't easy for her to say them out loud.

"He went back. He left us." Her eyes squeezed shut for a moment, a ragged breath leaving her before the next words fell like a brick. "And three months later, he was dead."

She dragged her eyes up to meet his, sadness rimming their edges. "I'm still not sure exactly what happened. No one really ever wants to tell us at home the whole truth. His commanding officer said he was on patrol in a small town, performing reconnaissance. They met with resistance and he was shot and killed."

She shrugged, her lips turned down in a frown. "All I know is that I never got to see him again because I was advised to have a closed-casket funeral."

She was proud of herself for keeping her voice steady. She looked up to meet Drew's gaze. His eyes were closed tight.

"Drew?" She touched him on the shoulder.

His eyes opened slowly. "I'm so, so sorry, Hannah."

"There's more though. And this is the part that I'm not proud of."

His face remained neutral, not giving away anything he was feeling. "You've told me enough. I don't need to know anymore. I can't imagine what you must have gone through, that loss and trying to raise a little girl by yourself ."

"But I want you to know. As much as I'm ashamed and afraid to tell you, I want you to know it all. Then maybe I can make you understand why I can't be with you."

ALL THE SYMPATHY he had felt was suddenly washed away in a wave of frustration. "Yes, please tell me then. Because I don't understand why you can't be with me if you aren't married anymore."

Hannah wrung her hands in her lap, nodding as she continued. "After the funeral, which I barely remember, I didn't know what to do or how to cope. I felt so angry, and so empty. I couldn't believe I would never get to talk to Jackson again. Or that Grace would never get to know how wonderful her father was. My brother came and stayed in our little apartment with us. He tried so hard to help. But I couldn't look at him, or even at Grace, without seeing Jackson."

There was a pause as her eyes met his. He nodded. "Go on."

Fidgeting in her chair, she continued. "So, I disappeared. I just didn't come home one day. I went to a bar and started drinking. And I didn't stop for two months. I went home with anyone who would have me, as long as it meant I didn't have to go to my home."

She grimaced at the memories. "And I did drugs. Anything that would keep me in a permanent haze so I wouldn't have to feel. I was walking a tightrope and barely hanging on. But the thing was, at the time, I didn't care. If I had fallen, I wouldn't have cared one little bit."

He understood now why she had been nervous, but it was still a shock to hear about her drug abuse and sexual oblivion. "You wanted to join Jackson." It was a statement. He didn't need her to confirm it, but she nodded anyway, her cheeks reddening.

"After about three months of this, my sister Tammy found me and dragged me kicking and screaming into a mental health center. I wanted to kill her. But of course, she did the right thing.

After another two months of dealing with my anger and

my loss, I went home. And I promised myself that from that point on, everything I ever did would be for me and Grace. I will never let myself be vulnerable like that again. Ever."

Hannah's timid eyes met his. He should try to be kind, but anger and confusion clouded his judgment, his voice coming out harsher than intended.

"I don't understand. Are you an alcoholic? An addict?"

"No, my doctors didn't classify me as an addict. Depression, yes."

Her hair fell forward as she glanced down at her entangled fingers. "I used it as a crutch to hide from my real problem. Although I never did drugs before Jackson's death. And I haven't touched them since I got help. I just used whatever was handy to make me forget about my real life. I just wanted to be numb. You've seen me drink socially. I can take it or leave it. But it's not something that I need. If that makes any sense at all."

"I don't know if it makes any sense. I've seen you drink, and I do think you may have a problem knowing what your limits are."

She shifted in her seat and her face turned a light shade of pink. She uncrossed her legs and made a move to stand, but Drew stopped her with a hand on her arm.

"Stay. I'm sorry if I'm making you uncomfortable. I'm just trying to understand."

Her body relaxed back in the chair and she folded her hands in her lap. "This is uncomfortable. I basically just told you I whored myself to forget my dead husband. It's not my proudest moment."

He winced. "Ouch. That's being a little harsh."

She shrugged. "It is what it is. I'm not going to pretend otherwise."

He gazed at her a moment, watching her chest rise and fall quickly, waiting for her breathing to slow before continuing. "I'm sorry your husband died, and I'm even sorrier that you had to go through so much pain because of it, but I'm not going to let you push me away because you're afraid to get hurt again. That's not living."

"But I am living. I'm living a life that I chose for myself. It's safe. Grace is happy. I'm happy."

He stood up then and walked over to one of the full-length windows, shoving his hands in the pockets of his jeans before closing his eyes and lifting his face into the sun.

"Come here and stand next to me."

Her clothes rustled as she rose from the chair and then her boots tapped over to him. He peeked at her through one eye before turning back toward the window.

"Close your eyes."

He couldn't be sure she was following his commands, but she wasn't arguing or questioning him, so he trusted she had complied.

"Do you feel it, Hannah?"

"Feel what?" He could hear the confusion in her voice.

"The sun. The heat. Do you feel it?" He chuckled at her continued stubbornness.

"Umm, yes. I can feel it."

He opened his eyes and watched her nod. "Tell me what you feel."

She raised her head up higher to the light, her eyes scrunching up a bit more tightly. "It's warm, and bright on my lids. My skin feels lighter somehow."

"Keep your eyes closed."

Drew walked away from her and flipped a switch, closing the motorized blinds. The room grew darker and the warmth from the sun faded.

"Drew?"

He stepped up behind her and whispered in her ear. "Don't open your eyes yet. Just tell me what you feel now."

"Cooler. Darker."

"Is it better?" He asked softly.

"Better than what?"

"Than the sun and light you felt?"

She opened her eyes and spun around, coming face to face with him. Instead of stepping back, he leaned down and grasped her arms gently. "To me, you are the sun and the light. You brought warmth into my life again. And I think I did that for you as well. I know it feels safer to stay inside where you can hide in the shadows, but is that really living?"

His hands moved up her arms to grasp her more tightly around the shoulders, his tone pleading. "Let me show you the light again. Even if it's one ray at a time, don't you want to feel that warmth again? Don't you want to share that with your daughter?"

She bit her lower lip and responded shakily, "I'm scared. So scared, Drew. I can't go through that kind of pain again and I think-" She shook her head as her eyes locked on his. "I think being with you could break me."

"I'm scared too. But I'm more scared of not seeing you again. We can go as slow as you want." He leaned in then and, ever so tenderly, kissed her.

As his lips met hers, she sighed in defeat and returned his kiss. Gently at first, but then she clutched his neck with one hand while the other bunched the fabric of his T-shirt on his chest.

His hands left her arms and wound through her hair as he held her fast. She parted her lips and darted her tongue out, swiping it against his mouth, which he gladly opened to her. As their kiss intensified, her body melted into his.

Drew broke the kiss but continued holding her in his arms. Looking down into her eyes, he chuckled. "See? Aren't you already feeling warmer?"

He pressed several more small kisses to her face. "Tell me you'll at least try. Let me see you again."

She nodded once, brought her eyes up to his, and breathed out her response. "Okay."

CHAPTER
Four

"OKAY?" Drew couldn't believe his ears. She was agreeing to see him again.

She nodded shyly. "Yes. I'm terrified, but I'm even more scared of not feeling the way I do again when I'm with you. I'm a mess, Drew."

Instead of speaking, Drew pulled her back to his lips to kiss her with more passion than she could ever remember feeling before. His hands stayed tangled in her hair, but he gently turned her and, using his body, backed her up until she hit the shades covering the window. His body was now flush with hers, his hard length pressing into her.

Her hands wrapped around his neck and shoulders while she hooked one leg around his waist, as if she were trying to fuse herself to him. He released her hair, sliding his hands under her bottom, lifting her, her other leg finding its way around his waist as she locked herself around him.

He rocked his hips into her core. She moaned as her

head fell back against the window. He took advantage of her exposed neck and trailed his lips down to her bare shoulder, his hand pulling her shirt down further, his lips skimming the tops of her breasts.

Her hardened nipples peaked beneath her shirt, and he wanted nothing more than to take one into his mouth and suck. Grabbing her firmly around the waist, he spun and strode to the living room. "Hold on, Hannah."

Her grip around his neck tightened before he lowered himself into a seated position on the couch, her legs straddling his hips. They looked at each other for only a moment before their lips crashed together once again. Their tongues danced in a swirl of insatiable desire.

He grabbed a handful of her hair, pulling her head back to expose her neck. Hannah gasped in surprise, but then moaned in approval when he ran his tongue up her neck to her lips again, nipping the bottom one gently.

Keeping her hair fisted in one hand, he used the other to pull her shirt down below her breast. *No bra?* "Well, aren't you a wicked little minx."

He grinned wantonly, not waiting for her to respond as he crushed his mouth down on her nipple. He ran his tongue around and then over the hardened tip before covering it completely and sucking hard. Hannah rose up on her knees, grasping his head to pull his mouth tighter to her while sliding her core up and down against his hard cock.

He let go of her nipple with a small pop. "Fuck," hissed from his lips. "Hannah, you're killing me here."

"But what a way to go, right?" she purred, continuing to rub up and down his shaft as she yanked her shirt over her head. Drew's eyes lit up in approval as she dropped her hands to the hem of his shirt and peeled it off him.

"I want to feel you against me," she urged, leaning forward, wrapping her arms around him.

He buried his face in Hannah's hair and inhaled deeply, savoring the floral smell he had remembered so well.

"God, I missed this smell. Your touch." He stroked her hair and then brought his lips to hers in a scorching kiss.

He rose up off the couch just enough to turn and lower Hannah back down, never breaking contact with her skin. He thrust his hips hard into her center, his cock throbbing through the material of his jeans.

He wanted to be inside her, and now. He pulled back, eliciting a moan of protest from Hannah, but when he began to unbutton her jeans, she reached up to do the same to his.

BZZZZZZZ. BZZZZZZZ. Something vibrated under Hannah, and they both froze.

"My phone," Hannah replied, gently pushing Drew back with one hand so she could reach into her back pocket to retrieve it.

Drew sat back on his heels as she looked at her screen, her brows furrowing in question before she answered. "Hey, Tammy. What's up?"

The expression on her face went from mild curiosity to alarm, her head bobbing up and down as she spoke. "Okay." Silence for a moment. "But is she okay?" Her voice was edged with panic now. "All right, all right. I'm downtown so I'll get there as fast as I can."

Hannah hung up, then reached for her shirt, pulling it quickly over her head before standing up. "I have to go.

Grace fell off the monkey bars at the playground and cut her head open. Can you have George call me a cab?"

Drew stood up, pulling his shirt back on again as well. "Don't be silly. I'll drive you. Let me just get some shoes on."

Hannah was pulling her jacket on now and pacing at the same time. "Okay, but hurry. She's hurt." A small cry of worry escaped before she clamped her hand over her mouth.

He pulled her into his arms. "Hannah, I'm sure it's going to be okay. Kids fall all the time."

She pushed out of his arms in frustration. "How would you know? Do you have kids? Were you the one sitting here about to fuck someone when your child was bleeding on a playground somewhere?"

"See?" She pointed a shaking finger back and forth between them, her eyes wild with anger. "This! This is why I can't do this again."

He blew out a slow breath, not wanting to incite her further. She was just scared for her daughter.

He walked toward the hallway and opened a closet. He pulled out a pair of sneakers, quickly slid them onto his bare feet and then pulled on a soft-looking leather jacket. He turned to her then and took one of her hands. "Come on. Let's get to her then."

A FEW SHORT MINUTES LATER, they were pulling out of the hotel parking garage in his Jag. Hannah had sent another text asking Tammy for an update but hadn't received a reply. "Which hospital?"

"The NYU ER on First Avenue. Do you know where it is?"

"I do." He shifted the car into a higher gear and weaved in and out of traffic. He was doing everything he could to get her there as fast as he could, and she was being ungrateful.

She placed her hand over his on the gearshift and squeezed. He glanced at her, startled.

"I'm sorry, Drew. I shouldn't have snapped at you like that." She gave him her most apologetic smile.

In turn he tangled her fingers into his and smiled. "I know you're scared. You weren't doing anything wrong though."

She looked down at the hand in her lap, fidgeting with her phone. "It's just that after all the time I wasn't there for her, I make sure I always am now. Then the one time I'm not, something happens."

"It's not your fault, Hannah. It's not." He frowned. "Kids play hard and accidents happen. They also bounce back quickly too. This could have happened even if you were right there in the park with her."

"But I wasn't." She shook her head as she repeated herself. "I wasn't."

Drew squeezed her fingers, then let go and pointed out the window. "Look, almost there. It's one block up. I'll drop you off in front and go park the car. Go find Grace and I'll meet you inside."

She reared back. "You're coming in?"

He tilted his head as he pulled up in front of the hospital.

"Yes, of course. I want to make sure your daughter's okay. That you're both okay."

She blew out a deep breath, trying to expel some of the nerves coursing through her veins. "I'd rather you didn't. I'll call you later. Tammy can give me a ride home."

Drew shook his head, then nodded, his lips pursed. "Okay, fine."

"Thank you for the ride and for understanding. I'll call you." She opened the door, stepped out of the car and hurried through the entrance.

After a brief exchange of information with an attendant at the front desk and the signing of what seemed like a hundred insurance forms, she was finally brought down to Grace's exam room.

Instead of the scared, crying child she had been expecting, Grace was sitting up in bed, a bandage on her forehead, a grape Popsicle clutched between her fingers, a purple smile lighting up her face.

Tammy was sitting on the bed with Grace, her back to the door. From the doorway, she watched her daughter for a moment to make sure she really was okay, then walked in.

"Hey, peanut. You doing okay?"

Grace held her arms out as soon as she saw her mom. "Momma!"

Hannah sat on the bed and pulled her daughter into a tight embrace, kissing the top of her little fluffy head at least six times before letting go. "Hi, baby. How's your boo-boo?"

She stroked Grace's hair away from her face and touched her lightly on the skin below the bandage. She turned to Tammy then. "What happened? What did the doctor say?"

"This doctor says she's going to be just fine," said a male voice behind her. A middle-aged man with a shiny bald head came into the room and extended his hand. "Mom, I presume? I'm Dr. Brothers."

Hannah took his hand and shook it. "Yes, hello. I'm Hannah, Grace's mom. She's going to be okay?"

The doctor nodded and smiled warmly. "Yep, this little lady is going to be just fine."

He walked over to Grace then and tickled the bottom of her foot, making her squirm and drip some of her Popsicle onto the bedding.

He turned back to Hannah. "We put a couple butterfly strips on her forehead, but the cut wasn't so deep that it required stitches. No loss of consciousness and very little swelling, so I don't see any reason to worry about a concussion. She's got a good hard head on her."

Hannah smiled in relief. "Oh, thank god. And thank you, Doctor."

"Just doing my job. The nurse will come by in a few minutes to sign you out so you can take her home."

"Thank you again." Hannah shook his hand again before he left the room.

Tammy got up off the bed and pulled Hannah into a hug. "I'm so, so sorry. I was standing right there, helping Emma climb up the jungle gym to sit with Grace. She reached down to grab Emma's hand and lost her grip and fell right through the middle of the bars. She smacked her head on one of the bars going down."

Hannah pulled away from her sister and patted her on the arm in reassurance. "It's okay. It was an accident. And she's fine. I trust you with Grace's life."

Tammy's eyes moved to the doorway and grew a bit wider. Hannah twisted around to see what had her sister's attention. Drew was standing in the doorway, a pink, stuffed teddy bear in hand.

"What are you doing here?" she hissed, too low for Grace to hear.

Instead of answering, Drew nodded at Tammy and extended his free hand to her.

"Andrew Sapphire. Nice to meet you."

Tammy looked back and forth between them before finally placing her hand in his, practically swooning as she responded. "Hi. Tammy, Hannah's big sister."

"Yes, she's told me about you. Very nice to meet you." He gently extracted his hand from hers.

Tammy turned to Hannah, keeping her back to Drew. Her eyes were wide in astonishment as she mouthed silently, "Oh my god!" Then in a normal voice, "Okay, well, now that you're here, Hannah, I'm going to go ahead and head home. I had one of the other moms take Emma for me so I still need to go and pick her up."

She gave Grace a big kiss and hug and did the same to Hannah before walking past Drew. "Nice to meet you, Andrew."

Drew walked further into the room as she passed. "You as well."

He squeezed Hannah's arm and tilted his head toward the bed in question before moving any closer. "Is she okay?"

"She is. Just a bad cut. No concussion."

He raised the stuffed animal in his hands slightly. "Is it okay if I give her the bear?"

She stared down at the bear in his hand a moment

before nodding, silently wondering how this was going to go. She had never introduced any other men to Grace. Ever.

Drew took a couple steps closer to the bed and then knelt down so he was face to face with Hannah's daughter. "You must be Grace."

Grace bit her lower lip and lowered her eyes, nodding up and down.

"My name is Drew. I'm a friend of your mom's. I heard you had quite a fall and hurt your head."

Again, Grace just nodded up and down. Drew brought the teddy bear up and placed it on the bed next to Grace. "Well, the nice lady at the gift store said this teddy bear is so soft and cuddly it's guaranteed to make you feel better."

Grace looked up at Hannah in silent question. Hannah nodded. "It's okay, Gracie. You can take the bear."

Grace finally released her lower lip from her teeth and tentatively reached for the teddy bear Drew offered. She pulled it into her arms, a smile breaking wide across her little face. "Thank you, Mr. Drew."

He smiled warmly at her, patted her hand and then stood up. "You are so very welcome. I hope you feel better really soon."

"What's her name?"

Drew tilted his head, surprise on his face. "Whose name, honey?"

"The bear. She has to have a name."

Drew scratched the scruff on his chin. She couldn't help enjoying the obviously new territory he had ventured into. "Oh. Hmm, I guess we need to give her one, eh? Any ideas?"

Her daughter stroked the bear's soft fur and then smiled brightly. "How about Pinky?"

"I think Pinky is perfect."

Right at that moment, the nurse came in carrying the discharge paperwork. "All right, is this little one all ready to go home?"

She and Grace responded in unison, "Yes!"

After all the paperwork was signed and Grace was back in her shoes and jacket, Hannah lifted Grace off the bed and into her arms. Grace clutched the teddy bear fiercely.

"Do you want me to take her for you?" Drew asked.

Hannah smiled appreciatively at him. "No, I've got her. Would you mind walking me out though? I could use some help getting a cab."

"A cab?" His brow furrowed. "Nonsense. Let me take you home. I'll bring the car around."

"But your car is a two-seater." Hannah screeched to a halt. " And oh jeez, I don't have a car seat either."

"Hannah, it will be fine. We're only a few blocks from your place. We'll buckle you both in nice and tight, and I promise I'll drive extra carefully."

She blew her breath out in surrender, her arms already getting tired from holding her daughter. "Okay. But extra careful!"

He reached out and gently ruffled Grace's hair as she started walking again. "I promise. Precious cargo on board. I'll go get the car and meet you at the main entrance, okay?"

She nodded in agreement. "Okay, meet you there."

Ten minutes later, she and Grace were all buckled up in Drew's car as he pulled away from the curb.

"You remember where the flower shop is? Grace and I live upstairs."

"Yes, I know."

Hannah whipped her head around. "You know?"

Drew shifted the car to a lower gear and cleared his throat. "Yes, I know."

Hannah stared at him for a good long time before responding. "I would ask how, but at this point, I really don't think I want to know."

At a red light, Drew turned and looked her directly in the eyes. "It's your fault, you know."

"What's my fault?" Hannah pulled Grace a little tighter into her lap, making sure she was still secure. She was busy having a very serious conversation with Pinky about the other animals she would meet when she got home.

"The reason I couldn't stay away from you."

"What reason was that?"

He closed his eyes for the briefest of moments and inhaled deeply. He opened them again and accelerated, the light green. "Your smile, the way your hair smells, the way you have to turn every conversation into a challenge, the way you respond to me, the way you taste."

His voice trailed off and a small electric shock ran through her body at his admission. She looked at him, her eyes hooded with a new surge of desire. "Oh. I'm sorry then."

This time a wicked smile curved his lips. "I'm not. Not even a little bit."

Her cheeks went crimson as blood rushed through and heated her body. When he darted a glance her way, she widened her eyes and tipped her head at Grace, silently pleading with him to end this conversation.

He raised his hand, brushing it lightly over her cheek

and then turned his eyes back to the road. "Here we are, ladies."

Hannah turned forward and realized he had pulled into the alley of the shop.

"Would you like some help in with Grace?"

She shook her head and looked down at her daughter. "No, thank you. I think it's been enough for one day."

His lips pursed, he nodded curtly. "Let me at least help you out of the car."

Before she could answer, he had swung his door open and stepped out. In another moment, her door was open and he was bending down, lifting Grace up and placing her gently on the sidewalk. Hannah stepped quickly out and took hold of Grace's hand.

"Thank you for the ride. And for getting us home."

His hand dragged roughly over the light stubble on his chin, his eyes looking toward the sky before he responded. "Of course, no problem. Can I call you later?"

She looked down at Grace, who was looking up at her curiously, the teddy bear hugged to her chest in her other arm. Grace had to be her priority right now.

"I'll try and call you later tonight after I put Grace down." She started walking toward the door, pulling her daughter gently along. "Thank you again."

"Hannah, wait."

She stopped and turned as Drew closed the gap between them. He reached into the back pocket of his jeans and pulled his wallet out.

"What?" She wasn't sure what he was doing.

He pulled out a white business card and handed it to her. "This has my cell number on it. I'm pretty sure you only have my office number. Or you could have called the hotel, I guess."

"Oh." She took the white card and, without looking at it, slipped it into the front pocket of her jeans. "Okay. Thanks again."

She turned and walked to the door before he could say anything else. His footsteps retreated in the other direction as she pulled her keys out of her jacket pocket and breathed a sigh of relief.

CHAPTER

Five

DREW TWIRLED the stem of the martini glass in his fingers as he debated whether or not to have another. He was sitting in one of the leather upholstered stools in the bar of his hotel, so it wasn't like he had to get into a car and drive. It was ten p.m. Monday evening and Hannah still hadn't called him.

"Another Hendrick's martini, Mr. Sapphire?" the bartender asked, taking the empty glass from his hands.

"Please."

Fuck it. One more isn't going to hurt at this point. The pretty bartender filled a new martini glass with ice to chill it and then poured a healthy amount of gin and vermouth into the shaker.

She caught him watching her as she shook the container. She smiled shyly, her cheeks blushing a light pink, before she looked away to finish preparing his drink.

She placed a new napkin in front of him before setting the full glass down on it. "Sir."

He raised the glass in a toast before bringing it to his lips for a sip. "Thank you."

The bartender's eyes followed the glass to his mouth and stayed there until he lowered it back to the bar. She raised her gaze again to meet his stare.

"Can I get you anything else, sir?" Her voice was husky, lower than before.

Her question implied more than a polite inquiry for a dish of nuts. She would happily accompany him to his room and serve him anything he wanted if he asked.

Three months ago he probably would have done just that. She was attractive and attentive, and best of all, the way she called him "sir" suggested she would be more than submissive.

"No, thank you." He smiled kindly to take the sting out of his rejection.

The only person he wanted now was Hannah. No one else was even remotely tempting. But after two days with no phone call, it looked like she didn't fucking want him.

The bartender nodded. "Just let me know if you change your mind." She turned and walked to the other end of the bar to tend to another patron.

Drew raised the glass to his mouth. Just as he was about to take a large swig, someone slapped him on the shoulder and sat down beside him, sloshing some of the gin out of the glass and onto the bar. He spun to give the person a piece of his mind, then stopped abruptly.

"Son." His father made himself comfortable on the stool next to him, then raised his hand to get the bartender's attention.

"Dad." Drew brought the glass up again and this time managed to take that large swig.

"Give me three fingers of the Talisker, straight up please."

The bartender poured the scotch and had it sitting in front of his father on a fresh napkin in less than thirty seconds. She was good. He picked it up and sniffed the warm, brown liquid before taking a drink.

"What are you doing here this late?" Drew asked as his father sipped his scotch.

"Business." There was an edge to his voice.

His father often worked late into the night at their various hotels to avoid going home before his mother went to bed.

He knew his father loved his mother. And she loved him. The loyalty Gavin and Caroline Sapphire still showed each other more than proved that to him. But after his sister had died, something between them had died. His mother could never seem to pull herself completely out of her grief, and his father escaped in his work instead of trying to help her.

"Will we see you at the house for dinner on Thursday? I believe Benjamin may actually join us."

"I'm not sure yet. I may have other plans."

His father's face pinched in anger. "Your mother will be disappointed." His father sighed. They tried to have a family dinner once a week, one of the only times his mother seemed fairly happy.

"I should know better by tomorrow. But if I can't make it, I'll call and set up a lunch date with her."

His father nodded. "I'm sure she'd like that."

He brought the glass up, drained the rest of his scotch

and placed it back on the bar before standing up. "Well, Carl's waiting with the car. I saw you sitting here and just wanted to say hello."

Drew raised himself up off the barstool and faced his father. "Send Mom my love."

"Jesus, what happened to your eye!" His father reached out and touched the left side of Drew's face. That side must have been hidden when he'd been sitting at the bar. Drew pulled away from his father's hand and grinned.

"Benny took me boxing. I lost."

"Is this why you cancelled our meeting the other day?"

Drew nodded in response.

"God damn Benjamin." His father laughed and shook his head in dismay. "He always loved to give you a beating."

Drew shrugged. "Nah, it's all good. It wasn't Benny. I was in the ring with some other guy and he was just better."

His father touched the side of Drew's face again, gently this time, and then wrapped one arm around his shoulder, clapping him on the back before turning away. "Good night, Andrew."

"Good night, Dad."

His father walked out of the low-lit lounge into the lobby, toward the front doors. Drew picked up his martini glass, finished what was left and motioned to the bartender that he was leaving.

After signing the slip and leaving a fifty-dollar tip, he headed up to his suite. It was a good thing he didn't have Hannah's cell number or he'd be drunk dialing it right now.

Tomorrow. Tomorrow he was going to talk to her. Even if he had to go to her again.

HANNAH'S HEART leapt into her throat as she pulled into the alley. Drew stood in front of the shop doorway. She had a feeling he would show up sooner or later. She'd just hoped it would be later, like at least a week later, so she had more time to build up some resistance to his charm. She shut the engine off, steeling herself to defend her decision not to see him.

She stepped out. It was freezing. How could he stand there in just a sweatshirt and sweats as the wind whipped around him?

He pushed his hood off his head as she approached. "You didn't call." His voice was low but not demanding.

She unlocked the metal casing and then the interior door. "Come in, Drew. It's cold."

The bell above the door tinkled, announcing their arrival as they stepped inside the warmth of the shop. She walked to the back and into the work room, taking her jacket off as she went.

She was trying to appear confident, but if she started speaking, her voice was going to wobble. She just wanted another minute to gather her thoughts. She hung up her coat, then pulled a stool out from under the table and sat on it.

Drew pulled one out to her right and sat on it, facing her. "You didn't call."

She stood up abruptly.

"Do you want some water? You ran here, I assume?" Her eyes scanned up and down his athletically dressed form.

"I don't want any water. Just tell me why you haven't called."

She lowered herself back onto the stool and began fidgeting with some ribbon lying on the table.

"You said you would try." He reached across the table and pulled the ribbon from her fingers.

She finally looked up at him. "That was before."

"Before?" His forehead creased.

"Before Grace got hurt—while I was about to have sex with you. I made a promise to myself that my daughter would always come first. And the first time I'm with you, the first time, something happens to her. It's a sign."

"It's a sign?" He didn't bother to hide his disbelief.

"Call it whatever you want." She waved her hand in the air. "It was a reminder to me about what my priorities need to be."

His hand slammed on the table, making her jump. "Jesus fucking Christ, Hannah! Really? Do you think for one second I would ask you to ever turn your back on your child or your responsibilities to her? Are you really going to try and hide behind that excuse?"

"Don't you yell at me! You have no idea what it's like to have to raise a child on your own. Especially after the things I did to her. I won't desert her like that again!" She lowered the finger she had been pointing at him, hiding her shaking hand. Before it hit the table, he grabbed it between his two palms.

"You didn't do anything wrong. There's a big difference between leaving your child in someone else's care when an accident happens and deserting her. I can see what a good mother you are. You don't have to keep punishing yourself to prove that."

His voice was as gentle as his caresses. "I'm not asking you to turn your back on Grace, nor would I ever. I'm just asking you to make a little room for me. To see if maybe we have a chance. And 'we' means all three of us, not just you and me. I understand that."

"I don't think you understand how hard this really is for me. There's never been another man in my daughter's life because I've never let another man in my life. This is huge for me. And I asked you not to come into the hospital, and then you did, further complicating things and not respecting what I asked. That was about my daughter. Not about me."

Deflated, Drew lowered his head. "I know. I'm sorry. I realized that after the fact. I acted on impulse and that was stupid of me. I should have known better. I only wanted to make sure you were okay. That your daughter was okay."

"I appreciate that, but I've been taking care of myself and her for a very long time now. If I needed your help, I would have asked."

He met her eyes with an apologetic frown. "It won't happen again."

"I wish I could believe that." She shook her head in doubt, continuing. "You like control. Giving that up to someone isn't in your nature."

"In the bedroom." He glowered back. "Not over your life. Not over your child. I know where the line is. I won't cross it again. Give me another chance. Give us another chance.

Please." He brought her hand to his lips and kissed the fingertips gently. "Please."

She liked him. She wanted him. She wasn't going to lie to herself about that. And when he touched her like this, even just small kisses to her fingers, she remembered what it felt like to be held by him. But how did she balance that and what was right for her daughter?

As if he could read her mind, he spoke again. "What if the three of us have dinner so I can meet your daughter properly?"

Her heart finally gave in, but it needed to find some common ground with her head. "Okay, dinner. But it has to be at my place. I think it will be easier for Grace if she's in her own environment."

A smile broke across his face. "Your place is perfect. Is tonight too soon?"

"Now who's anxious?" She laughed despite herself. "Tonight is actually good. Besides, I'm making your favorite."

He cocked his head. "My favorite?"

She grinned. "Yep. Grilled cheese and tomato soup."

Drew broke into a wide grin as well, obviously remembering with fondness the very same lunch they had shared together after their first time in the playroom. "That sounds perfect."

"Okay, come by around six."

CHAPTER
Six

AT PRECISELY SIX P.M., Drew rang the doorbell and waited. Within moments, the door swung open and Hannah stood before him. She was dressed in a pair of black leggings and an oversized long-sleeved T-shirt, her hair up in a ponytail. She looked simple, but beautiful as always.

"Hi! Come in! It's so cold out there." She shut the door behind him.

He bent and kissed her on the cheek. "Hi. Is it okay that I'm nervous?"

"Yep, 'cause I am too." She grinned up at him and then looked down at his hands. "Whatcha got there?"

"Oh! It's cupcakes. Since getting you flowers is out, I got a dozen of these instead. In all flavors, of course, because I didn't know what you girls liked."

He laughed when she jumped up and down and clapped her hands like a little kid. *Thank god I took Felicia's suggestion.*

"Oh this is perfect! We love cupcakes!" She grabbed the

box from his hands and started up the steps. "Come on, let me introduce you to Grace again and show you our home."

At the top of the stairs, she showed him where he could hang his coat. As he took it off and hung it on one of the proffered hooks, he looked around and absorbed the essence of her home. Grace came running in, stopping in her tracks when she saw Drew.

"Honey, do you remember Mommy's friend Drew from the hospital?"

Grace kept her eyes glued on him as she inched her way to her mother's side, wrapping her little arms around her leg once she was there.

Drew bent down to eye level and smiled warmly. "Hey, Gracie. How's your head doing?" He pointed to the small teal Band-Aid on her forehead.

She probed her forehead with little fingers until she found it, then shrugged her shoulders. "It's okay now. Mommy says I only have to wear the Band-Aid one more day."

She let go of her mother's leg then and walked closer to him. "Your face has prickles!" she said, brushing her hands back and forth against Drew's cheeks.

He couldn't help but grin broadly at her assessment of his unshaven face. "Yep, I guess it does."

Hannah stared down at them.

"What?" His brows raising.

"Nothing." She lifted a hand to her face in an attempt to hide her turned up mouth, turning quickly. "Come on, I'll show you the rest of the place."

He followed her and Grace down a short hallway that opened up into a large eat-in kitchen. She put the cupcakes down and then swung around in a little circle with open arms. "Welcome to my kitchen."

Grace twirled, mimicking her mother and echoing, "Welcome to my kitchen." She giggled freely as she continued to spin.

"All right, little monkey, not too much." Hannah placed her hands gently on Grace's shoulders to stop her from spinning. "We don't want you to knock your head again."

"Okay, Mommy." She grinned widely. "Can I go watch TV?"

"Sure, sweetie, go ahead."

They both watched as Grace danced her way out of the room through an open arch into the living room. Drew walked slowly around the kitchen, taking in everything.

Squiggly, colorfully lined drawings hung on the fridge, a box of crayons and a Cinderella coloring book lay open on the table, a pink cup sat in the strainer, and a pile of unopened mail lay next to it.

"Sorry, it's a bit messy. I don't usually get time to pick things up until after I put Gracie to bed." She shook her head. "If you had asked me this morning, I definitely wouldn't have said you'd be standing in my kitchen by nightfall."

He took another step closer, laying his hand against her cheek. "Me either, but I'm really glad I'm here."

There was a moment's pause between them before she pulled away. "Let me show you the rest."

She brought him through the arched doorway into the large living space. Grace was lying on a purple velvet bean-bag, watching cartoons in front of the TV. A large, dark gray, wrap-around couch took up part of the space. End tables, lamps and several large bookcases took up the rest. The bookcases were filled with picture frames and books. So many pictures of Grace from an infant till now decorated the shelves.

One picture was of Hannah. She was wearing a beautiful white sundress and had flowers in her hair. She stood in profile, holding the hand of another man, looking directly at him, sunlight spilling around them. His breath caught, surprise at seeing her looking at another man with so much love and devotion.

He started at her hand on his arm. "That was my wedding day. That's Jackson."

"It's a beautiful picture." He didn't want to be jealous of a ghost, but he was. And he was a total prick for feeling that way. The guy had died for his country.

"Come on, I'll show you upstairs."

He followed Hannah out a doorway off the living room and up another set of stairs. At the top were Grace's bedroom, a full-sized bath and another smaller bedroom.

"Is this your room?" It was pretty sparse. Just a full-sized bed covered in a simple quilt and a bureau with a few items on top.

"No, this is for Danny when he crashes here. My room is downstairs. Come, I'll show you."

She turned and retraced their steps back through the kitchen and out across the hall. She stopped at a set of French doors, turning the handle of one and pushing it open.

"I think this was actually supposed to be the dining room, but I made it into a bedroom so Danny could have the extra one upstairs."

He walked in and was immediately assaulted with her scent: roses and lilies and tulips and jasmine. The room was quintessentially female.

A soft white comforter covered a large bed, and yellow and pink throw pillows filled one side of the room. A long dresser up against another wall was covered with loose jewelry, pictures of Grace, perfume bottles and makeup. A white, fluffy rug lay in the center of the hardwood floor, and a soft gray chair sat in a corner, discarded clothing strewn across it.

"Sorry, it's a mess. Like I said, I wasn't expecting company." She paced in place, her cheeks turning a light pink.

"I love it. I love your home. It's lived in, filled with love." He gathered her into his arms and rested his forehead against hers. "You've made a wonderful life here for you both. Thank you for sharing this with me."

"You're welcome."

He ran his hand up her back and her neck before grasping her face gently, bringing his lips to hers. Their breath became one as their lips fused together, their bodies pulling closer to one another. He walked her backward until she hit the door, making it bang against the bedroom wall, but he didn't stop until his body was caging hers.

He tore his lips from hers and brought them to her ear, tracing his tongue around its edges, then blowing lightly. She shivered against him. "I can't get enough of you, Hannah. Being this close to you is killing me."

She turned her mouth to his and caught his lips in a biting kiss before pushing him away. She was breathing hard and her face was pink. "I know but we have to stop."

She tilted her head toward the living room. "Grace."

Drew nodded in understanding, trying to still some of the desire racing through him. "Maybe I should go?"

"No." Hannah shook her head. "No, stay. Please. I'm going to make dinner for us and then put Gracie to bed. We can spend some time together then. Okay?"

Drew bobbed his head once and was surprised to feel relief that she wanted him to stay.

HANNAH COULD HEAR Drew washing up the last of the dishes as she pulled Grace out of the tub and wrapped a towel around her little pink body.

She had a gorgeous, billionaire dominant down in her kitchen, cleaning up her soup and sandwich dishes. *How in the fuck did I get here?*

She dried Grace off and quickly slathered her in baby lotion before pulling her favorite Disney princess nightgown over her damp curls. "Okay, monkey, hop up in bed and I'll read you a story."

Grace climbed up in the bed and under her covers. "Mommy, is Mr. Drew staying at our house tonight?"

Hannah froze. *Shit. How do I answer this question?* "Why would you think that, sweetie?"

"Cause when Uncle Danny stays for dinner, he sleeps over."

She smiled down at Grace. "Well, I think Mr. Drew will be going home in a little while. He just wanted to have dinner with us. Okay?"

Grace yawned and smiled. "Okay. Can we read

Cinderella tonight?"

"Again? Aren't you tired of that one?"

"Never!" Grace clapped her hands.

Hannah chuckled and sat down on the bed, cuddling up next to Grace. "Alrighty then, Cinderella it is. Once upon a time . . ."

Ten minutes later, Grace's eyes were closed and she was snoring softly. Hannah tucked her in, turned off her light, shut the door behind her and made her way downstairs.

She found Drew sitting on the couch in the living room, a glass of water in hand and another waiting for her on the coffee table.

She reached for it as she sat next to him. "I'm surprised you're still here."

He tilted his head. "Really, why?"

She laughed dryly. "It's a lot of simple domestic bliss I've thrown at you tonight. Not exactly what our relationship was founded on."

He shook his head and blew out a slow breath. "I'm not going to lie. It's a little strange. But being here with you, seeing the real you is exactly what I asked for."

"And you're not ready to run for the hills yet? I mean, I have a child. You see how much of my life is about her. Do you understand that now?"

He brushed her cheek before taking her hand in his. "I have loved seeing this side of you. If this is going to work between us, I need to get to know all of you, and Grace is a part of that. From what I've seen so far, you seem like an incredible mother. But you are so much more than just a mother, Hannah. I've seen the other side of that. The side of you that comes alive under my touch. The side of you that is hungry to be loved and to be seen as a woman too. I'm hoping you'll allow yourself to be both."

She took a drink of her water, trying to quench some of the fire his words sparked. "I'm trying, Drew. I just don't want to get lost in this. And you are so much more."

"So much more?" His head cocked in confusion.

"More man, more money, more beautiful, more dominant, more everything than I've ever experienced before. It's a lot."

He put his glass down on the table and slid closer to her. "It doesn't have to be. It can be a little or a lot, really slow or really fast. I don't care. I just want to be with you. Whatever makes you feel good."

Her head fell back as she laughed. "That's just it. Everything you do makes me feel good. Too good. I don't want to get lost in that and forget everything else."

"Would that be a bad thing?"

She looked down at the water in her glass and then up at him. "It could be. That's what I'm afraid of. I've done it before. Of course, under different circumstances. But what if things really work out between us and I give you everything I have, and then you decide you don't want it anymore? That loss I felt when Jackson died, I can't go through that again. I can't. And I can't risk breaking Grace's heart either."

"This isn't something I thought I'd ever want again. And I definitely didn't factor a child into things. Being a member at the club gave me what I needed and what I thought I wanted. But then you walked up on that stage, and everything changed for me."

She frowned in realization. "I guess it changed everything for me too."

"I suppose we both got a little more than we bargained for, huh?"

She nodded, chuckling. "Speaking of unexpected. You were really good with Grace tonight. Do you have nieces or nephews?"

He shook his head. "No. It's just Benny and me and he hasn't ever married. And I don't think he has any kids that I know of."

He laughed at his own joke before continuing. "But you know about my sister Lizzie. She was five years younger than me. I loved being her big brother. Gracie reminds me of her in a funny way. Not in looks, but in the sweet, innocent way she does things. I remember being twelve or thirteen and how Lizzie would follow me around everywhere."

Drew was silent for a minute, lost in thought.

She went in an entirely different direction with her next question. "What about the other stuff?" Her cheeks turned pink. *Smooth, Hannah.*

"Other stuff? Which stuff?"

"Well, we met at an auction where you bought me for your sexual pleasure. You are a Dominant. What about that part of things?"

Drew ran a hand through his hair, then scratched at the stubble on his chin. Someone was nervous.

"Well, I guess that depends on you. You know what I like. But having you is more important to me than anything else right now."

"Right now?"

He looked directly at her, his tone more serious than she'd heard it all night. "Yes, right now. I'm only thinking about right now. I'm not sure about tomorrow, next week or even next month. But right now, I know what I want is you."

"Are you still going to the club?" she whispered, afraid of what his answer might be.

He flinched. "Is that what you're worried about?"

She shrugged. "Well, you're a man. You have needs. And it's been months since you and I . . ."

He leaned forward, his eyes growing darker, his voice low as he responded, "There's been no one since you."

"Oh" slipped from between her lips. "Did you quit?"

He shrugged. "Why would I go back?"

She stared at him in quiet disbelief as his response sunk in.

He broke the silence for them. "Why did you join the club? You said it was a job to you and you needed the money, but not just anyone can become part of that lifestyle."

"I wanted to buy this shop and I needed the money."

"But I was your first auction. I know how much a shop like this costs and I certainly didn't pay that much for you." A wry grin fell across his lips.

"Well, no, of course not. Things changed after that weekend. I thought I could have sex without the emotion, but I was wrong. So, I quit." She shrugged, trying to end the topic, but Drew persisted.

"What made you think you could do the job? Have sex with strangers. Without any emotion."

"I guess I have to go back to the beginning to explain."

"Okay."

"I've worked at the shop for several years. We're lucky enough to have some very good clients. You remember Mr. and Mrs. Downing from the ball, right?"

His eyebrows rose. "Harold? Yes. I wondered how you knew him."

"Would you believe he comes in every week and personally picks out flowers for his wife?" She smiled warmly. "Anyway, Baton Timide is, well, was one of our biggest clients. We delivered flowers there three times a week. One day I made the delivery and Domme Maria saw me."

Hannah looked at him and quirked a brow. "You know how she is: no holds barred. She walked right up to me and told me I was beautiful and asked if I liked women. I started laughing at first, but then she gave me that look. You know the one, right?"

Drew chuckled. "Oh yes, I know that look."

"She sat me down and explained what occurred at Baton Timide and told me if I ever wanted a job, to come back and see her. I didn't take her seriously of course. Until I needed money."

"Just like that?"

"No, not just like that." She scoffed. "I'm twenty-seven. I like sex. I like it a lot. And I always liked it a bit rougher than most. But before I had sex with you, it had been two years. I was looking forward to just having sex, to turning everything off and just doing what I was told. And it was in a safe environment. I thought it could be the best of both worlds: have some fun and make the money I need."

She raised her eyes, locking them with his. "But you, I wasn't ready for you. You made me feel so good physically, but when you made my heart start beating again-"

She paused and looked up at him apologetically. "I didn't sign up for that. So, I ran. Just like I always do."

"So, you like it? The sex. The domination." His eyes were dark, a feral gleam in their depths.

"Yes. I like it." Her voice was soft and husky, reacting to the change in his demeanor.

He leaned forward then, grasping her lightly around her neck, and brought his lips to hers in a scorching kiss. This, this part with him was always easy. She opened her lips and welcomed his tongue as it swept across hers, teasing and inviting. Their breath became one as the kiss intensified, his heart thudding against the hand that was now up against his chest.

He pushed her away, panting. "More?"

She tilted her head and in less than a second breathed, "More."

"Will Grace wake up?"

"There's a bell above her door. It jingles if she opens it."

"Good." His eyes darkened. "Go to your room and strip naked. Assume your position. Wait for me."

CHAPTER
Seven

DREW CHECKED his watch one more time to make sure he had given Hannah enough time to undress and prepare. He would have normally made her wait longer to build up the anticipation, but they'd already had three long months leading up to this moment.

The French doors to her bedroom were closed and the windows curtained, but low light shone under the edge. He turned the handles and pushed.

He froze and sucked in a breath at the sight before him: Hannah, naked and on her knees. Her head was cast downward, her blonde hair spilling over her face and breasts. Her legs were spread open into a V, and her hands were lying palms up on top of her thighs.

The sound of her quick breathing and her trembling fingertips betrayed her nervousness—or her excitement. He stepped into the room and then turned around to shut the doors behind him.

Before turning back, he pulled his T-shirt over his head,

took a deep breath and tossed it to the floor.He stepped forward until he was directly in front of her. He reached down and stroked her hair.

He could practically feel her purr under his touch. *Fuck, she is going to kill me.*

"Hannah, give me your hand." His voice was hoarse with desire.

Not lifting her head a fraction, she raised her hand up to him. He took it and placed it over his cock, pressing her hand against it. "Feel how fucking hard you make me."

Her fingers spread around his length and began slowly rubbing up and down, over the rough material of his jeans. From under her blonde curtain, a breathy reply reached his ears. "Yes, Sir."

He didn't think it was possible, but his cock grew even harder, twitching in his pants. *Jesus fucking Christ.*

He brushed her hand aside and unbuttoned his jeans, shoving them down and freeing his cock at the same time. Sweet relief.

Until she placed her hand back over his length and continued to rub.

"Look at me," he growled through gritted teeth.

Her gaze met his, her mouth now in perfect alignment with his throbbing cock. Not saying a word and keeping his eyes glued to her face, he fisted his cock and brought it to her lips. A groan escaped him as her pink tongue darted out and licked a drop of pre-cum off the tip of his cock before she opened wide.

Her eyes stayed glued to his as she sucked his cock deep into her mouth, swirling her tongue around it as she went. When she had it in as far as she could take it, she sealed her lips around him and sucked hard. He threw his head back with a loud moan, grasping her hair in both his hands.

She continued to suck as she slid her mouth up and down his cock. Just when he didn't think he could feel any fucking better, she started to hum. The vibration drove straight down his cock to his balls, which drew up tight, more than ready to spring.

He hadn't been with anyone since Hannah, so it wasn't going to take long for him to come. Tightening the grasp on her hair, he pulled himself free from her mouth with a loud pop before he could explode.

"Get on the bed. I want you on your hands and knees. Now," he panted.

She was up and on the bed in less than five seconds, her ass facing him. He gripped his cock as he strode over to her and smacked her ass hard with his free hand. "Shoulders down on the bed. I want your ass in the air."

Hannah let out a small yelp of surprise with the smack but instantly complied and fell onto her shoulders, her ass straight up.

He rubbed his cock with one hand and traced the outline his palm had left on her ass with the other.

"Jesus, Hannah, your ass is so fucking beautiful." He fondled her ass with one hand while the other stroked his cock. His balls started to tighten and he stepped closer, palming her ass firmly as he exploded onto it with a loud groan.

As the last drop fell from his softening cock, he dropped to his knees before he could fall and pushed Hannah's legs farther apart. "Don't move."

"Yes, Sir."

He grinned like the Cheshire Cat at her compliance. He brought his nose between her legs and inhaled deeply, taking in every ounce of her essence, and then ran his tongue up the inside of her thigh.

Wetness had dripped down from her core onto her leg. He lapped at it with two long strokes before moving to her center, dragging his tongue down in one long swipe.

She arched her back lower and pushed herself into him, but instead of punishing her, he drove his tongue into her pussy.

She let out a soft groan, his name on her breath. "Oh, Drew."

"You're so fucking wet." Not waiting for or wanting an answer from her, he continued tonguing her center. He started to get hard and moaned at the thought of finally sliding into her again.

He skimmed his hand up her ass and began running his thumb around her hole, using his cum as a lubricant. Instead of resisting, she mewled, pushing back into his thumb. His cock went rock hard.

He trailed his tongue up her pussy, found her clit and pulled into his mouth, sucking hard as he pushed his thumb into her ass.

"Ohhh, please don't stop . . . "

Drew smiled and continued sucking lightly on her clit, pumping his thumb in and out of her ass. He loved hearing the moans spilling from her mouth but wanted more from her. He released her clit and pulled his thumb away. Hannah whimpered her disapproval.

"What are you doing?" She started to straighten, but

before she could sit up, Drew pushed her back down and slapped her ass hard.

"Did I tell you to get up?"

"No, Sir." Her reply was instant.

"Where do you keep your vibrator?" Drew waited only five seconds before slapping her ass again. "Don't feign silence or pretend you don't have one. Tell me."

"In a shoe box in the bottom drawer of my dresser," came the timid reply from the front of the bed.

"That's better. Don't move." Drew rubbed her red ass affectionately before walking over to the dresser and opening the bottom drawer. He found the shoe box under a scarf and pulled it out, removing the cover. He raised an eyebrow in surprise.

"Three, Hannah?" He chuckled as she bobbed her head in silence. She really was made for him.

He took the smallest one out before placing the box on top of the dresser and walking back to Hannah.

"You really are a naughty little minx, aren't you?"

He kneeled down in front of her head and pulled her face in for a passionate kiss. Their tongues met amid a tangle of mixed groans from them both.

He broke away from her, leaving her breathless, then stood up. He trailed his fingers over the length of her body as he strolled back to her bottom.

He laid the vibrator on the bed next to her knee and caressed her ass before running his fingers up the insides of her thighs to her pussy. She was so wet that his fingers easily slipped inside. He gathered her juices and slid his fingers up to her ass again, mixing it with the remains of his cum, circling around her hole.

"Have you ever used one of these in your ass, Hannah?"
He picked up the small vibrator and ran it around her wet
asshole.

"No, Sir." Her hair swished as she shook her head back
and forth, an excited edge to her voice.

He groaned inwardly at her willingness and his cock
jerked in eagerness. He turned the base of the vibrator, and
it whirred to life with a quiet hum. He touched it to her ass.
He didn't push, just laid it there while he bent down and
sucked her pussy into his mouth. Her whole body arched
into him and she moaned, low and guttural.

He released her pussy. "Are you okay?"

"Yes! Oh my god, yes! Don't stop."

He chuckled lightly. "Always so eager, my little kitten."

He obeyed her command though and ran his tongue
down the length of her pussy before suckling gently on her
clit. He continued to rub the vibrator gently against her
hole until she pressed back into it.

Grinning through his work, he complied with her silent
request, slowly pushing it inside her. He remembered the
bliss at taking her ass for the first time at the club and
although this wasn't his cock, her complete trust in him
filled him with an overwhelming sense of possession.

She arched low, pushing her ass up. She was ready. He
released her clit and stood up behind her. He moved his free
hand down to her pussy and continued to stroke it as he
pushed the vibrator deeper into her ass.

"Ohhh that feels so good. I'm—I'm going to—"

Drew took his hand away from her pussy and smacked
her ass hard three times, pushing the vibrator in all the way

at the same time. He wasn't sure if she was yelling in pain or pleasure, but he wasn't about to stop.

"Not yet, Hannah. Wait." Sweat coated his body and his cock was throbbing as he gripped it to line himself up with her core. In one swift motion, he thrust his cock deep inside her pussy.

Hannah groaned and pushed herself up off her shoulders as he drove himself deeper. Drew yanked both of her arms behind her back, grasping her by the elbows, and began thrusting.

With each thrust of his cock, he hit the vibrator, ramming it deeper inside her. Hannah's chest was driven forward, her head thrown back, hair falling loose over her shoulders, mewling sounds leaving her rounded lips. Drew's cock swelled larger with each thrust, and he gripped Hannah tighter, bringing her head close to his lips.

He whispered in her ear, "Come, Hannah. Come now."

As soon as he said the words, her body tightened and convulsed around his cock, a cry rolling off her lips. He wrapped his arms around her middle, jerking her against him as he thrust one more time, his release bursting into her as he sank his teeth into her shoulder, muffling the groan coming from his own throat. He held her tighter as her body spasmed in response to him, then ran his tongue over the mark he had left on her.

Without disconnecting from her, he reached between them and eased the vibrator from her. Upon its release, her pussy squeezed and pulsed around his cock. She melted into him and whimpered as another small release took her.

He clicked the vibrator off, dropped it on the floor and

then lowered them to the bed. As he spooned her, her heart beat against his chest like a bird taking flight. He pressed small kisses up her neck and across her cheek until he found her lips.

She turned her head and pressed her lips hard against his, thrusting her tongue into his mouth. He darted his tongue out to meet hers and licked her softly, gently, trying to cool her down and bring her back to earth. "What have you done to me? I want more of you. I can't get enough of you."

Her kisses more frantic, she began nipping at his lower lip. She tried to turn and face him, but he gripped her tight. "Let me go!"

"Hannah, shhh." Drew loosened his grip a little, but not entirely, and started stroking one hand lightly up and down her body. "You need to let your mind catch up to your body."

"My body wants more. Who cares what my mind says!" She wriggled in his arms, trying to break free. This time he let her loose. She turned toward him.

"How can I still want you? After what you just did to me?" She looked at him, wide-eyed. "I've never felt like this before."

Drew chuckled as she straddled him, her fingers roaming over his chest.

"Are you laughing at me?" She was starting to look a bit wild now.

He shook his head and then stroked his hands up and down her arms before hauling her down and against him. "No, not at you. Just the situation."

She pulled herself back up into a sitting position, a look

of despair on her face. "What situation? Me wanting more of you?"

"This is actually a pretty common occurrence for a submissive."

"A submissive?"

Drew pushed up to a sitting position, leaving Hannah straddled on his lap, but now looking her in the eye. "Well, yes. You gave yourself over completely to me. It's not unusual after that happens the first time to want to give even more of yourself. Your only longing is to please your Master."

"My 'Master'?" She spat it out like a dirty word.

Drew rolled his eyes in dismissal. "Obviously, I'm not your Master. But you did allow me to be your Dominant. And you gave me complete power over you. Whether or not you realize what you did, you surrendered yourself completely. And your endorphins loved it. Your body loved it. It's what drives most submissives."

"But this wasn't the first time I was submissive to you."

Drew's head fell back as he laughed. "Are you kidding me? When we were at Baton, getting you to submit to me was a challenge. You did only what you had to. Tonight, you gave yourself to me because you wanted to."

Hannah was silent for a moment, staring into Drew's eyes. "You're right."

"I know."

Hannah shook her head in feigned annoyance, a small smile forming on her lips. "I hate when you're right."

"I usually am. Get used to it."

Hannah ran her fingers up Drew's chest and neck before wrapping them around his head and weaving them into his hair. She leaned forward and ran the tip of her tongue along his lower lip before biting down gently on it.

Drew pulled her flush against him, moving his mouth against hers in a kiss. One hand latched onto the back of her neck, while the other one trailed down her back, pulling her closer. She rocked her pelvis into his, releasing her grip on his hair, clutching his biceps for leverage.

Drew broke the kiss and pushed her back a bit, a smile on his face. "I guess you don't know how to take no for an answer?"

Hannah continued rocking her core against his pelvis, a pout forming on her lips. "This is your fault. You've created a monster."

"Ha! My fault? I say it's your fault. If you weren't so fucking perfect, I wouldn't have gone crazy trying to find you again."

She surged forward, crashing her lips to his in a bruising kiss, their mouths melting together once again. When she pulled away, she kept her forehead against his. "I'm so glad you saw me in the hotel that day. I'm so glad you didn't leave me alone."

Drew brought his lips to hers again and kissed her quickly. "Me too, Hannah. But I'm still not having sex with you again."

Her eyebrows shot up as he lifted her off him in one smooth motion before sitting her back down beside him. "At least, not for another half hour." And then he waggled his eyebrows at her as he grinned.

HANNAH ROLLED over and hit the snooze button on her alarm clock on the bedside table without lifting her head off her pillow. *Why am I so goddamn tired?*

And then, as the fogginess of sleep left her head, a smile broke across her face as she remembered her night with Drew. *Shit, Drew!*

She sat straight up in bed and looked next to her but found only rumpled bed covers where he had been the night before. She brought her hand to her mouth, trying to cover the smile that refused to disappear, and giggled. She was like a little school girl with a mad crush. It had been a long time since she had let herself feel this happy. It felt almost criminal.

She stretched her arms over her head, feeling every muscle and every wonderful ache from the amazing sex. Yum. She wanted more of this feeling and stat.

As she swung her feet out of bed, she reached for the folded piece of paper with her name on it next to the alarm clock.

Good morning beautiful,

I'm sorry I stole away like a thief in the night, but I didn't want to confuse Grace. Dinner Thursday? I have a meeting tonight I can't change. Call or text me.

xx Drew

P.S. You're even more gorgeous when you're sleeping.

Hannah pressed the note to her chest, still smiling. Good lord, I need to get a grip on myself!

Her door burst open and Grace ran in, climbed up on her bed and started jumping up and down.

"Mommy, Mommy, Mommy! I'm hungry, Mommy!"

She picked Grace up off the bed. "Good morning, monkey bean. No jumping on the bed."

"But Mommy, monkeys love jumping on beds!"

"Yeah, yeah. Okay, let's go get ready for our day. Come on." Hannah shepherded Grace out of the room and into the kitchen to start their day. One hour later, she had dropped Grace off at Miss Daisy's and was back at the shop, unlocking the door.

She was humming through the store, a silly smile still plastered on her face, when her phone dinged. Digging through her bag, she found her phone and checked the screen.

What do you send a girl to thank her for an amazing night if she owns a flower shop?

A smile broke across Hannah's face. She hit reply and typed in a quick response.

I could think of a few things . . .

It took less than a minute for a new reply to appear.

You really are a naughty little minx. I'm missing you this morning. Can you do dinner Thursday night?

Hannah thought for a moment before responding.

I'll have to see if I can get a sitter. I'll let you know later today. I miss you more.

Another message popped up on her window.

I'll be waiting.

Hannah clutched the phone to her chest. Was she taking things too quickly?

Before she could overthink it, she texted Tammy to ask

if she could take Grace on Thursday night. It wasn't unusual for them to take each other's kid for the night every now and then, but it was rare that they did it during the week. Of course, predictably, her phone rang three minutes later.

"Hello, Tammy."

"Hannah Banana. Why do you need me to take Gracie on a Thursday night? Does it have anything to do with Mr. Tie Me Up and Take Me Home from the hospital?"

Hannah laughed. "Jeez, Tammy. Mr. Tie Me Up? Really?"

"Well, he's the one. Right? From that weekend?"

Hannah sighed, silently wishing she had held back some of the information about the weekend she had spent with Drew.

"Yes, he's the one."

"Oh. My. God. I knew it. Hannah, he's fricking gorgeous. What the hell were you thinking trying to stay away from him?"

"You know what I was trying to do."

"Well, what are you doing now then? Make up your mind girl!"

Hannah groaned, hating that she had to explain herself to her sister. "I know, I know. Believe me, I was trying to keep my life separate from all that, and from him. But he doesn't care. He likes Grace. I talked to him. He made me feel better. Safer about things. So, I don't know."

"Good for you. It's about time you found some happiness again."

"Well, so far he makes me happy. We'll see what happens. I mean, he's a freaking gazillionaire. What do I do with that?"

"Whatever he'll let you!" They both laughed then.

"Seriously, Hannah. This is a good thing. Just go with it. And of course I'll take Gracie on Thursday. I'll pick her up from Miss Daisy's, so just send her with a bag tomorrow, okay?"

"Thanks, Tam. You're the best, really."

CHAPTER
Eight

HIS PHONE DINGED and he picked it up, scanning the screen, a smile stretching across his face.

"Felicia?"

She popped her head in his office doorway a second later. "Yes, sir?"

"Could you make a reservation at Marea for 7:30 tomorrow evening?"

"Of course. For how many?"

"Two please. Tell them it's for me and ask if I can have a booth by the window."

"Consider it done. Anything else?"

"That's it. Thank you." Her head disappeared from his doorway. "Actually, one more thing, Felicia."

This time her whole body framed the doorway. "Yes?"

"Can you ask the maître d' to arrange a round vase of red roses on the table?"

Felicia looked down, trying to hide the smile breaking out across her face. "Of course."

He waved her away. "Okay, I'm done."

She turned and disappeared from view again. Drew shook his head. He was turning into a regular sap. But damn it, he would do anything he could to make Hannah feel special.

He hadn't expected to meet anyone who made him feel this way again. After the betrayal of his first wife, he'd closed his heart and satisfied his physical needs at Baton Timide.

That had been a fine arrangement up until a few months ago. Something had changed for him the moment he'd seen Hannah and then when he'd heard her voice. He hadn't believed in love at first sight, but now, maybe.

Love was something he hadn't thought he'd ever find again, and now that he possibly had, he was going to do everything right. His first wife had felt slighted by the demands of his job. He didn't want to make that mistake again with Hannah.

He needed to make sure she realized she was special to him, especially because Hannah's heart wasn't the only one at stake here. She had a beautiful little girl who was obviously her whole world. Another thing he had never factored into his life.

He shook his head in an attempt to clear his thoughts. As usual, he was trying to force all the pieces into place before they were even laid out. Him and his damn control issues.

He pushed back from his desk, grabbed his jacket out of the closet and left his office. "Felicia, I'll be out for a few hours. I have my cell if you need me."

"Yes, sir."

Drew took the elevator down to the lobby, strolled out

of the hotel exit, then headed toward Fifth Avenue. He was going to make sure Hannah knew how special she was to him. How special she was period. He walked into Saks with a smile on his face.

"HANNAH, THERE'S A DELIVERY FOR YOU," Robin called from the front of the store.

Hannah stood and walked out to the main showroom to find three black boxes wrapped in a red satin ribbon on the counter. "What's this?" She looked at Robin curiously.

Robin shrugged, then grinned and handed Hannah an envelope. "Not sure, but a delivery guy just dropped it off and said it was for you. And it's from Saks!"

Hannah regarded the packages warily and took the envelope from Robin. She ran her finger under the closure to open and pull the note card out. The initials AMS were embossed on the front of the card in dark sapphire ink. Drew. She brought the card up to her nose and inhaled. She closed her eyes as she picked up the lingering scent of him on the paper.

Opening her eyes, and then the card, she read the short note:

Hannah,
I'd be so pleased if you would wear this to dinner this evening.
And just this.
XX Drew

This felt unsettlingly familiar. She thought her days of being told how to dress were over. She placed the card down on the counter and pulled the ribbon from the boxes. What was inside?

She quickly slid the cover off the smallest box and pulled the tissue paper aside. She blushed at the black lace garter and nude silk stockings, knowing Robin was watching.

"Sexy!" Robin squealed and tried to reach inside to touch them, but Hannah quickly folded the tissue paper back into place.

Yes, definitely starting to feel like a submissive at Baton Timide again.

"Too personal," Hannah chided.

"Let's see what's in the next box!" Robin prompted, undeterred.

Hannah pulled the cover off the second box. Her heart screeched to a halt. A tan Christian Louboutin Paris shoe box.

These types of purchases were so out of her league. She bought her shoes off the sale rack at Macy's, and they never ever had a red sole on them.

Her mouth open in shock, she turned toward Robin. "Are you seeing what I'm seeing?"

"Holy hell. Open that damn box already, woman."

With trembling hands, Hannah pulled the Louboutin box out of the larger box and set it on the counter before yanking the cover off. Inside was a red felt bag, which she took and set on the counter. Loosening the draw string, she reached in and slid out a pair of three-inch black satin pumps with delicate ankle straps.

She placed them on the counter and ran her fingers over

the material. "These are too much. I could never wear something like these."

"If you don't, I'll figure out a way to squeeze my size eight feet into them." Robin picked one up and turned it upside down, exposing the red sole. "They're gorgeous."

"Do you know how expensive shoes like this are?" Hannah snagged the shoe from Robin. "Seriously, these would probably pay half my monthly mortgage on this place. This feels so wrong to me. I don't need something like this."

Robin's fisted hands fell to her hips, a frown appearing on her face. "Why shouldn't you be spoiled like this? It's about time someone realized how special you are and scooped you up."

Despite her queasy stomach, Hannah smiled warmly at her friend. "No more special than you."

"Are you going to open the last box or what?" Robin pressed.

Hannah's hands wrung together as she viewed the rest of the packages. "God, I don't know. This is already too much. I feel like I should just wrap everything back up and return it."

"Don't be ridiculous. He wanted you to have these things. And let's face it, it has to be something to go with those shoes. Maybe it's a trench coat and he wants you to show up in just that, the heels and undies."

Hannah slapped her friend lightly on the shoulder. "Oh my god, don't even go there!"

"I know, right?" Robin let out an excited giggle. "This is totally bananas! This only happens in the movies!"

Hannah slid the cover off of the third box and started to

pull back the tissue paper but stopped abruptly at the sight of a blue tiffany box. Her breath caught in her throat even as her heart started galloping in her chest.

Not another blue box. Hadn't he heard her when she'd said they needed to take things slow? Having sex was one thing, but there was no way he was putting any type of collar on her. This was not Baton Timide. She was not his submissive anymore.

She wanted to be his girlfriend, his equal. Well, okay, he could boss her around in the bedroom and she wouldn't complain about that.

"Oh my, Tiffany's too?" Robin cooed enviously.

Hannah just shook her head in disappointment. Instead of opening the Tiffany box, she just took it out and placed it to the side.

"Wait, you're not going to open it?"

She shook her head and murmured, "Not right now. Maybe later." She pulled back the rest of the tissue paper to reveal a black wrap-style dress.

"That's an Alexandre Vauthier dress."

While Robin's voice was filled with envy as she pointed at the label, Hannah's insides were twisting into knots. She didn't want to be dressed like a doll. She wanted Drew to trust her enough to dress herself. She felt like she was being bought all over again.

She picked the dress up and shook it out so she could see it in its entirety. The material was gorgeous. It had a soft, rayon feel to it, but with more structure. It looked like an oversized suit jacket with a deep V in the front, but without the lapels. The dress wrapped around at the waist and was held together with a wide belt in the same material.

"It looks like a coat. That's going to be mighty short on those long legs, Hannah."

"I was just thinking the same thing." Not really, but she would at least let Robin enjoy the moment. She folded the dress and placed it back in the box, replacing the cover.

"Are you sure you don't want to open up that blue box?" Robin urged, a look of desire on her face.

Hannah shook her head again. "Positive."

"Ya know, it's already two o'clock. I can handle the store if you want to head upstairs early and start your beauty prep now."

"I wouldn't mind leaving early if you think you can handle the shop?"

"Go. But promise me that you'll tell me all the details tomorrow!"

"Of course!" Hannah gave Robin a hug, wondering as she did, what in the hell she was going to do with these "gifts."

Hannah went into the back room to put her jacket on before grabbing all the boxes and heading up to her apartment. As soon as she put the boxes down, she dug her phone out of her purse to text Drew.

Thank you for the lovely gifts, but it's too much. I insist you take them back.

Several moments ticked by as she waited for him to respond. Staring at her phone wasn't helping, so she went to the fridge and pulled out a bottle of water. As soon as she turned the cap to open it, her phone dinged.

You're welcome. And I insist you keep them. It makes me happy to buy gifts for you. Besides, I can't wait to see you in that dress.

Hannah slammed the water bottle down and began typing.

I'm not a sub at Baton that you can dress at will. Please take them back. Especially that damn blue box.

More than several minutes passed. Her mind was racing at what his reply would be. Finally, a half bottle of water later—and a half mile of pacing—her phone dinged.

I wasn't trying to dress you like a sub. I simply wanted to make you feel special. Wear whatever makes you comfortable. My apologies.

She felt a pang of regret. Had she overreacted? Was she being too sensitive? She'd never dated a man with money before and wasn't used to receiving gifts of any sort.

Sorry. This is still all new to me. And the blue box may have pushed me over the edge.

His reply came only a second later.

Apology accepted. It's not a collar. Bring it with you tonight. I'll see if I can change your mind. Pick you up at 7?

She frowned in confusion as she replied.

See you at 7.

DREW STEPPED out of the town car and adjusted his jacket. He was wearing a dark slate suit, a crisp white shirt and a gray and black print tie. He pulled on his overcoat and walked into the alley beside the flower shop.

It was exactly one minute until seven; he was nothing if

not prompt. He rang the apartment doorbell and waited, pacing back and forth.

A few moments later the door swung open and he spun around to a stunning Hannah. She stood in the doorway, still as a post, clutching her coat and purse with white knuckles, her lower lip caught between her lip. She was wearing the outfit he'd sent.

He raked his gaze over her, starting at her softly curled hair and ruby red lips, down to the swell of her breasts exposed in the deep V of the dress, farther down to her silk-covered legs and, finally, to feet clad in the sexiest pair of pumps, strapped tightly to her ankles.

He let out a slow whistle. "Good evening, Hannah."

"Drew." She cast her head downward as a small smile danced across her lips.

He put a finger under her chin and lifted it a fraction so that he could look into her eyes. "You may be the sexiest thing I have ever seen."

Her cheeks turned a light shade of pink. "Thank you. You are looking pretty handsome yourself, Mr. Sapphire."

He bent and brushed his lips against her painted ones. "Thank you for wearing the dress. It suits you. But, just to be clear, you would look amazing in anything."

He watched as she swept her hand down the short length of the dress, trying to pull it down lower when she reached the hem. "There's not very much of it."

A mischievous grin lit up his face as he pulled her hand away from the hem. With a single finger, he pushed the hem up her thigh an inch, stopping at the strap of the garter belt attached to the top of her stocking. He slid his finger to the inside of her thigh before slipping it farther north. When he bumped against her bare core, she inhaled sharply and stopped his hand with hers.

He tilted his head before whispering in her ear. "You just got me so goddamn hard."

He trailed his finger back down her thigh as he leaned in further, languorously kissed her neck . She tipped her head to the side and let out a small stuttered sigh. He pulled his lips away from her neck and stepped back, taking her coat from her hand at the same time.

Her eyes locked with his in desire as he held the coat open for her. She turned, gracefully stepping into the coat. He gently spun her around, holding her eyes again as he buttoned her jacket up.

"Ready?"

"We could just stay here." Her response was breathy and filled with longing.

He chuckled and shook his head. "Nope. I'm taking you on a date."

He placed his hand on the small of her back and guided her to the waiting car.

"We could just have our date here." She looked coyly over her shoulder at him.

"Oh, you are always so anxious, my little kitten. I've got plans for you tonight."

They reached the town car, and the driver opened the back door.

"You're not driving?" she asked.

"Not tonight." He turned and held her hand as she sat down in the car. "I wanted to keep my hands free."

Her eyes widened at his statement and a smile curved her lips, her eyes darting to the driver. Drew waited until she was seated comfortably, then moved to the other side of the car and climbed in beside her. "Come closer."

She scooted across the seat until she was up against his thigh. He pulled the bottom of her jacket open and rested his hand on the inside of her thigh. He leaned in and inhaled deeply.

"You always smell so good, Hannah. Like springtime."

"Really? I'm not wearing perfume." She brought the back of her hand up to her nose and sniffed.

"I know you aren't. It's just you. It's one of the things I love about you."

She looked over at him quickly and then back down at her hands. "So where are we going?"

He moved his thumb in small circles on the inside of her thigh, loving the soft feeling of the silk. "A restaurant called Marea. Do you know it?"

"I've heard of it. I've never been of course."

He trailed his fingers higher until he reached bare thigh, moving his thumb in small circles.

He bent closer. "Open your legs wider."

Her eyes shot to the driver and then back to him.

"Don't worry about him. David's worked for me for years."

Hannah scooted up higher in the seat and snapped her legs shut in the same motion. Drew shook his head, then used his trapped hand to pinch her inner thigh. She squeaked in surprise, and her legs popped open again.

He leaned down and whispered in her ear, brushing his lips against her skin as he did. "Don't fight me."

He ran his tongue around the rim of her ear, then down

the side of her neck. He grinned at the low whimper that escaped her, and her legs widened further.

Her breath faltered when his finger brushed against her clit, and then his own hitched when he felt how wet she was. He moved his lips back up to her ear.

"You're already so fucking wet."

She turned her head so that her lips were against his and started kissing him hungrily. He slid his free hand around the nape of her neck, pulling her in tighter, pushing his tongue against her lips in demand.

She complied immediately, their tongues dancing as their kiss deepened. He slid his finger back and forth against the hard hood of her clit, teasing a deep growl from the back of Hannah's throat.

He pulled his mouth away from hers and brought it back to her ear. "You like that?"

She nodded, pushing her core harder against his fingers. He chuckled low and deep at her neediness before thrusting not one, but two fingers into her.

Her hand gripped his arm tightly, her teeth clamping onto her lower lip as her eyes opened wide in surprise.

"Drew, please!" She was practically panting as she whispered.

He looked at her, a feral gleam in his eye. He fucking loved seeing her wither for him. His cock was like a damn piece of marble in his trousers. "Please what?"

"Make me come or stop," she breathed, continuing to clutch his arm, her face pinking at her bold request.

The car suddenly stopped and a voice came from the front. "We're here, Mr. Sapphire."

"Very good. Just give us a moment please."

"Of course." David left the car running but opened the door and stepped out, standing beside the now closed door.

Drew turned his attention back to Hannah, his fingers still working in and out of her pussy. "I'm going to make you come so many times tonight, you'll be begging me to stop."

And then he hooked his fingers, driving them deeper into her, pressing hard against her clit at the same time. "Come, but don't make a sound."

Her muscles clenched tightly around his fingers and then pulsed, her grip on his arm tightening even more, her teeth biting down on her bottom lip as breath whooshed in and out of her nose. He rocked his fingers slowly now, riding out her orgasm until she started to relax and her grip on him loosened.

He bent down and bit her bottom lip, pulling it from her teeth, and then kissed her hard, stealing her breath from her.

"That's number one. Let's keep count, shall we?"

Her eyes closed tightly and she exhaled heavily before she spoke. "You're going to kill me."

He slid his fingers out of her slowly, watching her lips form a small O when he pulled free from her. His throbbing cock twitched.

He brought his fingers to his mouth, sealing his lips around them, closing his eyes as he sucked, savoring the taste of her. He slowly drew them out, his gaze finding Hannah's wide one. "So unbelievably fucking good. I could skip dinner and just eat you."

"Okay." She didn't even miss a beat.

He shook his head in disbelief at her eagerness. "As

appealing as that sounds, it will have to wait. I need to feed you if you're going to have enough energy tonight."

Hannah's eyes lit up. She was so responsive to his every wish or command. "Okay."

He covered his cock with her hand. Her eyes flew up to his. "Do you see what you do to me? So fucking hard, Hannah."

She started stroking up and down his shaft but he dropped his hand over hers, stilling her motion. "No. I'll explode in two minutes if you do that."

She mewled desperately. "Let me make you feel good."

He shook his head. "No, I can wait."

She stuck her lower lip out in a pout and shrugged her shoulders. "If you're sure."

"I am." He leaned over and kissed her lips roughly and then broke away from her again. "I'm going to step outside for a moment and cool down. Take a moment if you need it."

She used her fingers to wipe away her lipstick from his mouth. He smiled at her attention and then pulled his overcoat closed as he opened the back door to step outside.

HANNAH SHOOK her head at what she had allowed Drew to do to her in the car—while someone else had been two feet away! She blew out a breath and then reached into her purse to find her powder and lipstick. She quickly reapplied both and then did her best to pull the very short dress down and back into place.

The sight of the garter straps, visible when she was sitting, made her turn crimson. She had never worn anything this provocative. While it felt so terribly indecent, she couldn't help feeling incredibly sexy at the same time. And the way Drew had looked at her in it, had made her core instantly tighten.

This man made her feel things and want to do things she had never imagined. And the worst of it was, she wanted more.

Shaking her head at herself, she pulled her jacket closed around her and pushed her door open. Drew was there, waiting, and before she could even step out of the car, his hand was there to guide her up.

When she was fully out, he pulled her to his side and kissed the side of her temple. "All set?"

"Yes. I'm good."

"Okay, right this way then."

He kept his hand on the small of her back as he led her into the restaurant. Inside, light piano music tinkled from somewhere, and lit candles decorated every table. The restaurant was decked out in beautiful reds and whites, romantic lighting and a gorgeous fire burning along a back wall.

He checked their coats and then approached the hostess. She followed as the hostess led them to a table in the back of the room, close to the fireplace. Hannah felt like every set of eyes in the restaurant was watching her as she walked to their booth. Like they knew she was playing dress-up and was an imposter at their party. Goose bumps broke out across her arms and a shiver ran down her spine.

Drew turned toward her, his face concerned, "You okay?"

She nodded once, smiling. "Just a chill."

"Will this do, Mr. Sapphire?" The hostess swung her hand wide at the table in question. The table, lit by a silver candelabra, held a round vase full of red roses.

"It's perfect."

Drew held out one of the chairs for her. As she sat, the hostess came over and presented her with a menu and then one to Drew, who was now sitting. She smiled and told them to enjoy their evening before leaving.

Hannah could still feel eyes looking at her and opened the menu up in an attempt to block them out.

Drew's fingers fell on top of her menu and pushed it down. "Hey, you okay?"

She shook her head back and forth and glanced around the room before whispering, "Everyone's looking at me."

Drew glanced around the room and then back at her. "You're a beautiful woman. It's normal for people to admire a beautiful woman when they see her."

"I feel like everyone here knows I don't belong."

His brow furrowed deeply. "Why would you ever feel that way?"

"I grew up in rural New York and I work at a flower shop. The fanciest thing I've ever done is go to the masquerade ball you brought me to."

He pulled the menu completely from her hands, placed it on the table and then took her hands in his. "When you walk, when you talk, the way you treat people; it is nothing short of graceful. That's not something that comes with money."

She extricated her hands from his and sat up straight in her chair. He was trying so hard and she was ruining things. "I'm sorry, Drew. The restaurant really is lovely."

He smiled back at her but it was strained. "Thank you for coming with me. I don't think I've ever had a more beautiful date."

Her features softened. "Nor I. Thank you."

"I'd give you the moon and the stars if you'd let me," he murmured before turning his attention toward the wine menu, as if the admission embarrassed him. She flushed at his confession and reached for her own menu.

The waitress came over and took their order for a bottle of red wine. She was back in moments, popping the cork and pouring Drew a sample to taste. Upon his approval, she filled each of their glasses and took their order for dinner. Well, Drew's order for their dinners.

He ordered them both a four-course dinner consisting of antipasto, mushroom risotto, thyme-crusted lamb with baby fingerling potatoes and chocolate soufflés for dessert.

She leaned forward and hissed through clenched teeth, "What if I had wanted something different?"

A look of surprise crossed his face. "I'm sorry. I should have asked. I'm used to ordering. It was presumptuous of me. Would you like something different?"

Hannah looked around before answering to make sure no one would overhear her. "No, it's fine, but I can't eat all of that. The risotto would have been plenty and this place is very expensive. It will be wasted."

A wide smile broke across Drew's face. "You know I'm a billionaire, right?"

She did not smile back. "So? Does that mean you should

waste your money? And once again, you're treating me like a submissive." She lowered her voice to a whisper edged in anger. "Are you going to feed me my food too?"

Drew's lips pursed into a tight line. "First, I love that you're worried about spending my money. That's a new one for me. But believe me, I'm fine." His tone was clearly edged with sarcasm. "And as far as the way I'm treating you, I'm simply trying to be a gentleman. It's not uncommon or considered in bad taste to order for your date."

Hannah looked down in embarrassment. She kept jumping to conclusions about the way he was treating her and it was ruining the evening. "I'm sorry. You're trying so hard to treat me like a lady and I'm just treating you awfully. I'm so out of my depth."

Drew took her hand from across the table. "Hannah, being with you . . . the feelings you stir in me . . . I'm the one that's out of my depth."

She stared in shock at his admission. "Really? I'm speechless."

Drew huffed, a wide smile breaking across his face. "Finally!"

She rolled her eyes, relieved the tense moment was broken, and let out a nervous laugh. A moment later their first course arrived and they started to eat. The antipasto was amazing. The strained silence was not.

"Do you normally eat out every night?" She needed to know more about his everyday life if she was ever going to understand him, and frankly, the silence was deafening.

He shook his head. "No, not usually. Unless I have a business meeting. David—my driver from the car?"

"Yes?"

"He is also my head of security and personal protection detail when required. He and his wife Julie have a suite of their own at the hotel. Julie cooks and cleans for me when I stay at the hotel. Takes care of my dry cleaning, makes sure my fridge is stocked."

"Wait, all I got out of that is *personal protection detail*. What does that mean?"

Drew shrugged. "I'm rich. Sometimes I need someone to have my back."

"You mean, like a bodyguard?" She set her fork down on her plate.

Again, he shrugged. "Eh, call it what you will."

She scoffed. "I call it a bodyguard."

She frowned, her brow crinkling. "But I've never seen David or anyone else with you before."

"I don't need one in most circumstances. There are occasions when I do though, and then I have David."

Her eyes widened a bit. "So, is he your driver or your bodyguard tonight?"

He shook his head and chuckled. "My driver."

"The rich are very complicated people." She took another bite of her food.

"Not just the rich." He tilted his head, sarcasm dripping from his tone.

Her brow furrowed at his slight dig, but before she could respond, a server interrupted them to clear their salad plates and set the risotto down in front of them.

"Okay, I'm changing the subject. Where does your family live? Ben and your mother and father? Do they live at the hotel too?"

"Twenty questions tonight?" He had a tired smile on his

face.

Her voice grew quiet. "I just want to know you better."

He stared at her a moment while he took a sip of his wine. "Okay, I have a question for you then."

She nodded. "Okay."

"Did you bring the Tiffany box with you?"

She sat up straighter. "Oh, not what I was expecting."

He raised his eyebrows. "What were you expecting?"

"Not sure." She reached down to the floor and brought her purse up to the table. "But yes, I brought it." She opened her purse and pulled the box out, placing it on the table between them.

"Open it." His eyes locked onto hers.

"No." She reached for her wine glass and took a sip.

"Open it, Hannah." Commanding this time. His eyes remaining locked in place.

She hesitated a moment and then muttered, "I don't want to. I'm afraid of what's in there."

"I already told you it's not a collar." His reply was gentle this time.

"I know. But it's a Tiffany box."

He tilted his head in confusion. "And?"

"So out of my depth again, Drew."

He pulled her fingers into his. "Stop saying that. And just open the damn box."

He released her and slid the box directly in front of her.

She looked up at him warily and then, with shaking fingers, lifted the lid off the box. Her eyes flew up to his, her cheeks lifting in a smile. "It's lovely."

She lowered her gaze back to the contents, her fingers grazing lightly over a silver chain necklace that ended with a tassel made of small pearls, held together by a delicately decorated silver cap. Also inside were matching pearl drop earrings.

"See, nothing bad." His lips lifting slightly.

She looked away from the box to meet his eyes. "But why? Why do you keep doing these things? It's too much."

He moved his finger lightly over the cap holding the pearl tassel together. "Do you see this?"

Hannah nodded.

"This design is made up of olive leaves. And I'm thankful —" He stopped and looked up at her then, removing the necklace from the box before standing up. Stepping behind her, he brushed her hair over one shoulder and then draped the necklace around her neck, fastening it.

"I'm grateful you gave me a second chance. Extending the olive branch, so to speak." His fingers trailed down the length of the necklace, which fell between the curve of her breasts, and then back up, before moving her hair back into place. He bent down, kissed her cheek and returned to his chair.

Hannah looked down. The necklace sat perfectly in the low V of the dress. Everything Drew did had a purpose.

A pang of guilt shot through her for her belligerent behavior toward him all evening. She ran her fingers down the silver chain, stopping when she reached the silver tassels.

"Thank you, Drew. You keep doing things for me out of the kindness of your heart, and I keep accusing you of bad behavior. I'm not sure I deserve your gratitude."

He nodded at her admission. "We'll figure it out. Both of us."

She sighed. "You're probably too good for me."

He rolled his eyes and let out a small, dark laugh. "I could punish you. And before you say anything, yes, now I am taking control."

"That kind of control I like." Her voice grew hoarse.

"You definitely are going to keep me on my toes."

"Can we go please?"

"Are you not hungry?"

Her eyes met his, her reply raspy. "For you."

Drew raised his hand and motioned for the waitress. "Check please."

CHAPTER
Nine

WITH A HAND at the small of her back, Drew steered Hannah through the lobby of the hotel and to the elevator. Stepping inside, he keyed in the security code to his suite. Then, without warning, he turned and shoved Hannah up against the wall. She gasped in surprise but melted into him.

"Always my eager little kitten." He bent down and nibbled on her neck as he worked the buttons of her coat open. He reached inside and splayed his hands around her center, pushing her harder against the elevator wall.

He grinned wickedly and then trailed his tongue down the base of her neck to the bottom of the V in her dress.

Hannah's head rolled to the side and a breathy sigh escaped her parted lips until Drew leaned back up and slammed his mouth over hers. He hissed as her hands wrapped around his neck, pulling at the hair at his nape.

The elevator dinged and the doors slid open to deliver them to the entryway of his suite. Not breaking their lip-lock, he turned her at the waist and guided her into the suite, pinning her back up against the wall in the hallway.

As he continued stroking her lips with his own, he ground his pelvis into hers, showing her how hard she made him. She pushed him away and started shaking her coat off.

"Too hot" was all she said before dropping the coat on the floor, watching as he also shed his. He chuckled as she reached for his shirt to pull him closer. She loosened his tie and tugged it over his head, then started working on the buttons of his shirt.

"Let me help." He pushed her hands away and, with a smirk, took both sides of his shirt and yanked it apart, buttons popping off. He slid it off his shoulders.

Her eyes flew open and she licked her lips before dropping both hands to his bare chest and running them lower to his belt.

"Stop."

Her hands stilled and her eyes peeked up at him in question. He raised her hands above her head, pushing them against the wall.

"Leave them like that."

She blinked slowly and looked down submissively. "Yes, Sir."

His cock jutted in his pants at her obedience and he rewarded her with a searing kiss. "Good girl."

He slid his fingers under the wide belt holding her dress together and unclasped the hooks. The belt fell loose as he spread the dress apart, exposing her breasts and bare center.

He placed both of his hands on her taut stomach and trailed them slowly up until they were each cupping a breast. He massaged them gently before taking one hard pebble in his mouth, biting down gently.

Hannah's back arched off the wall as she cried out. He shoved her back flat against the wall, not releasing the nipple, instead sucking it harder into his mouth. Mewling sounds left her lips each time he alternated between biting and sucking, and he had to keep his hand pressed firmly against her center to keep her from rocking into him. He finally released her nipple, laving his tongue over it and then up her neck until his lips found hers again.

She kissed him desperately, shoving her tongue deep in his mouth, moaning as she did. Drew pulled back and looked her in the eye, her mouth red and swollen.

"What do you want, Hannah?"

She blinked once and whispered, "You."

"I'm yours." He growled. "What do you want?"

She looked at him in silence for a few moments before answering. "I want you in my mouth."

Drew let a moan fall from his lips and leaned his forehead against hers. "You are fucking perfect."

He kissed her then, slowly, tenderly. "Put your hands down."

He stepped back and watched her lower her hands and shake them a bit. "Take your dress off."

She let the dress fall off one shoulder, then pulled the other side off and let the dress fall to the floor. He just stared at her.

She wore only the necklace, garters and heels and was the most fucking unbelievable sight to behold. "Walk to the living room and stand by the couch."

He wanted to watch her ass as she walked. The lace of

the garter fell halfway down each ass cheek, where it met the strap attached to the stockings. As she walked, her ass exposed and lifted high from the heels, he couldn't help but reach down and shift his cock before it shot out of his pants. She reached the couch and stood, head down, waiting.

He followed, then grabbed one of the cushions off the back of the couch and dropped it flat on the floor in front of her. "Get on your knees."

She dropped immediately to the cushion. "Unbutton my pants and release my cock."

Hannah looked up at him through her lashes and moved her hands to his pants, working his belt and then the button on the trousers before pulling them down. He was commando, so his hard cock jutted free as it was released from its prison.

He sighed in relief when her hand grasped him around his base and slowly sucked his cock into her hot mouth. She hummed around his length, and he had to grab onto the top of her head to steady himself from the fucking pleasure of it.

She brought her other hand up, grasping him now with two hands, squeezing tight, while continuing to suck his shaft in and out of her mouth. He growled at the sensation and knew he would come if he didn't stop her. He tightened his grasp on her head and pulled her back off his cock.

She looked up at him, her eyes wide. "I'm not done."

He snarled, tugging on her hair in an indication she should rise. "Yes you are."

When she was standing straight in front of him, he crashed his lips to hers, yanking her body flush. His cock, wet from her mouth, slid against her belly. The friction was enough to drive him over the edge, so he tore his lips from hers and grasped her by the shoulders, separating them gently.

His pants were still around his ankles, so he leaned down and pulled his shoes off, then his pants.

"Go over to the window and stand in front of it."

HANNAH LOOKED at him and blew out a breath in frustration. She was getting tired of being made to wait for what she wanted. What she needed.

She took a moment to assess the man standing naked in front of her. He stood tall, lean and muscular, but not bulky. She loved the soft dark curls that started at his chest and sprinkled down into a thin line like an arrow pointing the way to his manhood. She looked longingly at its hardness, licking her lips unconsciously.

"Do it, Hannah. Now."

She turned and stepped lightly to the wall of windows next to the dining room table. She looked at Drew for his next instruction, anxious to get her hands back on his body. He stood watching her from the living room before closing the distance between them, stopping a foot away.

"Turn around, bend over, and place your hands flat on the window."

Her eyebrows raised in question, she looked at the window and then back at him.

"Don't worry, no one can see in. It's one-way glass."

This made her feel a little better. She didn't mind putting

on a show for Drew, but not half of Fifty-Ninth Avenue. "Yes, Sir."

She faced the window and bent forward at the waist, placing her hands on the glass as Drew had instructed. When she leaned forward, the necklace around her neck swung forward and the pearls clacked softly against the glass. They continued to swing slowly back and forth in the space between her breasts and the glass as she waited for what came next.

Bending over like this exposed her core to Drew, but instead of feeling embarrassed, she felt empowered and sexy. Knowing she shouldn't, but not being able to resist, she looked over her shoulder at Drew.

His fist was around his cock, stroking it languidly, his eyes dark and heavy with lust as they met hers. Not letting go of his length, he took two steps until he was standing directly behind her, shaking his head once.

"Tsk, tsk little kitten. Always so curious." And without warning his free hand smacked her hard across the ass. She sucked in a breath at the contact and opened her stance wider to try and keep her balance. He seized her stinging cheek, rubbing it in small circles with the palm of his hand.

"I think sometimes you want me to punish you. Do you like when I spank you, Hannah?"

She shook her head back and forth in response and was met with another smack on her ass.

"It's 'Yes, Sir' or 'No, Sir.'" His hand fondling her ass again. Her core growing more slick with each touch, whether it be soft or hard.

"No, Sir."

He chuckled and then he slid his hand down her ass and

trailed his fingers between her pussy lips, finding her wet and slippery. She couldn't help the soft moan that stole out of her mouth. "Your pussy tells me a different story, Hannah."

She tried to be still as he worked his fingers back and forth over her clit but she thrust back into him when he plunged two fingers into her. The constant teasing had left her throbbing and his fingers only made her crave more.

He crowded forward, dominating her body with his, as he thrust another finger into her and rocked them in and out of her slowly.Panting, she tilted her hips, trying to push her clit into his fingers, but Drew withdrew before she could trigger a release.

She let out a small whine of discontent and whipped her head around. Drew had his fingers in his mouth, sucking, a sly grin on his face. He slid them out, then grasped her by the hips and rubbed his cock up and down the seam of her ass.

"What do you want, Hannah?" His voice was gravelly and thick.

She tried to push back into him, but the grasp he had on her hips made it impossible, frustrating her further. She growled under her breath and was met with another chuckle.

"Just tell me what you want."

Dropping her head in defeat, she sucked in a breath and pleaded, "I want you to fuck me."

"Why didn't you just say so?" In one swift motion, he plunged his cock into her slick center. Every muscle in her core clenched around him as he seated himself fully. She groaned in satisfaction.

He paused like that for a moment, apparently savoring the feeling, then withdrew almost entirely. He surged forward again, driving himself back into her in one hard thrust.

Her entire body surged forward, shoving her face and breasts up against the glass, her necklace clinking. Her peaks grew harder from the cold as she braced her head. Drew's hands encircled her waist, and he pushed down, raising her ass higher as he pulled back out of her slowly again. She knew what to expect this time, and when he thrust again, she welcomed it.

He slid his hands up her waist until he broke the seal between the window and her breasts, cupping each one to pull her back into him and away from the window. She left her hands braced on the glass for support but threw her head back with a loud moan as Drew rolled her hardened peaks between his fingers, thrusting in and out of her at the same time.

He was grunting from the exertion, sweat dripping off of him and onto her back. Each thrust pushed against her throbbing clit, her climax building. As if Drew could sense her impending orgasm, he tugged her back against his body and thrust harder, bringing his lips to her ear, panting.

"I'm going to come, Hannah. Are you ready?"

She swung her head back and forth. "Oh my god, yes! Yes!"

Drew's release exploded like a rush of hot lava, detonating her own climax, her muscles clamping down around his cock before detonating a thousand pulsing beats. She cried out, her fists clenched, her fingernails scraping across the window. Drew's mouth clamped down on her shoulder, muffling a low roar, his arms tightening around her.

After several moments, Drew's hold on her loosened, his lips brushing kisses across her shoulder as he pulled them both upright. He spun her around in his arms and brought his mouth to hers in a slow, gentle kiss.

She wound her arms around his neck, fusing their naked bodies together. His lips left hers and she rolled her head to the side as he dropped kisses down her neck and then back up to her ear.

He ran his tongue across her ear and then blew lightly on it, sending chills over her skin. Her grip tightened, pulling his hair. "Oh my god, that felt so good."

His grip on her intensified. Then with the softest breath of air, his lips brushed her ear whispering in a low chuckle, "That was only number two."

He picked her up then, wrapping her legs around his waist, and carried her to the bedroom.

HANNAH WOKE EARLY the next morning and blinked until her eyes adjusted to the light. Drew lay next to her still sleeping soundly, his breath drawing in and out of his mouth in a slow rhythm.

Her eyes raked down his naked form admiringly, and for about the hundredth time she wondered how she had gotten here, in a gorgeous billionaire's bed. She shook her head in silent disbelief before slipping quietly out from under the covers.

It was already close to 7:00 a.m. and she needed to get home to shower and open the shop. She tiptoed over to the dresser against the wall and, as quietly as possible, pulled open some drawers until she found a sweatshirt and a pair of sweats. They would be huge, but there was no way she was doing the walk of shame across the hotel lobby in the dress from last night.

Shit. She realized she only had her pumps to wear and cursed herself for not getting up and going home last night. Grabbing the shoes in one hand and the stolen clothes in the other, she stepped softly to the door so she could dress in the living room.

"Stay," a low voice grumbled from the bed.

She swung around quickly, a smile breaking across her face. "Sorry. I was trying not to wake you."

"Why are you sneaking out without saying goodbye? Come here." He sat up in the bed and motioned her closer.

She shook her head, her eyes scanning his chiseled torso, the playful smile on his face. "No way, mister. If I come any closer, I know exactly what's going to happen."

"Exactly. So come here."

She started backing away and toward the door again. "Nope. Gotta go home and shower and open the shop. Call me later, okay?"

"I want to see you later. Can I?"

She stilled just for a moment, opened her mouth to speak but then clamped it shut.

He sat up, concern on his face. "What?"

She shook her head. "It's just that I have to work all day, and then I have Grace. We have a bit of a routine. I don't want to confuse her." As much as she wanted to spend time with him, she was also afraid they might be moving too quickly.

He threw the covers off the bed and swung his legs onto the floor. "What if I bring dinner to both of you then? After five? Keep things simple?"

How could she say no to that? "Okay. That sounds good."

He rose up out of the bed and stalked over to her, grabbing her naked body around the waist and pulling her close.

"I'm not letting you leave me until I get at least a good morning kiss." He bent down and pressed his lips to hers in a warm, sultry kiss.

She sighed in resignation and kissed him back, loving the taste of him on her lips. Before things could get any more heated, she broke off and pushed him away.

"Only a kiss. I don't have time for more, as much as I'd enjoy it." She grinned shyly, trying hard to keep her eyes away from his hardened length.

"I'll have David take you home. Let me just call him." He walked over to the phone sitting on the table.

She was going to argue, but the thought of everyone in the lobby seeing her in sweats and heels changed her mind. "Okay, if he's available."

He began speaking on the phone and then hung up. "He's available. Take the elevator to P1 and he'll be there waiting."

She smiled gratefully at him and walked over, leaning into him for another kiss. "Thank you."

"Go," he growled through their kiss. "Because if you stay another minute, I'm not letting you leave."

She laughed and pulled away, turning from him to flee from the room.

"Hannah?"

She stopped and looked back over her shoulder.

"I hope last night was okay. I know it was a little awkward in the beginning."

She nodded in agreement. "It was good. Next time, we'll do better."

"Okay, get out. Go to work."

She blew him a kiss over her shoulder and left.

TEN LONG, busy hours later, Hannah locked the shop door behind her and headed up to her apartment, holding Grace's little hand.

The shop was extremely busy prepping and ordering for the upcoming Thanksgiving holiday, and the lack of sleep the night before had kicked in.

She was exhausted and all she really wanted to do was crawl into some pajamas and then into bed. She wondered if it was too late to call Drew and cancel. Dinner at her place was going to be nothing like their dinner at the restaurant the night before.

Before she could pick up the phone, the doorbell rang. Sure enough, when she opened the door, there stood Drew. He smiled and held up a large brown paper bag. "I hope Chinese is okay? Maybe eat out of cartons and keep the dishes to a minimum?"

She sighed in relief and motioned for him to come in. "You have no idea how perfect that sounds."

As they made their way into the kitchen, Grace appeared

and began chattering away as Drew unpacked the food. Her worries about a stressful night melted away when she saw how easily the two of them were getting along. Now knowing the relationship he had with his sister, it made so much more sense to her.

After they ate, Drew offered to clean up so Hannah could give Grace a bath and get her settled down for the night. Forty-five minutes later they were both snuggled on her couch together.

She had changed into a pair of yoga pants and a loose T-shirt that hung off her shoulder. Drew's fingers were running in a lazy circle over her exposed skin as they talked about their days.

"By the way, I have to go to Boston for a few days next week. Hotel stuff."

"Oh, really? How many days?" She couldn't help the small frown on her face.

"Just a night, I think. I leave on Tuesday."

"Is it wrong that I already don't want you to leave?" She looked at him shyly, not sure if he was feeling the same way.

"Come with me."

Hannah scoffed. "Drew, you know I can't. I have Grace and the shop. I just can't take off on a whim."

"How were you able to leave for three days to work at Baton Timide?"

The question took her by surprise. Not his tone, the fact that he had wondered how she got the time off.

"One weekend a month, Grace goes and stays with Jackson's parents. I planned my first auction around that. I wasn't even sure I'd make it past the first auction, so I really hadn't planned on what would happen next."

He shook his head and a lopsided grin appeared. "Yes, well, we see how well that worked out. For me anyway." He brushed his lips lightly against hers.

"Yes, not too bad at all." She smiled.

"So, when does Grace go visit her grandparents again? Let's plan something then."

"Actually, it's next weekend. Sometimes they take her for Thanksgiving weekend because I get so busy at the shop, but now that she's getting older and will remember things, I told them I wanted her for the holiday."

"What about your family? You don't spend it with Tammy or your brother? Your mom and dad?"

She shook her head as sadness filled her eyes. "My mom and dad died in a car crash about six months after I married Jackson. I wasn't even pregnant then."

He pulled her closer into his arms and hugged her. "I'm really sorry. You never mentioned them, so I wasn't sure."

"It was really hard at the time. Jackson and Danny were both gone, and Tammy and I had to deal with everything. The funeral, packing up their house, trying to sell the house for enough to cover their mortgage. We discovered pretty quickly that neither one of them had been very good with money."

"I'm sure it was difficult."

"It was, but it's over now. I just wish they had gotten to meet Grace."

"You've had more than your fair share of loss. I'm really sorry."

She frowned. "I guess. But you have too. It's why it's so important to me that Grace sees Jackson's parents, and probably why I'm so protective of her. She's just a little girl. She deserves all the happiness and stability I can give her."

"Well, if it's too hard for you to get away, I certainly understand."

She looked up at him and smiled. "I'd like to go away with you. I really would. I just have to make sure the girls can cover the shop on Saturday."

Surprisingly, she was excited at the prospect of spending several days and nights with Drew. "What should we do?"

He smiled. "Do you want to go to my house on the shore? We can bring some food and just be hermits. Eat, sleep, have lots of sex. We could stay naked all weekend long."

His eyes grew dark at his own suggestion and before she could respond, he cupped her face and kissed her tenderly. "I don't care where we are or what we do. It will be nice to just spend some more time with you."

She leaned into his cheek and turned her head to kiss the soft spot in the center of his palm. "It sounds absolutely perfect, Drew."

"I'm exhausted, let's go to bed." Hannah rose up off of Drew.

Drew stood up next to her and pulled her into his arms. "Is it okay for me to stay?"

She tried to cover her mouth as it opened wide in a yawn. A small smile hit her lips. "As long as you let me sleep."

He kissed the tip of her nose and smacked her lightly on the ass before releasing her. "Done. I'm as tired as you."

They made their way to the bedroom, and Drew pulled off his T-shirt and jeans. With him in his boxers and her in a night-shirt, they both climbed into her bed, sliding under the covers and up against each other. Hannah rested her head on Drew's bare chest and listened to his heartbeat under her ear.

"Drew?"

"Hmmm." His fingers were tracing back and forth over her arm.

"Do you mind leaving before seven? That's when Grace usually wakes up. I just don't want to confuse her yet."

"Sure, no problem. I'm generally up much earlier than that."

She nodded her head on his chest and whispered, "Drew?"

"Yes?"

"I'm glad you're here."

DREW WOKE and tried to open his eyes but they were covered. Hannah's long hair was draped over his face. She was curled around him like a boa constrictor.

He enjoyed the feel of her against his body, his cock twitching in agreement as it jutted against her backside. He brushed her hair out of the way and raised his wrist to look at the watch still strapped to it. It was just after five thirty a.m. Too early to wake her; she was exhausted.

He kissed the back of her head, savoring her floral scent as he did, and then slid out from under the covers. He grabbed his clothes and then carried them out to the bathroom so he could dress.

He made a quick stop in the kitchen to drink a glass of water. He placed his empty glass in the sink and then walked through the arch to the living room to grab his shoes.

He came to a screeching halt. Grace was sitting on the floor, coloring. He started to back up as quietly as he could but she swung her head up and saw him. A big wide grin broke across her face.

"Hi, Mr. Drew! Want to color with me?" She held the crayon in her hand up at him.

"Grace, what are you doing up so early?"

She shrugged, then wiped at her nose and started coloring again. "I woke up. But I saw you and Mommy sleeping so I came to color."

Shit. Hannah is going to freak.

Oblivious to his own freak-out, Grace continued to color, concentration etching her forehead, her tongue peeking out of her mouth. He had a flash of his sister when she was young, her face scrunching up just like that when she was working something out. He wanted to scoop Grace up and give her a hug. Best not to push his luck.

"Gracie?" He spoke softly and her head swung up to look at him. "I've got to go. Will you be okay in here by yourself?"

He realized he was asking a four-year-old if she was okay to be alone and shook his head at his own stupidity. She stood up then, came over to him on her tiny feet and took his large hand in hers.

"Let's have some cereal. Mommy says we need breakfast every day."

He thought his heart would combust. He realized two girls were laying claim to his heart, not just one. He wrapped his large fingers around her small ones and let her lead him into the kitchen.

She stopped in front of a pantry cupboard and used her free hand to pull the door open. She turned her head and looked up at him.

"Do you like Cheerios? Mommy won't buy me the Froot Loops." She stated it so matter-of-factly, making it clear that Froot Loops would obviously be the better choice. He nodded his head up and down.

"I do."

She let go of his hand then to pull the cereal out, then turned and put it down on the table. Then she walked over to a drawer and pulled out two spoons. She pointed to a cupboard up on the wall.

"Can you get the bowls, Mr. Drew?"

He jumped into action and did as she requested while she walked over to the fridge to take out a carton of milk before meeting him back at the table. She scooted herself up into one of the chairs and sat up on her knees to pour some cereal in each of their bowls. He opened the milk and poured some on top of the cereal.

She lifted her spoon and brought it up over their bowls and looked at him expectantly. He wasn't sure what she wanted.

"Pick up your spoon and clink mine. That's what me and Mommy do."

He couldn't contain the grin that stretched across his face, and lifted his spoon and clinked it against hers. "Bon appétit!"

She scrunched her little nose up in confusion. "What's that mean?"

"It means I hope you enjoy your food."

Her lips creased into a little frown and she dipped her spoon into her cereal to take a bite. "Me and Mommy say cheers."

Drew chuckled at the defiance he was already so familiar with but wrapped up in this much more compact person. He lifted his spoon over his bowl and waited for Grace to tap his spoon again. "All right then. Cheers."

She smiled then and sat back on her knees as she continued to eat her Cheerios. He ate his bowl as well and watched in delight.

Each time she chewed her food, she hummed at the same time. Neither one of them spoke as they ate, but instead just enjoyed the company of one another.

When they were done, he was delightfully surprised as she took both bowls to the sink. She came back then and returned the milk to the fridge.

"You can go now if you want."

He chuckled at her bossy little nature. He didn't want to leave her alone if Hannah was still sleeping. He looked at his watch. It was a few minutes before six. He'd stay with Grace a bit longer and then wake Hannah up.

"Actually, I thought I'd color with you, if that's okay?"

She jumped up and down and clapped her hands together before clasping onto one of his to lead him into the living room. She pulled him down on the floor with her and reached for a coloring book from a stack beside her. She handed it to him with a big smile on her face.

"You can have Toy Story."

"Perfect."

She placed the box of crayons between them and

returned to the picture she had previously been coloring. He watched her for a moment before pulling a brown crayon out of the box. He started working on a picture of a horse.

"That's Bullseye."

He looked down at the horse he was coloring and smiled. Grace chattered away as they completed their current pictures and started a new one.

"Hello." Hannah's tentative voice came from the doorway. Her hair was mussed, her eyes still sleepy. Grace popped up from her spot and ran to her mother, wrapping her arms around her legs in a hug.

"Mommy! You're awake!"

"Yes, and I see you are too. How come so early?" According to his watch, it was 6:30 now.

Grace lifted her arms and shrugged. "I woke up."

He rose to his feet and walked over to Hannah, bending to place a tentative kiss on her cheek. "Good morning, beautiful."

Her cheeks turned a light pink as she glanced down at Grace, nodding her head in question. "Good morning?"

"She was up when I got up at five-thirty. I didn't want to leave her alone and I wanted to let you sleep."

Grace pulled on the hem of Hannah's T-shirt to get her attention. "Mommy, me and Mr. Drew had breakfast too."

He reached out to stroke Grace's hair. "Gracie you can just call me Drew. You don't have to call me mister."

Grace looked up at her mother for confirmation, who nodded. Grace chanted, "Drew, Drew, Drew. Just Drew."

Hannah sighed. "I need coffee."

He pulled her into the hallway. "I actually do need to go

if you're up. Are we good? I'm really sorry Grace saw me. I was trying to sneak out."

"She seems totally fine with you being here." She shrugged. "Either my brain isn't awake yet, or I was being overly protective."

He looked down at the floor and then back up at Hannah, scratching his chin again. "Yeah, I think I'm just going to stay silent on this one."

Hannah's head was shaking in disbelief, but a slow smile spread across her face. "Welcome to my world, Drew. Single mothers who don't know if they are coming or going and who protect their babes like momma bears."

He took her face in his hands. "Like you said, we'll figure this all out. I just wanted to make sure you were okay with everything."

She nodded in his hands, and then he bent down to kiss her. She covered her mouth. "Morning breath."

He kissed her cheek instead. "I'll call you later."

CHAPTER
Ten

A WEEK LATER, Hannah waved goodbye to Grace one more time as Jackson's parents drove her away. They lived in one of the boroughs outside the city in a small Cape Cod style house with a large, fenced-in yard that sat on the edge of a field.

They loved having Grace for any amount of time and she loved spending time with them as well. It was a way for both of them to keep their connection to Jackson alive.

Hannah looked down at her watch. Drew would be here any moment to pick her up. Her bags were packed and she had gone to the market at lunch and purchased groceries for them to bring as well.

She was excited to spend two full days and nights with Drew. They had only spent that much time together during their weekend at Baton Timide. Hopefully this time would end differently.

She turned to head back into her apartment when a

black Mercedes SUV pulled into the alleyway. She stopped and waited as the door of the vehicle swung open and a jean-clad Drew stepped out.

A smile graced her face and she closed the distance to greet him. He cupped her cheek as placed a kiss on her lips.

"Hello, gorgeous. I missed you."

She wrapped her arms around him as he pulled her in for a hug. "You just saw me yesterday."

"That's too long. You ready to go?"

She nodded. "So ready. All my stuff is in the hallway."

He released her and they walked to the door together to retrieve her things. He took her bags and coat, insisting he carry them all, and stood by the door while she locked up. He stowed her bags in the back of the SUV and then opened the passenger door for her.

"Is this your car too?"

"It's one of the hotel's. I thought it would be more comfortable than the Jag."

She shook her head with a laugh as she climbed into the front seat. "Oh it's hard to be Andrew Sapphire."

He leaned into the car, then took her hand and placed it on his cock. It was hard and straining against his pants.

She looked up at him in surprise.

"Only every second I'm around you, Hannah Rose."

He released her hand and shut the door, securing her inside, before she could utter another word.

He opened the driver door and slid in. "Buckle up, baby. You're in for a wild ride." He looked over at her with a devilish gleam in his eye.

She pulled her seatbelt over the shift dress she wore. She startled when Drew placed his hand behind her neck and pulled her to him in a heated kiss. After several moments of tangled tongues, he broke the kiss and pulled out of the alley.

"Even one night away from you now is starting to feel too long."

She looked down at her hands in her lap, swooning. How can one sentence make me feel so wanted? Over the last week, he had come to her place for four of those nights.

They seemed to be moving into an easy routine each evening. As good as it felt, she was still a little nervous to believe in happily ever after quite so soon.

When they were on the road, Drew rested his hand on Hannah's leg. He inched the hem of the dress up, resting his hand on her bare thigh. His need to feel her seemed to match her need for his touch. She squeezed his hand softly before entwining her fingers with his.

"I'm really looking forward to spending the next couple of days with you," she said.

"Me too. It's supposed to be stormy tomorrow. It will give us the perfect excuse to be lazy all day."

"I hope by lazy, you mean stay in bed." She arched a brow.

His eyes met hers and the corners of his mouth rose. "Your wish is my command, princess."

TRAFFIC WAS heavy given it was a Friday night, and they stopped for a light dinner on the way, so it was a little after nine by the time they arrived at his house.

Hannah was impressed all over again by the high windows, clean lines and warm light that made up his home. He told her to go inside, giving her the security code to the door, as he retrieved all their belongings from the car.

She walked inside to the living room, remembering the meal they'd shared together after the masquerade ball, and a smile formed on her lips. She walked farther into the house and ran her fingers over Drew's stereo until she figured out how to turn it on and retrieve the playlists. When she found the one she wanted, she pressed play, turned the volume up loud and ran swiftly up the stairs and into his bedroom, leaving the room dark.

She raced over to the side of the bed and pulled her dress quickly over her head. She was wearing the necklace Drew had given her, and it bounced back down between her naked breasts as she dropped the dress on the floor. Next, she pulled off her shoes and slid her barely there panties off her body.

She climbed up onto the bed and, before she lost her nerve, laid her body flat, raising her hands above her head clasping onto the headboard. Then she waited.

The last time she had been in this room with Drew, things had started out like a dream and ended like a nightmare. She wanted to erase that night and create a new memory, a better memory for both of them. Was she doing the right thing, or was she pushing things too quickly?

The door slammed below, and then Drew called out to her. She didn't make a sound, but her breathing quickened in anticipation. She listened intently, trying to determine where he might be downstairs.

He called for her again from what sounded like the

library, and then his footsteps were on the stairs. Her heart beat wildly in her chest and she fought to keep her breathing controlled.

The door swung open and then Drew was silhouetted in the doorframe, illuminated by the light in the hallway. She waited, but he stood absolutely still. Finally, he slunk forward until he stood at the end of the bed.

"HOLY FUCKING SHIT, HANNAH."

Drew's eyes roamed the length of Hannah's body laid out before him. She was offering herself to him like a sacrifice.

He scrubbed his face to make sure he wasn't dreaming. From the bed, the delicate sounds of Hannah's voice reached his ears.

"I'm yours, Drew."

He couldn't contain the growl of possession that tumbled out of his mouth as his cock throbbed to life inside his jeans. He reached down and ran his fingers along the inside of Hannah's leg, widening them further. Even with the low light from the hallway, he could see that her core was glistening. *How the fuck did I get this lucky? She is perfection.*

"Are you sure about this? This room doesn't have the best memories attached to it."

Her tongue darted out to wet her lips and she nodded. "I'm sure. I want to wash away all of that with something better."

He reached down and unbuckled his belt, yanking it free from the loops. He stalked around the bed until he was standing at the head of it. "Do you trust me? Do you know I would never hurt you?"

Her head nodded up and down in the shadows.

"I need to hear you say it, Hannah."

"I trust you, Drew. Completely."

Without saying another word, he wove the belt around her wrists in a figure eight, then pulled it tight before securing it to the iron headboard.

Her chest rose and fell quickly in response, the pulse at the base of her neck beating wildly and the nipples of her small, supple breasts peaking into hard beads.

He loomed above her, wanting her to see and feel the desire he felt for her as he released the buttons on his shirt, sliding it off and dropping it to the floor.

Her tongue peeked out of her mouth and wet her lips before darting back inside her mouth. He leaned down then and kissed her roughly, splaying his hands on each side of her head for traction.

He pulled her tongue, her breath, her heat into his mouth and made it his own. He released her mouth, leaning back a fraction before licking his own tongue around her lips. He hovered over her and whispered, "Mine."

She nodded her head again and whispered back, "Yours."

His cock threatened to explode right then and there. She was his every fantasy come to life. He pushed himself off the bed and shucked his shoes and jeans.

When he was free and naked, he leaned down again. "What's your safe word?"

She blinked up at him in surprise. "Safe word?" She bit

her lower lip and then spoke barely above a whisper. "Ghost. But Drew, the last time I used—"

He placed a finger over her lips to quiet her. "That will never happen again. Never. This is just to make sure I don't push you too hard."

She nodded and Drew took his finger away, dropping a chaste kiss there instead. He walked over to his dresser and pulled something out of the top drawer. He went to the end of the bed, grasped one of her ankles and pulled her down the bed until her arms were taut above her head.

He looked at her for approval. "Okay?"

"Yes," she breathed.

He chuckled and widened her leg, using a tie to secure the ankle to the corner of the bed frame. He moved to the other side and did the same thing with another tie. He walked to the head of the bed again and sat down next to her, bending until his face was right above hers.

"Still okay?"

"Yes," she panted.

The Dominant in him stirred. "Yes what?"

Hannah's eyes widened. "Yes, Sir."

"Don't forget again or I'll punish you."

"Yes, Sir." Not a moment of hesitation. She liked this just as much as he did.

Instead of moving away from her, he rose up over her body. Bracing his weight on his knees between her legs, he splayed his hands on each side of her head. Using his tongue, he started at her lips, tracing their outline before nipping the bottom one gently to pull on it. She yipped at the bite of pain and then licked the tender spot.

He took the opportunity to suck her tongue into his

mouth until she was breathless. He released her mouth with a small pop and then trailed his tongue down her chin and to her ear.

He ran it lightly over the lobe before brushing his lips against the tiny hairs and breathing hot and heavy into her. Her body surged upward, bumping into his, but he pushed it back down into the bed.

"You are so fucking perfect." His proclamation escaping his mouth on the lightest of breaths.

He trailed his tongue down her neck and then further, until he reached her breasts. Her skin was hot, the areola of her nipples dark and taut. He laved one of her nipples, the peak growing under his attention. He dragged his tongue, hard and flat, over it again and again until she fought her bindings, moans of desperation falling from her lips.

"Please, please," she whimpered.

"Please what?" Drew growled, " what do you want, Hannah?"

Hannah wiggled, her body in search of some kind of relief."More, I want more. Please . . . I need to feel you inside me."

Drew cooed, "Soon, my kitten, soon."

His cock wasn't throbbing, it was pounding, matching the drum beat of his heart, his balls drawn up tight and hard. He needed relief as much as she did, but not yet. He moved down her between her legs and used a finger to swipe between the lips of her pussy.

"Oh, Jesus. You're so wet."

"Fuck me already," a frustrated Hannah mewled.

Drew pulled his hand back and slapped down lightly on

her clit. Hannah's hips bucked off the bed and a cry came from above.

"Fuck me already, *Sir*," Drew repeated.

Hannah's head was rocking back and forth as she dug her heels into the bed to try to push up into Drew. He clucked his tongue and slapped the inside of her thigh.

She yelped again but stilled, her body lying flat once more. Drew brought his mouth down to her core and ran his tongue up and down her pussy, sucking lightly at the juices that had built up.

Moans were falling freely from Hannah's lips now and her hands were wrapped in a tight grip around the iron bed rail, her knuckles white.

He found her clit and began teasing it, flicking his tongue back and forth over the nub, increasing the pressure until he felt her core begin to tighten. Before she could come, he pulled back and ran his tongue down the length of her leg. Hannah crying out in frustration.

"Drew, please, please fuck me. I can't take anymore."

He knew he should punish her for using his name instead of "Sir" but he wasn't sure how much longer his cock could stand it either.

He untied each of her ankles and then quickly covered her body with his, lining his cock up to her core, sliding his way home in one slow thrust.

They both moaned low at the action. Drew levered Hannah's knees up so he could drive deeper into her. He plunged into her again and again, each time slamming harder, pushing against her legs for traction. Amazingly, she took everything he gave her and begged for more.

"Harder, Drew, harder! I love when you fuck me like that!"

Drew's cock pulsed at her words and he slammed into her two more times before she began clenching around him.

"Oh yes, yes, yes! Don't stop. Please don't stop!"

He didn't have to command her to come. He knew what was coming and as her pussy tightened in a final grip around his cock, he exploded his release into her in one last hard thrust, his hands clenching her knees as they yelled in unison. He held his cock deep inside her until she relaxed, and then slid slowly out of her, releasing his hold on her limbs.

He got up on shaky legs and quickly unhooked the belt and her hands from the headboard. She lowered her arms, wincing in pain. Drew sat down beside her and massaged each one of her arms gently to restore blood flow to her muscles. She hummed her contentment as a small smile curved her lips.

He bent down and kissed her. It was soft and it was slow and it was full of love. *God, I love this woman.*

The realization slammed into him like a truck, his heart stilling in his chest, his breath leaving him as he tore his lips from hers. Her eyes flew open.

"What is it?"

"Nothing. I'm okay." *I'm so fucked.*

He had told himself he wanted this, but did she love him back? Or did she just love fucking him? Everything between them was still so tenuous.

She wrapped her arms around his neck and brought him back down to her. "More."

He shook his head in disbelief. "More? I think I'm done for a little while, you sexy minx."

His heart had begun beating again, but his brain was still foggy as he responded to her on autopilot.

She smiled up at him sweetly. "Just more of those lips please."

He smiled back at her and submitted to her request, trailing kisses over her neck, face and finally her lips. After several moments, he broke away and lay down, pulling her into his arms. He needed some time to regroup his thoughts.

"Are you cold?" he asked.

"No. I'm perfect." She scooted even closer to him.

"Yes you are. And you're also full of surprises."

She pushed her face into his chest and mumbled, as if embarrassed by her confession. "I love when you tied me up at the bungalow."

Drew's cock actually twitched at her admission. No matter what his head might be thinking, his damn cock had a mind of its own. "What else did you like?"

She shook her head quickly. "No, no more. I'm too embarrassed as it is."

He looked down at her and couldn't keep the surprise from his voice. "Embarrassed about what? Do you know what you did to me when I walked in here and found you waiting for me, splayed out on my bed? My heart fucking stopped. Stopped. I wasn't sure if what you did at Baton was for the money or because you liked it. And I didn't want to push you."

She peeked up through her lashes, speaking quietly. "I

liked everything you did to me, Drew. All of it. The spanking, tying me up, even you in my ass."

His breathing quickened as she spoke, not because he
was excited, but because she was confirming again how
much she liked having sex with him. But not a word was
about how she felt about him.

Because he didn't know what to say, he kissed her and
then pulled her into his arms so he could hold her. It wasn't
long before her breathing evened out in sleep. If only he
could get his brain to shut down now.

HANNAH WOKE SLOWLY and rolled over, finding the
bed empty. She raised her arms above her head and
stretched, feeling aches in all the right places.

She and Drew had made love once more during the
night and had also gotten up around three for some water
and a snack. She looked over at the clock on the nightstand.
How was it almost 11:00 a.m.?

Feeling guilty for oversleeping and not checking in on
Grace yet, she hopped out of bed to find her clothes and
then her phone. She smiled when she noticed that Drew had
left her bag on a stand outside the bathroom door. Sitting
on top was her purse.

She grabbed her phone and called Grace. After a ten-
minute conversation filled with happy chatter about going
to the zoo, she hung up. She threw her hair up in a tight bun
before taking a quick shower.

After dressing and fixing her hair, she applied a light

coat of lip gloss and left the bedroom to find Drew. As she reached the top of the stairs, she heard two male voices and wondered in surprise who might be here.

Drew had told her that it would be just the two of them this weekend. She padded down the stairs and made her way into the kitchen.

Drew and his brother Ben were sitting at the bar. They both stopped talking when she entered the room, a wide smile breaking across Drew's features as he stood up and greeted her.

He bent down and kissed her softly on the lips. "Good morning, sleeping beauty."

He turned and motioned toward Ben. "Look who decided to pop in for a surprise visit."

Ben stood up as well. He wasn't using a cane this time; was it more for show than for purpose? It wasn't a subject she would broach with him, especially after their last shaky encounter. He was standing in front of her now and nodded his head in greeting.

"Hannah?" He said like a question.

Her forehead scrunched in confusion, but then it clicked. She had originally been introduced to Ben as Scarlett. Had Drew told Ben how they had actually met? Oh lord, how am I going to explain this one?

She leaned forward and surprised him by pecking him on his cheek. "Ben. Nice to see you again."

He tilted his head and looked at her for a moment. "I feel like this is the first time we've met, actually. Drew hasn't told me anything except that you're Hannah, not Scarlett. But you were Scarlett."

"Scarlett O'Hara, for the masquerade ball."

She replied quickly, not even sure how she had just pulled that out of her ass. Drew's eyebrows shot up at her quick response, and then he nodded in approval. Ben, however, continued to scrutinize her.

Drew stepped between them and put an arm around her, maneuvering her to the table to sit. "Are you hungry, Hannah? Coffee maybe?"

She could feel Ben's eyes on her as she sat in the chair Drew pulled out for her, but she tried to act unaffected. "Yes, coffee would be lovely."

"Coming up." Drew pulled a mug down from the cupboard before popping a coffee pod into the brewer. When it was done, he took the peppermint mocha creamer she had brought and poured some into her cup, stirring it before placing it in front of her. As he did, he brushed a kiss against the top of her forehead and sat beside her.

Ben snatched his cup of coffee off the bar, where he and Drew had been talking, and sat across from her at the table.

She turned toward Drew and placed her hand over his. "What time did you get up?"

"I think around seven. The rain hadn't started yet so I went for a run down the beach for about an hour. When I came back, I found a message from Benny, saying he was coming out for the day."

"Sorry, I didn't realize Drew would have company. That hasn't been an issue for a long time."

I'm an issue? She shrugged off his comment and nodded instead. "No worries. We were just planning to sit around and be lazy anyway."

She hoped Drew wouldn't bring up that their definition of lazy involved a bed, but he gave her a knowing smile and kept silent. He took her hand instead and raised it to his lips, turning it to kiss her palm.

"Ben wanted to get out of the city for a few days and my secretary told him I'd come out to the house, so he headed out early this morning to beat any traffic."

A couple days? He's staying? So much for being naked and alone all weekend. She nodded and took a sip of her coffee. Ben stared at her intently. "Is something wrong?"

His forehead creased. "Sorry, I don't mean to stare. I feel like we've met before. Like I know you from somewhere."

"Well, we met at the ball. I was wearing a mask, so maybe it just feels different seeing my whole face?"

"No. It's not that." He shook his head. "It will come to me. Or maybe it's nothing. My head got banged up pretty good in my accident."

Drew punched his brother lightly on the arm. "Your head was screwed up way before that accident, Brother."

Ben snorted. "Fuck you." Then he whipped his head back to Hannah. "Sorry. Shouldn't swear like that in front of a lady. It's the soldier in me."

Hannah smiled, understanding better than he could have realized. "No apologies. My brother was in the army. Every other word out of his mouth is foul. I practically need to wash his mouth out with soap when he's with Grace."

He tilted his head. "Who's Grace?"

She hesitated for a moment. This was new territory for her. This was her first serious relationship since Jackson and she hadn't ever had to explain her situation before. Before she could speak, Drew did.

"Grace is her daughter. She's almost five. She is a beautiful, precocious clone of her mother."

Ben looked at Drew, shock evident on his face, before turning back at Hannah. "She with her dad this weekend?"

It was an innocent enough question, but one that caused her face to heat and her heart to pick up its pace.

"She's with her grand—"

"Hannah's a wido—"

So much for the simple answer. She looked at Drew, her expression turning angry, even though it made no sense to feel that way. This was her information to share if she wanted, not his.

Before she could say anything, Ben spoke quietly. "I'm sorry, Hannah. Truly."

His genuine sorrow at her loss cooled her anger and also made her feel that perhaps she had been too quick to judge Ben.

"Was he military? Overseas?" He continued, his brow raising slightly. "That's why you got so angry at me when I showed you my leg at the ball. Isn't it?"

Hannah was surprised he'd put the very few exposed pieces of her life together so quickly, but she nodded. "Yes. Yes. And yes."

He reached across the table then to place a hand over hers, his shirtsleeve stretching up to expose a forearm covered in tattoos. But the one that caught her attention again was the black rose with a gold leaf cluster that started at the base of his wrist and wound a few inches up his forearm. That damn tattoo.

Without any warning, she jumped up and pushed his shirtsleeve higher, exposing the words "Never Forget", just like she knew would be there.

Both Drew and Ben looked at her, astonishment on both

of their faces. Drew spoke first. "Hannah, what are you doing?"

Her body chilled as the blood drained from it. Her hands shook as she pointed at the tattoo. "Why do you have that?"

Ben looked up at her and then down at the tattoo, and as if lightning had struck, his expression changed to one of comprehension.

"Holy Fuck. You're Jackson's Hannah and Grace. You're Danny's sister."

CHAPTER
Eleven

"HOW DO you know Jackson and Danny?"

Hannah felt stupid for even asking the question. It was obvious they must have served together.

"And why do you have that tattoo? Danny has the same tattoo over his heart. He got it to honor Jackson after he was killed."

Ben stared at her wide-eyed, apparently still stunned at his own discovery, before looking down and running his finger over the tattoo. "I served with them both in Iraq. Jackson and I were in the same unit. We were together in the Humvee when we struck that IED."

Hannah pushed her chair back and started pacing, wringing her hands together as she tried to put the new pieces of this puzzle together.

She spun back around and threw her hands up in the air. "How come I never met you? All of Jackson's unit came to his funeral. And Danny has never mentioned you."

Ben glanced down at his leg and then back up at her. "I

should have come to the funeral. I should have. I'm sorry. I just couldn't see beyond myself and my own pain then. I was still in the hospital when I heard that Black Jack—" He looked up at her again and frowned. "Sorry, that's what we all called him. He won enough money beating us at poker to feed half a country."

He laughed then. The hollow sound just stoked her anger higher. She shook her head as if it to clear the emotions swirling in it.

Drew stood up from his chair and tried to wrap his arms around her, but she shrugged him away. He reeled back, surprise etched on his face. "Hannah, I just want to help."

She looked at him, dumfounded. "And, just how do you think you're going to help me, Drew? You think a hug is going to make this all right?"

Drew gripped one of her hands. "I don't understand why you're so upset. Isn't it a good thing if you found someone who knew your husband and can share things with you about him?"

She shook her head again and let out a small disgusted laugh before looking at Drew. "You really don't get it, do you?"

She wrenched her hand away from Drew's grasp and stormed over to where Ben was still sitting, eyes downcast.

"You know why I'm mad, don't you Ben?"

He pushed his chair back and stood, then sighed, "You think it's my fault he got killed."

She shoved his chest with both hands as she yelled, "It is your fault!"

Ben took two stumbling steps backward and looked like he was going to lose his balance, but grabbed the back of a chair, righting himself before falling. At the same time, Drew reached out and pulled her back and away from Ben, but she twisted free and turned to glare at him.

"Don't, Drew."

"Hannah, you're angry. I get it. Sit down so we can discuss this more calmly."

She scoffed, raking her hands through her hair in frustration. "I don't want to be calm, Drew. I'm pissed. Don't you get it? If your darling brother hadn't made my husband feel guilty for not being injured, he would still be here with me today. My daughter would have a father. The man I love would still be here and my life would be perfect."

As soon as the words left her mouth, a look of such hurt and devastation crossed Drew's face, instantly fueling her with regret. She didn't want to hurt Drew. She cared deeply about him too.

She took a quick step forward and pulled his hand into both of hers. "Drew, I'm sorry. I didn't mean it like that."

Drew stood before her, his head tilted, eyes crinkled in his examination of her, as if he wasn't sure who she was. He slipped his hand out from between hers. He took two steps back away from her, still silent, still staring at her. Her anger at Ben was temporarily forgotten as panic rose up and claimed her nerves.

"Drew, please. Don't look at me like that." She took two steps toward him to gain the ground she had lost, but he countered again and just shook his head, holding a palm out flat.

She raised her hands up to her sides, palms up, trying to open herself up to him. Seeing him look at her like this and knowing she could lose him made her realize just how much she had come to care for him. *Am I in love with him?*

She stepped toward him again, more confused than ever. "I'm sorry. I'm so sorry. I lost my temper."

"Hannah—" he started, but then he exhaled, rubbing at the stubble on his chin. "Hannah, just stop for a minute."

She cocked her head to the side. "Stop?"

"Yes, stop. Stop yelling, stop making assumptions. Just let Ben talk, for Christ's sake."

The words were like gasoline on the simmering flame of her anger. "Let Ben talk?"

Her voice dripped with sarcasm before turning quieter. "He's had over two years to come and talk to me. Two years. Why didn't he?"

"Hannah, don't you thin—"

"She's right." Ben interrupted.

Both she and Drew gawked at him. Ben met her gaze. "You're right."

He let go of the chair and took a couple steps closer. His voice was firm, but it was low and apologetic. "I should have come to see you. A long time ago. Maybe I could have saved you some of the pain you still feel."

Tears started to roll in slow trails down her cheeks. She smiled wryly through them. "I'm always going to feel that pain. You can't fix that."

She brushed aside the tears, angry for letting them fall at all. A small, sardonic grin fell on her lips and she shook her head before addressing Ben again. "You got the last of him. You know that?"

His eyebrows furrowed in confusion.

"He went to see you every day in that hospital when he

came home for the funerals. He spent every day with you. Grace was less than a year old, and it was as if she didn't exist for him anymore. He barely came home, and when he did, he wouldn't even look at me. He gave everything he had left, to you. After that, he gave everything to his men. And I was left with nothing."

She wasn't yelling anymore; she was just sad. Sad that this man was the reason her husband was dead. Sad that Jackson had chosen this man over her. And even sadder that he was Drew's brother. There was no way to escape him and the feelings he exposed if she wanted to stay with Drew.

At this last thought, she turned and looked at Drew, utter grief engulfing her. "I want to go home."

She turned and before either of the men could say a word, she ran from the room and up the stairs to the bedroom. She grabbed her bag and flung it on the bed, quickly stuffing her belongings into it.

Just as she zipped it up, the bedroom door flew open and Drew stalked in, his face pinched and hard.

"Hannah, what the fuck are you doing?" He grabbed each of her arms, turning her toward him.

She hung limply in his grasp, all strength having left her system when she understood what she needed to do.

"I'm leaving. Can I take your car? Can you go back with your brother?" She didn't even want to say his name.

He bent down so that his face was even with hers. "What do you mean, you're leaving?"

Her head swung back and forth, her hair swishing over her shoulders from the motion. "I have to go. I can't stay here. This is all wrong now."

His grip around her arms tightened, but she didn't fight him. She deserved this for what she was about to do to him.

"I can't be with you, Drew. Not after this. I will never be able share a space with your brother, and I won't make you choose between us."

"Hannah, no!" He shook her lightly and then yanked her body against his, wrapping his arms around her tightly.

She didn't reciprocate. She left her arms dangling loosely by her sides. If she reached around and hugged him, she wouldn't be able to let go.

His breath was hot against her ear as he pleaded with her. "I just got you back. I'm not losing you again. We can figure this out."

She squeezed her arms up between them and pushed out of his hold. Tears were rolling freely down her cheeks, leaving large wet droplets on her sweater. Pieces of her hair were stuck to her face where Drew had hugged her, but she made no motion to wipe them away. "Please, just let me go. It's too much."

"It's not too much. Let me talk to Ben. He can leave. You and I will figure this out. Please, Hannah."

She turned away and grabbed her bag off the bed. He tried to pull it from her, but she held on firmly and looked up at him with desperation in her eyes. "Please . . . please don't make this any harder for me. I can't be with you."

Her words finally seemed to sink in as Drew released his hold on the bag and staggered back two steps, his face pale, his mouth open in shock.

Before she could change her mind and before Drew could try and stop her again, she sprinted out of the room and down the stairs. She found the Mercedes's key hanging on a hook by the front door and grabbed it as she escaped out into the rain and sleet.

DREW WATCHED her run out of the bedroom and felt his knees give out from under him as he fell back onto the bed. This bedroom was like a goddamn curse.

Every time she left him, it was in this fucking room. He had an urge to burn the house down so he could remove it from the equation, but when he heard the front door slam shut, he bolted up. All thoughts about the house vanished.

Was she actually going to leave? His question was answered when the engine of a car roared to life, making him bolt out the room and down the stairs. He flung open the front door and ran down the driveway, watching as the Mercedes pulled out into the street and sped away.

"Fuck!" He kicked at the loose gravel and threw his hands up in the air, screaming again. "God damn fucking fuck!"

He spun around and stormed back into the house, slamming the door behind him so hard the glass rattled in its pane. He stomped toward the kitchen. "Ben? Where the fuck are you?"

He twisted around as a voice called out from behind him. "Upstairs."

Drew took the stairs two at a time and strode down the hallway to the guest bedroom. The door was open and Ben was moving his stuff from the dresser into a small duffel. "I'm leaving, don't worry."

"Good, I'm going with you. Hannah took my car."

He turned to leave the room so he could grab what few things he had brought with him, but Ben's hand stopped him. He shifted back around to look at his brother. "What?" Impatience dripped from his voice.

Ben dropped his hand from his arm. "I'm sorry. I don't know what the fuck just happened."

"The woman I'm in love with just left me. That's what the fuck just happened."

Ben staggered, transferring his weight to his good leg. "You love her?"

Drew's eyes lowered. He had actually said it out loud. "Yeah, I guess I do."

"Okay. I'll be ready in five minutes."

"Good. I just have to grab a couple things and I'll meet you downstairs."

Fifteen minutes later, Drew and Ben had locked up the house, loaded their bags into the trunk of the car and were backing into the street.

The weather was shitty. It was sleeting more than it was raining and he hoped that Hannah was driving carefully. He was thankful she was in the more solid SUV, not the Jaguar he'd left in Manhattan.

He pulled out his cell and tried to call her, but after two rings it went to voicemail. That goddamn stubborn woman had just declined his call.

He didn't want her to text and drive but he also wanted her to know he wasn't letting her slip out of his grasp that easily. He sent a quick message.

On my way to you.

The message was received and then read, but after

several minutes with no reply back, he put the phone in his pocket with a sigh of frustration. In the driver's seat, Ben stared intently ahead.

"Did you know?" Drew had to know the answer.

Ben turned to him for a second, eyes dark, before looking back at the road. "Know what?"

"Did you know who she was?"

Ben shook his head and huffed. "Seriously, Drew? What kind of person do you take me for? Of course I didn't know. Not until she asked about the tattoo. Not until she said her brother had the same tattoo, did the pieces click together. Only three of us got this tattoo. Me, Danny and Tyler. And Tyler lives in California."

Drew nodded in understanding but still needed more answers. Not only for himself, but for Hannah. "Why didn't you go see her? She's right, you know. It's been over two years since your accident."

Ben's knuckles tightened around the steering wheel and his breathing increased. He was silent for several long minutes before he spoke. "You know what it was like for me. When they made the decision to take my leg."

Ben's grip loosened and then his hands stretched out flat as he banged them several times on the top of the wheel.

"When I found out Jack had been killed, I felt like I was in that explosion all over again. And I felt like a failure. I couldn't even get out of bed without help, could barely take a piss without getting it all over myself. I was a fucking mess. I felt so goddamn helpless. And angry. Angry that I wasn't there to help him. Angry that I was still alive and everyone else kept fucking dying without me."

Drew remembered that time well. He'd gone to visit Ben

in the hospital almost every day after they'd taken his leg, and every visit had been hell. Ben wouldn't talk to him, and he had refused to speak to anyone that wanted to help him. Things had been really dark for a long time. So dark that no one had been that surprised when Ben took a bottle of Vicodin one night.

He had already lost one sibling, and he thanked God every day that Ben hadn't died. Something had changed in him after that, and he'd slowly emerged from the dark place he'd been in and begun quietly learning how to live again with his new body.

"I remember, Ben." Drew whispered.

"I couldn't help her then. And when I was finally feeling whole again, it felt like too much time had passed, and I couldn't bring myself to go and see her. I figured she would have moved on by then and I didn't want to make things harder on her. Danny said she was doing okay, and I believed him."

Drew studied him intently for a moment before challenging him. "You mean, you didn't want to make things any harder on you by going to see her."

Ben's grip clenched and unclenched around the steering wheel a few times before he finally responded. "Maybe, maybe. But I'm telling you right now, I never told Jack to go back. Never. I told him to stay."

The rest of the drive was spent in tense silence. Drew tried calling Hannah several more times, but each time he went straight to voicemail.

The traffic going back into the city was almost nonexistent due to the weather, and Ben's confident driving had them back in under two hours.

"Do you want to go to the hotel?"

"No, take me to her place. It's on Third, closer to Thirty-Ninth Street."

Ben turned the car in that direction. Drew told him to pull into the alley when they reached her shop several moments later. Her van was there, but he didn't see the Mercedes.

It was just before three, so the shop was still open. He opened the car door, stepped out, then bent down. "Wait here."

He walked into the shop, the familiar bell tinkling as the door pulled open, and looked around. No one. "Hello?"

A second after he called out, a woman appeared from the doorway at the back of the shop. He recognized her as the woman who had walked in on him and Hannah the day he had finally confronted her.

She walked toward him, and recognition crossed her features as she got closer. Then her brows creased in question. "What are you doing here? Aren't you and Hannah supposed to be in the Hamptons?"

Drew ignored her question and asked his own instead. "So, Hannah's not here?"

"Um, no. I thought she was with you." She put her hands on her hips, attitude starting to make its way into her posture. "Did you do something to Hannah?"

He sighed in frustration. "Listen, just tell her I came by and to call me."

Without waiting for her to respond and dreading the possibility of the third degree, he turned and left as abruptly as he had entered, running back to Ben's waiting car.

"Was she there?"

"Nope. Maybe she stopped somewhere?"

Ben shrugged. "Maybe."

"Let's just go to the hotel. I'll come back later if I don't hear from her soon."

Ben backed the car out of the alley and made it to the hotel in ten minutes. They pulled up to the valet and put the car in park. "You want me to come in with you?"

Drew stared out the windshield. "Look, it's the Mercedes. She's here."

He jumped out of the car and flew into the hotel, looking for the valet. He found him just inside, one of the regulars Drew knew by name.

"Mr. Sapphire. Welcome back. Bad weather bring you back early?"

"Bobby, hi. The SUV outside? Where did the woman go that was driving it?"

Bobby's face broke out in a grin as he walked over to the valet desk. "Oh yes, sir. The woman that dropped it off said to give these keys to you when you returned. She didn't stay though. I put her in a cab."

"A cab?" *Shit, she's not here.*

"Yes, sir."

"Did you get the address where she was going?"

Bobby shook his head. "No, sir. She didn't give me one. I'm sorry."

"How long ago?"

Bobby pulled up the sleeve of his coat to look at his watch. "Maybe fifteen minutes ago?"

"Fuck!"

Bobby shrank back at Drew's outburst. "I'm sorry, sir."

Drew ran a frustrated hand through his hair. "No, no, it's not your fault. Thank you."

Ben was walking into the hotel then, Drew's bag in hand. They met midway and Ben handed over the bag. "Anything?"

He scowled. "Nope. She dropped off the car about fifteen minutes ago and left in a cab. Not sure where."

"Back to the shop?"

"I don't know. I'll go back there in a little bit if she doesn't answer my call."

Ben clapped him on the shoulder. "You going to be okay?"

Drew looked at his brother and nodded. "I will be. As soon as I find her."

Where the fuck was she?

CHAPTER
Twelve

HANNAH CLIMBED into the back of the cab and told the driver to just drive. She didn't want to go back to the shop or the apartment for fear that Drew would come looking for her. She wasn't expected back at the shop until Monday, so she had two days to try and pull herself together.

She looked down at her phone again as it buzzed. Drew trying to reach her again. She hit the decline button and wiped away the stray tear falling from her eye.

"Do you have somewhere you want to go, miss?"

"Can you just drive for a little bit? Maybe through the park?"

The driver nodded in acknowledgement.

"Thank you."

She didn't know where to go. For the thousandth time since she'd left Drew's house, she wondered what the hell had happened.

How? How was it possible that out of the million men in

Manhattan, she'd gone and fallen in love with the one man whose brother was the reason her husband was dead?

And she loved Drew. It took her having to walk away from him to realize it, but she did. She loved him. But she also knew seeing Ben would be a constant reminder of her husband's loss.

How did she balance the two? She didn't know how. And she absolutely refused to make Drew choose between her and his brother. She knew how much his brother meant to him, especially after already losing his sister.

She had lived without his love before and would survive this and manage to do it again. That thought squeezed her heart and a small sob escaped her throat.

This is why she shouldn't have opened herself up to love again. In the end, there was always just so much pain. She rested her head against the cool glass of the window and watched the scenery in the park slide by. Even in the rain, people were out jogging and walking hand in hand with loved ones, huddled together under umbrellas. She ached, knowing she had lost the very thing she had feared most, but ultimately found anyway.

They had been driving around the park in circles for about forty minutes when the driver spoke again. "Miss, you're at forty dollars. Do you want to keep driving?"

They were near the center of the park. Light rain was still falling. "I'll get out here please."

The car slowed and came to a stop at the side of the road. She handed the driver a fifty and told him to keep the change, taking her bag and moving to leave the car.

"You going to be okay?" He was an older gentleman and had probably seen his fair share of women crying in the back of his cab before, but his concern was no less sincere.

She nodded, grateful. "Yes, I'll be okay, thank you."

He just nodded in return and turned back around in his seat. She shut the door and gripped her bag tightly in one hand as she began to walk through the park.

She was wearing a peacoat without a hood, her face and hair bare to the fine mist. She didn't mind. The cool air was refreshing on her warm, tear-streaked face.

Her mind wandered as she walked and she thought back on her time with Drew. From her first stolen glimpse of him from the stage at Baton Timide, to walking on the beach outside his lovely home. From dancing in his living room, to just lying in his arms less than twelve hours before.

How quickly life could change. She knew that, of course. After losing Jackson, she knew how unpredictable and unfair life could be.

Ben. He was the one. The one that had stolen the last bit of time she'd had with Jackson. The one who'd made him go back and avenge the deaths of their lost friends. The one who'd ripped her life away.

What would life with Jackson have been like if he had never gone back to Iraq? It was strange. When she thought of her future now, she could only picture Drew.

Exhaustion overwhelmed her as she reached the edge of the park and made her way out to the street. A bench sat against the high stone wall that surrounded the park, and even though it was sopping wet, she collapsed onto it.

She shifted the bag to her lap, clutching it like a life preserver. She stared ahead at nothing, unable to process anything more. The sky was darkening. She wondered if anyone mind if she just stayed here on this bench for the night?

DREW PACED BACK and forth in his suite at the hotel, his pulse in overdrive at not being able to find Hannah.

He had called her several more times, leaving messages pleading for her to call him, and had also gone back to the shop but to no avail. Telling Drew to call him if he could help, Ben had gone back to his place about an hour ago .

Not sure what else to do with his restless energy, he went down to his office to see if he could find something to keep his mind busy. Instead of taking the elevator, he took the stairs, emerging into a very empty office space. It was late on a Saturday, and the few people that may have come in for the day were long gone.

He walked into his office, choosing not to turn on the overhead lights, and sat in his chair in the dark. He checked his phone again, just in case. Still nothing.

He spun around and let his gaze wander outside. It was still raining, and people darted in and out of cabs, or walked hurriedly down the sidewalk, scrunched under umbrellas, the collars of their jackets turned up high to keep dry.

His eyes drifted to a lone person sitting on a bench next to the entrance to the park. His heart stilled. There she was. Sitting there, clutching her bag, wet hair falling forward over her bowed head. Hannah.

He jumped out of his chair and ran for the elevator, punching the call button furiously, willing it to come more quickly. The elevator finally dinged, announcing its arrival, and then the doors slid open.

He stepped in and hit the button for the lobby, praying it didn't stop at any other floors on the way down. When it finally came to a stop, he surged through the doors as they slid free and he ran to the side exit of the hotel that faced the park.

She was still sitting there in the same exact position. He looked both ways, checking the street before darting across, dodging an oncoming car, its horn blaring, and reaching the other side.

He knelt down in front of her on the bench. Her whole body was shivering and she was soaked from head to toe. He touched her knees through her wet jeans.

"Hannah?" He kept his voice soft and gentle, as if he were speaking to a child. Tears were running from her eyes, but she didn't move, nor did she speak. He brought his hands up to her arms and shook her gently. "Hannah?"

This time her eyes did move, but when she tried to speak, gibberish poured from her lips. At a loss, he scooped her up in his arms. She fell into him like a limp noodle, whimpering dully. He strode back across the street and into the lobby of the hotel.

George was suddenly rushing up in front of him, concern etching his features. "Mr. Sapphire? Is that Hannah? What happened? What can I do to help?"

He didn't slow down, walking past George and toward the elevator. "Can you just put the security code in for my apartment? My hands are kind of full."

His arms were starting to ache. George scurried in behind him on the elevator and quickly typed in the code for Drew's suite. He backed out again before the doors could close and tipped his head at Hannah.

"Just call me if you need anything at all."

Drew thanked him as the door slid closed and the elevator started its ascent. Hannah was shivering furiously in his arms, her head lolling up against his chest each time he moved, but she still hadn't said a single word.

When the doors slid open, he walked straight through the suite and into his bedroom, gently setting her down on the bed. She remained in a sitting position, but her head hung as limp as her wet, tangled hair.

He unbuttoned her coat and slid it off her. It had been useless against the rain, and her sweater underneath was as soaked as the rest of her. How long was she sitting out there? He continued to undress her, then scooped her naked body up in his arms again and walked to the bathroom.

He turned on the water in the shower and waited for it to get hot, then stepped in, holding Hannah close to him in his arms. He was still fully clothed, but his only concern at the moment was getting her warm. When the hot water hit her skin, she cried out like she had been whipped and curled her body further into his.

"Shhh, Hannah. I need to warm you up." He spoke softly into her ear and set her down on the bench seat at the end of the shower. He turned on the manual shower head and moved it over her hair and skin.

He reached for a sponge on the ledge and used it to rub her skin in small circles, trying to get her circulation moving again. She moaned and her head fell back against the tile, her eyes closing tightly.

He continued to speak quietly, trying to comfort and

assure her she would be okay. When her body had turned back to a normal pink and its touch was warm again, he shut the water off. He pulled a large towel off the rack and wrapped it around her.

Before stepping out of the shower, he peeled off his wet clothes and left them in a pile. He grabbed another towel and wrapped it tightly around his waist before moving back to Hannah.

He scooped her up again and carried her back to his bed. He reached down and awkwardly pulled back the covers before sliding her in between them. He laid her down flat and pulled the damp towel from around her body before pulling the covers tight around her. He walked around to the other side of the bed and dropped the towel from his waist before sliding in next to her, wrapping his arms around her and pulling her close.

She didn't resist. She melted into him as a soft whimper left her. His heart broke into a million pieces for the pain she was feeling. Everything he wanted was right here in his arms, yet she was so far away.

He would fix this. If it was the last thing he did, he would make her realize that their love could conquer anything.

WHY AM I SO HOT? She tried to roll over but found herself wrapped up tight in a pair of strong arms and legs. Her eyes shot open as she remembered the hazy events of the night before.

Rain, wet and cold. Drew lifting her up. Hot, burning streams of water pinging her skin and then circles of softness warming her. Covers sliding over her and then heat, hot and pliant against her skin before she fell unconscious. She had somehow ended up in his arms, in his bed.

She tried to pull herself out of his embrace, but he moaned and tightened his hold on her. His head nuzzled into the back of her head and she felt his breath, hot and steady before his lips pressed against the back of her neck.

"You're not leaving," he crooned against her neck, the vibration of his lips raising goose bumps across her body. He continued kissing her neck, brushing his nose against her hair to nudge it out of the way and then moving his lips back again.

"Drew, stop," she protested, but her body betrayed her and rocked back against him, her core already throbbing at the simple pleasure his lips brought her.

One arm loosened around her center and trailed up her side. His hand cupped her breast and slowly caressed it, his fingers plucking her nipple as it hardened.

She let out a soft sigh and gave in to his touch. As her body relaxed, his hold around her slackened. He pushed his hard member up against the cleft in her ass, never stopping his attentions to her breast or the small kisses he kept raining on her neck, her shoulders, her back. She arched into him and wrapped an arm around his head, turning back to meet his lips with hers.

He kissed her then. Torturously slow, his lips brushed against hers with the lightest touch, his tongue tracing the outline of her lips and then sliding inside to tease. She surged back, fusing their lips together, wanting to taste all of him. She inhaled deeply, taking his breath into her as if she needed it to survive.

His hand clasped her face, holding her to him, while the other one adjusted his cock behind her and then slid it into her wet pussy. A moan rolled out of her mouth and into his as he thrust forward, and she fisted his hair.

He released his hold on her breast and slid down between her legs until he found the hard hood of her clit. She bucked as he rubbed his finger against it, his dick slamming into her harder.

He stroked her clit back and forth, his finger in sync with his cock plunging in and out of her. With each thrust, his cock throbbed larger inside her. His mouth was against her ear and his breath was heated as he began whispering.

"I'm never letting you go, Hannah. Ever. You're mine. I own you. I own your body. I own your love."

He drove into her harder and harder and her body began the familiar climb toward orgasm he brought her to every time. Her only response was to nod frantically as she felt herself getting ready to detonate.

On the next thrust, he pinched her clit between his fingers and she shattered into a tiny million particles of light. Her body tightened and she chanted, "Yours, yours, yours," over and over again. Then Drew's release burst inside of her, and his grip around her tightened before he let out one more strangled word: "Mine."

As she came down from the high his touch gave her, reality washed over her like a bucket of cold water. He was trying to pull her snug against him again, but this time she wrestled free and sat up. She turned to face him and the look of shock on his face.

"I should go. This shouldn't have happened. I'm sorry."

"No." His expression morphed to one of anger as he sat up as well. "We are not doing this again."

She closed her eyes, trying to force her heart to stop beating so wildly, before opening them again. She brushed a loose strand of hair falling across his lashes back against his forehead.

"Drew, this didn't change anything that happened yesterday. This situation is just too much."

He took her hand in his and pressed it flat against his chest over his heart. "Do you feel this?"

She could feel the strong pulse of his heart under her hand and nodded. "Yes."

"It beats only for you now. If you leave, if you go, I don't know how to keep it beating, how to keep breathing."

"Drew, please," she begged, drawing her hand away. "Please don't make me do this all over again."

"Then don't." His voice firm before turning soft at his next declaration. "I love you."

Her body stiffened at his words. "What?"

"I'm in love with you. And I think you love me too."

Instant denial forced her lips into a frown. "It doesn't matter anymore. Ben is your brother. And I can't make you walk away from him. I can't. He's your brother. You've only known me three months."

Drew raked his hand through his hair. "I'll keep you two apart. Or we'll talk together and figure this out. He said he didn't ask your husband to go back."

Her pulse raced again. "What?"

"I don't know." He shook his head. "He just told me that he didn't ask him to go back."

Hannah let out a deep sigh and stood. "This is all just too weird. Of all the people I could have ended up with, and then to find out about this connection your brother has to my husband."

"He's gone, Hannah. You have to move forward." His tone was hardening with anger.

"How can I move forward if every time I see you, I think of Ben, and then I think of Jackson and that maybe he should be here instead? That's not fair to you!"

Drew's head dropped into his hands as he growled in frustration. "Goddamn it, Hannah. How many more excuses are you going to find to push yourself away from me? First it's your daughter, then I spend too much on you, then I treat you too much like a sub, and now it's your dead husband."

Time to move this along. Where were her clothes? She saw her jeans and rose to pull them out of the damp heap beside the bed.

Drew jumped out of the bed and yanked the jeans out of her hands. "You are not running away again. If I have to lock you up and keep you here, I will."

She tugged at the sodden denim in his grasp. "Fuck you. You can't keep me prisoner. Give me my damn pants."

"No."

She looked at him, so angry she could scream, and stalked around him. She jerked open drawers in his dresser until she found what she was looking for. She pulled out a pair of sweats pants and threw them on before he could stop her. Her hands were shaking as she pulled out a T-shirt next.

"Who the fuck do you think you are, Drew? You think you can tell me what to do? How I choose to live my life?"

He dropped her jeans on the floor and parked in front of her. "I am the man that's in love with you. I'm telling you not to throw this away because you're scared. I want you to choose to live your life with me. I love you, Hannah. I want to spend the rest of my life with you. With Grace. Maybe make another little Grace. Don't you get that? You own me."

She stilled, every frantic muscle in her body frozen in astonishment. "What?"

He took her face into his hands and pulled her close. "I love you so much it fucking hurts. I can't imagine a world without you in it."

Anger taking over, she wrenched away from him, looking around the room. *Where the fuck were her shoes?*

"I can't believe you're going to say this to me now. Now! Why not two days ago? Before you thought you were going to lose me? I can't hear your words of desperation. I can't believe them."

She found her wet shoes and bag and grabbed them as she dashed to the elevator.

"Hannah, stop."

"Stop?" she replied sarcastically as she mashed the elevator button.

Drew stomped after her. "Yes, stop. Stop being scared. Stop being so angry. Stop loving Jackson. Please."

The elevator dinged and the doors slid open. She stepped inside, Drew coming to a halt at the threshold.

"Fuck you, Drew."

CHAPTER
Thirteen

DREW DROPPED TO HIS KNEES, his fist punching the door, his heart plummeting to the ground with the elevator. He realized as his bare knees slammed against the cold marble that he was still naked.

He'd thought he had her back when she didn't resist him this morning, but he had only been fooling himself. And now she was gone and he had no idea how he was going to get her back again.

She truly believed this couldn't be fixed, but he would find a way. It wasn't going to happen on his knees though, so he pushed himself up and walked back into the bedroom.

He found his phone and dialed. It rang only once before Ben's strong voice answered. "Drew."

"Can I come over?"

"I'm in the middle of something, so give me an hour?"

"Okay. See you then."

The line went silent. They'd never required a lot of words between them. He wanted to call Hannah so badly, but for once, he listened to his head, not his heart, and took a shower instead.

He was assaulted with thoughts of her in the bathroom, still a mess from caring for her the night before. The scent of her lingered in the room, and his clothes still lay in a damp pile on the floor. He scooped them all up and threw them in a clothes hamper in the closet.

He turned the water on and, without waiting for it to heat up, stepped in and washed away the sour coating this morning's events had left on his skin.

After scrubbing his skin raw, he just stood under the shower head, letting the water run over him until he felt like a wet, pruny sponge.

He finally shut the water off, stepped out, dried off and walked to the closet to pull on some clothes. He was moving mechanically, no feeling, no emotion. All he wanted was to get out of this suite.

Every room he walked into smelled like her. It had only been a half hour and he'd probably arrive at Ben's early, but he didn't care. He grabbed a jacket and his phone and took the elevator down to the lobby.

He checked his phone on the way down to see if Hannah had called or texted, not that he expected she would have. There was nothing.

The valet brought his Jag around and he got in the car and sped off. Fifteen minutes later he pulled up in front of Ben's converted warehouse in SoHo. He was shocked to actually find a parking space less than a block from Ben's place and he pulled into it gratefully. He got out and was surprised to find Ben walking toward him.

As Ben approached, his eyes scanned Drew. "You look like shit."

He scoffed. "I feel like shit."

"Take it things didn't go well."

Drew stuffed his hands in his jacket pockets to warm them from the cold. "Things went to hell in a hand basket."

"Can you eat? I'm hungry as hell and there's a place around the corner I like."

Drew shrugged. "Whatever you want."

"It's this way." Ben walked past Drew and headed back in the direction his car had been parked. Ten minutes later they were walking through the doors of The Cupping Room.

It was crowded, but it was obvious Ben was a regular when the waitress greeted him by name and gave him the first table that opened up. They sat down and two steaming cups of coffee were sitting in front of them in seconds.

"She doesn't want to see me again. I told her I loved her and she told me to fuck off." His soul resembled the liquid sitting in the cup in front of him. He cupped his hands around the mug. At least it didn't feel as cold as his heart right now.

Ben's good foot kicked him under the table.

"What the fuck?" He barked, glaring up at Ben.

"A part of her life that she thought she had come to terms with just came crashing down around her. She's pissed." Ben stopped talking as a waitress came over to take their order. He ordered the special but Drew waved her off.

"I understand that, Ben, but none of it's my fault. She won't even try to figure something out."

"Listen, Drew, if there's one thing I know about, it's

anger. Nothing you say to her right now is going to change how she's feeling. You're just going to have to give her some space to digest everything."

"And what do I do in the meantime?"

"You wait brother."

Drew ran a hand through his hair and blew out a breath. "Waiting fucking sucks."

HANNAH RINSED another dish and placed it in the strainer as she watched Grace and Emma play in her sister's backyard. Tammy brought another bowl in from the dining room and set it on the counter.

"I love having everyone over for Thanksgiving, but this part blows."

"What are you complaining about? I'm the one washing all these dishes."

Tammy grabbed a dry towel and started wiping. "May I remind you that I did do all the cooking."

"But look at all the beautiful flowers I brought to decorate."

"Are you two arguing again?" They both turned their heads as Danny walked in and tore the towel out of Tammy's hand. "Go watch football with your husband. I'll do this."

"Okay, I won't argue with that." She stuck her tongue out at Hannah and giggled as she escaped the kitchen.

"You've been pretty quiet today. Everything okay?" He

took a dish out of the strainer and picked up where Tammy had left off.

She hadn't seen much of her brother in the last month. She hadn't spoken to him about Drew, but Tammy had filled him in on some of the details. "Danny, can I ask you something about Jackson?"

"Of course, you know that. Anything." He came to stand next to her.

"Did he talk to you about going back? After the accident? After the funerals?"

He shifted, leaning back against the counter, folding his arms at his chest. "We talked about a lot of things, but he didn't want to talk about that. I tried to get him to withdraw his request for another tour, but he told me he had already made the decision to go back before he had even come home. He did say that the accident only made it more clear that he was still needed over there."

The dish she was washing slipped from her fingers and fell with a clank into the soapy water. "What?"

"What?" His expression was one of confusion.

"What do you mean he decided to go back before? Before the accident?"

His head tilted. "Yeah. Didn't you know that?"

She threw her hands up in the air, soap suds flinging in different directions. "How would I know that? He barely spent any time with us when he was home then. He had promised me he was coming home after the last tour. I thought he signed back up because of the accident!"

He unfolded his arms and hauled her into an embrace. "Hannah, I'm sorry. I thought you knew that. I didn't realize."

She rested her head against his chest and blew out a tired breath. A thousand thoughts were running through her mind, but number one was that Ben wasn't the reason her husband had reenlisted. "I've made such a mess of things."

Her brother pushed her back and looked down at her. "What things? Why are you asking me about this now? It's been over two years."

She took the dish towel that was sitting on the counter and dried her hands before sitting at the kitchen table. "How come you've never mentioned Ben Sapphire to me?"

A frown appeared as sat beside her. "How do you know Ben?"

"Tammy told you about Drew?"

He nodded. "She told me you were dating a rich guy named Drew but that you had a falling out and to be extra nice to you today. That's about it."

She shook her head at her sister's overview of events. "His name is Drew Sapphire." She flashed a wry smile. "Ben's brother."

He shrugged, still not connecting the dots. "Okay, and?"

She rolled her eyes in frustration. "Do you know how I figured out Ben knew Jackson?" She pointed at the area above her brother's heart. "The tattoo. He has it on his arm."

His eyes grew wide as he finally put things together. "Jesus, it really is a small world, isn't it?"

She shook her head and muttered, more to herself than to him, "You have no idea."

"But I don't understand what's wrong. Ben's a good guy. He was pretty messed up after the accident though."

"I know. His leg. All that. But how come you never told

me about him? I mean, you obviously have a bond if you all share a tattoo together."

He looked down at his hands. "I don't know. A few reasons, I guess. Like I said, he was a mess after that accident. There was no way he could go to Jackson's funeral. When he heard what happened to Jackson, he tried to kill himself. He never said it was because of Jackson, but I think it was the last straw for him."

"Wait, he took that overdose because of Jackson?"

He cocked his head at her. "How'd you know it was an overdose?"

"Jesus, Danny. Are you listening? He is Drew's brother. Drew told me, but I thought it was before."

"I was the one who went to the hospital and told him about Jackson. He overdosed that night." He shook his head, dragging a hand down his face. "Want to talk about feeling responsible?"

"Why didn't you tell me any of this? I should have known."

He spoke quietly then. "Hannah, you were a mess. When you disappeared after the funeral—"

He reached out then and took one of her hands in his. "When we got you back, when you got home again, the last thing you needed was to deal with another soldier in pain. I wasn't going to do that to you."

Realization made her voice tremble. "Danny, I blamed him for Jackson. For everything. For going back. For his dying. For leaving us. I thought he was the one that told Jackson to go back. That he had talked him into reenlisting."

He squeezed her hand. "Then we'll go see him and you can talk to him."

She swallowed hard. "It's also the reason I told Drew I couldn't be with him. I said awful things to him. To both of them."

"Then you'll talk to both of them."

"What if he won't see me? What if I can't fix it?"

He shrugged, letting go of her hand. "There's only one way to find out."

HANNAH EYED the big brick warehouse in SoHo as Danny turned into a parking lot across the street. "Must be nice to be neighbors with Justin Timberlake and Jay Z".

He raised an eyebrow. "Don't judge a book by its cover, Sis."

"What does that mean?" They were walking across the street toward the entrance of the building.

"You'll see." A knowing smile split his face.

When they walked through the front door of the building, she paused to take everything in. The entire first floor of the warehouse had been converted into a gym and rehabilitation center. There were several men, and a few women, all disabled in some way scattered throughout the gym, working out. Some were being assisted by trainers, while others worked with each other. But what caught her eye and stilled her heart was the sign on the back wall.

BAKER-LANDON-ROSE MEMORIAL GYM

The names of the three men in Jackson's unit that had died.

"What is this?" she asked quietly.

"Ben started this about a year ago. Set up an entire gym with equipment disabled vets needed to get stronger. He hired specialized trainers and therapists who could work one on one with anyone who needs it. The membership has blown up in the last six months."

"This is amazing." She looked around at the people working out and marveled at the strength and determination she could see in many of their eyes.

"And that's not all. He doesn't charge any of them a dime. He also has mental health providers on staff with an open-door policy on the second floor. He wants to make sure he doesn't lose another soldier on his watch."

She had taken Ben at face value and had totally underestimated him. She continued looking around but stopped when her eyes locked with Ben's curious gaze. He leaned over and said something to the man he was working with before walking toward her. Her palms turned ice cold and sweaty as her heartbeat kicked up another notch.

His gaze slid from her to Danny, and Ben broke into a wide grin. He slapped a hand on her brother's shoulder in greeting. "Danny Boy! This is a surprise."

"Hey, Little Boy Blue." They shook hands and then Danny turned toward her. "I brought someone to see you."

"I see that." Ben's gaze shifted to Hannah and he extended a tentative hand to greet her. "Hannah."

Instead of taking his hand, she lurched forward and wrapped her arms around him in a quick hug. An "Oh!" fell from his lips as she backed up just as quickly.

"Hello, Ben." She brought her hands together, fidgeting as she spoke. "Could we talk? Do you have a few minutes?"

"Sure. Let's go to my office." He turned to Danny. "You coming?"

"Nah. I'm going to hang out and say hi to a few of the guys."

She gave her brother's hand a grateful squeeze. "Thanks, Danny."

She followed Ben's lead as he turned and walked through the gym, saying hello to some as he passed, until they reached a door on the other side. He held it open for her and closed it behind her again, then sat behind a desk in the room.

She scanned the room quickly and noted the American flag that hung on the wall and the bookshelf that contained numerous framed pictures of him, Drew and fellow soldiers, books and several medals.

Her eyes stopped on a box on his desk containing a dozen loose black-stemmed roses. "You're the one that leaves the roses on Jackson's grave?"

His cheeks reddened as he looked at the roses and then back at her. "It's just my way of honoring them. I don't want them to think I've forgotten."

He pointed to a chair next to the desk. "Sit down if you'd like."

She did before he could see that her knees were practically knocking together from nerves. "That's a wonderfully thoughtful thing to do."

He just nodded curtly, dismissing her praise. "So, this is a surprise."

"I know." She cleared her throat. "I'm sorry, I hope it's okay that I just showed up."

He stared at her a moment before responding. "What can I do for you?"

Her hands were in her lap, fingers fidgeting again. She met his wary gaze. "I came because I realized I owed you an apology about Jackson. "

She inhaled as if trying to drag in more courage and continued in a rush. "I know now that you didn't ask him to go back. I know it wasn't your fault."

She drew in another deep breath and exhaled. "And I'm sorry. So sorry, Ben. Because I know what happened to him was just as hard for you as it was for me. I'm sorry I didn't listen to you. And I'm sorry for what I said to you. I was so wrong."

She hung her head then, afraid to look him in the eye. Afraid that he might tell her to go to hell. Afraid he wouldn't accept her apology. She heard his chair scrape back and she tensed, waiting for the inevitable order to leave.

A hand on her arm towed her up and then into an embrace. "Thank you."

He hugged her tightly. After a second of profound surprise, she wrapped her arms around him and hugged him back. He pulled away after a couple moments and turned quickly, wiping at his cheeks before leaning against the desk. She looked at him with new eyes, taking in the man now, and not the enemy she had painted him to be. "I'm sorry too."

She shook her head in confusion. "What for?"

"I should have come to see you. After. Even if it was six months later, I should have."

He looked down at the tattoo on his hand and then back up at her. "I guess I thought I was honoring him with this tattoo, and by visiting his grave, but I really should have honored him by going to see you. And his daughter. I should have made sure you were both okay."

Her lips frowned in a sad smile. "I guess we both could have done some things differently."

He told her then that's why he'd started this gym. He wanted returning vets, physically or mentally damaged, to have a place to come to and feel safe. Every one of them had served their country, and he understood what they had been through. He wanted to believe he was helping in some small way. He wanted to make up for not helping Jackson when he needed it.

"I understand what it's like to be in that dark place. I went there after Jackson died."

"This is a really, really good thing you're doing." She touched his arm. "You're a good man."

He patted her hand and then pushed himself up off the desk. She stood then as well and was about to leave, but she couldn't without asking about Drew. "How is he?"

He grunted. "I was wondering if you were going to ask."

"I was afraid to, actually, but I need to know."

"Go see him. He hasn't left the hotel suite since you fought."

Her eyes opened in shock. "That was six days ago!"

"Yep. I tried to drag him out of there yesterday for Thanksgiving, but no go."

Her gut clenched in guilt. "Will he even see me?"

"Only one way to find out."

This was starting to feel too familiar.

CHAPTER
Fourteen

DREW HIT mute on the stereo remote at the ding of the elevator arriving. The doors slid open with a whoosh.

He stood up and slammed his glass of tequila down on the table. Goddamn it all to hell. He had told Ben yesterday to just leave him alone.

He stormed out of the living room and skidded to a halt when his eyes landed on the shadowed form in his foyer. "Hannah? Is that you?"

Her voice cut through the darkened room like a beacon. "Why are all the lights off?"

"I like it like this." His tone wasn't kind. "What are you doing here?"

Her footsteps sounded and then the click of a switch being flipped. Bright light flooded the foyer and he raised his hand to cover his squinting eyes.

He heard the sharp intake of a breath and then her hand was on his shoulder. He flinched.

"Drew, how long has it been since you've eaten or showered?" Her voice was soft and maternal.

His eyes were adjusting to the light so he lowered his hand, blinking rapidly, as if waking up from a bad dream.

"Are you really here?" He reached out to touch her and was surprised when he actually made contact. He stroked her hair, taking a lock in his hand and smelling it. He gave her a sloppy smile. "You always smell so good."

She gently pulled the hair from his hand, and a small smile graced her face without quite reaching her eyes. "Are you drunk?"

"Am I drunk?" He threw his hands up and laughed maniacally. "Not enough if I can still see you."

"Oh, Drew."

He swayed slightly as she dropped her purse on the floor and then her coat on top of it.

She took his hand. "Come with me, okay?"

He liked when her voice was soft like this. He let her lead him through his bedroom and into the bathroom. She turned lights on as she went, then let go of his hand and pulled a stool up to the sink. She grabbed a bottle of shampoo out of the shower.

"Come sit over here." She pointed to the stool, and because he didn't know what else to do, he went. Behind him, water started to flow. Her hands were at his waist and then his shirt was being pulled up.

"Lift your arms up, Drew."

He lifted and she pulled the shirt up over his head and dropped it on the floor. She took a towel then and wrapped it around his shoulders, brushing her hand over the thick scruff that layered his face. "Let's get you cleaned up, okay?"

She laid her hand flat on his chest and pushed him back. Her hand moved to his head and her fingers ran through his hair, pulling his head back gently.

She scooped water from the faucet and he sighed when the warm liquid made contact with his head. He closed his eyes and let himself relax as her fingers continued to weave through his hair.

He smelled the shampoo before its coolness hit his scalp, and then her fingers were massaging his head. He let out a contented sigh.

"Does that feel good?" Her warm breath at his ear made goose bumps break out across his chest and arms. More warm water spilled over his head as she rinsed the soap from his hair.

The water shut off and the towel around his shoulders was pulled free and settled over his head. He closed his eyes and enjoyed being in the darkness again for a moment.

The towel slid out of his hair and was draped back around his shoulders again. He blinked his eyes open.

She stood next to him, eyes on his face. "Can I shave you?"

He didn't have the strength or will to do it. He closed his eyes and shrugged his shoulders. "Okay."

She pulled open a drawer and he heard foam coming from a can and then felt the cool cream as she spread it over his face. Her touch was light and gentle and made him want to kiss her. He opened his eyes and watched her movements as she worked.

She locked eyes with his and her hand stilled. "Okay?"

He just nodded and looked away. He heard the water

turn on again and then she was standing over him with his razor in hand.

"Up or down?"

"Up my neck, down my face."

The razor touched the bottom of his throat and then scraped up and through the stubble. When she reached his chin, she rinsed the razor and began again. He shut his eyes and lay still as the razor rasped against his throat.

Ten minutes later, a hot wash cloth was rinsing his face, and then her cool hand was trailing lightly over his smooth skin. He sat up then, opening his eyes, and caught her wrist in his hand.

She met his eyes and pulled her wrist out of his grasp. "Better."

She turned, walked to the shower, opened the door and started the water. When she seemed satisfied with the temperature, she walked to the closet and took out another towel and handed it to him.

"Take a shower. I'm going to make you something to eat."

Not giving him time to digest her order or refuse, she left the bathroom and shut the door behind her. He sat on the stool and tried to remember what day it was.

He'd lost track between tequila shots. Was it yesterday that Ben was here? His head was foggy and he couldn't remember the last time he'd eaten or slept.

How many days had he been sitting here, waiting for her to come back to him? And now that she was here, he didn't know what to say, what to do.

The door opened suddenly. Her body leaned halfway through the opening.

"Drew. Get. In. The. Shower." The door banged shut.

Fifteen minutes later, in a fresh pair of sweats and a clean T- shirt, he left his room and walked into the kitchen. His stomach clenched and grumbled loudly as the smell of bacon assaulted him.

She had made toast and scrambled eggs and had fresh juice all sitting on the table. She was setting a plate of bacon down on the table when she spotted him.

She smiled and his heart stuttered. Just seeing her here, even if he didn't know what it meant yet, made his heart beat a little less painfully than an hour ago. She motioned for him to sit down. "Come eat. You look like you've lost ten pounds."

He looked down at himself, frowning, and then shuffled to the table. He picked up the fork and started eating. He was three bites in when he realized he was starving and began wolfing it down.

Her hand landed on his forearm, and he froze. "Hey, slow down. I don't want you to get sick."

He grunted, but did as she requested and started chewing his food instead of inhaling it. After several minutes, he put down his fork and picked up the orange juice, draining it in a few gulps. He stood and walked over to where Hannah was standing.

"Why are you here?"

His voice was edged with confusion and anger. The tequila was wearing off and he was starting to slip back into reality.

"I came to talk to you, but when I got here, and when I saw you—" She lowered her voice. "I needed to make sure you were all right first."

He scoffed. "You think I'm okay now?"

She shook her head. "No. I just mean . . . Drew, you looked so . . . so broken."

He barely spoke above a whisper. "Hannah, I am broken. And I'm tired. So fucking tired."

He stepped back, turned and starting walking to the bedroom. "I can't do this again. Please, just leave."

He didn't look back. He didn't want to see her face. He didn't want to hear anything else. He didn't want to fight anymore. He shut the door, shut off all the lights, climbed into bed and let the darkness claim him.

"HANNAH?" A hand gently swept hair off of her face as her eyes flickered open. Drew's smooth face was inches from hers, his blue eyes filled with concern. She sat up quickly as she remembered where she was.

"What are you doing here?" His voice was no longer angry or accusatory, just curious.

She rubbed the sleep out of her eyes before meeting his nervously. "Don't you remember last night?"

His hand ran through his hair and a small smile touched his lips. "I remember you washing my hair. That felt nice."

She returned his smile with a small one of her own. "You were a bit of a mess. I didn't know what else to do. It appeared you may have been overserved."

He sat on the couch next to her. "Tequila and I have been really good friends lately."

"I'm sorry, Drew." The apology fell from her lips before

she had time to think. "I came to tell you that last night and then when I found you." She shrugged before continuing. "You were just so sad. I had to do something. So, I washed your hair, and shaved you, and fed you."

His hand scrubbed down his face in memory as she described what she had done the night before. "And I couldn't leave again. Not until I had a chance to at least tell you I was sorry."

Her pulse was thrumming wildly and she was talking way too fast but she was afraid he was going to tell her to leave again and she just wanted to say what she needed to say before he did.

He didn't though. He just stared at her, his eyes pensive, as if he couldn't be sure he'd heard her correctly. "You're sorry?"

She scooted closer and touched his knee, needing contact. "I'm so sorry. Sorry I said the things I said to you. Sorry I didn't stop and listen to your brother. Sorry I didn't trust that we could have figured this out. I'm sorry for so many things, but when I saw you last night—" Out of air, she took a hasty breath. "When I saw what I did to you. My heart broke into a thousand pieces for the hurt I put you through."

A small frown appeared on his face. "I don't understand. Don't get me wrong, my heart leapt out of my chest when I walked in here and saw you sleeping on my couch. All I wanted to do was lie down beside you and pull you into my arms because I've missed you so fucking much. But, what's changed in a week?"

Her heart sank at the doubt in his voice. Was she too late? Had he already closed his heart to her?

"Everything's changed. Everything."

She shifted even closer and this time took one of his hands into her own. He tensed at first, but then relaxed as she wrapped both her hands around it tightly. "I talked to my brother, and to yours."

His eyebrows flew up in surprise. "You saw Benny?"

"Yesterday." She nodded. "But let me tell you why. I talked to my brother about what happened, and he told me that Jackson had reenlisted before the accident even happened. He had always planned to go back."

She shook her head angrily but rambled on as different emotions played across Drew's face. "I was so wrong about everything. About my husband and why he did what he did. About your brother. And for how I treated you because of it all. I should have had more faith in you. In us. And I didn't. Instead, I ran away and hid in my anger again."

She hung her head, trying to hide her shame and embarrassment, but also because she was afraid of what his face might reveal. "I realize now that no one but Jackson made that decision to go back. Even if Ben had asked him to go back, it was still Jackson. He made that choice. The choice to leave us. I just wanted— No, I needed someone to blame."

His hand slid out from between hers and any hope she had for reconciliation went with it. She whimpered.

His hand was under her chin then, lifting it up so that her face was even with his. He was inches from her. "Don't ever run away on me again. Ever."

Her heart lurched in her chest as hope flowed in again. She shook her head frantically. "I won't. Ever. I promise."

"I want to know everything, Hannah. I do." His hand

shifted from her chin to her cheek. "But right now, all I want to do is hold you. I've missed you so goddamn much."

He moved then and brought his lips to hers in the softest of kisses. His lips sealed tenderly over hers, his actions slow and deliberate as he seemed to taste every area of her mouth. When he broke away from her, he slid his arms around her and held her tightly.

He just held her and so she wrapped her arms around him tightly and held him back, so grateful for his forgiveness and to feel him again. His breath was hot on her ear as he whispered, "I missed you. So much."

She shifted then and straddled his waist. He cradled her face and began peppering kisses everywhere but her lips. When he had covered every inch of her face, he moved down her neck, pulling her collar aside to expose her shoulder.

His tongue grazed over the light mark of his love bite, and then he pulled her shirt over her head. Before it even hit the floor, Hannah began tugging his off as well. No words were spoken. They moved in sync, desperate to feel each other again.

As soon as his shirt was gone, she leaned forward and relished the feeling of his bare skin against hers. His soft chest hair tickled the sensitive buds of her breasts into hard points.

Their lips were fused together, their breaths becoming one, as she rocked her core slowly up and down the hard length of him. He broke away from their kiss and wrapped her hair in his fist, pulling her head back, and rained kisses down her neck, her clavicle and finally her breasts. He pulled one into his mouth and swirled his tongue around the elongated nipple before suckling.

Hannah pushed herself deeper into his mouth, lost in the slow rising heat he was bringing to her surface. He let go of her nipple, kissed his way across her chest and slid the other one into his mouth. She might combust just from the sensations he sent coursing through her. This was so slow and gentle and it meant so much more than the other times they'd had sex.

She pushed herself up and off Drew and started sliding her jeans down and off her legs. She pointed to Drew's sweats. "Off. Now."

He chuckled. "Always so anxious. I love that about you."

He quickly untied the string on the sweats and, raising his hips, slid the material down over his waist and off his legs. His cock sprang up, hard and ready.

"Don't you ever wear underwear?"

"Easier access." He crooked his finger beckoning her. "Come back here."

He didn't have to order her twice as she slid atop him. She didn't have the patience or restraint to wait another second and positioned herself over his cock, guiding it inside as she lowered herself down.

They both moaned in unison, her head falling back, before Drew's hand reached around her neck and pulled her to his lips. In between kisses, he breathed out a command: "Move."

Hannah began rocking her pelvis back and forth, sliding her pussy up and down his cock, leaving it wet and throbbing. With each forward motion, her clit rubbed up against the base of his shaft and pulsed in response. "Oh my god. You always feel so good."

Drew latched onto one of her peaked nipples, sucking hard, biting the tip gently. Her hips surged harder against him, and her core began to tighten.

"Drew, I'm going to come." Hannah's hips plunged quickly now, increasing the pressure of her clit against his cock, her breath leaving her in small gasps.

"Come, Hannah. I want to feel all of you."

His permission was all it took for her orgasm to detonate. She scrunched her eyes as her muscles clenched onto Drew's cock, sparks of light bursting behind her lids, a mewl of relief leaving her mouth. He clamped his mouth over hers with a growl, clutching her, as his release shot into her.

Her clit pulsed around his cock for a few more beats before both of their bodies relaxed. She lifted her head off his shoulder and brought her forehead against his, their eyes locking on one another. He leaned in and kissed her slowly, then drew back, meeting her eyes again.

"I love you, Hannah. I wasn't sure how you felt and I didn't want to push you. But I do. I love you."

Her breath caught at his words, but instead of being scared, she was relieved. She had been so worried he wouldn't take another chance on her, and it took almost losing him to make her realize she had fallen in love with him too. Before she could respond, he started talking quickly again.

"I know it's too soon. I know it's too fast. I know we've both made mistakes. But every single minute of every single day, all I want is to have you next to me. When you aren't here, I just feel empty."

She was struck speechless by his words so she simply nodded. Drew moved his hands up and gripped her lightly around each arm, breaking her hold from around his neck, pushing her further back.

"Can you say something? Anything?" His voice was laced with concern and worry.

"I think I love you too," she whispered. She was surprised to realize it was true.

A smile broke out across his face as he yanked her back into an embrace. Then he pulled away again. "Wait, you think?"

"I just— This is— I never thought I would be here again."

"I never thought I'd be here again either. Ever. But here we are."

She let out a shaky laugh. "Yes, here we are. And I'm terrified."

He shifted her into his lap, his arms holding her close. "Of what?"

"Of everything." She blurted as she shook her head. "Of loving you. Of losing you. Of what this means. We lead such different lives. I have a child. I thought I had my life all figured out and then, you."

"It's as simple or as hard as we make it. We'll figure it all out. We have to."

"We have to?" She couldn't keep the concern out of her voice.

He smiled wistfully. "Yes, we have to. I love you, Hannah Rose, and I'm not letting you go now that I have you."

"What about Grace?"

He looked at her in confusion. "What about Grace? She's a part of you. I'll love her as much as I love you."

"Just like that?"

"Just like that. People fall in love with single parents all the time."

"But you live so richly. I live in an apartment over a flower shop I barely can call my own. How does all this work?"

He shrugged. "I don't know yet. But we don't have to figure it all out today. Let's just be us for a little while."

"But—"

Drew placed a finger on her lips. "No more questions. Stop overthinking it. I only have one more question for you."

"Okay?" she mumbled around his finger. He lifted it again. "Do you love me?" His soft voice was laced with fear.

She brought her eyes up to his and nodded. "Yes, I do."

A wide grin broke across his face. "Say it."

She smiled back at him and then sat up straighter. "I love you. I love you, Andrew Sapphire."

He pulled her face to his and crushed his lips against hers, kissing her hungrily. "I love you too."

CHAPTER
Fifteen

HANNAH PULLED her jacket around herself tightly and tugged her scarf higher over her face. It was a cold, raw January day and the wind was unforgiving. She stood in the snow over Jackson's grave, a man standing next to her. He was using his cane today so he wouldn't slip in the snow.

He bent at the waist to lay a bouquet of black roses against the white marble. His hand rested against the top of the stone as he bent back up, his lips moving silently for a few minutes. He looked at her then and shrugged. "I wanted him to know I'll always look out for you."

She grasped his hand and squeezed it, not letting go. "Thank you, Benjamin."

A lot had happened in the two months since she had discovered that Drew's brother and her husband had served together in Iraq. Most important was the peace she had seemed to make with herself and with Ben over Jackson's death.

Now, with her hand in the crook of his elbow as they

walked across the snowy graveyard back to his car, she only felt love and respect for him. The anger was gone. When they reached his car, he opened the passenger door for her and helped her inside.

They were headed back to the city to meet with Drew and Grace.

"You okay?" He looked over at her.

"Yep." She glanced over at him. "You?"

"Yep." He smiled at her. "Excited about tonight?"

"Nervous. I hope your parents will be happy about everything."

He grinned. "Trust me, Hannah, they are going to be thrilled."

DREW HAD Grace wrapped up in one of his arms, her little arms around his neck, while his other hand held Hannah's as they entered his parents' house.

"Mom? Dad? We're here."

His mother appeared gracefully from another room and greeted them all with hugs and kisses. "Hannah, how nice to see you again. And Grace, you too."

They had begun joining his parents for their weekly family dinners shortly after he and Hannah had reconciled.

His mother wrapped her hands around his middle when he reached down to hug her, patting her hands on his back. "How's my baby boy?"

He rolled his eyes and placed a kiss on her cheek. "Mom, I'm not your baby anymore."

"Oh, you'll always be my baby." She stroked him lovingly on the arm and then turned and motioned for them to follow her through the foyer to the dining room. "Come, dinner is all set. Ben is already at the table with your father."

When they entered the room, his father stood up and met him with a half-hug and a slap to the shoulder. "Andrew."

His father's face lit up at the sight of Gracie. It always amazed him how such a little girl could wrap a grown man around her finger so easily.

She was a living reminder to his parents of what it was to have a little girl in the house again. They had loved his little sister fiercely, and having Grace here had brought them back to life.

His father scooped Grace out of his arms and gave her a big hug and kiss. "How's my favorite girl?"

She giggled and clutched his face in her two little hands and kissed him on the nose. His father's face turned a light pink, and his smile turned even brighter. Yep, Dad is a goner.

"Hi, Mr. Sapphire."

His father lowered Grace to the floor and then reached over to kiss Hannah on the cheek. "And my other favorite girl? How are you?"

Hannah brushed a kiss back on his cheek and smiled warmly at him. "We're good."

"Okay, let's sit down and eat then. I'm starving. Grace, come sit next to me."

Drew shook his head and smiled to see his father in this light. He hadn't been this happy and relaxed in a long time. They all took a seat and began passing food around the table, chatting and eating casually. After dinner, his mother brought out bowls of ice cream topped with whipped cream for everyone.

It was then that Drew decided to share their news. He reached over and took Hannah's hand, squeezing it before placing it in his lap. She smiled knowingly at him. He cleared his throat and tapped his spoon against his bowl to get everyone's attention.

"So, as much as we love coming to have dinner once a week with you now, Hannah and I actually wanted to meet with you tonight to share some news with you."

He looked over at Hannah again, smiling warmly, and then stood up. "As you know by now, when I met Hannah, she sent me into a tailspin and stole my heart in one fell swoop. We haven't been together very long, but neither of us wants to wait another second to spend our life together, so I'm happy to share with all of you that Hannah has agreed to marry me."

He pulled her up into an embrace and kissed her passionately on the lips. They were met with cheers of joy and congratulations from around the table.

When he pulled apart from her, his mother was at their side and pulling Hannah's left hand up to look at her empty ring finger.

"No ring?" She turned and looked at Drew in question.

"Not yet, Mom." He took Hannah's hand and brought it to his lips in a kiss.

"I just finally got her to say yes last night. But don't worry, it's coming."

HANNAH WALKED off the elevator into Drew's foyer and let out a gasp at what she saw. Lit candles were on every surface, bathing everything in soft twinkling light.

Van Morrison played softly from somewhere further in the suite, and the scent of roses was everywhere. At her feet, soft red petals were scattered in a path leading her further inside the room.

She ambled down the trail of petals, taking in every detail of the room as she went, until she was standing in the middle of the living room.

Drew had said he wanted to take her to dinner, so she was wearing a burgundy dress with the black heels he had given to her on their first "official" date. She looked around the room and marveled at the number of candles that were lit and the endless bouquets of red roses that filled every available space.

She flinched in surprise as Drew's hands slid around her waist and then tugged her into him in a hug. "Hello, princess. You look beautiful."

She spun and wrapped her arms around his neck, then pulled herself up to his lips for a kiss. Breathless, she broke free. "Drew, what is this? It's amazing."

He dropped another kiss against her mouth. "Do you like it?"

"Yes, it's absolutely breathtaking."

He nodded and began swaying with her to the music. "Do you remember this song?"

She bit her lip as she remembered the dance they had shared the first time she went to his house in the Hamptons. And then blushed when she remembered how they'd made love afterward. It was the first time she'd admitted to herself that she was falling for him. "Of course I remember."

"I remember too. I remember how beautiful your hair looked as loose strands blew in the wind when we walked on the beach. And I remember how happy you were eating leftovers from my fridge. And how your face lit up when you laughed while we danced. But mostly I remember making love to you and knowing in that moment that you were the woman I wanted to spend the rest of my life with."

He let go of her then and knelt down in front of her, taking her left hand in his. Her other hand rose to her mouth, trying to cover the smile that broke out across her face. He slid a ring out of his pocket and held it in his other hand.

"Hannah Marie Rose, I love you more than I could have ever thought possible. You are the very breath that makes my heart beat. You are the sunshine that warms me. You are everything that makes my world whole. Will you please do me the honor of becoming my wife?"

Tears of joy streamed down her face as she nodded and jumped up and down and then into his arms. He wrapped his arms around her tightly and spun her in a circle before putting her down and kissing away her tears. She was laughing and crying and trying to kiss him all at the same time.

She'd never ever thought her heart could feel this full again. He pulled away, and then lifted her hand to slide the ring onto her finger. It was a beautiful princess-cut diamond, completely surrounded by smaller diamonds and set in a diamond-encrusted band.

She looked at it on her finger and then crushed her lips to Drew's, pulling away after a moment to gawk at it again.

"It's absolutely beautiful."

"Is that a yes?"

She realized then that she hadn't even given him an answer. She grinned so broadly her cheeks hurt. "Yes, Drew. Of course, I'll marry you!"

He cupped her face in his hands then and kissed her lips gently.

"I love you so much, Hannah."

"I love you right back."

Epilogue

HANNAH WADDLED to the side of the bed and shook Drew awake. "It's time."

Drew bolt upright in the bed and looked at her in wild-eyed panic. "It's time?"

"It's time. My water broke an hour ago."

He jumped out of the bed and started running around, yanking clothes on erratically. "What do you mean an hour ago? Why did you wait so long to wake me?"

Hannah laughed under her breath as her husband struggled into his pants. "The baby isn't going to drop out of me, Drew. It could take hours. I have done this before, remember?"

He stopped what he was doing and darted another wild look her way. "Oh shit. Where's Grace?"

She shook her head, kind of enjoying the sight of him completely falling apart. "Tammy came and got her. That's why I waited to wake you up."

She waddled out of the bedroom. "I'll be waiting in the kitchen when you're ready."

She covered her smile as he swore in frustration while hunting for his shoes. *Men.* As she sat in the kitchen, she looked around and smiled at the wonderful home she and Drew had made together.

They had flown to St. John one month after he'd proposed and were married on a beautiful, white sandy beach. It was exactly how they both wanted it. Simple and just the three of them. Grace was delighted to act as flower girl and maid of honor.

They had both already been married before and didn't want to make a fuss over a big ceremony. All they had wanted, was to be married and start their lives together.

Just last week, she turned the keys of the shop over to Robin to run for her while she navigated having, and raising baby number two. She'd be there to help as needed, and would most likely go back again once they'd all gotten into a new routine, but she was thrilled to give Robin this opportunity.

Making things even easier was Robin's decision to move into her apartment when she and Drew had moved in together.

They still had the house in the Hamptons, but Drew no longer spent nights in his hotel suite. They'd bought a loft several buildings down from Ben and had it renovated into a home they could grow into. Four bedrooms, five baths, a huge kitchen and living space for them all.

The city was their playground. Grace was in first grade now and attended a private school that Hannah brought her to daily.

They saw Ben almost every day and were surprised if Drew's dad didn't stop in any less than three times a week. Gracie had her uncle and grandfather wrapped around her little finger and had become the apple of their eyes.

Yes, life was so much better than she could have ever imagined or hoped for.

Drew stumbled out from their bedroom, her hospital bag in hand, his hair in a thousand different directions. God, she loved this man.

"You ready there, Superman?"

He looked up and grinned at her. "I know, I'm a fucking mess. But Jesus, woman, you're having my damn baby today."

She looked down, rubbed her belly and winced in pain as a contraction hit her.

He ran over to her and took her hand. "Breathe, honey, just breathe."

She swatted him away. "Are you kidding me?"

The contraction passed and she stood up straight again. "Okay, let's go have a baby."

EIGHTEEN HOURS LATER, Grace stroked the dark, downy locks on her baby brother's head and then, frowning, looked over at Hannah lying in her hospital bed. "I think Brody is a weird name, Mom."

She chuckled and then raised her eyebrows in surprise. "What's so weird about it? Brody was my father's name."

"Mom, it rhymes with grody. Do you know how many

kids will pick on him when he gets older?" Grace shrugged her shoulders to indicate how obvious this should be.

She laughed again. "Well, I can't change it now. You'll just have to make sure that no one picks on him. That's what big sisters are for."

A knock came at the door then, interrupting any further discussion on the subject.

Grace jumped off the bed and over to the door to open it. "Grandma and Grandpa are finally here!"

Caroline and Gavin strode into the room, arms filled with flowers, balloons and a big, blue teddy bear, wide smiles on their faces. Caroline deposited her contents on the closest surface and walked quickly to Hannah, small tears of joy leaking from the corners of her eyes.

"Let me see my grandson!" She bent down and dropped a quick kiss on Hannah's forehead before leaning down further to place a softer kiss on Brody's head. "Can I hold him?"

"Of course!" Hannah lifted her son up toward her mother-in- law. "Meet your grandson, Brody James Sapphire."

Gavin had moved closer and was standing next to Caroline, and as she took the baby into her arms, he reached out and swept a gentle caress over the baby's head. "He's absolutely beautiful, Hannah. He looks just like Andrew did when he was a baby."

"Speaking of Drew, he should be back any minute. He went home to shower and change." Hannah looked up at the clock on the wall, noting that he had been gone a little over two hours.

She was just about to grab her phone to text him when

the door swung open again, and Ben and Drew walked in. Her face lit up to see her husband. He still made her heart race. "Look who I found out in the hallway."

Ben clasped Drew's shoulder as a wide grin broke across his face. "My baby brother is a dad!"

Drew walked over to the bed and sat down next to Hannah before kissing her softly on the lips. "Hey, gorgeous. How are you?"

"Happy that you're back."

"Do you need anything?"

"Nope." She looked around the room at the people she loved and was filled with a sense of absolute happiness, gratitude and peace. She smiled back up at him. "I'm perfect."

He dropped another kiss to her cheek, then moved his lips against her ear to whisper. "Wait until I tell you about Ben's news."

Hannah's eyes shot wide as she turned to face Drew. "You're going to make me wait?"

He shot her an evil grin, nodding his head.

The ULTIMATE Bid

The Auction Series Book Three

MICHELLE WINDSOR

THE AUCTION SERIES: BOOK THREE

The ULTIMATE Bid

MICHELLE WINDSOR

This is dedicated to all the veterans who came home missing a piece of themselves.
Thank you for your service, your sacrifices, and may God bless and continue to watch over you.

CHAPTER

One

I SHOVE two fingers between my collar and neck and tug hard as I stride through the revolving door of our newest hotel. This damn tie is strangling me. It's bad enough I have to make an appearance at these events, but Drew's insistence that I wear a suit and tie is pure torture for me and he knows it.

Fuck it. I grasp the knot of the tie, loosen it, and yank the noose-like silk over my head, shoving the offending article in my jacket pocket. I unbutton the top two buttons of my shirt as well, letting out a sigh of pleasure at the ability to breathe freely again.

What's Drew going to do, fire me? He can't. I own thirty percent of the company, just like him.

Just to really get under his skin, I stop at the coat check, swap my suit jacket for a ticket, and grin widely. I thank the attendant who has just unwittingly helped me to drag at least one eye roll out of my younger brother this evening.

Yep, Drew is my younger brother, but he does more to

keep me on the straight and narrow than the other way around.

After spending seven years in the Army, three of those years deployed overseas for active duty, he understands that my edges will always be a little rough. But that doesn't stop him from trying to smooth them out when he can.

Strolling into the grand ballroom, I smile as a swell of pride courses through me. The latest hotel in our chain, Sapphire Resorts, has turned out beautifully, and without a doubt, I believe it's going to be a big success, especially with the location so central to the financial district.

When did I start caring so much about this shit? I chuckle softly with a small shake of my head and then look for the closest bar. I need a drink if I'm going to get through the next two hours.

I head to the back corner of the ballroom, a spot I know will most likely be a bit quieter, but pause when a flash of gold catches the corner of my eye. I turn my head and draw in a long, appreciative breath as I scan the beauty making her way across the room. Her gaze seems focused on the bar at the front of the room, so I turn my body and casually drift in that direction instead.

As I'm walking, I scan from her gold-clad toes, up her bare, toned legs to mid-thigh, where the hem of her sheer cream dress ends. The sheer fabric is scattered with a thousand different types of golden gemstones that hug her tiny waist and perfect breasts, reflecting against every light in the room.

But what really draws my attention is the open back of the dress. Her entire back is bare, exposing skin so smooth, it appears flawless. I clasp and unclasp my hand as I fight the urge to press it flat against her skin as I move closer. It's hard to tell if her hair is long or short because it's all piled on top of her head, as if she knows the power her exposed back possesses.

I stop several feet from the bar and watch as she attempts to cut a path through the mingling throng, waving to try to catch the bartender's attention. The bartender is female; otherwise, I'm certain she would have had a drink in front her before she lifted a single finger.

I continue watching until a rather stout gentleman slides up beside her and attempts to make conversation. It's amusing to watch her try to be kind to the man until I see him reach out and slide his pinky finger down her arm suggestively, a look of disgust crossing her face at the action.

Anger surges through my body, and within seconds, I'm pushing myself between her and the man. A warning snarl slips from my lips as I glare at him and place my hand flat against the center of her back. It feels like silk. It's the single thought that flies through my head before I smile down at her and brush a kiss against her cheek.

"Hello, darling. Are you having a problem getting the cocktails?"

Her wide blue eyes look up at me in surprise and then in knowing relief as she immediately plays into my little game. "Yes! Have you come to rescue me, babe?"

I can't help the wide grin that breaks across my face when she gives me a small wink and mouths silently, "Thank you so much".

"I have." I give her my full attention for only a second, my gaze locking onto hers long enough to see light grey flecks mixed into the blue surrounding her pupil, reminding me of waves churning at sea.

I break contact and look at the bartender's name tag. "Excuse me, Greta?"

Whether it's because I'm a somewhat handsome male, or because she realizes a Sapphire is standing in front of her, suddenly, all of her attention is focused on me.

"Yes, sir, what can I get you?" Her cheeks turn a light pink as she fidgets with the bottle opener in her fingers.

I smile warmly to try to settle her nerves, nodding toward the back of the bar. "I'll have a couple fingers of that whiskey, please, on the rocks." I turn my head toward the vision in gold, locking eyes with hers again. "And, I'm sorry Darling, what did you want again?"

I watch as her eyes narrow, one side of her gloss-lined lips tilting up in a smirk as she tells the bartender that she'll have a Goose on the rocks, her eyes never leaving mine.

Greta sets our drinks down in front of us within seconds, then busies herself with the next person in line. I watch as her delicate fingers, tipped with nails painted black, wrap around the glass to raise it to her mouth, her lips kissing the edge as she draws in a small sip of the clear liquid before slowly lowering it.

"Thanks for rescuing me."

I look down in shock as the hand that was on her back is suddenly cold and empty. I watch her turn and walk away for only a second before I grab my whiskey off the bar and quickly follow, calling after her.

"I'm Ben, in case you were wondering."

She stops mid-stride, anchors her foot and then spins around, stopping in front of me, a cocky grin on her face.

"I wasn't. Wondering." She flashes a cocky grin and then continues, "But nice to meet you, Ben. Thanks again."

She raises the glass in salute and moves to turn again, but I take a step closer as she does, causing her to falter, one eyebrow raising in curiosity. "Yes?"

"You aren't going to tell me your name?" *Jesus, I sound like a desperate idiot who's never seen a beautiful woman before.*

She smirks and takes another sip from her glass, scanning me from head to toe then pausing briefly at what I'm sure are my tattoos peeking out of my open collar, and then shakes her head. "No, I don't think so."

I rear back in surprise and scoff. "You seriously aren't going to tell me your name?"

She shrugs and challenges me. "Why?"

"Why do I want to know your name?"

She nods and places a hand on her hip, jutting it out slightly as she does. "Yes, why? Are you planning on sending me flowers or are you just trying to get to know me better?"

She lifts her glass a little in the air. "Or do I owe you because you bought me a drink?"

A little unsure and a lot stunned by her response, I scratch my beard and frown down at her. "You're a spunky little thing, aren't you?"

She lifts her shoulders nonchalantly. "Maybe. Maybe I just know guys like you."

I raise my brows in surprise. "Guys like me?"

She nods and takes her hand off her hip to wave it up and down with a flourish around me. "Yes, guys like you: tall, dark and handsome."

She gives me another once over before continuing. "And I'd say rich based on your watch and shoes alone."

I give her my most dazzling smile. "You think I'm handsome?"

"See? That's all you heard." A small frown tugs her lips down. "Guys like you think they can throw their pretty little smiles around and we women are just supposed to fall at your feet."

"I wasn't expecting you to fall at my feet. I was just wondering what your name is."

She lifts the glass to her mouth, the ice clinking as she drains the rest of the vodka, and then takes a step closer to hand me the glass. "Like I said, thanks for the drink."

She looks me up and down one final time, shakes her head, muttering as she turns to leave, "Been there, done that. Not going there again."

As dumbfounded as I am, I can't help but chuckle under my breath. *Challenge accepted.*

I watch her walk back through the crowd, her beautiful bare back taunting me as she does. I raise my own glass in response, finishing the whiskey in one swallow, promising myself that this isn't over yet.

As I lower the glass, I notice Gage, my friend and photographer we hired for the evening, taking some pictures at the edge of the room. I quickly walk back to the bar, deposit the empty glasses, and ask Greta for two beers. Grabbing them, I relocate Gage and make my way over to him.

"Hey, man! How's it going?" I hold one of the beers out to him, which he takes, a grateful look on his face.

"Thanks, man. I need this." He takes a long pull from the bottle. "The shoot is going great. I'm just about done I think.

Just want to get some of your brother's speech and then I think I can wrap up."

"Thanks again for filling in last minute. I know Drew really appreciates it."

"No problem at all. It's easy work." He scowls and pulls at the collar of his shirt. "I just wish I didn't have to wear this damn thing. Hate having shit on my neck."

I can't help but chuckle, because I obviously know exactly how he's feeling, but I give him some crap anyway. "Toughen up and quit your bitching."

Gage points to my loosened collar and retorts. "Shut the fuck up! Where the hell is your tie?"

I grin broadly. "I don't work for my brother so I'll wear whatever the hell I want."

We laugh and take a couple more drinks in silence before Gage points his bottle toward the stage. "Looks like Drew might be getting ready to speak, so I'm going to go find a good spot."

"Okay, look me up after if you want to get another drink." I tip my bottle at him in goodbye and turn to see if I can find Hannah, Drew's wife. Scanning the crowd in front of the stage, I spot her and work my way over, a smile breaking across her face as she sees me, her hand lifting to wave me over.

I wave back and only miss half a beat in my step when I notice the woman in gold is standing next to Hannah, her features a mask of surprise as I approach and kiss Hannah on the cheek. "How's my favorite sister-in-law?"

She kisses me back and giggles. "I'm your only sister-in-law."

"Then you win, hands down."

I give her a wink and move to address the three people standing next to her, my eyes landing on my mystery woman, who is shaking her head, a small grin of defeat on her mouth. "Hi, I'm Benjamin Sapphire, Hannah's brother-in-law. I don't think we've met before."

"Oh, I'm sorry Ben." Hannah shifts quickly into hostess mode. "This is Drew's friend from college, Mika Kingsley, and his new bride, Raeva." She gives me a quick look of apology. "I thought you may have already known him."

"No worries at all, Hannah." I grasp Mika's firm grip in my own and shake it. "Nice to meet you both."

I give a warm smile to his wife and then move my attention to the woman on her right, extending my hand, unable to hide the devil in my grin. "And you are?"

She purses her lips and tilts her head, gracefully placing her hand in mine before finally bringing her eyes up to meet mine. "Jill Baldwin. Nice to meet you, Benjamin."

I'VE GOT to hand it to the man; he's very resourceful. His lips curl up into a triumphant grin. *Damn it.* Of course, he had to be Benjamin freaking Sapphire.

"Jill Baldwin?" He repeats my name, as if he's mulling it over in his head. The timber of his voice traveling up my spine, awakening every nerve inside my body. Sex is literally seeping from his pores, and he is one thousand percent the type of guy I need to stay far, far away from. "I know I've heard that name before," he muses, still staring at me.

Dear God, it feels as if he looking right into my inner thoughts. I feel the heat rise in my cheeks. Nope. *Tall, dark, and off limits.* I remind myself sternly, forcing myself to get it together.

"I think you were supposed to be at the meeting I had with your brother last week," I reply sweetly. "But you had to cancel last minute?"

"Jill owns that amazing spa downtown." Hannah chimes in. "Serenity."

I met with Drew last week after Mika set up the meeting. He thought a partnership with Sapphire Resorts would be a great way for me to expand my business.

Quite frankly, in retrospect, I'm happy Ben wasn't at that meeting. I don't think I could have focused. Drew Sapphire is handsome, but his brother—oh my God—that man should be illegal. From his dark hair that's screaming to have my fingers running through it, to the intense gaze in his deep blue eyes, every inch of his impressive six feet is drawing me in like a moth to a flame. And that is a sure sign that I need to run for the hills, and fast.

"Well, I was sorry to miss the meeting that day, even more so now," he replies smoothly as he flashes me a smile that could melt any pair of panties.

Good God, I need to get away from him. I force a tight smile. "Maybe next time. If you'll excuse me, I need to go powder my nose." I reach for Rae's arm. "Are you coming?" I ask her urgently.

Raeva raises a brow but nods. She kisses Mika on the cheek. "I'll be back in a bit, love," she tells him sweetly.

My heart is pounding against my chest as if it wants to

escape. I take long strides toward the ladies' room, practically dragging poor Rae with me.

"Slow down, Jillybean. These are six-inch heels."

I slow my roll. "Sorry, Rae. I just had to get away," I explain as we step into the fancy bathroom. I look around. The Sapphires really take things to the next level.

Raeva chuckles. "I take it that Ben is tall, dark, and hell no?"

I groan. "I can't possibly do business with Benjamin Sapphire."

Raeva rolls her eyes at me. "Are you seriously going to walk away from a huge opportunity, just because you find a man attractive? I know I don't have to tell you how ridiculous that sounds."

I sigh. "Rae, guys like him—"

"Guys like him?"

"Yeah, too handsome, too rich, too…"

"Too what exactly? You do realize that you've just pretty much described my husband? And you adore him; I know you do." She admonishes.

"I adore him because he makes you happier than I've ever seen you."

Rae's face lights up like a Christmas tree. "That he does."

"Benjamin Sapphire is just not what I need in my life right now. I've been down that road plenty of times. I'm not…"

"Whoa, let me stop you right there. We are talking about a business deal, not marriage. If you don't want to date him, then don't. It's that simple."

As usual, my best friend makes total sense. "You're right,

I'm being silly." *I am being ridiculous. No matter how gorgeous Ben is, I am in complete control of my emotions.* I tell myself in attempt to actually believe it.

"You good, Jillybean?"

"I'm good."

Raeva folds her arms around me and hugs me. After a beat, I pull away, holding her upper arms, and look at my beautiful friend. Her long, dark hair is cascading around her shoulders, and her full lips are painted the same red as the silky gown that seems to have been poured onto her. "Have I told you, you look amazing tonight?"

"Repeatedly, but thank you. And, might I add, right back at you. No wonder you had Ben drooling."

A girlish giggle escapes from my lips. "He was not drooling."

"Oh, please," Rae challenges.

We both are laughing as we walk out of the bathroom. "Is there any particular reason why you keep running off, Jill?"

I almost miss a step. I look up to find Benjamin Sapphire leaning against the wall across from the ladies' room.

"Well, that's my cue," Rae announces as she flashes me a wink.

"Traitor," I mouth at her. I watch her walk away for a moment, an enormous grin on her face, before I turn to face my accuser. "Going to the bathroom is running off?"

I'm surprised with how even my tone is. Judging from the look on Sapphire's face, it's thrown him off, too. But he recovers fast, a sexy grin lifting his lips as he approaches me.

"So, can I interest you in a drink at the bar then?"

"Look, um, Ben, is it?"

He closes the distance between us and cocks his head. "You know it is."

I bite my lower lip in an attempt to hide my smile; it's fun sparring with him. He's so close now, close enough for me to smell his cologne. Hints of clean soap and earthy scents tickle my nostrils, and it is taking everything I have to stop myself from inhaling deeply. Mercifully, I manage to collect myself.

Lifting my head, I look at him and smile sweetly. "I'm just not that into you."

His eyes sparkle brightly, a twinkle of amusement setting them ablaze. He takes another step closer, his right-hand slipping around my waist to pull me against him. It doesn't even occur to me to stop him.

Our gaze locks, and I feel his finger trail slowly from my shoulder to the very tip of my index finger. The gentle touch sets my body on fire. I gasp slightly, screaming inwardly to look away, but my irises are his willing prisoners. My body trembles against his, close enough now that I can feel how hard is chest is.

He leans in, agonizingly slow, and I know that I'm done for. His lips are mere inches from mine, his breath warm as it meets mine. My eyes flicker to his perfect mouth, and I swallow hard.

"Yes," he whispers against my lips. "I can see just *how little* you are into me." His lips gently brush my cheek as he releases me. The air is thick with desire, and I know it's not just mine. Ben shakes his head, a smirk on his face. "Stubborn little thing, aren't you?"

He takes my hand once more and lifts it to his lips. "I'll definitely be in touch."

And, with those parting words, he leaves me standing there in the hallway, somewhere between feeling bereft and dumbfounded.

CHAPTER
Two

"WHEN'S YOUR next meeting with Jill Baldwin?" I burst into Drew's office and make myself comfortable in one of the wing back chairs in front of his desk. Glancing up, I'm met with a look of utter annoyance.

"Well, good morning to you, Benny." He waves his hand to the chair I'm already in. "Won't you come in and have a seat? It's not like I was working on anything." His brow arches high as he finishes, his voice laced with sarcasm. "Can I get you a cup of coffee perhaps?"

"You can get me Jill Baldwin's number," I retort, shaking off his edginess. *He's too wound up for his own good.*

"I'm sorry, whose number do you want?" His fingers are tapping in irritation on his desk.

"Jill Baldwin. Mika's wife's friend. Owns Serenity Spas. You had a meeting with her last week."

Realization dawns and a knowing smile dances on his lips. "Ah, you must have met the lovely Ms. Baldwin at the

433

opening, and now you're interested in a meeting. Am I correct?"

"Did you see her? She's absolutely stunning." I stand from the chair and begin pacing, trying to expend some of the restless energy coursing through my system. "But damn if she isn't playing hard to get."

"Yes, she's hard to miss. I can see why you're taken by her."

I stop and turn in his direction when I hear his fingers cease their movement. "But?" I know there's a but coming. Drew may be my younger brother, but there is no doubt that he's generally the more reasonable one of us.

"But," he gives me a hard stare, "I'm actually quite interested in having her incorporate her spas into our hotels and don't need you to interfere with that."

"So, let me help. If you think it's a good business decision, let me work to make the deal happen."

Drew chuckles and shakes his head. "I think we both know what kind of deal you're interested in when it comes to Ms. Baldwin. Go chase another skirt. This one is too important for you to mess with."

I move to stand in front of his desk and slap my palm down hard. "Damn it, this girl is different! I feel it in my bones."

My brother stands to his full height, which is two small inches taller than me, his blue eyes turning to steel. "Different because she said no? I'm sure that's a new concept for you, big brother."

"Fuck you, Drew." I move to stand next to him to show I'm not intimidated by him in any way. "If memory serves correctly, I don't think it was too long ago that you found yourself in a very similar position. It was only chance that you ran into Hannah that day in the lobby that saved you."

I feel a little badly for shooting below the belt when I see Drew take a step back, his eyes widening in surprise, but the feeling goes away immediately when I hear his consent.

"Fine." He sits back in his seat and types something on his laptop. "I'll text you her information."

"No." Drew's eyes snap to mine in frustration. "I want you to set up another meeting with her, but I'll take the meeting, not you."

He stops typing and looks up at me, anger stewing close to the surface. "So, you're essentially going to trick her into a date with you?"

"No, it's a business meeting, but unfortunately, you aren't going to be able to make it, so I am generously going in your place to ensure discussions move forward." I flash him my cockiest grin and then continue. "Set it up for Thursday, 7:00 p.m. in the hotel restaurant at the new financial district location."

"A little late for a business meeting, don't you think?" His tone is wry and condescending at best.

"She won't say no to you. You're Drew 'Fucking' Sapphire." This time, I grace him with a genuine smile.

"You got that right." He finally cracks and lets a smirk escape before muttering, "You better not screw this deal up for us, Benny."

THREE LONG NIGHTS LATER, I stroll into the Blue Ivy and address the hostess. "Good evening. I've got a table reserved under Sapphire."

"Of course, Mr. Sapphire." She takes two menus and leads me to a table. "I have you here, but if you'd prefer something else?"

"Yes, actually." I look toward one of the more private booths along the wall in the back of the room and move in that direction. "I'll take this. Can you show Ms. Baldwin to the table when she arrives, please?"

"Certainly." She sets the menus down and places the wine list in front of me. "Jeffrey will be over in just a moment. Do you need anything in the meantime?"

"No, thank you." I open the wine menu in dismissal and begin browsing the selections.

I'm fifteen minutes too early but couldn't stand sitting in my apartment any longer and also wanted the element of surprise when she arrived. I'm generally a whiskey or beer kind of guy, but given this is supposed to be a business meeting, wine seems like the wiser choice.

"Good evening, Mr. Sapphire, sir." A smartly dressed waiter in his mid-thirties stands before me, a white napkin folded neatly over his arm, a black pad at the ready. "I'm Jeffrey and will be your server for the evening. Would you care for something to drink from the bar, or perhaps a bottle of wine?"

"Jeffrey." I open the folder and point to the row of Pinot Noirs. "Let's try one of these bottles. Do you have a recommendation?"

"The 2014 Gaps Crown is very nice. It's from Oregon

and has wonderful layers of floral and fruit flavors that aren't overly acidic."

"Great." I close the menu and smile up at him. "Let's do that then."

"Yes, sir." He walks quickly away to retrieve the wine, and I look at my watch for the twentieth time. Six-fifty. I wonder if she'll be prompt, but then consider what she must know is at stake if she goes into business with Sapphire Resorts and assume she will be.

Jeffrey is back before I can start another thought, twisting and turning the cork off with a soft pop and then handing it to me with a flourish. I smell it, pretending to know what I'm doing, and nod my head in approval. He pours a small taste into my glass, which I take, swish around, inhale, and taste.

My eyebrows fly up as the flavor of the wine bursts across my tongue and slides warmly down my throat. The wine is quite delicious, and I tell Jeffrey just that. He beams as if he had pressed the grapes himself and then pours more into my glass.

I raise my glass for another sip as he steps away, revealing a hidden Jill from his shadow, her lips pressed in a tight line, brows furrowed. Even with a grimace on her face, I cannot help but marvel again at how beautiful she is.

My eyes rake over her figure, hugged in a simple form-fitting dress of tan and black, made edgier by the cropped black leather jacket she's wearing. Her feet are also clad in black leather, but with three-inch heels, and she wears only simple diamond studs in her ears.

Standing, I greet her with my most charming smile, my hand extended. "Ms. Baldwin, you're so prompt."

She glares at my hand, ignoring it before responding tartly, "I thought I was meeting with the *other* Mr. Sapphire."

"Unfortunately, he had an unforeseen emergency and asked me to meet with you instead. He didn't want to cancel on such short notice or stall the discussions for the spas."

"Isn't that convenient?" One well-manicured brow arches sky high.

I chuckle lightly. "For me, perhaps." I move behind her and can't help but notice her eyes following, her neck craning as I place my hands on her shoulders. "Can I take your jacket?"

Seemingly resigned at being stuck with me, she shrugs as I slide the thin, soft material from her shoulders. Her arms are bare, and I notice, very tone, and wonder if she works out regularly or if it's great genetics. As I pull the jacket down her arms, I inhale her scent and immediately am reminded of coconuts and the sun.

She twirls around, seeming startled to realize she's only inches from me, and takes a sudden step back. "I don't know what game you're trying to play, Ben, but I can assure you right now that this is strictly a business dinner."

God, she's sexy when she's trying to be tough. I give her my most complacent smile and take her elbow, gently guiding her to the table and into the booth before sliding in next to her. "Of course. What else would it be?"

I lift the bottle that's been left by Jeffrey. "Wine?"

I REALLY WANT to take him up on the offer. God knows I could use a drink. But seeing that I am already struggling to string together a coherent thought when I'm in his orbit, adding alcohol to the mix doesn't seem like a smart idea. *Crap, why does he have to be this ridiculously good looking?*

After taking a deep breath to calm my nerves, I immediately regret it. He's sitting right next to me, and the scent of him—clean mixed with woodsy and musky tones—is intoxicating.

I can't believe it's *him* that showed up. I regret my choice in clothing; it feels too constricted, too tight. I can literally feel his eyes roaming all over me, like a ghostly touch. I cross my legs and don't miss the fact that his eyes track the movement, his gaze hovering at my legs for a long moment before traveling back up to my face.

He looks at me expectantly, flashing his pearly whites. Everything about him is drawing me in, and I can't allow that. Alarm bells ring inside my head, instantly causing imaginary walls to shoot out of the ground and up to the ceiling.

"I'll stick with water, thank you," I tell him with an eerily calm voice, one that doesn't match what I am feeling at all.

"You don't like wine?"

"Quite the contrary; I love a good glass of wine. But, like I said, this is a business dinner, and I don't mix business with pleasure."

"Ah, so, in your mind, you associate me with pleasure? I will take that as a win for me," he says with a smirk.

I scoff. "I associate you with a few things, Mr. Sapphire. Pleasure isn't on that list, I assure you. I am here to discuss business. If that isn't the case, then I will get up and leave right now."

When I move to do just that, he gently places a hand on my arm. "Listen, I'm sorry," he says sheepishly. "I think we got off on the wrong foot. Can we start over? Please?"

He actually looks contrite and sounds sincere, and I can't help but feel a little bad. I sigh. "Okay, let's start over," I concede.

He visibly relaxes, his shoulders dropping on an exhale, and I tense up more in response. "Ms. Baldwin, thank you for joining me tonight. I know you were expecting my brother, but I assure you that I am just as invested in the company as he is."

I realize it is entirely possible that I am putting too much stock in my belief that this is a set-up. After all, he is a Sapphire and this deal could be lucrative for all parties involved. To think that he would orchestrate this meeting just to get into my pants seems a little arrogant. I mean, I know I'm an attractive woman, but that man is sex on legs and certainly doesn't need to beg. Why would he go through all this if it wasn't for business?

I smile at him. "I've been looking forward to the meeting, Mr. Sapphire. I—"

"Please, call me Ben." He interrupts with a shake of his head. "Mr. Sapphire is my father; I have no desire to be called that."

"Okay... Ben." Just saying his name causes a tingling feeling in my belly. "And you can call me Jill, if you'd like."

"Perfect." He flashes a quick smile. "Thank you, Jill."

I nod my head and continue. "As I was saying, I have been looking forward to this meeting because I think a collaboration between your resorts and my spa would be a happy marriage."

Ben smiles, and I fight the urge to touch the dimple that appears. He hands me a menu, and I pretend to read it. Instead, I am inwardly trying to collect myself. My heart rate is accelerated, every single nerve ending in my body is at high attention, and my stomach is tied up in a thousand knots. *Why the hell does he make me so damn nervous?*

The server approaches the table and asks if we are ready to order. My eyes dart over to Ben, who is studying my expression. I force a smile and nod. I order the first thing I see and hand the waiter the menu. Ben orders his food, and the server pours us both some water before leaving us to our discussion.

"My brother tells me that one of the reasons he was so keen to meet you in the first place is the development of your own product line and special services. I understand it's quite revolutionary. Can you tell me more?"

"Of course." I pull my catalog from my attaché, place it on the table, and slide it toward him. I'm impressed he's actually done his homework. He opens it as I tell him about my skincare line, the painless hair removal, and about the special rejuvenating facials we offer. Much to my surprise, he actually hangs on my every word. He seems genuinely interested, asking me follow-up questions and taking notes. Now that I am talking about my passion, I feel relaxed and in control.

The food arrives, so I place the catalog back in my attaché while Ben stows his notebook away. Our dinners are placed in front of us, and I'm relieved to see I ordered a salad. The server pours more wine for Ben and asks me if I would like a glass, too.

"Actually, I'd love a glass," I say with a smile. I expect Ben to comment, but he simply smiles and cuts his steak. I accept the glass from our server and take a sip of the blood red liquid, nearly moaning at the taste. It's delicious. I tell him so and he beams at me.

"This is one of my very favorite wines," Ben confesses as the server strides off.

A chuckle escapes my lips.

"That's funny?"

"No, it's just that you don't really strike me as a wine guy."

"That is an astute observation. What, pray tell, would you say is my poison of choice?"

This is too easy. "Hmmm, that is a hard question." I purse my lips as I pretend to mull it over. "You definitely strike me as a bourbon kinda guy."

Ben raises a brow and a small smile tugs at my lips. "Is that right? What brings you to that conclusion?"

"I could lie and tell you that I guessed, but I won't. I remember what drink you ordered the night we met." I grin with a little wink.

"You remember what drink I ordered?" His brows arch in feigned delight. "Well, Jill, if I didn't know any better, I would swear that I made an impression on you."

He has no idea. "I'm glad you know better."

His lips curl up into a smile, revealing those dimples of his. I drain my glass and warmth spreads through my belly, knowing it isn't the wine causing this stir inside of me.

"Would you like some more wine?" he asks as he hovers the bottle above my glass.

I am inclined to say yes, because part of me wants to prolong the evening. But a nagging voice in the back of my head is telling me to go. I am not setting myself up for disappointment and heartbreak. I need to get off this road. "I think I have had enough. Thank you, Ben," I state politely.

He nods and places the bottle back on the table.

"In fact, I think I should probably call it a night. If you have any more questions, you can email me."

"You're right, it is getting late." Ben motions the server and requests the check, handing him his credit card without even looking to find out how much the dinner costs.

Our server returns swiftly, and Ben puts his credit card back into his wallet. He hesitates for a moment, but then slides out of the booth and picks up my coat. I follow suit and smoothly glide out of the booth. An involuntarily shiver courses through my body as he helps me into it.

"Let me walk you out," he offers. "I'll help you catch a cab."

"Actually, I have a driver waiting for me, but thank you."

"Let me walk you to your car then."

"All right."

We walk through the restaurant, which for the time of night is still very crowded. Ben places his hand on the small of my back, and my breath catches. I notice some longing looks being thrown his way, and I hate to admit that I loathe them. A chilly New York breeze greets us as we step outside onto the teeming sidewalk.

"Well, I think this was a very successful *business* dinner," he tells me as we walk toward my waiting car.

"I think so, too. I am very excited." Upon our approach, the driver gets out of the car and moves to open the door for me, but Ben beats him to it. I get into the back seat and look up at him. "I look forward to further discussions."

He presses the button on the window, lowering it before shutting the door. He holds out his hand, and I place mine in it. He brings it to his lips and presses a small, sweet kiss on the back of my hand before letting it go. "Goodnight, Jill."

"Goodnight, Ben," I croak.

Our eyes lock, and even as the driver starts to pull into traffic, I don't look away. He smiles at me, and I give him a small wave. I don't take my eyes off him until we turn the corner.

I'm so screwed.

CHAPTER
Three

I WALK INTO THE LOBBY, nod a greeting to the doorman, and stride toward the elevator. "I'm expected."

"Very good, sir." He moves to the phone to alert my presence. "I'll just let them know you're on the way up."

I step into the elevator, press the PH button, and stare at the wall during the thirty second ride until the doors swish open. I walk into the hallway, approach their door, and raise my hand to knock, but it's pulled open before I can connect.

"Benjamin!" A beaming Hannah stands in front of me, Brody seated firmly on her hip, his head leaning on her shoulder, thumb in his mouth. "What brings you over in the middle of the day?" She steps out of the way and motions for me to come inside. "Not that I'm complaining! You know I love seeing you."

I reach for Brody. "Here, let me take him. You look like your arm is going to fall off."

Sighing gratefully, she shifts him from her arms to mine.

"He's been a handful these last few weeks. He won't let me put him down."

I adjust him so that he's resting with his head down on my shoulder and kiss the top of his downy locks, inhaling and appreciating his baby smell. *Why do they always smell so damn good?*

He looks like a mini Drew; same dark hair and striking blue eyes. "No Gracie?" I think my favorite part of visiting Hannah is getting to see what kind of witty quips her six-year-old daughter will throw my way.

"School." She turns and starts toward the kitchen. "Come on, you want some coffee?"

"Sure, that sounds great." I follow her, stepping over toys along the way, and sit on a stool while she moves around prepping the coffee for us.

"You hungry?" She walks to the fridge and pulls the door open. "I can make you a sandwich or a salad if you want?"

"Just coffee is great." I smile at her and think how lucky my brother is to have someone this loving in his life. Although their beginning was definitely a little unconventional, nothing about their life today is.

They share a love and devotion for each other that I can't help but admire and hope to find myself one day. I'm thirty-six years old, almost thirty-seven. I'm getting tired of the chase, nameless girls, and my empty apartment.

"So, you going to tell me what's on your mind?" She lifts a brow as she sets a big mug in front of me, steam rising from the hot, black liquid.

I take a sip and grin. "What, you think I have a motive? Just couldn't stop by to see my favorite sister?"

"I see you almost every day, Ben." She comes up beside

me and pulls a now sleeping Brody out of my arms, and I watch as she places him gently in a nearby pack-n-play before walking back to sit on the stool beside mine. "That's how I know you've got something on your mind."

I smile sheepishly into my coffee before looking back up at her. "Guilty as charged I guess."

"All right, spill then." She pulls her cup of coffee closer and takes a sip.

"There's a girl." Before I can get another word out, she starts laughing. My brow scrunches up in confusion at her response.

She slaps her hand over her mouth and shakes her head as she gets her laughing under control. "It's Jill Baldwin, isn't it?" My eyes open wide, and she smacks her hand on the counter when she registers my surprised look.

"Uh-huh! I knew it! I saw the way you looked at her at the opening celebration!" She hits her hand on my leg this time and smiles wide. "And Drew may have mentioned you have a little crush on her."

"Fucking, Drew." I mutter, then sheepishly nod. "But yeah, it's Jill Baldwin."

"I knew it!" She claps her hands in delight and beams like she just won the lottery. Women are strange. "Okay, what can I do to help?"

"She's playing hard to get, and let's face it, Hannah, you wrote the book on that one."

Her mouth falls open as her brows shoot up. "Benjamin Sapphire, I did not play hard to get. My situation was completely different and you know it."

"Okay, if you say so." I raise a brow in doubt. "The point is, she says everything is about business and insists on keeping things that way, but there is a chemistry there. When we're together, talking, just being in the same space, it's different than anything else I've ever felt before, and I know she feels it, too. But, damn it, she's fighting it tooth and nail."

"Are you sure it's not just the fact that she's saying no?" She raises her hand to stop me from arguing. "Don't get mad at the question; it's a fair one. I mean, let's face it, Ben, you don't hear that word very often."

I roll my eyes. "I hear it more than you think, and no, that's not the issue. Because you're right; for every one person that says no, there are ten that say yes."

"Well, aren't you just special, little lover boy?" She's joking when she says it, but what she doesn't realize is that it's not a title I want.

I can't remember the last time I spent an actual night with anyone and felt happy about it the next morning, or had a conversation with a woman that intrigued me. Most of the time, women approach and proposition me, not the other way around. And spending every night by yourself gets lonely.

It fills a void but definitely not anything in my heart. I think she realizes she's hit a nerve because she reaches over and grabs my hand. "I'm sorry, Ben. I was only joking. You are one of the most caring men I've ever met in my life. Let's not forget that I know this better than just about anyone."

She's referring to her first husband, Jackson, who was killed in action shortly after I lost my leg. Losing him and two other brothers-in-arms was almost more than I could bear, especially while I was dealing with the loss of half my leg. With help, though, I did get through the losses and started a gym for disabled veterans. It's free and there for anyone that needs its services. It's named after her late-husband.

I squeeze her hand and force a smile. "I know."

"So, we need to figure out how to get Jill to take you seriously." She taps her finger on her chin, thinking, and then suddenly sits up straight and points her finger in the air. "I know what you need to do!"

"Okay, let's hear it." I can't wait to see what she's come up with.

"Well, you are definitely interested in her business, right? And, that seems to be the most important thing to her at the moment, right?"

"Definitely a top priority for her. And, yes, me too. It would actually be a great partnership." I waggle my brows. "In every way if I can help it."

She rolls her eyes. "Oh, Benny."

I frown at her use of Drew's nickname for me. "Keep going."

"Then you need to go check out her business. You can use it as an in to see her again. Go to her spa, say you want to see and experience the services in person. You need her to first believe that you're committed to the business partnership before she's ever going to take a chance on you personally."

"That's it?" It seems to simple.

"Yes, that's it." She reaches for her phone, brings up a number, and then puts the phone to her ear after pressing call.

"Hey, Jill! It's Hannah Sapphire. How are you?" She's silent for a minute, nodding her head as she listens to Jill.

"Yes, I had a great time at the opening, as well. I was so glad you were able to come. I was actually wondering if you could help me out with something?"

She gets up, pacing back and forth in the kitchen as she talks. "Drew and his brother Ben have worked so hard getting the resort up and running, and I was hoping to treat them to some services at your spa. They need to relax for a bit!"

She's nodding her head again. "Yes, you are so right! It's a wonderful way for them to see first-hand what you do!"

She nods her head a few more times and then gives me a big thumbs-up. "Yes, I can get them there on Thursday for you. Not a problem at all. Thank you so much. Let's get together ourselves soon, too! You, me, and Raeva for lunch! Okay, bye, Jill!"

Ending the call, she looks up at me with a victory grin on her face. "Step one of Operation Get Jill is complete! You and Ben have a full spa package scheduled for this Thursday at noon!"

I smile brightly back at her and wrap her in a hug. "You are the best! Thanks!"

TWO DAYS LATER, Drew and I walk into Serenity ten minutes before noon for our appointment. "This was a good idea, brother. The best way for us to determine just how top of the line their products and services are."

"You have your wife to thank for this, not me. She came up with the brilliant idea."

"Ah, yes, the 'Operation Get Jill' plan. Hannah did mention that." He shakes his head while giving me a hard eye roll. "I'm trying to forget about that part of this visit."

I grin over at him. "But that's the best part of the whole afternoon." Our conversation pauses as we're greeted at reception and then shown to a locker room where we can change. I thought Jill was going to meet us, so I voice my disappointment to Drew when I don't see her.

"I'm sure she's quite busy. Perhaps she got pulled into something else. Besides, we're here for several hours. I'm sure we'll see her at some point."

We're led to a medium sized room where two massage tables are set up. Two women are waiting in the room and smile when we enter, one of them speaking. "Good afternoon, gentlemen. Jill booked this room for you, in case you wanted to discuss business during your massage, but if you'd prefer a single room, we can accommodate that for you as well."

I look at Drew, and we both shrug in unison. "This is fine."

"Wonderful. We'll step out and let you get situated on the table. Just slide under the sheet, and we'll start face down."

The women leave and we both move to a table. I sit on the table, bend down and pull my prosthetic off below the knee, then lean it against the table. Drew's already sliding under the sheet as I stand and balance on one leg to take my robe off and then slide under my own. The room is warm, and soft melodic music is playing over speakers hidden somewhere. It's relaxing, and I chalk up one point for Jill and her business.

"So, do you really like her, or is it just the thrill of the chase?" Drew asks from his side of the room, his words slightly mumbled as his face is lying sideways on the table.

"It's not the chase." I scoff. "Well, you know, a little chase is always fun, but that's not it. Yes, she absolutely may be one of the most beautiful woman I've laid eyes on, but it's more than that. There's a spark there. She's challenging and smart and isn't afraid or intimidated by me one little bit. It's refreshing to find a woman who is utterly sure of herself and knows what she wants but also shows some vulnerability."

The door clicks open, and I hear two sets of feet shuffle quietly in. "Any objection to oils?" one of the women asks. Drew and I both grunt out a, "No."

I feel the sheet being adjusted and then a slight gasp as all movement stills for a minute. I'm never sure if it's because of the tattoos covering my back or if it's my leg, but the pause is so short, and I'm so used to it by now, that I dismiss it as quickly as it occurred.

"So, are you going to ask her on a real date?" Drew mumbles between a moan.

I feel oil on my back and then let out a long sigh when hands start to work my shoulders. I boxed for two hours yesterday, and I'm sore as hell today.

"That's the plan." I groan as the fingers dig hard into a knot on my back. "But, first, I think I have to get her to admit she likes me."

Jill 15 minutes earlier...

I COULD HAVE KILLED Anna a few minutes ago. Rationally, I know it isn't her fault that the daycare called to inform her that Casey—her little girl—has a fever, and thus per policy, needs to be collected from daycare. I know she had no intention of leaving me high and dry. But still, I can't help but feel annoyed that she put me in this situation, today of all days.

The spa is completely booked, and I have no other available staff. Seeing as today is all about impressing the Sapphire men, I have no other choice but to step in myself. We walk back into the room after a few minutes have passed by. Aisha asks if they object to oils, and neither does. She has already positioned herself beside Drew to start his massage and I chastise myself for my predicament. *I should have insisted before that she take Ben.*

I gently pull back the sheet, a small gasp escaping from my lips as I absorb the sight before me. Never in my life have I ever seen someone's back and thought it was sexy.

This man's back is a work of art—all muscle and sunkissed skin decorated with ink. I knew he had tattoos but would have never imagined that so many graced his skin. At first glance, I think it's just a tribal tattoo, but upon further inspection, I find several animals sketched into his back. The large wolf particularly grabs my attention, and I long to trace my fingers over the fur that looks so real.

Grabbing a few bottles from the warmer, I mix the different oils together in my hands. I smooth the oil all over his broad shoulders and his back, tracing each muscle. I've never really been a tattoo kinda girl, but his are beautiful, not to mention the canvas.

I am so enthralled that I nearly miss when Drew mumbles something about asking "her" out on a real date. My heart rate accelerates and begins to knock against my ribcage as my fingers kneed his firm flesh. *Is he talking about me?*

"That's the plan," he says as my fingers make short work of a knot in his back. He groans, and the sound of it causes a stir in my belly. He tells Drew that he has to get "her" to admit she likes him. And, I know then, without a shadow of a doubt, that he is talking about me.

Frankly, it annoys me, and not just because he is cocky enough to think that I might have more feelings for him than I am admitting to. Mostly, it's because I know that his pretentious self is right, even though I don't want him to be.

Drew chuckles."How are you planning to pull that off, Romeo? It's not like your charms have worked on her so far."

I bite my bottom lip to stifle my laugh. I'm beginning to like Drew more and more.

"What do you know?" Ben grumbles. He sounds sullen, and it is adorable. My hands continue to explore, and I have a hard time keeping my inner dialog under control. As my fingers sweep across his back and dip lower to his buttocks, I nearly groan myself. It's rare for a man to have a nice backside, but Ben? Yeah, the man wrote the book on having a great ass. I tell myself to focus. You'd think I've never done this before.

I pull the sheet back up to his shoulders and position myself at the bottom of the table. I'm about to lift the sheet when I notice a prosthetic leg leaning against the table. I tilt my head, glancing at the table beside me, but neither Drew nor Aisha is paying attention to me. I lift the sheet to position it so his lower half is exposed and see that it's indeed Ben's prosthetic. I had no idea that he had lost part of his leg.

Shaking my head, I attempt to clear my thoughts, becoming even more curious about the man beneath me. I rub some more oil onto my hands and start to massage his upper legs. He stiffens for a short moment when I slide my hands near his stump but soon relaxes under my fingers.

Maybe, I have been judging him unfairly? Maybe, my opinion of him has more to do with my own fears? Maybe, I should just give the man a chance? Maybe, I have been trying so hard to keep him at arm's length, to deny—even to myself—that there is an obvious attraction between us. But, honestly, I am not sure I can muster up the will to deny it anymore.

"You know what?" Ben says.

"What?" Drew mumbles.

"I'm just gonna ask her." I declare.

Drew lifts his head toward Ben and opens his eyes. His expression is one of complete surprise when his gaze lands on me, a smirk appearing on his face. A small smile tugs at my mouth in response as I shrug.

"You are just going to ask her what, Benny?" Drew continues to look at me as he continues his conversation with his brother.

I smile back at Drew and shake my head.

"I'm just going to lay it on the table."

"You are laying on a table."

"You know what I mean, asshole," he says, clearly a little irritated. "If I go to her and just tell her how I feel, ask for a chance to get to know her better over dinner or something, what else can she say besides yes?"

My brow shoots up, and Drew cocks his head, scratching his chin as he attempts to mask his growing smile.

I pull the sheet back to cover Ben, then make my way toward the head of the table. I lean in close until my mouth is right by his ear. "I'll tell you what else she can say." I grin wickedly when his head shoots off the table to lock eyes with mine. "I'm not your typical kinda girl. I expect gentle-man-like behavior—opened doors, pull out my chair type of thing. If you are running late, pick up a phone and call or don't bother showing up. If you can live with that, you can pick me up tomorrow night at seven," I inform him.

I stand straight and walk toward the door, just as Ben pushes himself up off the table. I reach for the handle but pause briefly. "Oh, and Ben, any man that wants to take me out to dinner has to bring me flowers. White lilies are my favorites, if you care."

Ben stares back at me, shock apparent on his face for only a second before he flashes me a stunning smile. "White lilies, huh?"

I smile and nod.

"Duly noted."

I close the door behind me and scurry to my office to catch my breath, or at least until my heartbeat slows down. I need a minute or two just to collect my thoughts. The Sapphire men are scheduled to be here for most of the afternoon, but luckily for me, I can hide in here while my staff takes over.

I try to focus on work for a while, but thoughts of Ben, his very naked body, and a date with him tomorrow keep distracting me. I need some girl time to help me collect my thoughts. I pull my phone out and go to the group text between myself, Rae, and Mik and tell them that I need an emergency cocktail meeting tonight. I press send, my fingers drumming on my desk as I wait for their responses, a knock on my door distracting me.

"Yes?" I call out to my closed door.

The door opens, and Sage, the front desk girl, sticks her head in. "Hey Jill?"

"Yes?"

"There is a delivery for you."

"Okay. Do I need to sign for it or something?"

"Um, no, but I think you might want to come and see this."

I rise and walk toward the door but step back when it opens wider and several delivery people enter, and begin filling up my office with white lilies. A girlish giggle escapes my lips as my cheeks heat up and flush a light pink. The last person to walk in is holding a bouquet so large that I don't notice it's Ben until he places the flowers on top of my desk.

"I see that you don't half-ass things," I say with a small chuckle.

He smirks and waves a hand across my flower-filled room. "Go big or go home."

"That is a dangerous precedent you are setting for yourself, Mr. Sapphire," A playful tone to my response.

"I'm okay with that," I inhale his scent as he leans closer. "I think you're worth it."

I'm smiling so big, my face hurts. I've got to hand it to the man. He is good.

"I'd like to properly ask you out." He looks at me, brow raised, an expectant look on his handsome face.

"By all means," I retort, happy to play this game.

He flashes me those dimples of his, and I know I am a goner. "Jill, I'd love to take you out for dinner tomorrow night if you are free?"

"It's kind of last minute. I will have to check my schedule," I deadpan, glancing around the large bouquet of flowers to feign a look at my calendar.

"Of course," he says, one side of his mouth quirking up.

"Hmmm," I tell him. "I think I might be able to squeeze you in."

We both smirk at one another, and he takes a step forward.

"Does seven work for you?" he asks.

"It does." I walk to my desk, jot my address and cell number down on my business card, and then stroll back to hand it to him.

Ben leans in to place a gentle kiss on my cheek as he slides the card from my fingers. I close my eyes and let out a sigh as his lips make contact against my skin. "See you tomorrow night, Jill."

"Looking forward to it, Ben."

Did I mention how screwed I was?

CHAPTER
Four

THE TOWN CAR pulls up in front of her building precisely five minutes before seven, and I realize I'm nervous. I can't remember the last time I felt like this; well, at least, about picking a woman up for a date. There were plenty of times overseas that I was more than nervous, but those were life and death situations. This is definitely not that. I take a deep breath and tell the driver I'll be just a minute.

I step out of the car and approach her building but stop in my tracks, my heart skipping two beats in my chest as I see her exit the building. Did I just say this isn't a life or death situation? Because what she's wearing literally knocks the wind out of me. She sashays up to me, hips swaying lightly back and forth as her heels click on the pavement, her smile brightening the dusky night sky.

I sweep my gaze up her body, clad in a little black dress, but not your typical LBD. Oh, no, not my Jill. This one hugs every curve of her body, starting with the high neckline that is followed by two, black sheer strips; the second strip revealing just a peek of her cleavage. The dress falls a few inches above her knees, but there's a slit in one side of the skirt that exposes almost her entire thigh with each step.

She's teasing me, and the smile she's giving me says she knows it. She comes to a stop in front of me, and I reach out to gently clasp her hand in mine, raise it to my lips, and brush a soft kiss against her knuckles. "You look exquisite."

Her cheeks flush just the lightest color of pink as she casts her eyes down to my feet and then leisurely up my body until she meets my gaze. "You look pretty fine your-self, Mr. Sapphire."

I grimace at being called Mr. Anything but don't want to start the evening off on the wrong foot, so I smile and nod my head in thanks. "I would have come up."

"I was ready. No need." She fidgets with her small clutch and smiles. "Am I dressed appropriately? You didn't say where we were going?"

"You're perfect." I move my hand to her elbow and guide her to the town car where the driver is already waiting with an open door. I help her in and then move around to the other side of the car, settling myself in beside her.

As soon as I sit in the enclosed space with her, I'm assaulted by her scent and close my eyes for a minute to try to identify it's origin. It's unique and not the overly sweet perfume other women often wear. This is light and fresh and reminds me of how the air smells in the forest after a summer storm.

"Are you okay?" Her voice is a bit timid.

My eyes fly open, and I turn my head so I can meet her gaze. "I was smelling you."

"Smelling me?" Her brows furrow in confusion.

"Yes." I lean my head forward so that my nose is almost touching her neck, and I inhale deeply. I lift my gaze back to her, not pulling away. "You smell like the rain, clean and crisp and pure."

Her hand moves to her neck as she pulls back from me just a bit, and I realize I might be invading her space a little too soon, so I pull myself back up straight. "Sorry. I didn't mean to make you uncomfortable."

She drops her hand down onto mine as she provides me with a warm smile. "You aren't making me uncomfortable. It's a nice compliment. Thank you."

I turn my palm so I can lace her fingers in mine, pulling it into my lap, my thumb sweeping back and forth across hers. Her skin is soft and warm against mine. "You're welcome."

"So, are you going to tell me where we're going?" She tilts her head to one side as she asks.

"You don't like surprises?" I raise an eyebrow in response.

"Only good surprises."

"This is a good one. I promise."

She chuckles. "Already making promises?"

I frown. "Is that a bad thing?"

"Only when you don't deliver, and in my experience, I've learned most men don't."

Immediately feeling challenged by her statement, I raise my brows. I grasp her hand a little tighter and yank her flush to me, a yelp of surprise escaping her painted red lips which are now a breath away from mine. I take her face gently in my other hand and meet her hard stare.

"Let me assure you, Jill, I'll deliver on any promise I make to you. And I also guarantee you won't be disappointed because I'm not like most men, and I don't like being compared to them." I cock my head closer. "Understand?"

My voice is just short of a growl, but she doesn't look scared. She looks aroused. Her breath is falling in short little pants, and her gaze keeps moving from my eyes to my mouth, her pink tongue darting out to run across her lips as she nods. "Got it."

I move my hand slightly and run my thumb over the same trail her tongue just took, her breath inhaling sharply as I do, her eyes fluttering shut. I lean in, but instead of kissing her and doing the expected, I trail my nose across her cheek, down her neck, and then up to her ear, brushing against her soft locks and finally whispering, "I could kiss you right now. I want to. So badly. But in *my* experience, *really* good things are worth the wait."

She pulls back sharply from my grasp and purses her lips, fire burning in her eyes. "You, Benjamin Sapphire, are a tease."

I give her my most devilish grin. "And you, Jill Baldwin, are fun to tease." Her mouth falls open to respond, but I point out the window and speak. "We've arrived, and just in the nick of time, I think."

"Just in the nick of time for you, I think," she retorts.

I step out of the car and motion for the driver to stay as I move to the other side to open Jill's door. "Is there a restaurant in this marina?" I watch as she swivels her head back and forth in search of one.

"Sort of." I take her hand and start toward one of the

docks where a large yacht is moored. "Come on, it's this way."

"Are we going on that?" She points to the boat, eyes wide.

I'm thrilled to have surprised her and maybe even a little proud that I can share such a luxurious experience with her. The yacht is actually my parents, but they rarely use it these days. They were more than happy to lend it to me, as well as the staff, for the evening. Especially after they found out that I'd be taking a date on board. I think, they're afraid I'm never going to settle down. "We sure are. Do you like boats?"

"Um, sure. I mean, this is more than a boat. But are you sure I'm really dressed for this?" She pulls back on my hand, stalling our forward progress.

I chuckle at her dress concerns. "Jill, this is a luxury yacht. You won't have to do any mooring or sailing on this. You're absolutely perfect."

"So, we're actually going to leave the dock and go out on the water?" Her voice rises an octave.

"Yep." I start moving forward again. "The staff have a wonderful dinner they're preparing for us, and we can relax and watch the stars as we eat and take in the New York City skyline."

"That sounds wonderful." She stammers as we reach the vessel. "I've never been on a luxury yacht before."

I help her onto the yacht and lead her to the main salon where the staff are waiting. Introductions are made before the captain excuses himself to get our trip underway. Heather, one of the attendants, pours us each a glass of champagne, and I usher Jill toward the deck.

"Isn't it beautiful?" I want to make sure she's comfortable, but I also am doing my damndest to try to impress this woman.

"It really is gorgeous. It feels so decadent." She wraps her arms around herself and shivers as we approach the railing. I shrug my jacket off and drop it over her shoulders as I move to stand behind her and shield the wind.

"Is it too cold for you? We can go back inside." I run my hands lightly up and down her arms to warm her.

"No, it's fine. I like the fresh air." She turns her head and gives me a smile. "Thank you for your jacket."

"Let me know if you get too cold. I can get you a blanket." I step closer to her so the heat of my body insulates her. She leans back against me and lets out a long sigh, which in turn makes my heart race. I want her to feel relaxed with me, comfortable. I want this to be one of the best nights of her life and feel like we're off to a perfect start.

"IS it too cold for you? We can go back inside," Ben asks with concern in his voice as he gently rubs my arms on either side, trying to warm me.

Oh, God, please no, not inside.

He's very sweet, and I hate that this date is probably going to be ruined by my seasickness. I am inwardly kicking myself, knowing I should have spoken up when I had the chance. Now, I have to put on my big girl panties and power through. He steps closer, pressing his body against mine.

I am a little taken aback by how natural this feels, but I don't dwell, and let myself enjoy the moment. I lean back against him, and a soft contented sigh falls from my lips. With my head resting against his chest, I listen to his heart beating. It's accelerated, like mine. Ben leans in and kisses the top of my head. I lift my gaze, and his eyes fix on mine. We stare at each other for a moment. Suddenly, he spins me around and pushes my back against the railing, caging me with one arm and cupping my face with the other.

"Fuck waiting," he snarls.

His lips press against mine, gentle little pecks at first but it's not enough. I throw my arms around his neck, the jacket slipping from my shoulders, my body no longer chilly. I deepen the kiss, and while it starts off sweetly, our tongues dancing around each other, exploring, tasting each other, it soon turns more frantic, almost desperate.

Any feeling of nausea or cold is forgotten as this man expertly invades my mouth. My entire body feels like it is on fire, and the heat between my thighs is almost unbearable. There is no denying that I want him. *Right now*. Unfortunately, we are interrupted by the clearing of a throat and both turn to face a very red-faced staff member, whose name currently escapes me.

"I am so sorry, Mr. Sapphire. I wanted to let you know that dinner is being served."

Ben recovers much faster than I do, because he flashes her a smile and thanks her. He holds out his hand, and I take it without a shred of hesitation. I'll follow him anywhere right now.

We head inside, and I inhale a sharp breath as I appraise the sight before me. The table is beautifully set, and the food smells delicious. I can't disguise the smile beaming from my face when I notice the vase of white lilies on the center of the table.

Ben pulls out my chair and I lower myself in to it. He makes his way across from me and gracefully drops into his seat, flashing that grin that makes me weak in the knees. The girl that caught us making out on the deck walks in with plates of appetizers, and I feel my cheeks heating when her gaze meets mine. She smiles at me sweetly and gives me a wink, putting me at ease.

"This is stunning."

"Thank you," he replies, eyes fixed on me. "You're stunning."

My cheeks heat under his scrutiny, lifting at his compliment. I place my napkin on my lap, and I begin moving some of the starters to my plate. The boat begins to sway, the rocking motion seeming to intensify with each bite I take.

I set my fork down and blow out a long breath, hoping to settle the roiling motion that's begun in my belly. Ben's brow furrows, concern evident on his face as he peers over the food at me.

"Are you okay?" He points to the pitcher of water on the table. "Would you like some water?"

I can feel my stomach contents coming up, and my eyes widen and flash over to meet his. Panicked, I scan the room, trying to search for a bathroom. I can't see myself, but I'm convinced that I must be a lovely shade of green at this moment.

"Bathroom," I gasp.

Ben jumps out of his chair and is over to me in a heartbeat. He lifts me into his arms and carries me swiftly to the bathroom. I drop to my knees in front of the toilet and am mortified as my insides gush out like a tsunami. Ben kneels beside me and holds my hair with one hand while stroking my back with the other.

When it finally feels as if the sickness is letting up, embarrassment rears its ugly head. I cover my mouth with my hand and stand, stumbling toward the sink. I turn on the faucet and rinse out my mouth, I look up and grimace when I see my reflection in the mirror.

"Are you okay?" he asks me. "Is it motion sickness?"

I bite my lip as our eyes meet in the mirror and I nod.

"Shit." He rakes a hand over his beard. "Has this happened before? I would have never taken the yacht out if I had known you were prone to sea sickness."

"It may have happened once or twice before." I reply sheepishly. I close the lid on the toilet and slump down onto the seat, my stomach still not feeling its best. "You went to so much trouble to set this beautiful dinner up. I didn't want to ruin it and hoped—well prayed, if I'm being honest — that the seas would be calm enough that I'd be okay." I force a weak smile. "So much for that theory."

"You could have told me. Dinner would have been just as nice moored to the dock." Ben kneels down in front of me, taking my hands into his. "You don't have to hide things from me. I'm not a fragile flower that will fall apart if plans have to change."

He rises to his full height, pulling me up with him. "Let's get this baby turned around and get you feeling better, yeah?"

"Please." I practically plead, my hand flat on my turbulent tummy.

He smiles and asks me if I will be okay for a moment, and I tell him I'll be fine. He comes back only a short moment later and wraps a blanket around me before he leads me back onto the deck. We sit in complete silence with his arm draped around me.

I am grateful when we make it back to the dock so quickly. We thank the staff, and Ben wastes no time ushering me off the boat and onto the dock. My legs are still a little wobbly, and he must notice, because he wraps an arm around me, pulling me up against his frame to steady me.

We make it to the car, and he helps me inside, closing the door once I'm settled, then moving around the other side to climb in beside me. His eyes, as dark as the night, analyze me. "Feeling better?"

I nod, my pride swallowing away any words I might have.

"I guess we're going to have to try this again." He flashes me a glimpse of his cocky grin as he continues. "But on land this time."

I look at the man that just held my hair as I lost every last bit of what was in my stomach, and am overcome with an unfamiliar feeling. Not able to put any words together at this moment in time, I just nod.

Screwed? I'm fucked.

CHAPTER
Five

FRUSTRATION REIGNS supreme as I walk around the car to climb in beside Jill. Have I made her feel so uncomfortable that she couldn't share the truth with me about her aversion to being on the water?

Reasonably, I know she was only trying to make the best out of what ended up being a bad predicament for her, but I want her to feel she can be completely open with me and know I won't be upset. I think it's the soldier in me. I'm used to my team letting me know any weaknesses so we can protect and keep each other's backs safe. And damn it if I don't feel like I need to protect Jill.

I open the door and lower myself into the seat next to her. One look in her direction has me doing a complete one-eighty. She's practically curled herself up like a kitten, the blanket from the yacht wrapped around her, making her tiny form somehow look even smaller. Her eyes are downcast, her skin still so pale from the turbulence her body felt

469

on the boat. She musters a small smile and peeks up at me from under her dark lashes.

"Feeling better?" It's hard to tell quite honestly, especially when she only answers with a nod.

"I guess we're going to have to try this again?" I chuckle. "But on land this time."

She nods again, and is silent for another moment before an apology tumbles from her. "I'm so sorry, Ben. I should have said something."

Not wanting her to feel one ounce of remorse over any time we spend together, including this disaster of a date, I slide closer and unbuckle her seat belt. I gather her in my arms and pull her into my lap and up against my chest. "No apologies. I understand you were only trying to brave it out to please me."

Her head bobs up and down against my shirt, her soft hair tickling the exposed portion of my chest. And, yes, I inhale again, because even though she was sick only a short time ago, she still smells fucking amazing.

"Will you give me a chance to redeem myself?" I whisper gently against the top of her head.

She nods again and snuggles her body into mine, resting her head against my shoulder. "I think I'm the one that needs to do the redeeming here."

"Dinner tomorrow? At my place? I'll cook for you, and I promise, I live on solid ground."

She nods again but then stops abruptly. "I actually have plans tomorrow night, but I can do the night after if you're free."

"I am now." I pull her petite frame tighter against me and drop another kiss on top of her head. I hate that she's feeling so terrible and that it's my doing. I guess I'll have to make sure I do a little recon work for our next date—find out what she likes and doesn't like to eat, and any allergies she may have. I am not going to put her in a position again where she feels like she may disappoint me.

The car comes to a slow stop as it pulls up outside of her building. The driver jumps quickly out of the car and opens my door for me. Jill moves to get off my lap, but I move my arms under her legs and pull her flush to me. "I've got you."

I turn and place both feet on the pavement and thank God I've strengthened my one good leg so it's strong enough to rise out of the car with her in my arms. She looks up at me, her eyes soft, her color finally returning to the lovely shade of pink it should be, the corners of her perfect lips lifting just slightly. "Thank you for taking care of me, Benjamin."

What I really want to do is crush my mouth against hers, but instead, I brush a soft kiss against her forehead and smile. "Nothing gives me greater pleasure." And I truly mean it when I say it.

The door to her building opens before I even reach it, a look of concern on the doorman's face. "Is everything okay, Ms. Baldwin? Can I do anything?"

"Everything's fine. Just an upset stomach. Can you get the elevator for us?" I stride in its direction, the doorman scurrying ahead of me to push the call button.

"Ms. Baldwin, you just ring down if you need anything. James or myself will run out."

"You're so sweet, Henry. Thank you." She smiles weakly as we pass by and into the elevator that has arrived.

I nod my head in thanks to Henry, and then look at Jill. "You okay to stand? I'll put you down if so."

She nods her head, so I lower her legs to the floor but keep one arm firmly around her waist to keep her close. "What floor?"

"Penthouse."

My brows rise in surprise as I lean forward and stretch my hand out to push the PH button.

"It's not like that. Really. I share it with Mikaela Kingsley," she says defensively.

"I didn't say a thing." But now it all makes sense. Mikaela is filthy rich, and one of the sweetest women on the planet. I'm happy to know she's living in good company.

"I saw the look on your face when I said penthouse," she retorts.

Ah, she's definitely feeling better. Her spark is flickering back to life, and this makes me smile down at her in relief. "That was simply surprise. No judgement."

"Well, I hope not. I've worked really hard for what I have. Mik has been a godsend and one of my best friends."

Unable to help myself, I bend down and peck a kiss on the very tip of her nose. "I agree. Mikaela is one of the very best people I know."

This seems to placate her, because she just nods her head tightly and then leans against my shoulder. I wish I could hold her against me all night, but know I need to put her needs first. The elevator comes to a stop and we step out into the foyer.

There are two penthouse suites on the floor so I turn and look at her. "Which door?"

"Oh, sorry, that one." Her delicate hand snakes out from

the blanket, and a finger points to the door on the left. I lead us in that direction and am about to ask her for the key, when the door swings open, Mikaela standing in the entrance.

"Jill! What happened?" She glances to her friend and then up at me with an accusatory expression on her face. "What did you do to her, Benjamin Sapphire?"

I'm about to speak my defense, but Jill beats me to it. "He's been wonderful, Mik. I just got a bit seasick."

Mik slaps my arm and then places her hands on her hips. "You took her on a boat? Are you crazy?"

I let out a sigh an in attempt to stay calm. "Can you step aside so we can come in?"

"Oh!" Her eyes pop wide as she realizes she's standing in the middle of the doorway and moves. "Sorry."

I lift one brow and frown as I walk past her, Jill still pressed to my side. "I had no idea she got seasick. She didn't tell me until *after* the boat left the shore and got sick."

I stop and turn my head toward a trailing Mik. "I would never have put her in a position to make her ill if I had known." I continue further into the apartment.

I look down at Jill and soften my voice. "Which way to your room Angel?"

She tilts her head to one side of the room. "Down that hallway. It's the second door on the left, but, Ben, I'm okay now. I'm feeling much better."

"I've got you." I don't care how uncomfortable she might feel right now; I'm not letting her go until I know she's safe in her room.

I follow the direction she's given and guide her into the bedroom. Mik's still trailing behind me and flicks on the light, then runs around me so she can pull back the covers on the bed. I gently place Jill on the bed and slide my arm out from around her waist.

She smiles up at me and trails her hand down my arm as it moves away from her, finding my hand and giving it a squeeze. "Thank you, Ben. Even though things didn't go quite as planned, you've been wonderful."

I lean forward, wrap my free hand around the back of her head, and pull her forward until my lips press against her forehead in a quick kiss. "I promise, our next date will be one thousand times better."

"I can't wait," she whispers back.

We release each other as I rise and turn to find Mik watching us like a hawk. Before she can squawk at me again, I raise my finger to silence her. "Just take care of her."

I stroll past her and out of the apartment before she can say another word.

"SURE SOUNDS like that date went well." Mikaela jests, amused as she sits on the bed next to me.

I dramatically bury my head into the pillow and groan loudly, much to her delight. "Glad that my misery is entertaining to you."

Mikaela pats me on the head. "I'm sorry, babe. I promise I'll try to wait and glee over your misery later when you feel better."

"Gee, thanks." I deadpan.

I stand and head to the bathroom so I can change and

brush my teeth, but both our heads snap to the door, which is thrown open as Raeva bursts in. "What the heck happened?" she demands.

Rae looks incredible; dressed to the nines in a stunning gown. She and Mika must have been on a date themselves. That man is always thinking of ways to sweep her off her feet.

"Well?" she urges as she lowers herself on the bed with Mik, watching as I grab pajamas from a drawer and walk into my attached bathroom. I can hear them loud and clear as I change and brush my teeth.

"He took her on a yacht," Mikaela explains.

"Is he crazy?" Raeva belts out.

"My exact response to him."

Mikaela says, frowning, "When we got back from dinner and James told us that you were carried in the building looking like a ghost, I nearly had a conniption! I left Mika standing in the lobby and ran into the elevator!" She throws her hands up in the air, her head shaking. "Ugh, I could kill Ben right now! What the heck was he thinking?"

"He didn't know. It's not his fault," I protest as I walk back into the room. "I swear, guys, he was amazing. So sweet. He held my hair and stroked my back and practically carried me to the car. Ben really was the perfect gentleman."

I look up when there is a lack of response and find my two besties gaping at me.

"Jillian Baldwin, are you swooning?" Rae teases.

I roll my eyes.

"Don't deny it, you totally are." Mik chimes in.

I sigh. What's the point in denying? My flushed cheeks

have already betrayed me. "He asked me out again," I admit reluctantly.

"Tell us everything," the say in unison. "And don't you dare leave anything out!"

I can't help the smirk that appears on my face when I start to talk about Ben. Up until the point that I started to hug the porcelain throne, it was a great date.

"Are you just going stare dreamily into space, or are you going to take us out of our misery and fill us in?" Rae prods.

"I mean, I have been sitting here all night waiting for you to come home!" Mik whines.

I roll my eyes in an attempt to mask my amusement.

"Did he kiss you? Or did you get sick before he had the chance?" Mik asks.

"Oh, he kissed me." I say with a sigh as I recall how his lips felt against mine.

The two of them squeal like school girls, and honestly, it's hard to resist the urge to join them. That kiss was amazing, and I'm pretty sure if the waitress on the boat hadn't interrupted us, I may have begun shedding my clothing right there on the deck; cold weather and seasickness be damned.

I share the details of the kiss with the girls, and they hang on my every word, sighing dreamily when I finish. As I recount the entire experience, I swear I can feel my lips tingle.

"Wow that sounds amazing. So, swoon worthy." Mikaela says, a soft smile on her lips.

"Yes, up until you started to expel your stomach's contents, it sounds like it was the perfect date." Rae agrees.

"I know, I know." I shake my head at my own mistake. "I

should have told him that boats and I don't mix. But, you guys, I didn't want to come across as high maintenance! Though, in hind sight, I guess that probably would have been better than having him watch me throw my guts up." I state, mortified at the memory.

"I actually think it is romantic." Mik gushes.

"Come again?"

"Well, he took care of you Jillybean. He didn't leave you to your own devices. I'm not even sure if I could have stayed with you to watch you hurl."

I already know this, but hearing her say it out loud makes it even more real to me; Benjamin Sapphire is pretty special. And even though I've agreed to go on another date with him, I wasn't completely sure if I would actually go through with it.

Between the mortifying evening and my reservations about dating, I was seriously considering he might be better off without me. The one thing holding me back was that damn kiss. That scorching as hell, soak my panties, tongue stroking, I'm so damn fucked, kiss.

CHAPTER
Six

I'VE LEARNED, after drilling Mik and Raeva, that Jill loves a good steak, french fries, and asparagus with hollandaise sauce. So, that's what's on the menu for tonight.

I've got the steak marinating, sides prepped, and a bottle of red already open to breathe. She's supposed to be here at 7:00, but knowing from our past meetings that she's always prompt, I expect she'll be arriving any minute.

While I don't live in a penthouse, I do live in a very nice loft. I had it renovated after I bought the building for the gym, which is located downstairs.

It's a large, open space that contains a restaurant-worthy industrial kitchen, a living space filled with a couple of couches, a large flat-screen television, and a bedroom in the back corner of the space that I had sectioned off with some retro glass bricking. I've got rugs scattered throughout on the hardwood floors, and retractable blinds cover the very large warehouse windows that surround three of the outside walls.

I lit some candles, actually ran a vacuum over the floors, and made sure my bed had fresh sheets on it. I wasn't sure what direction our date was going to take, but I certainly hoped that it might end up in the bedroom.

I dressed comfortably, in a pair of worn jeans and a black t-shirt. Now, all I need is my date. No sooner than that thought crosses my mind, the bell to the elevator dings.

The beat of my heart ratchets up a few notches as I make my way over to the call button. I press it and speak. "Come on up." I press another button that unlocks the elevator down below and hear the large doors clank shut and then some light rattling of the wires as it begins to rise.

My bare feet pace back and forth a few short steps, and then stop when the doors slide open revealing who I've come to believe is the most beautiful woman in the world. She seems to have followed suit with my casual attire, because she's also wearing a pair of jeans; although, hers are much darker and fit snug over her long legs. She's got some kind of light cotton top on that's sitting off her shoulders, in a pretty teal color, and has a jacket over her arm.

She holds up a bottle of red wine and beams brightly. "I brought wine!"

I stroll toward her, take the bottle, and using my free hand, cup her face. I tug her just close enough to place a soft kiss against her cheek. "All I need is you."

She flushes a light pink and lets out a soft sigh as a small smile graces her lips. "Hi, Ben."

"Hi." I release her and swing my hand over the space in front of us. "Welcome. Not a single wave in sight."

She chuckles and runs a hand down her face to hide her

embarrassment. "Ugh. Let's forget about that disaster. Please!"

"Done." I take her hand in mine and start toward the kitchen. "You look beautiful, by the way."

"I feel like I should take my heels off so we're on even ground." She giggles beside me.

"Angel, we ain't ever gonna be on even ground. You're always going to be floating in a space much higher than me." I turn and slide my gaze down her body. "No matter what you're wearing."

She tucks her chin in as she tries to hide the blush coloring her cheeks. "Ben, you have to stop saying things like that to me."

We reach the kitchen, so I place the bottle of wine on the island and turn, yanking her up against me by our joined hands, a small gasp of surprise coming from her as our bodies crash together.

I place a finger under her chin and raise it until I'm gazing into her eyes. "I don't know how other men have treated you, but you deserve to be told every day how goddamn beautiful you are. Every time I see you, you take my breath away." I give a small shake of my head. "I don't know how you do it, but each time I see you, you're even more gorgeous than the time before."

Her lips form a small 'o' shape, as her eyes grow wide.

"So, if you're going to be with me, get used to hearing it. You're fucking stunning. A literal angel walking on this earth. I'd almost bet you have wings hidden under that shirt if I didn't already see your bare back the night of the opening."

Her fingers, which were clutched around my biceps a

moment ago, have started to trail gently down my arms as something in her gaze shifts. I watch as her tongue darts out to swipe across her lips, leaving them wet and shiny, causing my restraint to finally snap. My hands move up the back of her neck, sliding around to capture her face, and then I crash my lips to hers.

It's not the first time I've kissed her, but it's the first time I've had sparks light up under my eyelids as the heat of her breath mixes with mine when our mouths fuse together. She groans, and I take advantage, sliding my tongue against hers, deepening our kiss.

Her fingernails dig into my arms where she's clutching them, her body pressing more tightly against mine. I know she's discovered the growing bulge below my waist when she rubs her core up and down my length, another small moan vibrating against my mouth.

I move my hands to clutch under her ass and lift, urging her to wrap her legs around me, and begin walking blindly toward my bedroom. Her hands are gripping my hair as she tries to control the heat of our kiss, her lips breaking away from me as they begin to nip down my neck. My head falls back, a low growl rolling from my chest as she latches on and sucks hard for just a second before releasing and moving lower.

My fingers dig into her ass as I yank her tighter against my now fully erect cock, her mouth leaving my skin as her head raises, her gaze locking onto mine, eyes wild with desire. My knees hit the bed at the same time, and I lower her back onto the bed, my body hovering just inches above hers.

"Are we really doing this?" Her question comes out breathy.

I CAN'T BELIEVE I'm lying here, on my back, in his bed, and it's only our second date. And it's not because I don't want to be here, I do. So badly. He runs his nose along my neck and across my cheek before he plunges his mouth on mine once more. Our tongues dance furiously with each other, stirring the flame of our desire higher.

He pulls back and captures my gaze with his. "Is it too soon?" he pants out in response to my question.

His genuine concern for me, and the fact that he seems to actually be asking my permission instead of talking me into something I might not want, makes the decision easy for me. I shake my head. "If it is, I don't care." Truer words have never been spoken by me.

Ben reacts by grinding his enormous length against my core, and I nearly combust on the spot. Our mouths fuse together once more, more frantic than moments ago when I would have sworn we could not feel more heat.

Both of us are wearing too many clothes right now, so I slide my hands down his back until I find the hem of his shirt, grasp it in my fingers and start pulling it up to take it off. When he realizes, his lips break away from mine long enough to assist me with the process before slamming back home. My nails dig deep into his back as I grind up against him, needing him urgently.

Ben shifts away from me and yanks me to a sitting position. I watch as his fingers skim down over my breasts until they find the hem of my shirt, which he bunches in his fingers and then lifts over my head. I automatically raise my arms as he does and shiver in delight when he takes my smaller hands in one of his larger ones and pushes me back on the bed.

"Stay right there." He orders, and it's so entirely sexy that even the little rebel on my shoulder nods her head obediently.

I suck my bottom lip between my teeth and bite down, welcoming the sting of it. Ben's gaze slides to my mouth, growling fiercely as he lowers his mouth onto my shoulder and starts peppers kisses in a line straight to my breasts.

His mouth finds my nipple over my bra, which isn't difficult since they are currently hard as rocks, and draws it into his mouth with a sharp pull. My hips jerk up into his, once again rubbing against his swollen center, and I moan loudly. He smirks briefly before moving to the other side, giving my other nipple the same attention.

My bra has a front clasp, and he seems to have no issue snapping it open. His strong hands slide the fabric off and grasp onto each breast, and I nearly scream out when he squeezes.

I can't help the moan that falls from my lips; it's loud and needy. I want his mouth back on my breasts, and I have no trouble letting him know. I grip his hair in both hands and force him back in their direction. He chuckles but obliges none the less. His tongue circles around my nipple before he sucks on it, hard. My body jumps in response. "Oh my God. Yes, Ben!"

He moves to the other breast, eliciting the same

response, before finally making his way down, lower, where I am literally aching for him. I am throbbing between my thighs. His mouth finds the button of my jeans, and I almost come when the man rips them open with his teeth! *Holy fuck, that is hot.*

He grips the waistband of the denim fabric and slides it off me with remarkable skill. In my dazed state, it takes me a moment to realize that my panties are coming down as well. I have no objections, and in compliance, lift my hips, making the process easier and faster. As my need for him grows to epic proportions, my patience dwindles at the same rate. In an effort to assist him in ridding me of my jeans and panties, I push at the back of my heels with my toes to release my shoes. They fall onto the floor with a loud thud, and then I am completely naked, entirely exposed to him. Both physically and emotionally.

Every wall has come down, and I want to join my body with his more than I want to take my next breath. He leans back over me, but he is still entirely too dressed, and I want him naked. "Uh-uh. I want yours off, too."

My hands move to his top button and tug it free. My eyes flicker to his, and I think I see him hesitate for just a moment before he tugs at the zipper and pushes his jeans down off his legs. When he is fully naked, I swallow hard. I felt him grind up against me before, and I knew he was... large, but Jesus, his cock is huge! He's going to destroy my pussy. I relish the idea. My eyes flicker a little lower, and I remember the prosthetic now that I have my eyes on it. I get it now; the slight hesitation.

"Do you need to take it off?" I nod my head in it's direction.

It's the first time I've seen his confidence stutter, his cheeks flushing just the slightest pink. "Do you mind? It's actually easier if I do, and more comfortable."

Shit, all I want is for him to screw my brains out. I catch his gaze and make sure he can see the look in my eyes when I tell him, "Ben, just do whatever you need to do to fuck me already."

His face lights up at my blunt reply, and he shakes his head slightly, as if he cannot believe the words that have just fallen from my lips. He sits up and pulls the prosthetic off with lightning speed, and before I can even blink, he's on top of me, caging me with an arm on either side. I take advantage of this position and allow my hands to explore that magnificent painted chest of his, gliding my fingers over the perfection above me. But hunger soon overtakes me. I need his mouth on mine. I have never been known for my patience, and I am not about to start now. I pull him down until his lips crash onto mine.

His swollen head is sliding against the throbbing between my thighs, now soaked with my need. I move my hips up and down to show him just how ready I am for him. He reaches over to the bedside table and pulls out a condom, rolling onto his side to slide it on.

He is taking too long; I don't want to wait another second, so I push him onto his back and straddle him. He looks up at me with wide eyes, his lips curled up in surprise. I lower my pussy against his length and glide over it back and forth, the pressure against my clit pure heaven.

He says something, but I am too lost in my nirvana to even comprehend words. I'm done waiting and move to position myself over him before driving him into me in one push. I welcome the sting, screaming out my relief as his impressive length impales me. "Yes!"

I rise up until he's almost out of me and drop down again, adjusting to his magnificent cock more quickly this time. Ben thrusts up at the same time and leaves me feeling so impossibly full that I think he's going to split me in two. We move in perfect sync, as if this was rehearsed a million times and we are competing for finals. I fall into ecstasy as the muscles in my core begin to tighten around his cock.

Tingles run across every inch of my skin, and I close my eyes as my orgasm starts to crest. I rock myself harder against Ben and moan as I pulse around him in such welcome relief. Just when I think it's over, he rolls me onto my back and starts to pump into me even more deeply than before.

I wrap my legs around him, locking him against me, meeting each of his thrusts with a loud grunt. His arms tighten around me as I crest yet again, a second orgasm exploding from me as I scream his name out. He thrusts one final time, hard and deep, his head thrown back as he bellows out my name, his cock jerking inside of me with his release.

We both lay panting for a moment before he rolls over, his semi-erect cock sliding out of me as he does. and then pulls me close. He wraps his arms around me, tugging me flush to him, kissing the top of my head. "That was fucking amazing," he says, out of breath.

"Yeah, it wasn't too bad," I say, like the smart ass I am.

He lifts his head to look down at me, brow arched. "Not too bad?"

I shrug against him. "Well, I usually at least get dinner

when I'm on a date." I smirk as I trace my fingers lazily over his chest.

"Oh, honey, this date is just getting started. I'm going to make you dinner, and then we're going to do this all over again. But better."

"It gets better?"

"For someone who just said it wasn't too bad, I think I'm going to have to do whatever I can to make sure it gets better." He flashes me his most devilish smile.

Yep, now I am quite literally fucked. But damn, did that feel good.

CHAPTER
Seven

I'VE SLEPT with my fair share of women over the years. But fuck me, I don't think I've ever felt this satisfied. Ever.

I haven't even scratched the surface with what I want to do to this woman. This was hard and fast and full of desperation, but I still need to explore every inch of Jill's delicious body.

I want to do it right now, in fact, but my date has requested I feed her, so feed her I will… more than my cock. I chuckle at my own internal joke and shift my gaze as her fingers stop trailing over my stomach then lay flat as she pushes to lean up and look at me.

"What's so funny?" One brow is raised over her gorgeous gray eyes.

The side of my mouth rises in a cocky grin before I lean forward and press my lips against hers. "Just wondering how I got lucky enough to get your gorgeous ass in my bed."

"Trying to distract me with compliments?" She grins back down at me.

"Oh, if I was going to distract you, I would do something like this." Before she can react, I roll her over and capture her lips in mine, slide a hand over her breast, and gently roll her taut nipple between my fingers. Her mouth opens as a soft moan falls from her lips, and I sweep my tongue inside, loving the feeling of her breath against mine. I kiss her for only a minute, making sure to leave her wanting, and then pull slowly away. "Didn't you say something about me feeding you?"

Her hands snake up and latch onto the longer locks of my hair as she pulls my face close to hers. "I've said it once, Benjamin Sapphire, but I'll say it again. You, sir, are a tease."

I grin salaciously. "Me?"

"Yes. You." She draws my face forward until it's only a hair's breadth from hers and then darts her tongue out, sliding it across my lips in one slow motion. I inhale deeply and force myself to keep my head still instead of crashing my mouth onto hers like I desire. "Just don't forget that two can play at this game."

"I like when you're feisty." I snake my own tongue out and trace it over my lips, following the same path hers did. "But you're right. Let's eat first. I want to make sure you have enough energy for what I'm planning to do to you later."

Her eyes widen, and I feel her body shift under me as her cheeks flush a stunning shade of pink. "I think I can live with that plan."

I lower myself the tiny fraction required and place a soft kiss on her lips before pushing myself up and off her. Her eyes roam down my chest so I look down in question and then back at her. "Too much?" I have a lot of ink. I don't see a single mark on her body.

She shakes her head. "No." Her fingers reach out and graze over the wings of the phoenix on my shoulder. "I want to trace every single line with my tongue. It's incredibly sexy." Her eyes shift to meet mine. "You're incredibly sexy."

My fucking heart skips a beat, then another, and then another. I want to throw her back on this bed right now, shove my cock into her, and claim her as mine. Instead, I muster every ounce of will power I have and push my animalistic needs away for the moment. "You just may be the most perfect woman I've ever met, Jill Baldwin."

Her eyes grow wide for just a second before she blushes and shifts her gaze to her lap. I honestly don't think she's used to receiving compliments, which staggers me because she is truly the most gorgeous and humble woman I can ever remember meeting. Not wanting to embarrass her further, I shift to the end of the bed and move to place my prosthetic back on. I look over my shoulder as I do to address her. "Ready for some dinner? I'm going to make you the best steak you've ever had."

Her face lights up as she smiles and hops out of the bed. "Yes! I'm starving." She wiggles her eyebrows and smiles even brighter. "Plus, word on the street is that I'm going to need some extra fortitude for the rest of the evening."

She reaches down, plucks the t-shirt I had on earlier off the floor, and yanks it over her head. I watch as she finds her panties and slides them up her legs.

Did I say she couldn't get any more beautiful? *Fuck me. I was wrong.* Seeing her in my shirt may be the hottest goddamn thing I've ever seen in my life. I rise off the bed, walk over, and draw her into my arms mumbling into her soft waves, "Where in the hell have you been hiding?"

Her arms tighten around me in response, clinging to me for a full minute before she loosens her grip to step away, her eyes meeting mine with a smile. "I guess good things are worth waiting for."

AFTER I PULL on a pair of shorts, and no shirt per her request, we head to the kitchen and work together to cook dinner. I'm pleasantly surprised to learn she's an amazing cook and gives me some great tips on how to grill the asparagus, rather than steam it, for optimal flavor. As soon as I sink my teeth into the tender green stalks and the smoky flavor bursts in my mouth, I moan. Out loud. It's that good. Not a single drop of the hollandaise is needed, not that it stops her from dipping every bite in the delicious sauce.

I love that this woman eats with gusto. She wanted her steak rare and her fries crunchy, and I smile as she devours every morsel without apology. Seriously, this woman just keeps getting better and better.

Even though I made promises to have her for dessert, after cleaning up the dinner dishes, we wander over to the big couches in the middle of my living space. We fold into one with full glasses of the wine I opened early, continuing the easy conversation that's been flowing between us. She curls her legs underneath her like a cat, her long bare limbs exposed past her thighs where my t-shirt sits.

"So, tell me all the things I don't know about you yet, Ben." Her lips kiss the edge of her glass as she takes a sip of the dark red liquid, her eyes locked on me.

"Tell me what you know and I'll fill in the blanks," I counter, not smugly but challengingly.

She tilts her head in acceptance. "Well, I know you're a Sapphire, which basically means you're rich."

I shrug my shoulders. It's not something I can deny. I was lucky enough to be born to a father who worked his ass off to build an empire. Now, Drew and I run it, and we're able to enjoy and reap the benefits of its success. "Does it bother you that I'm rich?"

She shakes her head back and forth. "No, because you don't act like you are. You could choose to do whatever you like, live wherever you want, but instead, you live in a loft. You joined the Army. And look what you've done downstairs. I mean, could you be any more selfless?"

I look down into my glass and think about how to respond to this, because I think, initially, when I started the gym, it was purely for selfish reasons. I decide to be honest and share this with her. "I'm not quite the savior you paint me to be, Jill. When I lost my leg, I went to a really dark place. I almost got lost there and may not have made it back if it wasn't for my stubborn brother and another really stubborn physical therapist at the hospital."

She shifts closer to me and, completely astonishing me, places her hand on the seam where my prosthetic meets my scarred leg. "This happened in the war?"

I'm not lying when I tell you that not a single person,

outside of medical staff, has ever touched my wound. Her touch shifts something inside of me, making me aware of how special this woman is.

Emotion threatens to steal my voice, so I clear my throat as I try to shake it away. "Yes. Our truck hit an IED." I stop to look at her and clarify in case she doesn't understand. "An explosive buried in the ground." She nods, so I continue before I lose my nerve. "It was bad. Really bad. When I woke up, I just remember seeing blood everywhere, and body parts, and feeling terrified when I looked down and saw how mangled my leg was. But it was nothing compared to looking beside me and seeing one of my best friends dead."

I stop then because the old anger of being the one to survive, of being alive when two of my friends are dead, is boiling under the surface. She doesn't need to see that. And, again, I'm astonished when she moves even closer and takes my hand in hers, squeezing gently. "I'm so, so sorry for your losses, Ben. I can't begin to comprehend what you must have suffered, but I'm really glad your stubborn brother saw you through."

Blinking rapidly to damn the emotion that's trying to break free behind my lids, I shake my head again in wonder. I clear my throat again and continue my story. "So, you see, I needed to do something with all that anger. Once I could stand on my own again."

I release her hand for only a moment to knock on my leg to expand on my statement, and then take it back in mine, "I found a way to release some of it and began boxing. When I left the hospital, I wanted a space more private where I didn't feel like everyone was looking at my leg, or if I lost my balance and fell, I didn't have people feeling sorry for me."

I shrug, regarding the space around me. "I bought this building and initially just put a punching bag in. Then I invited some of my brothers, and then they invited some more, and the next thing I knew, I had a full-fledged gym. It would have been selfish of me not to open the doors to other men like me who needed a place to go and didn't have it." I glance over to find her staring at me intently.

She finally graces me with a smile as she moves her head back and forth in a slow motion. "Do you understand how amazing what you've done is? I'm in awe of you, Ben, complete awe."

I stare into my glass and then take a sip of wine before replying. I'm embarrassed. I did this for me, and being able to help my other brothers-in-need just happened naturally, not because of anything I did consciously. "Don't be. Be in awe of the men and women who are still out there fighting and protecting us. And for the families here waiting with baited breath for them to come home. They are the ones to admire." I shake my head firmly. "Not me."

She scoots even closer to me, and I wonder if she's going to climb into my lap, but instead, she grasps my chin between her tiny fingers and pulls my face in her direction. "That is what makes what you've done so amazing. You take no credit for how much you help these people and feel less for doing it. That makes you one of the most giving men, and maybe, I'm now proud to say, one of the most admired men I have ever had the honor of knowing."

I'm stunned by her words and at a loss as to how to respond to them, so I lean forward and press my lips to hers. Her hand moves from my chin and slides around my neck to deepen the kiss, but it doesn't take a passionate turn. This kiss is different; it's filled with feelings I've never experienced and leaves me breathless with its meaning. Before I can think about it further, she draws back, places a kiss to my nose, and then slides down to curl into my body.

"Okay, so we've got rich, one-legged, selfless, and amazing kisser out of the way. What else should I know about you, Ben?"

I laugh out loud and pull her closer to me as I do, enjoying the feeling of her warm body pressed into mine. I tell her about my sister that died in a car accident at sixteen, how hard it was for my family, how much my brother Drew, although younger, has really always taken care of me. I tell her how we spent our summers in Northern California on the beach, surfing, playing football, and chasing girls. I tell her how much I love Hannah and the children she's brought into our lives and how they brought my parents back to life.

We talk for hours, her also sharing her story with me, until we finally grow quiet and just sit in each other's company. Sometime during the night, or early hours of the morning, we both drift to sleep on the couch, her safely encased in my arms. As her soft breaths whisper against my bare chest, my heart is fuller than it's ever felt before.

MY EYES FLUTTER open as little rays of sunshine dance across my face. Ben's arm is draped over me, and I can hear the steady beat of his heart under my cheek. A warmth spreads through me and my lips curl into a smile. I squeeze my eyes shut again, trying to keep reality at bay for just a little longer. I inhale his scent, a faint trace of his cologne mixed with my perfume. The scents compliment each other perfectly. I focus on his breathing, and everything inside of me just wants to sneak a peek at him while he's sleeping.

I carefully slip out from the warmth of his arms and park my backside on top of the coffee table and just stare at him. The cold surface under my barely covered ass bothers me at first, but is quickly forgotten as I admire him. He's sleeping peacefully and smiling contently while doing so.

I stare at him a little while longer, watching his gorgeous chest rise and fall. As I study his tattoos, I resist the urge to touch them, to trace them with my fingers. I feel my heart rate accelerate, and the butterflies are back. *There they are again.*

I blink. And then I blink again. My hand raises to cover my now open mouth. "No," I whisper.

My eyes widen when realization hits me. I am falling for him—hard. *I am fucking falling for Benjamin Sapphire.*

Suddenly, the butterflies make way for feelings of doom. Panic seizes around my throat. The little nagging voice in the back of my head tells me that a man like Ben doesn't stick around for the long run, and here I am stupid enough to let myself fall for him.

He makes a little growling noise, and it startles me. He turns over, and I release the breath I didn't know I was holding. I have to get out of here. I know I am going to need to wear more than Ben's shirt to get home, so I stealthily get up and tiptoe to his bedroom.

I gather my clothing, which is scattered all across the room, and shrug into my jeans. I pull Ben's shirt off, which still smells of him. I can't stop myself from bringing it to my nose a final time to inhale his scent before placing it on his bed. With my own top back on, I find my heels at the foot of the bed.

I don't put them on yet. I don't want the clicking to wake Ben. I go in search of my jacket, knowing that my cell phone is in the pocket. I don't have to look far; it's hanging on a hook near the entrance. I press the elevator button and am relieved when the doors slide open. I step into the elevator, press the button to go to the lobby and slip my heels on my feet, my heart beating in my throat.

I'm grateful I didn't wake him. I cannot bear the thought of an awkward goodbye. He got me in his bed, like he wanted, and now it's done. And that's okay.

Ugh, that's a lie. It meant so much more to me, but I need to cut this off before I get in too deep. If I am falling for this man already, after just a couple dates, what will I feel like in another couple weeks when he's ready for something new? And I guy like Ben always wants something fresh and new.

"I've made the right decision," I tell myself as the doors slide open.

WHEN I GET out of the cab, Rae is standing at the curb with some cash in her hand. Mikaela is pacing behind her. I didn't take my purse to Ben's last night, and I had no money for the cab I hailed. Tears burn behind my eyelids when I see my two besties. I sent a 911 text on my way back and here they are. No questions asked, they are just here.

Raeva hands the cabby the cash and tells him to keep the change. She turns toward me and must see the look on my face because she immediately pulls me into an embrace.

That's when the dam breaks. In the middle of the street, in the brisk New York City morning air. While hordes of people buzz around us.

"Awe, honey. Shhhh," she says as she ushers me into our building.

Mikaela has walked ahead of us and called for the elevator. We walk into it, and when the doors slide to a close, I realize that for the first time since I moved in to the building, I didn't even greet the doorman. I'm not sure why I am focusing on that right now. We ride up to the penthouse, but nobody says a word. The elevator is filled with echoes of my not so silent sobbing.

I'm not sure why I am crying like this; I feel ridiculous. After all, I am the one who snuck out of Ben's place. I am the one who allowed myself to start falling for him, and I am the one who fell into bed with him. The elevator door opens, and we step into the hallway just as Mika is stepping out of their penthouse. I use my sleeve as a makeshift hanky and wipe my eyes. When his gaze lands on me, his brow shoots up and his eyes flicker from his wife to his sister before landing back on me again.

"Everything okay?" he asks.

Raeva strolls toward him and gets on her tiptoes to plant a kiss on his lips. "Yes, baby. Just girl stuff."

He looks at me and gives me a half-smile and a nod. "Okay then, I'll leave you ladies to it then."

Mika kisses his wife and walks over to kiss his sister's cheek. Then he stops in front of me and places his hand on my shoulder. "I'm not sure what is going on, but whatever you need, I'm here." Then he leans in and kisses my cheek as well.

I smile weakly at him as I thank him, but I am genuinely grateful, because I know he means it. With that, Mika steps into the elevator, and we turn and step into our penthouse. We head straight for the living area where I curl up the couch, the girls following suit.

"So, Jillybean, what happened?" Rae asks.

"Did he hurt you?" Mik inquires at the same time.

"No."

My two friends share a look.

"You had sex and it was terrible?" Raeva says as she wrinkles her nose.

"Oh, God no. I mean, we had sex. In fact, it may have been some of the best sex of my life."

Rae looks at me skeptically.

"I swear. Ben is great. Last night was amazing."

The two of them look at me with brows furrowed.

"What's the problem then?" Mik questions.

I sigh. "I like him."

Mikaela frowns, but Raeva's expression displays an understanding. "You like him and you're running," she says, matter of factly.

I nod once more. "But it's not as simple as that, guys. I am a realist. This thing was never going to work out. Sure, Ben likes me just fine. Now. But he is not the settling down kind of guy." I arch a brow. "You both know his reputation as well as I do. He's a man about town and makes no secrets about it."

Raeva shakes her head. "So, you're not even going to give him a chance to fall in love with you?" She cocks her head like this should be so obvious. "Because you know he will, right?"

"I live in the real world, Rae." I lift my mouth in a forced smile. "And this girl would rather walk away now, before I get burned."

"But what if you're wrong?" Mik challenges. "What if he wants more? Isn't what you're feeling worth taking the chance?"

I frown. "My instincts are telling me to cut and run before I get hurt."

"Listen, you can still change your mind. You snuck out? He doesn't need to know you did. We can always tell him that you had an early meeting and didn't want to wake him?" Mik continues, still trying to convince me that I've made a mistake.

I shake my head. "No, I can't see him again."

"Jilly—"

"No, I mean it," I interrupt sternly.

They both hold up their hands.

"Listen, I know it's hard for you guys to understand, but I am doing this to protect myself. I just can't risk him breaking my heart. I know he doesn't intend to, but that is where this will end—in heart break." I sigh. "Besides, I am doing business with them. I should have never mixed business with pleasure."

My besties share another look, and I know that they are skeptical. But, never the less, they pull me into a group hug.

"If that's what you want, we support you," Mik tells me.

There is a knock on the front door, and the three of us look at each other. It's barely after 9:00 am, so no one we know would be knocking this early. Mikaela rises to her feet and goes to answer.

Rae and I duck down on the couch and peek over it as she opens the door. We both chuckle when we see it's one of the doormen. He hands her an enormous bouquet of white lilies then shuts the door for her.

Of course, I already know who they're from. My stomach knots up as Mik approaches me. She places the flowers on the coffee table and plucks out the card. She holds it out for me, but I shake my head. I can't bring myself to read it because I know that the words will be perfect and that my resolve will weaken the moment I do.

"Are you sure?" she asks.

I swallow hard, press my lips tightly together, and nod my head.

"Do you want to keep the flowers?"

I can't look at them without feeling an ache in my chest, so I shake my head. She nods thoughtfully, proceeds to pick up the flowers, and walks toward the kitchen.

Rae scoots over to me to wrap her arms around me. She pulls me closer and hugs me from the side. "Honey, I can't say that I understand your reasoning, or even that I agree with it. But I support whatever it is that you want, okay?"

I lay my head on her shoulder and nod.

Told you I'd be screwed.

CHAPTER
Eight

IT'S BEEN three days since I woke on my couch to find my arms empty and Jill gone. Three days of unanswered texts and phone calls. Three days that I've sent numerous bouquets of her favorite flowers to both her office and her penthouse.

Two days of calls to Mikaela, demanding she tell me what's wrong with Jill, and still no answers, only evasion. Mikaela says she's extremely busy working and hasn't seen her to even speak with her. Fucking girl code. I know without a doubt Mikaela's covering for her.

What I don't understand is what the hell happened between her falling asleep in my arms and waking up the next morning alone. The night we spent together was one of the best of my life. I have never felt a connection like the one I do with her. There is no way I am letting her run away from me now.

I punch the bag in front of me one more time for good measure and then lean my exhausted body against it in defeat. I've been punching the shit out of it for the last two hours, and my knuckles are red and swollen. I'm surprised they haven't bled out under the tape yet. I'm going crazy waiting for some kind of message from her and am at my wit's end over what I should do next. Letting out a tired breath, I push myself off the bag and head toward the shower.

After rinsing off two hours of sweat in steaming hot water, I change into a pair of jeans and a hoodie. I decide to go see the one person who might understand more than anyone what it's like when the woman you crave just disappears.

Leaving the building, I walk outside into the crisp fall air. It's days like this that I wish I could still ride my bike. I've talked to some guys that have had their bikes modified to allow them to be able to ride again, but I just haven't gotten that far yet. Instead, I walk into the alley beside my building and slide into my Dodge Charger. It's a badass car and makes up for the fact that I can't swing my leg over a bike on afternoons like this.

I put the key in the ignition and turn it, the engine roaring to life, and for good measure, I press on the gas, revving it loudly before I shift into reverse and out into traffic. I'm in front of our hotel on Park Avenue in twenty minutes and hand the keys to the valet driver who greets me by name as I exit the vehicle. "Keep it close. I won't be long."

"Yes, sir." He doesn't give me a tag. He knows who I am. Being a Sapphire definitely has its perks. I stroll through the lobby of the hotel to the elevator and press the floor number for his office. The elevator glides to its destination in seconds, and the doors swish open for me to exit. I stride down the hallway and smile at Felicia, sitting at her desk outside the large dual-office doors of my destination.

"Mr. Sapphire!" She smiles and exclaims in surprise. "Is the other Mr. Sapphire expecting you?"

I stop short of her desk and grimace. "Felicia, please, for the hundredth time, just call me Ben."

"Oh no! I could never do that, Mr. Sapphire." She shakes her head so hard you would think I just asked her to crawl across the floor on her hands and knees and lick the dirt off my boots.

"Really, you can. Actually, I insist." I watch as her eyes pop wide in shock at my order. "Just call me Ben. Mr. Sapphire is my father and makes me feel old."

"Okay, um, Ben." Her face turns an extremely dark shade of pink as she says my name, and I can't help the smile that forms on my lips. It's the first time it's happened in days. "The other Mr. Sapphire," she lowers her voice to a whisper, "Drew," she continues uncomfortably, pointing to his office doors, "he's in. He's alone, so you can just go in."

It's strange, but I just want to give her a hug to let her know that her protection of my brother, and her need to show us so much respect, doesn't go unnoticed and is appreciated. But, of course, I don't. I can only imagine what color she would turn then. Instead, I gently pat her hand as I thank her and then move past to knock on the door.

I don't bother waiting for an answer as I enter. Drew's attention shifts from his computer, a look of surprise and then subtle annoyance crossing his face as it lands on mine.

"Ah, I should have known. Only you enter unannounced, Benny Boy." He leans back in his chair and shakes his head, steepaling his fingers in front of him as he does. "I was wondering when you'd show up."

I cock my head as I plop myself into one of the leather chairs in front of his desk. "Why's that?"

"Jill Baldwin's disappearing act?" he counters smugly.

"How the fuck do you know about that? I haven't talked to you in almost a week." I sit up straighter in the chair, anxious to see what information he has.

"Oh, I'm not supposed to know a thing." His brows raise. "And, believe me, I wish I didn't. But those women had a little hen session the other day, and it's all I've heard Hannah talk about since."

I widen my eyes and wave my hands in exasperation. "Well, what the fuck is going on?"

"Apparently, Jill had some kind of melt down about how she may or may not be feeling about you and has gone into retreat mode." He shrugs his shoulders.

"What the fuck does that mean? Retreat mode?" I question hotly.

"Jesus, I don't know, Ben." He runs his fingers through his hair and blows out a breath. "She's been burnt pretty badly in the past by a couple of men. Not just one, from what Hannah says. I think she's cagey about trusting or caring for anyone again."

I shake my head in frustration. "Drew, I've been nothing but a perfect gentleman to this woman. Done everything I can to assure her I'm on the level here. I mean, I shared shit with her that I've never shared with anyone. Not even you."

I flinch as I see an expression of hurt slide over his face and then just as quickly disappear, and groan inwardly that I've offended him. I continue in an effort to try to explain my way back into his good graces. "It's just different with her. Even though we haven't spent a lot of time together, I feel like my soul has known her forever. She's awakened something in me."

"Look, I get it, Ben. I was there with Hannah." He chuckles as his eyes roll back in memory. "And you know how hard it was to get her to see me and believe she wasn't wrong for doing so."

"So, what the hell am I supposed to do now? Not see her? Sit around and wait? Not being able to talk to her to try and fix this is driving me crazy." I stand and walk to the large window behind my brother and stare down at the park entrance below.

"Go find her, man." He rises and comes to stand next to me. "Funny story." He points to a bench sitting just to the left of the entrance. "When I thought I had completely lost Hannah, I found her sitting in the pouring rain, right there. My destiny was sitting right outside, and all I had to do was go down and make her mine."

I look over at him, my brows creased. "What the fuck is your point, Drew?"

He rolls his eyes and slaps a hand on my shoulder. "You don't have to wait for her to show up, Benny. You know where to find her. Go get her."

"Yeah? Just like that? Go invade her space?"

"Yeah. Just like that." His hand grips around my arm and shoves me in the direction of the door. "What the hell are you waiting for? You've got nothing to lose, right?"

I tilt my head, shrug my shoulders, and meet my brother's challenging look. "If this makes things worse, I'm gonna come back here and kick your ass, little brother."

"You can come and give it your best shot. Now, get the hell out of my office." He scoffs and points to the door.

Ten minutes later, I'm back in my car and headed to Serenity. My gut tells me that's where I'll find her. She's completely invested in her company, and I'm guessing she's buried herself in work. I'm not sure what I'm going to say when I see her, but I pray, when she does come face to face with me, she'll tell me what the fuck is wrong.

Another fifteen minutes later, I pull into a parking garage a block from the spa and then quickly walk the distance to its entrance. It's after four, and the waiting room is empty and quiet. I'm assuming they are probably done taking appointments today, and most likely in the process of finishing up whatever clients may still be in-house. No one's at the front desk, so I take a seat in the lobby and wait for someone to appear.

I pick up a magazine on the table and begin absently flipping through the pages when I hear voices around the corner. I go on high alert and stand, tip-toeing a bit closer when I hear Jill's name being spoken in the conversation.

"Yes, that guy, the tattooed one with the missing leg!"

They both giggle and shush each other at the same time.

"Well, from what I heard, what he's missing from one leg, he makes up with another. If you know what I mean!"

Another round of giggles ensues, and I roll my eyes at their immaturity. Really, they're gossiping about my dick? My irritation comes to a screeching halt when I hear Jill's name again.

"Anyway, I heard Jill tell Maria that if he comes in here again that she wants nothing to do with him. Maria can handle any and all business with him."

"But why? One leg or not, the guy is smoking hot."

"Something about having had enough damaged goods in her life and doesn't need anymore."

My heart lurches in my chest, and the blood in my veins turns icy cold as it races through my body, every inch of my skin hardening at what I just heard. *She thinks I'm damaged goods?* I shake my head in disbelief. She seemed totally fine with me, and my leg, the other night. Was it all an act? I can't stand to listen to another word these women are whispering.

I take a step backward and move to spin around and slam right into a side-table, the potted plant on it smashing to the ground. *Fuck me and my goddamn leg that doesn't feel a thing!*

Before I can escape, the gossiping girls appear from around the corner, their expressions changing from wonder to shock as they recognize me. I'm quite sure, based on the expression on both of their faces, they realize I just heard every word they've said.

They both begin apologizing and move to help with the plant, but I place my hand out flat. "Just stop." They comply instantly and freeze. Without another word to them, I spin on my good heel and leave the building as quickly as I arrived.

MY BLOOD, moments ago cold as ice from the words I overheard between the two women at the spa, is now flowing like lava under my skin as my rage grows. *Damaged fucking goods?*

I shake my head in disgust. Not at her, but at myself. For believing that a woman like Jill saw past my disability to see the man that I am. Who the hell was I kidding? Pieces of me are missing. A woman like her deserves someone whole.

I reach my car and yank the door open, throwing myself behind the driver's seat. I stare at the concrete wall in front of me and have a sudden urge to start the engine, put the car in reverse, and then plow forward until I smash head-on into its hard surface. Closing my eyes, I shake my head again. I haven't had dark thoughts like these in a very long time. If caring for a woman drives me to thoughts like this, maybe her not wanting me is for the best.

Banging my hands on the steering wheel, I let out a roar of frustration. It doesn't help relieve one bit of the pain that now seems to be clenching my heart. How is it possible after knowing this woman for only a few short weeks that I could feel so thoroughly gutted?

I lay my head on the steering wheel in defeat, already knowing the answer to my own question but trying in vain to push it to the recesses of my mind. I need to force her and whatever I was feeling to the very back corner of my heart and forget about her. Forget her smile, the silkiness of her skin under my fingers, her fresh rain scent, the way she felt under me, and especially how it felt when she trailed her fingers over me.

I lift my head to try to shake it clear. Darkness creeps in along the edges of my brain, and I know I need to move before it takes over completely. I start the car and exit the garage, paying the attendant as I do. I drive aimlessly for an hour and then head back to the hotel. Grabbing my cell phone off the passenger seat, I tell Siri to call Drew. Seconds later, his voice sounds on the other end.

"Benny, how'd it go?" He's upbeat and eager to hear my news, but I'm in no mood for small talk.

"Meet me at the bar in ten." I hit end without waiting for a response. I'm sure that alone will tell him what he needs to know.

Traffic is heavier now, so it's another fifteen minutes before I walk in and see him sitting at the far end. He's got a drink in his hand and another waiting on the bar in front of the stool beside him. I slide onto it, grab what I know will be whiskey, and drink it in two long gulps. He doesn't say a thing, just lifts a finger and motions for the bartender to bring another. He does. Quickly. I tell him to leave the bottle. After a nod from my brother, he does and then scurries away.

We sit in silence for a few very long minutes before either one of us says anything. He finally breaks and starts the conversation. "You want to talk about it?"

"Not really." I drain my second glass of whiskey and grab the bottle to pour myself another.

"So, am I just supposed to sit here and watch you get fucked up? Because, really, I've got a few more important things I could be doing right now."

I turn my head and stare at him, my insides turning black with anger. "Can you just sit here with me and be my goddamn brother? If I want to get my feelings out, I'll call a fucking counselor."

He stares right back at me, reaches for the bottle to pour himself another drink, and shifts back on his stool, his gaze never leaving mine. "I'll sit here all damn night if you need me to, Ben, but I can't read your mind."

"She said I'm damaged goods," I spit out and turn my head to break our eye contact, heat flaring in my cheeks.

"What?" His glass slams down on the bar, and I hear liquid slosh out and land on the bar. "She fucking said that to you?"

I swallow my embarrassment and turn my attention back to him. "Not directly."

"Wait, what?" His brow creases as his head cocks to one side.

"I overheard some of her staff talking. They apparently are under orders to make sure I'm kept clear of Ms. Baldwin and mentioned it was because I'm damaged goods." My brows raise matter-of-factly as I finish explaining.

He's speechless for several long minutes before finally blowing out a long breath. "I don't know what to say to that."

"I do." I take a swig from my glass and slam it down. The warm liquid is starting to turn the black edges of my brain to gray and I like it. "Fuck her."

"Don't you think you should talk to her?"

I watch as he uses a napkin to wipe up the whiskey he spilled a moment ago. "What the fuck for? More insults? More fake smiles? No thanks." I shake my head and let more of the warm liquid slide down my throat.

"Ben, you know how gossip is. Shit gets misconstrued, made up, twisted, and honestly, this doesn't sound like the

Jill I met. I don't take her for someone to dismiss another over a disability, let alone speak about it to others."

I shrug. I'm tired of talking about this shit. "Whatever. I've been calling her for days. She's obviously made her choice."

"So, now what?"

"What do you mean?" I glance over at him.

"What's your plan? Are we ditching the Serenity deal?"

Ah, I knew business was going to play into this sooner or later. It always does with my type A, controlling as hell brother. I scoff. "My plan is to sit here and get fucked up. Then maybe I'll pick up the first gorgeous woman I see, bring her up to a suite, and fuck Jill out of my system." I grin wickedly at him, pretending that's all I would actually need to forget a woman like Jill, that I even want to be with another woman, and then continue. "You want Serenity still; it's all yours. But I'm out."

"I could give two shits about the deal, Ben. It's not like we need the goddamn money. If you're out, I'm out." He takes a sip of his drink and keeps talking. "But instead of wasting away here, why don't you head out to my place in the Hamptons? It's empty, and its quiet. You can do whatever the hell you need to for a few days."

I cock my head in his direction and consider his suggestion. Getting out of this city, away from my loft that still carries her lingering scent, to stare at the shore for a few days while I shake her out of my system actually seems like a good idea. "Okay."

"Really?" He's surprised and I don't blame him. I'm not usually this agreeable.

"Sure. What the fuck else have I got to do?" I take another drink and then say quietly, "My bed is haunted with her scent. I'm not ready to deal with that yet."

His hand reaches out and clasps around my arm in a tight, knowing grip. "Let me get David to drive you. He's got my car outside and waiting for me anyway. I'll take a cab home."

"Right now?" I question in surprise.

"Bring the damn bottle with you if you need to, Benny. Let's just get you the hell out of here."

I ROLL over on the couch, my arm smacking into the empty whiskey bottle sitting on the nearby coffee table, sending it crashing to the floor. I sit up, grabbing my forehead as I do, and listen. Did I just hear the doorbell ring? I stand, my leg stiff as fucking hell from being in the prosthetic all night, and glance out the window. It's pouring and the sky is a dark, turbulent gray, which matches my mood perfectly.

I turn my head abruptly again when I hear loud knocking against the door. Okay, so it wasn't my imagination. But then, who the hell would be crazy enough to come out here in the middle of a fucking raging storm? I stride to the door and yank it open, not bothering to look through the peephole first, and my mouth falls open.

Standing before me, looking like a drowned rat, is a shivering Jill. I stare at her for a long moment, trying to decide if I want to slam the door in her face, but of course, I can't. No matter how pissed off and hurt I am over what she said, I'm not a fucking asshole, and I'm not going to leave her standing in the freezing rain.

I step to the side and motion for her to come in. "What the hell are you doing here?"

CHAPTER
Nine

THE KNOCK on my office door startles me. Every time someone knocks, I am afraid that Ben will be on the other side of it. Or maybe I am secretly hoping that it will be him. I'm such a damn mess.

"Yes?" I call out.

The door opens, and Aisha peeks her head around the corner. "Hey, Jill, you got a minute?"

I smile. Relieved or disappointed, I'm still not certain. "Sure, come in."

Aisha steps into my office, closely followed by Anna. The two of them stand before me as if they are students in front of the principal. I raise a brow. "Did something break?"

They share a look, one that I don't like.

"Okay, what broke?"

"Nothing broke," Anna mutters. "But we did kind of mess up."

I frown. "Sorry, ladies, I'm very busy, so can you please spit it out?" My voice is laced with irritation I can't hide.

They share yet another look. "We were talking in the hall, and we think—no, we *know* that he heard us."

"What in the world are you talking about?" My brow creases in confusion.

Another shared look.

"Will the two of you stop doing that?" I bark.

Anna bites her lip. "We were talking about you and Mr. Sapphire... And, well, we may have been joking a little bit and he overheard us," Aisha says.

My stomach drops.

"I swear, we didn't know he was there," Anna defends.

My nostrils flare as I press my lips in a firm line. I close my eyes for a moment, pinching the bridge of my nose in an attempt to reign in my temper. "Where is Mr. Sapphire now? And don't you dare share another damn look."

"He left."

"He left?"

"And what exactly was said that upset him so?"

Both of their faces scrunch up, and I already know that I am *not* going to like what they have to say. "Well, I was telling Aisha that I overheard you tell Maria that she was to deal with Ben—um, I mean, Mr. Sapphire—and she asked me why. So, I told her that you said you were tired of damaged goods."

I'm stunned silent for a moment while I absorb what this means. *He thinks that I called him damaged goods? Oh my God.*

"The fact that you two know better than to talk trash in my place of business is one thing, but to gossip so openly about someone I'm dating is completely unprofessional. I promise you two right now, that I will not tolerate this if it happens again."

Aisha and Anna nod.

"Not that it is any of your business, but you were grossly mistaken. What I actually told Maria is that Ben is too good to be dealing with damaged goods. *Me* being said damaged goods."

Anna bites her lip, and I see tears glistening in her eyes. "We are really sorry. We promise, we won't ever do anything like this again."

Imagining how he must have felt when he heard them talk like that makes me sick to my stomach. "See to it that it doesn't. I wasn't kidding. Anything like this again and I will not hesitate to fire you on the spot."

Their eyes widen.

"Understood?"

They nod in unison.

I wave at the door, making it clear they should leave, which they do, fast and with their tails between their legs.

I pick up my cell and scroll quickly to his number. It rings and rings and rings. Fuck. No answer. I punch in a text, and seconds later, Raeva responds, informing me that she is on her way with a car.

I try Ben again, but this time it doesn't even ring; it goes straight to voicemail. Argh!

I grab my keys and my purse and head to the front of the building so that I won't waste any more time than I need to. I pace the pavement in front of Serenity, stewing, a mixture of anger and anguish flowing over me in waves. A town car pulls over just ten minutes after I text Raeva, and I recognize it to be one of the Kingsley vehicles. Raeva's driver-slash-security guard, Simon, gets out and opens the door for me. I smile at him and thank him as I slide into the car next to her.

"What is the emergency? Where are we headed?" she asks.

"Ben's place."

She raises her brow but provides Simon with Ben's address.

"Now, what the hell is going on?"

I am still shaking with anger when I tell her everything Aisha and Anna told me.

"Shit," she says when I am done talking.

"I know."

Raeva leans in and instructs Simon to step on it. "Yes, ma'am."

We pull in front of Ben's place just minutes later, and I practically fly out of the car before we have even come to a full stop. "Wait for me, please," I yell over my shoulder.

I run up to the elevator across from the gym and press the button. I wait a beat and press again. Damn it. I pull my cell from my pocket and try to dial his number again, knowing that he won't answer, but still, I try.

I sigh as I slide the phone back into my pocket. I turn around and see that the gym is open. Maybe he's there? I stride over to the gym entrance and walk to the front desk. A pretty redhead is on the phone, giving someone a piece of her mind. My first thought is that *I like this girl*. She's feisty. She smiles and holds up a finger before finishing up the call.

"Hi, my name is Stacy. Welcome to Baker-Landon-Rose Memorial Gym. How can I help you today?"

I flash a shy smile at her. "Hi, I'm Jill. I am actually looking for Ben."

She looks me over. "Hmmm, so you're Jill, huh?" she says with a smirk. "I've got to hand it to him; he's got excellent taste."

I feel my cheeks heat, and I'm not sure if it's the compliment, the fact that she clearly has heard about me, or both.

"Oh, and humble, too. Score," she jokes.

I nod, not quite knowing what to say.

"I'm sorry, Ben isn't here. He called earlier to say that he was going to be away for a few days. I actually assumed he was going to be out of town with you."

I'm not sure why that surprises me. But, also, now I am stuck. How am I going to find him? I thank Stacy for her time and make my way back to the car. Simon sees me coming and comes around to open the door. I slide next to Rae feeling defeated. I let out an audible sigh of frustration.

"Not home?" she guesses.

"Nope, and not at the gym either. The girl at the front desk told me that he is going to be out of town for a bit."

I drop my head backwards. "What am I going to do now? I can't bear the thought of him thinking that I would ever say something like that about him."

We drive home in silence, and when we get to the penthouse, I am not in the mood to talk to anyone. I kick off my shoes and crawl into bed, not even bothering to take off my clothes. I wrap myself in the duvet like a little caterpillar in a cocoon.

I try to call Ben once more, but it goes straight to voicemail again. So, I punch in a text, asking him to please call me. I sigh and bury my face in the pillow. And I don't emerge till morning…

LOUD KNOCKING on my bedroom door has me sitting straight up.

"Wake up, sleepyhead."

I groan. "What do you want, Rae?"

"Open the door, Jillybean. We have a phone call to make."

I walk to the door to flip the lock then crawl back into the bed.

"Really? You didn't even bother undressing?" Rae says as she wrinkles her nose.

"Are you here just to lecture me, Mom?" I say a little more irritated than I intended.

"Testy this morning, are we?" She tosses back at me, unaffected by my mood.

"I'm sorry, Rae. I'm just feeling like crap. I still haven't been able to reach Ben and I haven't heard back from him. I don't know what to do."

"Well, lucky for you, your person is brilliant," she says with a triumphant smirk.

I raise a brow. "That a fact?"

"Yup."

"And what brilliant idea do you have, pray tell?"

"I know how to find Ben…"

I sit up, my full, undivided attention on her. "How?" I say eagerly.

"We call Hannah." She cocks her head, grinning from ear to ear.

HANNAH IS AWESOME, even though she makes it abundantly clear how upset she is that Ben is hurt. She listens to my side of the story; seeming relieved that there was a reasonable explanation for what happened.

We are not particularly close, but I have always liked her. She tells me where to find him and makes me promise to make it better. I promise that I will try. She clearly loves her brother-in-law dearly.

I ask Raeva if I can borrow the faster-than-lightening car she received for her birthday so I can make it to Drew and Hannah's place as quickly as possible. She hands me the keys without hesitation, and smiling gratefully, I hug my bestie and thank her.

"Go get your man."

THE DRIVE SEEMS to take forever. It takes just a little under two hours from Manhattan to the Hamptons, and that's when there's no traffic. I am impatient to see him. And, let's be honest, patience isn't one of my strong points. I make good time, though. My mind is racing the entire time. There are dark clouds in the distance and I wonder if it's a sign of things to come.

The GPS tells me that I'm ten minutes out, which pulls me out of my thoughts and back to reality. It's only now I notice my knee is bouncing like its doing a jig. I feel restless and rake a hand through my hair. I've been gripping the steering wheel so tightly that my hands actually hurt. And, like the bad omen I was afraid of, the sky opens up and rain starts to pour down as if the heavens are flooding.

Just perfect.

I am grateful when I pull up and see lights on in the house. I park in the driveway and sit in the car for a few minutes, just staring at the front door. I try to control my rapid breathing and calm the nerves that have crept up from deep within. I finally get out of the car to brave the pouring rain. Trying to minimize the damage, I run as fast as I can, but by the time I reach the front door and use the knocker, I am soaked from head to toe.

After pounding a second time and becoming even more drenched, the door swings open and I actually flinch in surprise at his disheveled appearance. I realize instantly that no amount of preparation would have helped to control the array of mixed feelings swirling through me at this very moment. The hurt in his expression, and the unfamiliar flash of anger that mars those always sparkling eyes of his, is almost too much to bear.

"Hi," I whisper through trembling lips.

He steps aside and motions for me to come in. "What the hell are you doing here?"

"I had to see you. I had to explain."

"There really is no need. I think I get it."

I sigh. "Ben, you really don't understand. I—"

He puts a hand up to stop me. "I'm missing a leg Jill, but there is not a damn thing wrong with my hearing."

"Damn it, Ben!" I plead with force. "Will you just shut up for one second and let me talk?"

He raises a brow but gestures for me to continue.

"First, I should have called you back to thank you for the flowers and to explain why I stopped returning your calls. Please believe me when I tell you it had nothing to do with you."

I pause, hesitant to admit my truth, but knowing I need to in order to be fair to him. "This is all about me and my fear of letting people in. I swear." I take a step closer to him and fix my gaze on his. "What you heard those two women say; it was them repeating something I said but they got the context completely wrong."

I shiver, some of it from the wet clothes I'm standing it, but also because his stare is cold and unrelenting. He doesn't say a word, so I continue. "Yes, I told Maria to deal with you regarding business because I knew I needed to put some distance between us. But, I told her it was because you've had enough damaged goods in your life and didn't need more." I point to myself. "I'm the damaged goods here, Ben. Not you. My heart just doesn't work like everyone else's."

My voice becomes shaky as I try and control the emotions now beginning to seep into my tone. "I know that I pushed you away, but it most definitely had nothing to do with you. And yes, you may be missing a part of your leg, Ben, but there is not a damn thing wrong with you. I don't give a fuck about your leg. You are more of a man than anyone I have ever encountered."

He's silent for a moment and then speaks matter-of-factly. "You shouldn't have driven here in this weather. What were you thinking?"

An exasperated chuckle leaves me. "I had to see you. I had to try to explain. The thought of you thinking you were less than whole; I couldn't live with that. I tried calling, but you wouldn't answer. So, here I am." I shrug my shoulders.

"Yes, speaking of that. How *did* you find me?" He scratches his beard, still watching me.

"Hannah," I admit. "But don't be mad at her. She ripped me a new one before hearing my side."

He seems to relax, because he smiles for the first time since I arrived. "She can be a giant pain in my backside, but I love her," he confesses with affection in his voice.

Our gazes meet, and we gravitate to one another like magnets. But then, he stills, taking a step back. "We should get you out of those wet clothes. I'm sure Hannah has something that will fit, and you can use the shower in the guest room." He motions to the stairway. "It's the second door on the right up there. I'll leave some clothes on the bed for you."

I'm not sure what I was expecting, but I feel a twinge of disappointment. I know I have no right, since I'm the one who ruined any chance of us being together. So, I plaster a smile on my face and thank him before heading to the room he directed me to.

I take a quick shower and dry my hair, and when I emerge from the bathroom, I find a pair of jeans and a sweater laying on the bed. Thoughtfully, he also miraculously provided underwear that still has the tags on them. My bra is still soaked so I forgo wearing one. Once I am dressed, I go on the hunt for Ben and find him in the kitchen, making sandwiches.

"Hey there," I say, a bit shyly.

"Hey there, yourself." He favors me with a small smile, those dimples I love so much appearing. "I made some coffee, and I thought I'd feed us."

Ben hands me a plate with a baguette, which I gratefully accept. I didn't realize how hungry I was until I smelled the food. We head to the breakfast nook and sit. I want to tell him that I was wrong, that I've missed him, and that I want us to try to work things out. But before I have a chance to open my mouth, he starts speaking.

"I'm glad you came to straighten things out."

I smile at him, a glimmer of hope spearing through my heart.

"I had some time to think before you showed up." He drums his fingers on the counter for a brief second, glancing down at them as he continues talking. "I realized that perhaps you were correct all along and we should have kept things strictly professional from the start. I want you to know that what happened with you was special to me, but I understand if it wasn't for you, and that I'll let it go and move on."

I feel like he just punched me in the gut. As quickly as my appetite appeared, it disappears. I take a bite anyway, because I am not sure that I can keep my voice from breaking if I speak. So, instead, I chew and nod my head, averting my eyes from his.

"If you are still interested, we should push ahead with our deal. I don't want what happened to affect your willingness to work with us."

Forcing a smile, I take another bite and nod. "Thank you," I tell him with the most even tone I can muster up.

What the hell is wrong with me? This is what I told myself I wanted, so why does my heart feel like it just fell out of my chest. All I know is I deserve this, that I was right all along. I knew this would end in heart break, only the culprit wasn't Ben. It was me.

By the time we finish eating, the weather seems to have improved, so I inform him that I need to be headed back to the city. I thank him for hearing me out and offer work as my excuse to leave. He doesn't argue. We hug as we say goodbye, and I inhale his scent one more time before I whisper goodbye and practically stumble to the car and drive away.

Be careful what you wish for I guess.

CHAPTER

Ten

AS JILL LEAVES, I close the door behind her and lean my head against the door jamb, fighting an internal battle about whether to chase her or let her go.

For once, reason prevails, but it doesn't stop me from shoving off the frame to move to the closest window and watch as she slides into the sleek car she arrived in. It's several minutes before the engine come to life, and I wonder if she's feeling as much regret as me. The car pulls out of the long drive, but I don't look away until I can no longer see the red taillights through the mist.

I hope I didn't just make the biggest fucking mistake of my life. I believe every word that fell from her sad pink lips, and I also know without a shadow of a doubt that she feels as much for me as I do for her. But I also know, especially after feeling the darkness begin to creep into my soul yesterday, that I absolutely can't let that happen again. Opening myself up to her, even just the small fraction I'd allowed so far, had made me far more vulnerable than I wanted to be.

I stand at the window, staring at the rain pouring down, until my stump begins to throb in complaint. I've had the damn prosthetic on for way too long and my body has had enough. I tear myself away and decide a visit to the hot tub is in order. Drew was smart enough to build an enclosure around the tub so that it could be used year-round, and I could kiss him right now for his brilliance.

No one is here, so I decide to live on the wild side and strip naked instead of finding a suit. I remove my leg when I reach the edge of the tub, then slide my body down into the steaming hot water with a sigh of relief.

As hard as I try not to let my thoughts wander to Jill, it's the only place my mind seems to want to go. I know, even in the short time we spent together, that she could have been the one and it's the first time I'm allowing myself to admit it. Now that she's gone, of course. I chuff out loud as I think of the old cliché, 'you'll know when the right person comes along' and feel pissed that it's actually fucking true.

"So, why'd you let her go, asshole?" I say it out loud, even though I know there's no one around to hear it, but maybe to make sure I realize I may have just fucked up royally. I'm a coward for pushing her away instead of putting myself in the line of fire again, but damn it, the thought of any more loss in my life is more than I think I could bear right now. No, I made the right decision. I just need to learn to live with it. I'll find other women to spend my time with; that has never been a problem for me. I blow out a long breath, lean my head back, and force myself to push her out of my conscience.

I'VE BEEN BACK in the city for the last two days and know a visit to Drew and Hannah's is overdue, so I find myself leaving my loft and walking one block down to their place. Yeah, it's convenient having them so close, and nice. Knowing I have loving people only a few doorsteps away provides a comfort to me that I truly cherish.

I make my way through the lobby and into the elevator, the doorman nodding a friendly greeting at me as I pass. I punch the button for their place, wait until the doors slide open again when the elevator reaches their apartment.

They own the two top floors of the building. But, I mean, hey, they already have two kids and it wouldn't surprise me if they popped out a few more, so the space definitely seems to be a requirement for them. I knock on the door and wait for someone to answer.

The door swings open a minute later, and seeing no one at eye level, I shift my gaze lower to find my spunky little niece smiling up at me. "Uncle Benny!" She doesn't hesitate to run and hop up into my arms, her little hands wrapping around my neck to hug me tight.

She lets go after a moment and scrunches her face up at me, one little finger moving to point at me in a scolding motion. "Where have you been, Uncle Benny? You haven't come to see me in over a week!"

I lean over and pretend to bite her finger, which causes her to screech and clutch onto me tighter as giggles ensue. I place a few kisses on the top of her curly blonde locks and then give her my most practiced puppy dog look. "Sorry, Gracie. I went out of town for a few days."

Her head bobs up and down in understanding. "Uh-huh. Mommy said you were getting your head screwed back on." She leans over, cupping her small hand around my ear, and whispers into it. "But I don't think I was supposed to hear that."

One side of my mouth cocks up into a half-smile as I whisper back, "That can be our little secret then, okay?" Her head bobs up in down in silent agreement, her brown eyes wide with relief. "Where are Mommy and Daddy?"

Grace is actually Hannah's child with her first husband, my friend Jackson, who I served alongside with overseas. He was killed in action shortly after I lost my leg, and unfortunately, never got to raise this beautiful baby girl. Drew married Hannah a little over a year ago and, shortly after, adopted Gracie as his own. As I look down at her adoringly, I think she may be the most beautiful creature on this planet, except for Jill of course.

I stop in my steps as I realize she's managed to creep back into my thoughts and silently curse myself.

"Whattsa matter, Uncle Benny?" How are kids so damn intuitive?

I plop another kiss down on her head and smile at her. "Not a thing, funny face. So, where's Mommy and Daddy?"

"Mommy is giving Brody a bath 'cause he pooped all over himself. It was so gross! You should have seen it, Uncle Benny. I thought Mommy was going to barf!" She throws a hand over her mouth to try and contain her giggles.

"I think I'm glad I didn't, thank you very much!" I ruffle her hair and head toward the kitchen area. "And Daddy?"

"He's not home yet." Her mouth turns down in a little frown. She's got my brother wrapped around her little finger, and I'm sure that when he is home, she's probably got him playing dolls, or having tea parties, or whatever it is six-year-old girls do.

"Well, I guess it's a very good thing I came over then, isn't it?" I sit her down on the kitchen island and slide onto the stool next to her. I glance at my watch to check the time and then back at her. "Have you had dinner yet?"

"Nope." Her blond curls fly back and forth with each shake of her head. "Mommy said after Brody's bath."

"Well, why don't I make you something then? Grilled cheese sound okay?" I stand and wait for her response.

"Yes!" She claps her hands gleefully and bounces on the counter. "Can I help, Uncle Benny?"

I lower myself so that my face is even with hers and speak softly. "Yes, but only if you stop calling me Uncle Benny and just call me Uncle Ben."

Her brows furrow as her eyes squint in thought. Her tiny hands reach out, and she places one of each side of my stubbly cheeks, holding my face in place before speaking to me in a most serious tone. "But Daddy said you love being called Uncle Benny."

I laugh heartily, causing her to jump in surprise, a look of confusion on her face. "Your daddy is a troublemaker, that's what he is, Gracie!"

She frowns as if this can't possibly be the case and then turns her head and smiles brightly as her mother enters the room. "Who's a troublemaker?"

"Uncle Benny said Daddy is! Does that mean he's in

trouble, Mommy?" Her eyes shoot back and forth between Hannah and I, waiting for an answer.

Hannah's brow arches high as she shakes her head. "If Uncle Benny isn't careful, he's the one that's going to be in trouble."

I laugh out loud and then walk over and kiss her on the cheek in greeting. "Hey, Hannah." She gives me a quick hug and a gentle smile as she returns my greeting. "I was just going to make the doodlebug here a grilled cheese."

Her eyes open wide and turn toward her daughter. "Grace Rose Sapphire, you had a grilled cheese for lunch and for dinner last night, too. You're going to turn into a grilled cheese sandwich if you aren't careful."

"But, Mommy, I like them." She lifts her shoulders and blinks rapidly like this should be the most obvious thing ever and not a problem at all.

Hannah walks over, pecks a kiss on Grace's nose, and then lowers her to the floor. "I'll make you dinner. Go play for a little bit and I'll let you know when it's ready."

"Okay, Mommy." She smiles and waves at us both before skipping out of the room.

Hannah turns to look at me and offers me a sympathetic smile. "You doing okay?"

I nod. "Yeah, yeah, I'm good." I pace around her to sit back on the stool I occupied earlier. "Thank you, by the way."

She tilts her head, one brow raised in question. "For?"

"Cleaning my loft. Changing the sheets." I look down and fidget with a fork sitting on the counter. "I appreciated coming home to…" I look up at her again and shrug. "Well, you know."

Her hand falls over mine and squeezes gently. "We're family, Ben. We do what we can for each other, even if it doesn't seem like very much at all."

I look up into her soft caramel eyes and smile warmly. "My brother sure got lucky when he found you."

She shakes her head and laughs. "Well, technically, he won me in an auction, but that's another story."

I chuckle. "Do you happen to know if there's another one like you I could maybe look into buying?"

Her eyes darken and her smile disappears. "I think, Ben, that you may have already found what you're looking for. Maybe you just need to give it another chance?"

"Hannah, I love you, but I don't want to go there right now, okay? I came over here to try to get her off my mind. So, let's just drop it, okay?"

She sighs. "Fine, but I just want to say one thing."

I look at her, exasperation in my voice. "Do I have a choice here?"

"Not really." She shrugs like I just need to deal with it. "I just want you to know that I was at the spa the other day and saw Jill. She looked miserable, maybe even sadder than you."

"Hannah—" I try to interrupt her, but she slaps her hand over my mouth to shut me up.

"Quiet. I'm almost done." I nod and she removes her hand. "All I was going to say is that it doesn't make sense to me that two people who are so miserable apart should stay that way when they so obviously don't want to be."

I stare at her, my expression blank, and wait to see if she has anything else to add. If she slaps her hand over my mouth again, I may snap. When she remains quiet, I speak. "You done?"

She nods her head contritely.

"It's over." I move to stand in front of her and speak more quietly. "And I'm fine, okay? Or, I will be, so just drop it."

Her eyes shift to the floor, but she nods her head in acceptance. I change the subject quickly, trying to turn the mood in a better direction. "So, where's my baby brother anyway?"

"Work. Closing some deal." She looks at me and lifts her shoulders. "I didn't ask for details. But, hey, what are you doing this Friday? Want to come to dinner with us? There's a fabulous new restaurant that we got reservations for. It's called Indigenous. Have you heard of it?"

I shake my head. "Nope."

"Well, it's getting amazing reviews, and anyone who is anyone has been going, so I got Drew to snag us a table. What do you say?"

I shrug. "Sure. I'm always up for a good meal. Sounds good."

"Awesome!" She claps her hands in delight at my acceptance and I smile. Sometimes, it's the simplest things that make women happy. "Now, are you going to make those grilled cheeses? Because I'm sick of cooking them!"

I spend the next hour cooking, eating, and laughing with Hannah and Grace. She put Brody to bed after his bath, so I missed him but knew I'd see him soon. I leave around eight so Hannah can put Grace to bed, promising I'd see her again on Friday for dinner.

IT HAS BEEN seven excruciating days since I drove to the Hamptons to see Ben. Seven days since I left my heart laying on the floor of that kitchen. Seven days I've been burying myself so deep in work that I have barely seen anyone.

Even at work, I stay in my office. I get there before we open, and I leave long after we close. When the cleaning crew comes in, I've been sending them home and scrubbing the place from top to bottom myself. Anything to keep busy and people out of my hair. I haven't even done a single treatment this week. I just can't be around anyone right now.

Aisha and Anna have been picking up the slack without a single complaint, probably because they still feel bad about what happened the last time Ben was here. I still cringe when I think about it. It's even worse when I remember the look on Ben's face when he opened the door for me in the Hamptons. How gutted he looked. All I wanted was to take that pain away.

I shake my head. I need to stop thinking about him. I need to stop missing him. I need to accept that it is over. My phone buzzes on my desk and I glance at it. It's Raeva, and I know what she wants. Mikaela and Rae have been worried about me, and have been relentless with the well-meaning nagging.

I let it ring. But it doesn't take long for me to realize how naïve I was for thinking she would let that slide. Rae is tenacious when she has her mind set on something. Raeva and Mik storm into my office without knocking, armed with boxes of Chinese food and wine.

I glance at them and arch a brow. "Come in, please. Make yourselves at home." Sarcasm drips from every word.

Neither of them seem bothered..

"I called, but since you didn't answer, here we are." Rae shoots back. She places the take-out boxes and some chop sticks in front of me. "Now eat."

I know better than to argue with her when she uses that tone of voice. It's her stern nurse voice, and let me tell you, she knows how to use it. I open a box and shovel some noodles into my mouth. I'm sure they are amazing, but I don't even taste them. Mikaela fishes a corkscrew out of her bag and opens the bottle of wine. My two besties sit on the chairs across from me, and for a while, we eat in silence.

"Do you remember my new friend Mackenzie?" Mikaela asks me.

I nod. "The chef?"

"That's the one," Mik says with a smile.

"Well," Rae continues. "We are planning a little dinner tomorrow night for River, to celebrate the new software program he designed. And we are having it at Indigenous— Mackenzie's place."

"I really am too busy, but thanks for the invite."

"Oh, please. Too busy doing what?" Mikaela rolls her eyes. "Wallowing in your own self-pity?"

"I'm not wallowing. I am trying to run a business." I retort.

"A business that will run just fine without you while you

go out for dinner, particularly because you close around that time anyway."

I realize how lame my excuse is the second it rolls out of my mouth. Leave it to my friends to call me out.

"River really wants you to come. You know he adores you and hates our dinner parties. He says it'll be bearable with you there."

I groan. Of course, she is playing the guilt trip ploy. The last thing I want is to go out in public and entertain people. But, River has always been like a little brother to me; the two of us are thick as thieves. He is brilliant, dresses quirky, and makes me laugh. Maybe, hanging out with River for a night is just what the doctor ordered. Rae and Mik stare at me expectantly.

"Okay," I concede. "I'll go."

"Good," Raeva states smugly.

"I'm picking you up from work at 5:00 pm sharp. I have dresses for us, and we need time to get ready," Mik informs me with excitement.

She gets a little zealous about clothing, and she should; her designs are amazing. Mikaela Kingsley is a fashion queen. Clothing, interior, she does it all. In fact, she did the design for her friend's restaurant. I've not seen it yet, but I'm excited to see her work. I know picking me up and dressing me is a guarantee to make sure I don't cancel last minute, and I appreciate the gesture. I muster up a smile.

"Okay. I'll be ready."

"Good girl," Rae says as she refills my cup. "You've earned some more wine."

Mikaela smirks at Rae's joke, and I roll my eyes. When I

look at my friends and see how much effort they are putting into making sure I am okay, it fills me with warmth.

"Hey, guys?"

"Yeah?" they say in unison.

"Thank you."

"What's family for?" Rae tells me.

"Cheers to that!" Mik chimes in.

CHAPTER
Eleven

I TAKE the elevator from my loft down to the lobby and walk into the brisk night air to wait for Drew and Hannah. They texted a moment ago and told me they were on their way. I glance at my reflection in the glass window from the lobby and note that what I've worn definitely reflects my mood. I'm dressed completely in black. Black Prada suit, black dress shirt, and black shiny shoes. *All the better to go with my black heart.* I shake my head in defeat over how I feel as of late.

Before I can mull over it any further, a sleek black—*how fitting*— Escalade pulls up to the curb, the window lowering to reveal Drew, a smirk on his face. "Looking for a date?"

I walk to the vehicle, open the door, and step inside to sit across from Drew. "If I was, you certainly wouldn't be my first choice."

"No, I don't suppose I would," he drawls back at me, brow raised knowingly.

I shift my gaze to Hannah, who looks radiant, dressed in a striking blue dress, her long blonde hair falling in waves around her shoulders. "You, however, could be." I flash a playful wink at her. "You look stunning."

"So do you!" Her eyes sweep over me quickly. "I like you in black, Ben. Very dark and sexy."

"Uh-um." Drew clears his throat and tilts his head in his wife's direction, brows creased. She turns her attention to him and smooths a hand down his chest, over his waist, and then rests it on his thigh. "Do you really need me to tell you that I think you're the most gorgeous man to walk this earth, honey?"

One side of his mouth cocks up before he leans over and presses his lips against hers for several seconds. When he pulls away, she lets out a soft breath. "Nope, but I don't want you admiring anyone else either, my love."

While I'm happy my brother is so completely in love, it's difficult not to be irritated. It feels like I came so damn close to having the same thing within reach, but instead of holding tight, I foolishly loosened my grip, any chance of love slipping through my fingers.

"I'd be happy to get another ride if you two would rather be alone." My tone is snarky, but hey, so is my mood.

"Sorry, Ben," Hannah offers, moving her hand from Drew's thigh and placing it in his hand instead. "We'll behave. I promise." She produces a smile that makes it difficult for me to stay grouchy.

We chat about dinner at our parents' the following week, moving on to what the kids are dressing up as for Halloween, and then we seem to be at the restaurant. We exit the luxury vehicle and move forward to enter the restaurant. When we walk through the doors, I stop in my tracks, my dick practically getting hard at the decadence before me. The front of the restaurant boasts a whiskey bar unlike any I've seen before, and I know instantly Indigenous just became my favorite restaurant.

I tap Drew on the shoulder and then point to the bar. "I'll meet you at the table. I want to see what they have to offer."

"Ten minutes, Ben." He looks in the direction our table seems to be in. "Don't make me come looking for you."

"Ten minutes." I repeat, confirming his request. I make my way to the bar, pick up the whiskey menu sitting on its surface, and begin browsing. The choices are magnificent, making it difficult for me to decide what to choose, but it also gives me even more reason to come back again. I finally decide on a glass of Highland Park, the Ice edition, and my mouth waters to taste one of the rarer single-malts to be had.

The bartender places the glass in front of me, and I lift it to my lips, pausing when I notice some familiar faces breeze through the door. Mika and Raeva, along with Mikaela stop at the hostess station for only a moment and then carry forward into the restaurant, not noticing my presence. I make a note to stop and say hi to them when I find my table.

I bring the glass to my nose, inhale deeply, and my mouth waters as I take a slow sip, drawing just a small taste into my mouth. I close my eyes to savor the taste but blink my eyes open when I think I hear a familiar voice.

I turn in the direction of the doorway and freeze when I

see who it is. Of course, where Raeva and Mik go, Jill is sure to follow. My heart starts to gallop in my chest as I question whether I should go over and say hello or leave her alone, which is very much what I told her I would do.

I stare at her, my eyes raking down her body to admire the very short dress that displays every curve on her perfect body, down her bare thighs and to the black suede knee-high boots she's standing in, making her legs impossibly longer than the already are. *Fuck it.* There's no way I'm not saying hello.

I take my drink in hand and begin to stroll in her direction but pause again when I see the expression on her face change to relief and then joy as a strangely dressed man bursts through the door and waves her purse in the air. "Found it!"

She meets him halfway and throws her arms around him, depositing a kiss to his cheek as she does. "Oh, River, you're my hero! Thank you!"

I'm once again frozen in my tracks, my eyes glued to the scene unfolding before me. I can feel my pulse throbbing in my neck and the flow of my blood roaring in my ears. Who the fuck is this asshole? And what in the goddamn hell is he wearing? A fucking Hawaiian shirt? Under a suit that I know cost easily over a thousand dollars? This is what Jill is trying to replace me with? And what is he, twenty? He looks like a baby compared to her.

Before I have a chance to respond or move forward, he sweeps his arm around her shoulders and ushers her into the restaurant. I know my ten minutes is up, and if I don't get my ass to the table, Drew will be on the war path. Wasting what should have been a savored drink, I raise the glass of Highland Park to my mouth and down it like a shot. I walk forward, slamming the glass on a random table I pass, and enter the dining room to look for Drew and Hannah.

I don't have to go far. And, *Jesus fucking Christ*, can this night get any goddamn worse? As I move closer, I see Hannah instructing a busboy to merge some tables so that we can all eat together as one large party. I scrape my hand down my face, trying to gather some sense of calm, and approach tentatively. When I'm standing beside Drew, who happens to be looking at me with a 'don't fucking ask me' expression on his face, Jill finally notices my presence, which is made obvious when her mouth falls open, the grip on her date turning white.

"What the fuck, Drew?" I growl under my breath.

He shrugs. "The Kingsleys walked in, we started talking, Hannah invited them to join us, and here we are." He throws a quick glance in Jill's direction and then back at me. "This was obviously *before* Hannah realized Jill was with them."

"I thought this was just going to be a quiet dinner," I growl again.

"Then leave, Ben. No one is forcing you to stay," he snarls right back.

I turn toward him, fire blazing in my eyes. "You think I'm going to leave her here alone with that little fucking prick over there?" I cock my head in Mr. Aloha's direction. "No fucking way."

"Then sit the fuck down and shut up." He walks away to rejoin Hannah, effectively ending our conversation.

"Ben," Hannah calls to me. "Come sit here next to me." She pats the chair next to her, a look of apology in her eyes.

I nod and move behind her to slide into the seat she's offered. I lift my head, and my heart stutters when I find a pair of stormy gray eyes staring back at me, as wide with disbelief as mine.

I purse my lips but know I have to be a gentleman, even though my inner caveman is bursting to come out, and force a small smile. "Jill." I nod curtly in greeting.

She offers me a small smile in return and replies, "Ben."

My eyes shift to her right as the man-child she arrived with sits down next to her and drapes an arm across her shoulder. "This okay, Jillybean?"

She nods her head, her eyes darting from him to me, and then back to him again. He's not a complete moron because he obviously notices the tension between us and rises out of his seat to extend his hand to me. "I don't think we've met. River Ray."

I stare at his hand, one I could easily crush in mine, and then lift mine off the table to grasp his. I give it a quick shake and then release it quickly so I don't unintentionally follow through with the dark thoughts running through my mind. "Benjamin Sapphire."

I think I see him falter for a moment as he glances at Jill, but can't be sure, because his movements are as smooth as glass. "I've heard a lot about you, of course. It's nice to finally meet the man in the flesh."

I quirk my eyebrow up, shifting my gaze back and forth between him and Jill and then finally respond. "Unfortunately, I can't claim the same about you. River, you said?" There is no way I'm letting this guy think he's anything but a passing fucking thought in my brain. "What do you do for a living?"

He reaches out, grabs a piece of the fresh bread that was just delivered, butters a slice, and then takes a bite. He shrugs, a smug look on his face as he responds. "A little of this and a little of that."

Without a care in the world over whoever this fucking man-child is, I turn my attention back to Jill and cock my head in a show of disbelief. "Perhaps you should teach him to not talk when his mouth his full. I mean, really, Jill, are you sure he's even old enough to drink?"

Her eyes squint dangerously, and then her red painted lips move to form a sinister smile. "Oh, don't you worry, *Benny*, he more than old enough to drink. In fact, he could probably teach an old dog like you a few new tricks."

"I highly doubt *that* boy could teach me anything." I snort, looking over at her date again, scanning my eyes over his lean frame, and then bring my gaze back to hers. "But if you need a reminder of what I do and don't know, Jill, I'd be more than happy to show you." I run my thumb over my lip, darting my tongue along its tip as I do, a subtle reminder of just what I can do, and chuckle when I see her cheeks flush pink.

She rises abruptly from her chair, tossing her napkin to the table, excusing herself before stalking in the direction of the bathroom. Her man-child stands to follow, but I reach across the table and grip his arm in warning. "Stay. I'll go after her. I'm sure I owe her some kind of apology now."

He nods curtly and slides back down into his seat. "Just stop being a dick, man. She deserves better."

I meet his eyes for a moment and nod, knowing he's right, and then stride after Jill. Instead of going to the restroom, though, she walks to the entrance of the restaurant and steps outside. By the time I follow after her, she's walking in long strides back and forth in front of the building.

When I exit, she stops, spins on her heel, and marches up to me, her finger spearing me in the chest as she begins yelling. "Just who the hell do you think you are, Benjamin Sapphire? You have no right. None! How dare you insult my friend like that, and then blatantly come on to me in front of the entire table!"

I open my mouth to speak, but she stabs her finger into my chest again. I know I shouldn't feel this way, but seeing her angry like this only makes me realize how much I want her. She's so goddamn sexy when she's trying to be tough with me. "No! I don't want to hear one word you have to say! I've heard enough out of you!"

"You know what, Jill?" I pluck her tiny hand from my chest, wrap it in mine, then push my body against hers, backing her up until she's forced up against the brick wall of the building. I take her other hand and press it above her head, stepping forward into her body so mine is completely flush with hers, ensuring there's no question about how I feel. "There's not a goddamn thing I want to say to you anyway. But I sure as fuck know what I want to do to you."

Before she can say another word, I slam my mouth against hers in fury. I kiss her until I feel her knees weaken underneath her, and her chest is rising in short pants against mine. I kiss her until I feel her hand grip onto the back of my neck and her fingernails dig into my skin. I kiss her until I finally feel her soften under me, and only then do I let her go.

We both are breathing hard and staring at each other in

confusion. "Jesus Christ, Jill. What the fuck are you doing to me?" I rake my hand through my hair and then shake my head in an attempt to clear it. I take a step closer and cup her face in my hand, a feeling of regret washing over me.

"I'm sorry. So fucking sorry." And then I turn and walk away from her, fleeing the restaurant and her as quickly as I can.

Jill - 3 hours ago....

AS PROMISED, Mik shows up at five sharp in one of the Kingsley vehicles to pick me up. I am under no illusion that I have any say regarding any of this, so I am ready and waiting for her to arrive. As soon as I'm home, I'm ordered to my bedroom to take a shower to get prepped. After I dry my hair, I shrug into a robe and head to Mikaela's room, where I also find Rae, both of them in Mik's dressing room.

"Champagne?" Rae asks as she holds a glass out for me.

I gratefully accept. If I am going to be any fun tonight, I need a little buzz.

"Look what I got for you," Mikaela says in a sing song voice.

She holds out a beautiful leather dress that has thousands of little spots in a variety of colors painted atop of it.

It almost looks like dragon skin; it's beautiful. I tell her so and she beams.

"Put it on," she says.

I eagerly accept the gorgeous garment and slip it over my head. Raeva helps me zip up while Mikaela stands in front of me, appraising her masterpiece. She claps her hands together and squeals with glee. I think she approves. Her reaction makes me giggle, and I realize that I have just laughed my first genuine laugh in a week. Maybe tonight is exactly what I need.

"Wait!" Rae exclaims. "I have the perfect boots to go with these. Be right back."

She runs off to her own penthouse to get them, leaving me with Mikaela.

"I can't tell you how happy I am to see you smile, Jill."

"I'm not going to lie, it feels good."

I sit at Mik's dressing table, and she positions herself behind me and starts to brush my hair.

"I know how it feels." I look up at her in the mirror. I know that she does, even though she never speaks about it. "And I understand why you walked away."

She searches for my gaze in the mirror and captures it. "I just hope that Ben doesn't turn out to be your Eric, your one and only, because I wouldn't wish this feeling on anyone. Pining for the one man you know you can never have. Knowing that no man will ever understand you the way he does, or who truly see who you are. I love you, and I don't want that for you."

A tear rolls down her cheek. I rise to my feet to pull her into a hug. "Hey," I tell her. "No crying allowed, remember. This is supposed to be a fun night." I pull back enough so that I can wipe the tear from her cheek with the back of my hand and then pull her into another hug.

"Jeez!" Rae exclaims. "Can't I leave the two of you alone for one second?"

Mikaela and I share a look, and she holds her hands up. "My bad." She smiles in apology at Rae. "We're good now."

Raeva nods and then holds up her phone. "River just texted that he's headed this way, so we need to finish getting ready."

Raeva approaches me and whispers in a conspiratorial tone, "I am making him wear a suit."

I scoff. "No way."

"Yeah way."

I laugh. "Now, this, I have to see. Let's finish up, girls!"

When we get downstairs, both Mika and River are standing in the lobby, their backs facing us. The first thing I notice is, not only did River get a haircut, but he is in fact actually wearing a suit. When he turns around, though, I'm pleased to see the River we all know and love is still present.

"River! You promised!" Rae complains with a wrinkled nose. He holds his hands up in defense. "Hey. I held up my end of the bargain. You said wear a suit. I am wearing a damn suit." He cocks his head, unable to mask the delight on his face. "I even wore the suit you sent over."

I chuckle. Typical rebellious River. He's right, of course; he is wearing a suit—a very nice one at that—only instead of a dress shirt, he has paired it with the loudest Hawaiian-print shirt known to man. I walk over to him and kiss his cheek.

"I, for one, think you look fantastic," I state in support.

River beams at me. "That's because you have excellent taste, my friend."

And, with that, we walk outside and all pile into the silver Lincoln that is waiting at the curb. River blows out a long whistle. "Fancy ride, brother-in-law. New toy?"

"Are you in the market for a new toy, brother-in-law? Because I can set you up with my guy," Mika says with encouragement..

"Boys and their toys," Mikaela says as she rolls her eyes.

Everyone happily chats and jokes during the short ride to Indigenous. When we pull up to the curb, I'm the last one to climb out, River waiting to assist me. We step into the restaurant, and I notice my hands are empty and slap myself on the forehead. "Crap, I left my purse in the car. I'll be right back," I say as I turn to leave.

"Don't be silly, I'll get it." Before I can even respond, he's already shot back outside in search of my purse. I linger at the hostess stand for only a few moments before the door opens, and River steps in waving my purse. I do a little dance as I make my way over to him and throw my arms around him, placing a kiss on his cheek in thanks.

"Oh, River, you're my hero! Thank you!" I beam.

"You're very welcome." River slides his arm around my shoulder to lead me into the restaurant, where we spot our table mates quickly. Only, it seems that we now have a few more guests in our party. Drew and Hannah Sapphire are also here, and the girls are working to have our tables joined for dinner. A bolt of pain flinches through me, followed by relief when I realize Ben doesn't seem to be with them.

I move to greet Hannah and introduce her to River. I ask

where Drew is, and she points somewhere behind me. I turn around to wave at Drew, and that's when I see him. The entire planet tilts and falls off its axis, making it feel like the room is spinning out of control. I can feel the color drain from my face as my jaw goes slack. *What the fuck is he doing here?*

My first instinct is to run as my eyes dart to the exit. But, no, I can't let him see that he affects me in any way. I don't want him to think he has power over me, even though I know the truth. *Damnit, he totally does.* I'm not sure if he's noticed me, but everyone starts to take their seats, and of course, by some damn misfortune, the only two chairs available are directly across from Ben and Hannah. To make matters worse, when River pulls my chair out for me, he reaches for the one directly across from Ben.

What am I supposed to do, act like a child and tell him I don't want sit across from the mean boy that broke my heart? Ugh, that's not even accurate because he doesn't even know he broke my heart. I plaster a smile on my face, thank River, and then gracefully sink into the chair. I can't help myself, but my eyes are fixed on Ben to gauge his reaction. I can't believe my heart is betraying me like this; beating out of control, as if she is trying to escape from my chest and jump into Ben's arms. He looks up and our eyes finally connect. The look on his face speaks volumes; he doesn't want to see me at all. And fuck me if that doesn't hurt like hell, especially after the curt greeting he gives me.

River sits next to me and puts his arm around my shoulder. He knows I always get cold in restaurants. He gestures up, and my eyes follow, noticing the vent blowing cold air above our heads. I see now why he chose this seat for me. He's the one directly under the vent. "This okay, Jillybean?"

I nod my head. I seem unable to keep my eyes from wandering back to Ben. It's as if he is silently calling to me. Or am I making this shit up in my head? I'm not sure what Rae has told River about Ben, but I do know that River can scope out a situation like no other. He introduces himself to Ben, and I get a real strange vibe from the interaction. There is definitely some kind of silent pissing match happening between them, with me being the object of their attention, which is a ridiculous thought. Ben is the one who stated he wanted to keep things professional between us. Ben looks at me and cocks his head, a look of contempt marring his chiseled features.

"Perhaps you should teach him to chew with his mouth closed and not talk when his mouth his full. I mean, really, Jill, are you sure he's even old enough to drink?"

Are you fucking kidding me?

I narrow my eyes as my temper tries to get away from me, smiling to disguise my anger. "Oh, don't you worry, *Benny*, he's more than old enough to drink. In fact, he could probably teach an old dog like you a few new tricks."

He scoffs. "I highly doubt that boy could teach me anything." His lip rises in a sneer.

Dick.

"But," he continues, "if you need a reminder of what I do and don't know, Jill, I'd be more than happy to show you."

I can't believe he just said that. I'm so pissed. I sit and stew for a second, watching as he takes his thumb and traces it sexily over his lip, his eyes locked on mine. When he sees me looking, he chuckles. He's such an ass, and I've had enough. I rise to my feet, deposit my napkin on the table, and grab my purse.

"Excuse me, please."

I intend to go to the ladies' room, but I am so angry I know I need more than a moment. When my gaze falls on the exit door, I make a snap decision. "Fuck it," I mutter angrily under my breath.

When I get outside, I realize the car has left. Damn it. I pull out my phone and order a cab. Impatiently pacing on the sidewalk, I wait for my ride when Ben storms out of the restaurant and stands in front of me, forcing me to stop pacing. And I just snap. "Just who the hell do you think you are, Benjamin Sapphire? You have no right. None! How dare you insult my friend like that, and then blatantly come on to me in front of the entire table!"

He opens his mouth, but I don't want to hear a damn thing from him anymore. I am over it. Done. And I tell him so while poking him in the chest.

"You know what, Jill?" he says as he grabs my hand. He towers over me and closes the distance between us. I try to retreat, but not out of fear; I am not scared of Ben. No, I back up out of self-preservation. Because even though this man has just acted like a gigantic ass, my body screams for his. I want him. Suddenly, there's nowhere else to go. The brick wall that is halting my escape is cold against my back. Ben pushes into me, and I can feel how hard he is. I swallow, raising my eyes to find his blazing ones staring back at me.

"There is not a goddamn thing I want to say to you anyway. But I sure as fuck know what I want to do to you."

The next thing I know, his lips slam against mine and the world falls away. Just when I think my legs are going to collapse under me, he pulls away and looks at me in confusion. Before I can even gather my wits, he's apologizing and then walking away.

I watch in a daze, unable to react. *What the fuck was that? How could he kiss me like that and then tell me he regrets it? You don't kiss someone like that and regret it. No way. Benjamin Sapphire owes me some answers, and I am going to go get them.*

What a fucking mess.

CHAPTER
Twelve

WHAT THE FUCK did I just do? I tell her we need to keep things professional and then I go and act like a jealous school boy the moment I see her with another man—okay, I still contend he's a child.

My strides are long and heavy as I walk away, afraid to look back, because I'm not sure I'll be able to stop myself from turning around and dragging her back home with me. Why does she have to be so goddamn beautiful, so smart, so irresistibly challenging?

I head closer to the curb so I can hail a cab and am happily surprised, and extremely relieved, when I see the Escalade pull up beside me and the passenger window sliding down. David, Drew's right hand man, is leaning toward the window. "You want me to take you somewhere, Mr. Sapphire?"

I nod and move to open the back door and then settle myself inside the vehicle. "Thanks, appreciate it."

"That's what I'm here for, sir." He pulls smoothly out

into traffic and then meets my eyes in the rearview. "Where can I take you?"

I scrub my hand over my rough beard, wondering momentarily if it's time for me to actually shave it, and then shrug. "Home, I guess. I don't think I'm going to be good company for anyone tonight."

"Home it is." Minutes later, we arrive in front of my building, and I help myself out of the back seat and slam the door shut behind me. I give David a short wave of thanks and then turn toward the front doors. I'm about to go in when my phone starts vibrating against my chest. I reach inside my jacket and pull it out, knowing already it's either going to be Hannah or Drew. I grimace when I see Hannah's name on the screen and swipe left to read her message.

-What in the world is the matter with you? How dare you treat Jill and River the way you did! I'm so mad at you right now, Ben!

I shake my head, knowing I'm going to have to go over and see her tomorrow with my tail between my legs to apologize. Because, of course, she's right. I acted like a complete asshole. My phone buzzes again, and I read the next text from Hannah, a smile small forming on my lips, thinking again how goddamn lucky my brother got.

-David said he took you home. Are you okay? Call me if you need to talk.

I slide my phone back in my jacket pocket and then enter the lobby of my building, taking the elevator up to my loft. I walk in, shrug my jacket off, and walk straight to the kitchen to pour myself a drink. I think some whiskey is in order, if I do say so myself. Lots and lots of whiskey. Whatever I have to do to get Jill out of my goddamn head.

I grab the first bottle I see out of the cupboard—I have many, mostly gifts from clients and staff—and a glass, then pour myself a good four fingers of the amber liquid. Just smelling it makes my mouth water, and as I take a long pull, I moan in relief. I head to one of the couches, pulling my shirt from my slacks, working the buttons undone as I go, and am about to sink down when the buzzer for the elevator sounds.

Shit. Maybe Hannah decided she was going to rip me a new one tonight instead of tomorrow. I must have really pissed her off. I stride quickly over to the call button and press the intercom button. "Yep."

"Ben?" I rear back in surprise when Jill's curt voice reaches my ears. She's definitely not who I was expecting.

"Jill?" I respond. "What are you doing here?"

"Let me up, Ben. I have a few things I want to say to you."

Shit. I can hear the anger in her voice and sigh deeply as I press the button to release the elevator. *This should be fucking fun.*

I set my drink down on the table and, moving to stand in front of the elevators, shove my hands in the pockets of my slacks as I wait for her. After what feels like an eternity, the doors slide open, my breath once again catching at her beauty.

She stomps her foot on the floor of the elevator, rolls her eyes, and then storms past me. "Jesus Christ, Ben! Really? Do you have to stand there and look like... like that?" She waves her hand up and down the length of my body.

I look down to scan myself and then back up at her, my

brows creased in confusion. "What the hell are you talking about, Jill?"

"Argh!" She slams her purse on the table, twirls around to face me, and places her curled up little fists on her hips. *Jesus, she's fucking adorable when she's pissed.* I can't help the smirk that dances across my lips as I watch her, fascinated.

"You really have no idea, do you?" she spits out. "And wipe that look off your face!"

I watch as she takes a few steps closer to me, her eyes trailing down my bare chest, and then I realize what she meant. Well, fuck, I just scored a point and wasn't even trying. I take a step closer, purposely trying to invade her space, and cheer internally when I see her falter and stand in place.

"Where's your man-child? Won't he be upset that you left him and came running back to me?"

I know I'm pushing my limits here, but if I don't do something to really piss her off, really make her want to leave, I'm going to do something both of us may regret.

"You are such an asshole." She stomps her foot in place again, her hair swishing back and forth as she shakes her head in anger. "First of all, *River* is a friend. He's Rae's younger brother, whom I have known since he *was* a child, so why don't you just put that jealous shit on a shelf and move on!"

My brows raise at the fact that River wasn't her date at all, and I'm immediately torn in two by feelings of relief and then embarrassment for my assumptions and behavior. She must read the emotion on my face because she doesn't wait for me to reply before continuing.

"Yes, not feeling so high and mighty now, are you, Mr. Sapphire?"

I growl and take another step toward her. "Don't call me that. You know I hate it."

She's taunting me now, because she takes a step closer, the distance between us mere inches, and tilts her head up to mine to smile sweetly. "And I hate that you tell me in one breath that we need to keep things professional, but then you act like a jealous beast the first time you see me on another man's arm."

Her breath is coming out in short pants, the heat of it invading my nostrils every time I inhale, reminding me exactly what she tastes like. My gaze flicks to her mouth, her eyes, and then back to her mouth again. The angle of her head changes and rears back slightly, and I know she's registered what I must be thinking.

I want her. I want her so fucking badly that having her this close is making it very goddamn hard not to do what every instinct in my body is screaming at me to do.

I surprise myself, and, I think, her, when I reach forward and cup her face gently in my hands and speak softly. "And that's why I said I was sorry. You deserve better than this, Jill. I'm a fucking mess. You deserve someone whole, and good, and who isn't afraid to love you the way you should be. I'm a broken man, Jill. Maybe beyond repair."

Her eyes crinkle as she scrunches her forehead and looks directly at me as her voice, soothing and sweet, leaves her mouth. "We're all broken, Ben. All of us, in some way. Won't you even try and give us a chance?"

I let my head fall back as I blow out a long breath, my

eyes closed as I consider what she's asking me, and then bring my gaze back to hers. "I don't want to hurt you."

Her teeth clench around her bottom lip, her cheeks flushing pink as she looks up at me from under her lashes, and then releases it. Moving herself closer to me, her next words come out in a whisper. "Not being with you hurts more."

That's it. I'm done. It's all I need to hear. I slide my hands behind her head as I pull her body flush to mine and finally, finally, seal my lips against hers. Her hands snake over my chest, against my bare skin, and wrap around my back as she holds on to me. I don't care if this ends with my heart turning to stone. There is nothing I can do to stop the floodgates she's just opened.

THIS ISN'T what I came here to do. I came here to give him hell. But, now, all I want is to rip every last article of clothing he's still wearing off his body. His lips are on mine, his tongue invading my mouth, our breaths becoming one. My entire body is pressed tightly up against him, but it still doesn't seem close enough.

I moan into his mouth, and he responds by grinding up against me, demonstrating just how much he wants me too. Hands are everywhere, as if neither of us can decide where we want to touch first. Ben tears his lips away, panting, his eyes locking with mine as he rests his forehead against me. *Has he changed his mind again?*

I stare back at the stormy blue gaze I always seem to find

myself drowning in and am rendered speechless. The virility in his disposition is the sexiest thing I have ever seen.

"If we do this tonight, Jill, no more running. I'll be yours. Every piece of my brokenness will be yours, and you... you'll be mine." He trails his lips from my forehead, slowly moving down until he's peppering my neck with small kisses and little nips. "Every last fucking inch of you will be mine. Is that what you want?" he demands.

I can't find my voice to speak. I'm too mesmerized with him, too consumed with need. So, I just nod. I tremble as his tongue slides across my clavicle. "Say it," he growls. "I need to hear you say the words."

"I do. I want that," I manage to croak.

That seems to be all he needs. In a flash, my dress is pooled around my ankles, and I stand before him in only black lace panties and Rae's knee-high suede boots.

"Jesus Christ, Jill. No bra? Are you trying to kill me?"

I suck my lower lip between my teeth and swing my head back and forth. "It didn't work with the cutouts on the dress." I step demurely out of the material around my feet and push Ben's shirt off his shoulders sending it swishing to the floor. A mischievous grin appears on my face, and I push against his chest, indicating that I want him against the wall. He cocks his head and raises his brows in delight as he willingly obliges.

Darting my tongue out, I run it quickly over my lips and look up at Ben as I sink to my knees in front of him. I undo his belt, then his button, then grab onto the metal tab of his zipper to slowly pull it down. I tug his slacks down, making sure to take his boxers down as well. His magnificent length springs free and stands in attention in all its glory.

I wet my lips again. I want to taste him so fucking bad. I've not taken my eyes off his once, and I feel an electric spark run through me at the desire in his eyes. I smile, wrap my hands around his cock, and then slide my mouth over its wide crown. I stroke his length with my fingers as my tongue swirls around his head.

I suck, alternating between gentle and a little rough. His hands fist my hair, and he rocks his hips against my mouth. I relax my throat and take him—all of him. I don't take my irises off his when he hits the back of my throat, moaning around him instead, thrilled when I see his head finally fall back, a long groan escaping his lips. The little sounds he makes every time he slides in serves as motivation to keep going, but Ben has different ideas.

He slides out of my mouth, pulls me to my feet, and then hoists me up in the air over his shoulder. I yelp when he smacks my lace-covered bottom and then practically purr at the warm feeling that spreads after. When he reaches the bed, he tosses me onto my back, my body bouncing slightly on its soft surface, a short gasp of excitement leaving me. I like this man-cave act he's displaying.

He sits on the edge of the bed, removes his prosthetic, and then rolls over onto his hands and knee and begins prowling toward me. "My turn," he says with a wicked grin on his face. He pushes my legs apart and buries his head between them. I can feel his hot breath through my panties, and I let out a soft mewl. His large hands grip either side of my lacy underwear, and in one smooth tug, he yanks at the material, turning it into scraps.

A surprised squeal escapes from me and he chuckles. "I'll buy you new ones," he mutters before diving back down. I forget about the damn panties the second his tongue makes contact with that little bundle of joy he's zeroed in on. He sucks and nibbles and licks long strokes up and down, over and over, driving me to the brink of insanity.

His stroking stops, and I feel the heat of his mouth cover my entire core before he sucks, hard. I surge off the bed, and he shoves me back down with one hand. "Uh-uh, you stay right there, Angel."

His talented tongue keeps playing with my clit as he thrusts two fingers inside of me. "Yes." I nearly come right then and scream out loud. He plunges his digits in and out of me, changing directions and applying pressure that has me writhing underneath him, all the while continuing his oral pleasure. I can feel my orgasm building in the depths of my belly, and I beg for it, for the sweet relief my body so desperately aches for. "Ben, please," I whimper.

"Please what?" he teases.

"For the love of God, make me come already." I gasp.

He smirks before he takes me in his mouth sucking my clit roughly, and I combust on the spot, screaming his name as I fall over the edge.

I hear the ripping of foil, and before I even have time to come down from my orgasm, he positions himself over my throbbing core and plunges inside of me in one smooth stroke. All of him, every last inch, fills me completely, and I finally feel whole.

He stills for just a moment and then begins to rock against me. It only takes seconds until we're moving in tandem, our bodies slapping slamming into each other. It feels incredible; I don't want this pleasure to ever end. Just as I think those words, he pulls out of me, a loud yelp of protest falling from my lips.

He flashes me that devilish grin of his, then grips my waist, flipping me onto my front. In one second flat, his hands slide to my hips, lift them, and then his cock is thrusting into me from behind. I rock my ass back into his hips, a moan of pure bliss rolling out of me.

One hand snakes across my belly and grasps onto my breast, while the other holds on to my hip, his grip tightening as he begins to piston in and out of me. Long moans fall from my lips as my core starts to tremble once more. I know what's coming and I want it. I want it so, so bad.

"Oh my God," I croak over and over until I explode around him and collapse forward onto my chest, my ass still in the air. He grasps my hips tighter as he starts to chase his own release, pounding into me without mercy. Inwardly, I beg for him to come, while simultaneously praying he'll never stop.

I WAKE up tightly nested in Ben's strong arms. When I try to move, he clutches tighter.

"Don't you even think about it," he grumbles.

I inwardly swoon, murmuring. "I was just turning around."

He loosens his grip, and I turn to face him, wrapping my arms around him. "Good morning," I tell him with a smile.

He kisses the top of my nose. "Good morning."

"I hate to be all cliché about this, but I have to ask; what now?"

Ben rubs his nose against mine. "I'm not sure what now. All I know is that I am miserable without you."

"I was miserable without you, too," I confess.

"Then let's not be miserable together," he says, grinning.

I giggle, then tease, "Oh, how poetic."

Ben cups my face in his hands and angles my head so that I am staring directly into his eyes. "I wasn't kidding last night, Jill. You're mine now. You chose me, broken and all, and I am not letting you go."

"I need you to hear me when I tell you this, Ben," I plead earnestly. "I am lying here naked in your arms, not just physically naked, but emotionally stripped down. For you. Just for you. You say that you're broken, but dammit, so am I. But when I am with you… Ben, when I am with you, I feel whole."

A tear rolls down my cheek. Ben leans in and kisses it away. "Well, shit."

I frown. "What?"

"Your speech just blew mine out of the water."

I roll my eyes and playfully slap him on the chest. Ben grabs my hand and brings it to his mouth. "I'm sorry for being a complete asshole last night. Can you forgive me?"

"Can you promise me it will never happen again?"

"I solemnly swear," he says dramatically.

I grin and kiss the tip of his nose. "Then, yes, you're forgiven. But you better apologize to River."

He grumbles but concedes. "I'm glad you came over to rip me a new one," he says with a smirk.

"Stop trying to beat my speech. You won't win," I admonish jokingly.

"Fine," he tells me before flipping me onto my back. "But I bet I can show you a bunch of things I am a champ at."

"Oh? Those sound like fighting words to me," I tell him with a smirk.

"I think I'm up for the challenge," he counters, his gaze turning dark and smoldering.

I look to where his need his pressing firmly against my belly and then back up at him. "I'd say that's more than obvious."

"You better get ready then, Angel, 'cause the games are about to begin."

Now this is the kind of fucked I want to be...

CHAPTER

Thirteen

Two glorious months later...

I ROLL over and smile when my eyes land on the angel taking up residence across half my bed. She's managed to pull almost all of the covers off me and has them wrapped haphazardly over her body, one naked leg curled over the top, seemingly holding all of the blankets prisoner. She starts out at the beginning of the night curled up against me like a kitten, and every morning ends up looking like a caged tiger gone wild.

I move to the side of the bed, fit my prosthetic on, and then rise silently, glancing at the clock. It's still early, just a few minutes after seven in the morning. I smile again because I remember what day it is. It's Christmas, and I couldn't ask for a more perfect gift to wake up to on this day. To have her here in bed every morning when I wake up is still a surprise to me.

But here she is, like she has been almost every single

morning since our blow-out at Indigenous back in October. Every single fiber of my being wants to force myself back under the covers and wake her up in a way that will never have her thinking about Christmas morning the same way again, but I don't. We were up late last night celebrating with Mika, Raeva, and Mikeala, and I know we have another busy day ahead of us today, so I tiptoe out of the enclosed space and head toward the kitchen.

When I reach the room, I press a button to open only the kitchen window shades and stare in wonder when I see the sky outside. Large, fluffy snowflakes are floating down through the air, landing on every available surface to create an enormous blanket of white. I walk closer to the window to marvel at its simple beauty, my heart filling with joy at everything I have to be thankful for today. I've always thought New York City was beautiful, but witnessing the scene before me leaves me stunned.

Warm hands wrap around my waist from behind, and I sigh as Jill presses her body to mine, resting her head on my shoulder. "Good morning, handsome."

"Merry Christmas, my Angel." I turn in her arms and cup her face in my hands, placing a kiss on her lips. "I was trying to let you sleep. I'm sorry if I woke you."

She smiles up at me and leans forward to press her lips against mine. "You didn't. I had to pee." She giggles and then pushes her body against mine in a hug. "And, Merry Christmas to you, too, babe."

I hold her against me, close my eyes, and savor this simple moment. It doesn't last long because she pushes against me and does a little hop-dance move in front of me, her hands clapping together. "Do we finally get to open presents?"

I throw my head back as I laugh out loud and then beam down at her. "How old are you, Jill Baldwin? I don't even think Gracie gets this excited."

"Ben," she drawls out in frustration, "you've been making me stare at wrapped presents under that tree for two weeks. I can't take it anymore!"

I bend down, peck her on the nose, and deliver a slap to her backside that causes her to jump out of reach with a squeal. "Well, Miss Little Impatience, you're going to have to wait ten more minutes because this man needs coffee."

"Ugh." She scampers over to the coffee maker and begins preparing a pot for us, looking over at me while she does, and sticks her tongue out. "Fine, but only because I desperately need a cup, too."

I grab her favorite creamer out of the fridge and place it on the counter near her, dropping a kiss on her head as I pass, and then continue past to pull two mugs out of the cupboard. I hand them to her, and she scoops one sugar and some of the cream in a mug, leaving the other as is. We've developed an easy routine that I, for one, never in my life imagined would happen for me.

"Do you want me to open the rest of the shades, or leave it a little dark so we can enjoy the lights on the tree?"

"Open!" she exclaims with glee. "I want to watch the snow falling. It's so pretty!"

The coffee is almost done brewing, so she fills both mugs before carrying them over and handing one to me. We move in unison to the tree and, without words, both sink to the floor in front of it, looking at the lights twinkling above us, both of us admiring the beauty.

"Ben?" Her voice is soft and quiet as she says my name.

"Yes?"

"This is so beautiful, and it's so romantic, but if you don't let me open a present right this minute, I swear I'm going to scream."

I chuckle and set my coffee on the floor beside me. "Oh, my little Angel, always so anxious." I reach under the tree, pluck out the first gift I have for her, and place it in her eager little fingers.

Her eyes light up, just like a kid on Christmas morning, and she rips into the packaging, tearing it to shreds as she does. She's left with a flat, 8 x 10 box, which she spins around in her hands a few times, shakes, and then finally tears open. She flips the tissue paper open and pulls out the envelope laying inside, her brows creasing in curiosity as she looks up at me.

She lifts the fold and then pulls out the contents, revealing two plane tickets. I wait a minute as she reads the destination, and then grin broadly when she looks up at me, her eyes wide with wonder. "Bora Bora?" She looks back down at the tickets again as if she can't believe they are real, and then back up at me. "You're taking me to Bora Bora?"

I nod enthusiastically, so fucking content that she's happy with my gift. "I overheard you talking with Rae one day about your dream vacation, so..." I shrug and point to the tickets. "Because, baby, I want to make all your dreams come true."

She drops the tickets and lunges herself against me, her arms wrapping tight around my neck as she tackles me.

"Thank you, thank you, thank you, Ben!" She pulls her face back enough to press her lips to mine for a few seconds, delivering enough passion to make me want to drag her back to the bedroom, and then leans back to look at me. "You are seriously the most amazing man I could have ever hoped for."

I kiss her now, tugging her back into my arms for another hug. "You deserve this and so many other things I intend to give you, my Angel."

When we release each other, I can see she's blinking rapidly, but don't worry because I know it's happiness. I've given this to her, and it fills me with a peace like none I've ever known.

She reaches under the tree to grab a present for me, but I hold up my hand. "Wait, I've got one more for you."

Her mouth falls open and then just as quickly, closes and forms a smile. "I was going to say you should have, but no, if you want to give me more presents today, I'll take them." She's bouncing up and down, her legs under her, and holds out her hands for another offering, her mouth curved into a huge grin.

I laugh and then reach under the tree to pull out a smaller box, wrapped in pretty gold, sparkling paper and place it in her wiggling fingers. Again, no hesitation, just ripping, the paper sitting in shreds on the floor in seconds. She holds it up to her ear, shakes it lightly, and then lowers it into her lap before lifting the cover off the small, square black box.

She gasps when the lid is off, her hand flying to cover her mouth, her wide eyes jumping up to lock onto mine. Her hand slowly lowers from her mouth, and my name rolls quietly from her lips. "Ben..." Her gaze shifts back to the box and then to me again. "This is beautiful."

I reach over, slide the box from her fingers, and run my fingers lightly over the contents. "I had this made just for you." I lift the necklace out of the box, undo the clasp, and then lean forward to secure it around her neck. It's a delicate gold chain, and on the end, her name, Jill, has been spelled out in diamonds. It looks stunning on her.

"The first time I ever laid eyes on you, it was in a dazzling gold dress covered in a million sparkles." I move my gaze from the necklace to look down into her eyes, now even more moist, and offer her a warm smile. "You were the most stunning woman I had ever seen, but you wouldn't tell me your name."

She laughs and nods at the memory. "I remember, Ben. But, to be fair, you were insanely sexy looking and that scared the crap out of me."

I chuckle and grasp her hand in mine. "This is just my way of honoring you, your name, and everything you mean to me. I'm so fucking thankful and happy you're in my life, Jill."

"Oh my God, Ben, me too." She throws herself in my arms again, this time delivering a kiss that has me dragging her onto my lap, our breathing turning heavier as it grows more heated. I'm about to lower her to the floor when she rips her lips from mine and shakes her head back and forth.

"Not yet!" She scoots herself off of me and wags her finger at me. "You are so naughty, which normally I like." She grins wickedly. "But, first, you have to open your presents!"

AFTER ALL THE amazing gifts that he has just given me, I feel a little silly. I hand him a hand-carved square wooden box. It's secured shut with a tiny padlock. Ben pulls at it for a moment before looking at me with his brow raised. I chuckle and hold up the key. He reaches for it, but I pull it away. "Uh-uh, you have to listen to the story attached to this gift first," I direct with a smile.

He pulls me toward him, and I nestle up against him. "Well, let's hear it then."

"So, my grandmother and I were very close. When I was younger, she used to tell me this story about a rich woman whose heart was broken and bruised by several men. The woman became jaded and scared to love. One day, she decided she'd had enough and carved a heart from the wood of a hickory tree. She cut out her own heart and replaced it with the wooden heart. She believed that, this way, nobody else would be able to hurt her heart or bruise it, because it was made of the hardest wood."

I turn my head to look at Ben to find him staring at me with adoration. I feel my cheeks warm from this single look and turn away so I can finish the story. "One day, she meets a man, and this man didn't want her money. He didn't want her jewels. All he wanted was her love, but she was afraid she couldn't show her love because her heart was now made of wood. So, to show him that she loved him, she took her wooden heart and presented him with it, knowing he would always care for it and for her."

Now that I've shared the story with Ben, I become nervous and avoid looking him in the eye. I reach out to tentatively hand him the key and watch as he opens the box. There, on a bed of purple satin, lays a wooden heart. Ben looks at it for a second, and then his eyes flash up to mine. I bite my lip.

"Does this mean what I think it means?" he asks me.

I bob my head up and down and finally meet his gaze. "These last few months have been the best of my life, Ben. I can honestly say that I have never been this happy, ever. So, yes, it means what you think it means. I love you, Benjamin Sapphire."

He pulls me into his arms and peers into my eyes. "Thank you for giving me the best Christmas present I have ever had, Jillian Baldwin. No contest."

"Really?"

"Really." He places a kiss on my lips and gazes into my eyes. "I'll take your heart, Jill, and I'll keep it safe, because I love you, too. More than I ever thought possible."

CHAPTER
Fourteen

JILL steps out of the bedroom, and I can't help but admire her with pride. She always looks amazing, but today, she's dressed entirely in white, and she looks more like an angel than ever. The pants she's wearing are loose and flowing like silk, and she's topped them with a soft cashmere sweater that falls off each shoulder, her entire neck area exposed, highlighting the necklace I gave her earlier.

I'm dressed for the day as well, and have on a charcoal gray, three-piece suit, sans tie of course, with a fitted white dress shirt. I walk to her and nod in appreciation. "If I didn't know better…"

She tilts her head and scrunches up her cute little nose. "If you didn't know what any better?"

I pull her flush to me and smooth my hand down her back. "I would swear there are wings hidden here somewhere."

She laughs and tilts her head up to me, a smile shining on her face. "And if I didn't know any better, Benjamin

Sapphire, I'd think you were trying to sweet talk your way right into the bedroom again."

I grin wickedly at her and then shake my head. "As much as I would love to do that, we've run out of time. There's some place, or I guess, some thing, that I'd like to share with you."

I give her a quick squeeze before letting her go, and look down at her feet, currently clad in a pair of white heels lined with silver edging, and frown. "Do you think you could humor me and throw on a pair of boots? It will make where I want to take you much easier."

Without hesitation, she shrugs and nods her head. "Sure. Let me go see what I might have in your closet. I can't remember."

I follow her into the closet along the back wall, and slide my feet into my black leather biker boots, but I also grab a pair of dress loafers to take with me. Jill glides up beside me, a small tote bag in hand, and takes my shoes from me and stores them in the bag with hers. She looks down at her feet and clicks the heels of her boots together, then back up at me giggling. "Yee-haw." She's wearing a pair of black cowboy boots. "It's all I could find."

I chuckle and nod approvingly. "They'll do. At least, better than the heels you had on."

After pulling on our jackets, hats, and gloves, we take the elevator downstairs and exit into the lobby of the building. "Give me one second, okay?"

"Of course."

I unlock the door to the gym, quickly stride across the large space into the kitchen, and grab a box I've stored in the large industrial refrigerator. Then, I make my way back to Jill.

Her brows rise as she eyes the content of the box. "Um, morbid much, Ben? Wouldn't red or white roses be more fitting on Christmas?"

I look down at the bouquets of black roses stored in the box and then back at her, my lips trying to form a small smile. "I'll explain in the car. Come on." I offer her my hand, and we make our way out into the snow and down the alley where I'm parked. I help her into the car, ask her to hold the box, and then climb in on the driver's side.

The alley seems to have blocked the car from much snowfall, because the wipers clear what little snow is on the windshield and the back window is barely covered as I start the car and reverse out into the street. I head in the direction of the parkway and then reach over to take one of Jill's hands. She's taken off her gloves, and her hand is warmer than usual in mine. She hasn't said a thing, intuitively seeming to understand that what I'm sharing with her isn't easy for me. When she sees the direction we're headed, she turns to me. "We're going to Brooklyn?"

I nod my head and figure there's no time like the present to start explaining. "Yes, to Cypress Hill Cemetery."

Her hand squeezes mine more tightly as she looks down at the flowers and then back over at me. "The military cemetery?"

"Yeah." I grip the steering wheel a little tighter in the one hand I'm holding it with and blow out a sigh. "I go there a lot." I shake my head. "Well, probably not as much as I used to over the last few months, but always on Christmas."

"Sorry. I'm guessing that's my fault," she lets out meekly.

I squeeze her hand. "Don't apologize. Believe me, Jill, none of these guys would blame me one bit for blowing them off to spend a little more time with you."

"So, tell me about your friends." She turns in her seat so she can face me. "I want to know about them."

I turn my head and give her a loving smile. "Jesus, I know I just said this an hour ago, but damn if I'm not the luckiest bastard in the whole world."

"I'd say we both got pretty lucky." She lifts my hand to her mouth and places a soft kiss on the back of it before lowering it back to her lap.

"Well, you know, of course, about the gym, and that it's dedicated to the guys I served with. Baker and Landon were in the truck with me when we hit the explosive that took my leg. Baker was one of my closest friends, and when I woke and saw him dead next to me, it was like someone had stuck a goddamn stake into my heart. I didn't find out until after I woke up in the hospital that Landon had died as well."

I close my eyes for just a second, the pain from the memory causing my heart to contract tightly, but breathe out, trying to push it away. "I was sent home, of course. And pissed as hell, of course. Pissed my friends had died and I couldn't even go to their funerals or help their families. Pissed I lost my leg and couldn't go back and blow those mother fuckers up. And pissed that our country didn't seem to give a flying fuck about what was happening to those still over there serving."

"So, basically, you were pissed." She chuckles lightly, and I can't help but let out a laugh in return.

"Yeah, I guess that about sums it up," I joke. "I think the

worst of it for me, though, was Rose, er, Jackson; Hannah's first husband. He was actually a Marine, not Army like me, but we were all stationed in the same area, and somehow, this squirrelly little fucker got under my skin and seemed to be everywhere I was. We became friends… good friends."

"I've seen pictures of him in Grace's room. Did you know that there's one of you and him together on her dresser? You look so young in it!"

"Yeah, I actually gave that to Hannah a while back. It used to be in my office, but I don't know, it just seemed like something she should have. Hannah said she wanted Gracie to know that her daddy and her uncle were friends, so she thought her room was the best place for it." I can feel I'm starting to get a little more than nostalgic, so I shake my head to try to clear away some of its weight.

"You okay?"

Jill reaches out a hand and places it softly on my cheek. I turn my head and place a kiss on her palm and then nod. "I'm good. Just a lot of memories."

Her hand moves back to her lap, covering the one that's holding her other hand, and rests there, her fingers grazing back in forth in comfort over my skin.

"Yeah, so Jackson came back to the States on leave when Grace was born, and came to see me. I was still in the hospital healing, still angry as fuck. He was even madder than me, and was so eager to get back and, as he put it, 'get even'. I begged him to reconsider. He just had a baby, for Christ's sake. He had a beautiful wife. He had both goddamn legs. But he wouldn't listen to reason. He died a few weeks later, killed in action."

I look over at Jill and am surprised when I see tears

streaming down her face. "I'm so sorry, Ben. I wish there was some way I could take all this pain from you and carry it instead. You've lost too much already."

We're in the cemetery now, so I pull the car over and put it in park, but leave it running to keep it warm, and then pull her into my arms. This is why I love this woman so much. To want to take my pain and have it be her own. Who says things like that? Who wants to do things like that? She lives up to my nickname of Angel more every day. I kiss her head and whisper, "I love you so much, Jill."

"I love you right back." She hugs me hard and holds on until I slowly pull us apart.

"This helps me." I lift my hand and point a finger out my windshield toward the gravestones in front of us. "Coming here. Honoring them. Making sure they know I'll never forget them or what they meant to me, to this country."

"And the black roses?" She looks down at the box she placed on the floor between her legs some time ago.

I point to the tattoo on my arm. A few of us got these to honor Baker, Landon, and Jackson. The rose specifically for Jackson, and well, you know all about my black heart." I shrug.

"I know all about your heart, Ben, and it's nowhere near black."

I look at her and smile. "Not anymore."

She goes with me then, and we walk through the cemetery, stopping at the grave of each of my friends, my brothers, as we place a bouquet of the roses on each their stones. I tell her a little more about each of them. Hannah is the only other person I've brought here, but Jill is the only one who has ever made my heart feel lighter while doing so.

AN HOUR LATER, we pull back into the alley and park the car. We run up to the loft and grab three big bags of presents and a couple bottles of wine, and then head back outside. The snow is still falling gently, so we decide to leave our boots on and just walk the block over to Drew and Hannah's place. Jill tries to catch snowflakes on her tongue as we walk, and I think my cheeks might actually crack if my smile grows any wider as I watch.

We reach the building in minutes and stomp the snow off our feet as we enter the lobby and share Christmas greetings with the doorman. He knows us by name, our familiarity a product of the frequent visits we both make here. When we step off the elevator, Gracie is already standing in the hallway waiting for us, arms thrown wide as she runs over and hugs us both.

"Merry Christmas, Uncle Benny and Jill!" I drop the bags and scoop her up in my arms, swinging her around before giving her a large hug. When I look up, I see my mom standing in the doorway to the apartment, a very content Brody on her hip, sucking on a green candy cane.

"Merry Christmas, Mom." I smile and set Grace on the ground so I can retrieve the bags and enter the house. I give my mom a one-armed hug and watch with warmth as Jill hugs her with both.

"You two are all covered in snow." My mom already beginning her fussing. "Put those bags right there and take off those wet shoes and coats before you come in any further. Hannah will have a fit if you dirty up her floors."

"What will I have a fit about?" Hannah strolls in carrying a large tray of cut vegetables, placing them down on a table before moving over to give Jill and I a hug. "Merry Christmas, you two."

She takes a step back, places a hand on her hip, and cocks her head at us. "You two are practically glowing. Any news you want to share?" She glances toward Jill's left hand and lifts her brows in hope.

Jill's eyes pop wide, and her head begins shaking back and forth. "Oh God, no! Hannah!" She slaps at her playfully and then lays her hand flat against her breast bone under the necklace I gave her. "I mean, wouldn't you be glowing if Drew had your name put in diamonds?"

That's all it takes for all three women to gather round and start chatting about presents and shoes, and whatever it is women go off and talk in circles about. I chuckle as they all head off in the direction of the kitchen, and then look down when I hear crinkling behind me.

"Gracie, what are you doing?" Her little blonde head pops out of the bag, her wide eyes meeting mine.

"Nothing, Uncle Benny. Just looking to see which presents are mine." She starts bouncing up and down in place, and I can't help but laugh out loud when I realize she's the spitting image of Jill a few hours ago.

"Well, let's go find Dad and Grandpa and see if we can't gather the troops so we can open these puppies up. Sound good?"

"You got me a puppy?" Her eyes light up as her face widens in delight, and I freeze in place.

I let out a long sigh and realize it's going to be a very long day as I try to explain my choice of words. I wonder where the hell my brother is hiding because I need his help pronto. And, damn if I wasn't ready for a Christmas drink, too.

We spend the next few hours opening presents,well, Gracie doing most of the present opening, and then have a wonderful dinner together. I realize as I look around the table, surrounded by the people who mean the most to me, who I love the most, that I may just be the luckiest man alive. And for the first time in a really long time, I don't feel guilty anymore for being the one that survived.

I smile over at Jill and take her hand into mine and squeeze it softly. "Thank you for the most amazing Christmas I've had in a long time."

"You're so welcome." She raises her eyebrows and smiles wide.

CHAPTER
Fifteen

One Week Later...

MY EYES FLUTTER OPEN, and I lift my head off the pillow to look down to try to figure out what's woken me up. One side of my mouth cocks up when I see the top of Jill's head hovering over my stomach, her finger tracing over the lines of one of my tattoos. "Morning, beautiful."

She hums as she places a soft kiss against my chest. "Morning."

"Whatcha doing down there? Come give me a proper kiss," I growl, reaching to pull her up.

"I don't think I've gotten to know this one yet." She pushes my hand away and continues moving her finger lazily over my lower abdomen.

I chuckle softly and move my hand to rest it in her hair instead. I know where this is headed, and I have absolutely no intention of interrupting her. "Angel, I think you know all my tattoos pretty well by now, but by all means, investigate further if you must."

She raises her head just enough so she can peek up at me under her lashes, licking her lips as she flashes me a very sexy smile, and then leans back over me, replacing her finger with her tongue. My head falls back against the pillow, and I close my eyes, letting myself bask in the attention she's giving me right now.

I feel her tongue lift off my skin and then the vibration of her voice as she speaks. "I don't think I ever noticed the way these feathers curve up here around this muscle." And then her tongue is back against my skin, the tip dragging along the edge of one of my lower muscles, and then lower still, my skin breaking out in goosebumps as she goes.

"Last time I checked, there wasn't any ink below my waist, love," I murmur, but don't hesitate to lift my hips when her hands make quick work of removing my boxers.

"Shhh, I'm just looking to make sure." Her fingers trail up my stomach and then rake back down slowly, stopping when they circle around the base of my cock and tighten, her tongue dragging up its hard length, and then her hot, wet mouth sliding down to cover me.

My hips thrust up involuntarily, and a loud moan rolls up from my chest. *Now, this is a great fucking way to wake up.* My hands find her head, and I tangle my fingers in her downy locks, helping to guide her up and down as she sucks me in and swirls her tongue around me, my cock growing even harder. She moans and the vibration against my cock almost causes me to explode right then and there.

I tighten my grip in her hair and pull her off me with a soft pop, guiding her back up my body. When she's close enough, I slam my lips against hers and yank her body flush to mine. She's naked, and her hard nipples brush against mine as she adjusts herself over me. She thinks she's in control, and for a moment, I let her believe it as she slides her wet center up and down my throbbing length.

When she shifts to move higher so she can impale herself with my cock, I grab her arms and roll over, trapping her beneath me, a small gasp falling from her parted mouth as her wide eyes look up at me. "You don't think I'm going to let you do that yet, do you?"

Her teeth find her lower lip and she bites it, as if trying to quench the obvious hunger stirring within, shaking her head softly. I don't give her a chance to reply verbally, because I crush my mouth to hers, my tongue twisting with hers, her body pushing back against mine in desperation. She wraps a leg around me and tries to rock her center against my cock, but I release her lips and slide down her body, effectively breaking the hold she has, and suck one taut peak into my mouth.

I smile around the nipple when I feel her hands clutch the sheets next to me and hear a moan from above. My minx is on fire, and my lips on her only seem to fan the flames higher. I release her hard bud, run my tongue over it with one hard swipe, and then rake a wet trail down her stomach until I reach the apex of her legs. Without hesitation, her legs fall open wide in invitation and I enter greedily, plunging my tongue into her sweet core. I stroke softly until I land against her hard nub and then wrap my lips around her and suck.

Her hands are instantly in my hair, clutching wildly, her knees rising to push her feet into the bed as I grasp her hips tightly and suck even harder. "Oh my God, Ben. I'm going to come if you don't stop."

I want her to come, I do, all over my goddamn face, but I want her pulsing around my cock even more, so I release her and move like lightening up her body and between her legs. Her hands move to my arms, her nails digging into me as she clings to me, and I lean over and slowly ease myself into her. Her hot walls clench and then pulse, pulling me in deeper, holding tightly as I arch my back and plunge all the way in.

We both groan when my center slams against her, and I still, but only for a moment before I slide back out and then drive back into her again.

"Oh my God, yes. Harder, Ben!" I need no further encouragement and surge back and forth against her body, thrusting my cock as deep as it will go, my arms flexed tightly as I hold myself over her. After only a few moments, I feel her tighten around my cock like a blood pressure cuff, her head thrashing back and forth on the pillow, her hands reaching out to grasp me around the neck. She lets out a long, guttural moan, followed by my name in a whisper.

As if it was even possible, hearing my name from her pink lips causes my blood to surge straight to my cock, turning it to stone. I move faster now, my hips pummeling against hers as I feel my balls tighten and then finally explode, my release coating her insides. I clutch onto her, pulling her flat against me, my hot breaths against her ear as I moan out her name again and again.

When my pulse finally slows down enough for me to think reasonably, I roll off her and lay flat on my back, my breaths still coming out in pants. *Holy fuck. How in the world does this just keep getting better and better?*

She lifts herself and lays the top half of her body across my chest, her hand under her chin as she looks up at me. "Did I say good morning yet?" And then she breaks into a fit of giggles as her face flushes a beautiful shade of pink.

AN HOUR LATER, we're both showered and in the kitchen. I'm drinking a cup of coffee as I watch her move around, cooking for us. She's humming and moving her hips softly to the rhythm, and I realize I could never feel more content. "Move in with me."

She freezes, spatula suspended in mid-air, and turns to me, eyes wide, her mouth forming a small 'O' shape before finally speaking. "What?"

"Move in with me." I set my mug on the counter and move closer to her. I slide the spatula from her fingers and wrap my arms around her. "You're here all the time anyway now."

"Ben…" Her face scrunches up in thought for a second. "I mean, I don't know. What about Mik?"

"What about Mik?" I counter. "She's a big girl. And Rae is right across the hall from her. I'm quite sure she'll be just fine."

She chews on her lip in contemplation, and I can tell there are a hundred thoughts swirling around in her head. "Listen, just think about it, okay?" Her head nods up and down, her expression dazed. I tug her closer to me. "Jill, I love you. I love having you here. I love waking up with you every day. I didn't mean to freak you out or scare you."

"I'm not scared." She peeks up at me. "Nothing has ever felt more right to me."

"Really?" I can't help the smile that spreads across my face.

"Really." She nods again, almost like she can't believe what she's saying. "I just have to figure out how I'm going to tell the girls."

"So, you're moving in? That's a yes?" I have a hard time containing the joy in my voice, but I don't give a shit. It gives me a sense of relief and anticipation knowing what else I have planned for her tonight.

Her face breaks into a huge smile. "It's a yes."

"Woohoo!" I tighten my arms around her and swing her around in a large circle, crushing my lips to hers in delight. She squeals out in laughter and then slaps at my arms to put her down.

"Ben, put me down! I have to finish breakfast." Her cheeks are flushed and I know, even though she's trying to play it cool, she's just as excited as me for this next step. "If I'm not at Rae and Mik's by eleven, they will kill me. You know how they feel about preparations."

"Well, if this is the start to our New Year, I think it's going to be fucking amazing." I plant one more kiss on her cheek and let her go so she can finish cooking. "So, what does that crazy duo have in store for you this time?"

"Oh, you know them… Of course, the entire afternoon will be spent at the spa. My rules, not theirs. There's no way I'm showing up to your charity event tonight looking anything less than fabulous."

"Angel, you could show up in a plastic bag and I'd still think you were the most gorgeous woman in the world." I slap her ass playfully and wink.

"You, Benjamin Sapphire, are biased." She turns and smiles sweetly at me. "But thank you. After the spa, we're going to go to my place for dressing. Mik has designed some stunning new creations for us to wear. I can't wait to see them!"

"And I can't wait to see you in it." I raise my brows suggestively.

"You're insatiable!" She grins back. "Are you sure you don't mind me meeting you at the event? It's just going to be so much easier riding over with Mik and the gang instead of coming all the way back over here."

I move up behind her, wrapping her in my arms, and lean my head down on hers. "I told you already, it's fine. It's good, actually, because I have a ton of stuff I need to do before the event. Need to make sure all ducks are in a row and what not."

She spins in my arms, throwing hers around my neck, and smiles up at me. "I love you, Benjamin. I know I tell you all the time now, but I do. I just want you to know that. And I'm still so glad every day that you chased after my stubborn ass."

I soften at her words, knowing without a doubt that everything I have planned for this evening is happening at the perfect time. "I love you, too, Jill." And I kiss her, hoping to show her just how much.

CHAPTER
Sixteen

AFTER WE HAVE SPENT the entire day at the spa getting pampered, we arrive at the penthouse with the girls in full-blown party mode. I go to my room, take a quick shower, and then head to Mik's dressing room to see what kind of magic she's created for me. I walk in just in time to hear the cork pop.

"Jillybean!" They greet me in unison.

"Hey girls." I stroll in wearing my robe, a smile on my face.

Raeva hands me a glass of champagne, smiling like the Cheshire cat.

"What's with the face breaking smile?" I ask with a chuckle.

"I'm just excited about tonight. Whoever came up with the idea for this party is brilliant. Oh, and wait until you see what Mikaela has got for us to wear tonight."

I don't even have to see the outfits to know they will be spectacular. Everything Mik designs is fabulous. It's New

Year's Eve, and we're going to a party being held at the Sapphire Resort; the very one I met Ben in, which seems like such a good omen to the start of our night and the year ahead.

Someone came up with the amazing concept of working the party into a charity. Every guest must donate money into a pot in order to attend. The guests then divide into teams for a scavenger hunt, with the winning team getting to choose the charity they want the total funds donated to. Not only does it sound like fun, but we get to help a good cause.

"Is Ben meeting us here?" Mik asks.

I shake my head and take a sip of the champagne. "No, he said he had tons to take care of for the event and that it would be easier for him to just meet us there."

"Ah. Okay, well, when he sees you, he might not get up."

I frown. "I'm sorry… what?"

Mikaela rolls her eyes. "Because you'll look so amazing; you'll knock him out. Duh."

Raeva and I burst out laughing. "You're a nut, Mik."

She smirks and holds out a hanger with a gorgeous black sequin dress. The dress has a rounded neckline, with a scoop back and three-quarter sleeves. And, it's short, falling a good four inches above my knee making it incredibly sexy. Ben loves when I show some leg. Of course, it fits like a glove. Mikaela is a magician when it comes to things like this. She knows exactly what looks good on anyone or anything.

"You will need a pair of amazing shoes to go with that, of course," Rae chimes in. "Lucky for you, your person has just acquired these." She passes me a shoebox, and my brows rise in delight when I read Jimmy Choo on the box and know they are going to be fancy. I lift the lid and gasp. Inside, I find a pair of black and silver, coarse-glitter-covered, pointy toe pumps. They are perfect. I hug my friends and thank them.

I start to work on my make-up, and watch in the mirror as Rae and Mik begin dressing, all of us continuing to chat about this and that. Mikaela is wearing her signature gold. The color matches her eyes, and she looks stunning. Raeva is dressed in a gorgeous silk top and pant set.

Yes, we look amazing, and we beam in pride at each other. I do make-up and hair for each of us. Mika must be getting impatient for our company, because he's already sent three texts in the last twenty minutes. We take the final one as our queue to leave and all rise and take one last look in the mirror.

We squeeze each other's hands and look expectantly at each other before I finally speak. "I think we're ready, girls." We all nod in agreement and leave the dressing room to head to the party.

ONCE DOWNSTAIRS, we climb into a gorgeous white limo and head to the financial district. I pull my phone out of my purse, check the screen, and frown. Still nothing from Ben. It's a bit strange, as he usually checks in, but I try not to think too much about it, knowing he had so much to do to prepare for the event. I'll see him very soon and can't wait for him to see me in Mik's latest creation.

I've been wondering all day how I am going to tell Mik that I am moving in with Ben. I know she will be happy for me, but I hate the thought of her being alone in that big place. I know I've spent almost every night since meeting Ben at his place anyway, but I still can't help but feel bad. I know she's lonely, especially in the evenings, when she's wishing she could be with Eric.

When we pull up in front of the building, a large smile breaks across my face as my mind drifts back to all those months ago—the night Ben picked me out of the crowd, my knight in shining armor, even if I didn't know it then, at the opening gala for the hotel. I shake my head when I recall my unwillingness to even have a drink with the man, and whom I now can't imagine being without.

We head into the lobby where we are all greeted and directed to the coat check. I scan the room for Ben, but still see no sign of him. We make our way to the large ballroom on the second floor as a group and marvel at the opulence before us. The room is gorgeously decorated with flowers dipped in glitter scattered throughout and candles burning on every surface. After securing drinks at the bar, we find our table and take our seats.

A staff member gets on the small stage in the center of the room and begins the evening by requesting our donations and then directing us to a list containing the name of our assigned team mates. Of course, because I know some strings must have been pulled, my team consists of Hannah, Mikaela, Raeva, and of course, myself.

The rules are explained again, and we each listen intently. Each team has until midnight to try to solve the clues provided to them. Each clue will lead to the next and so on until we get to the last one. The first team to get to the last clue will get to pick the charity of their choice to donate the combined money to. We are instructed to assign a team captain, and without hesitation, Raeva gets the job with a unanimous vote.

"Okay, first things first," Rae says, holding a little card. "According to this, we have to declare our charity before we start. Any suggestions?"

"Get Vets Set!" Hannah and I say in unison.

We look at each other in surprise and then giggle.

"It's Ben's charity." I explain. "He offers free gym memberships and physical therapy for vets. It is such a great initiative, and I would love it if we would support him."

"I second that," Hannah chimes in.

"I'm three for three," Mik says with a grin.

"Get Vets Set, it is!"

Raeva fills out the card and hands it in, and we receive our very first clue. It's a balloon. There are some numbers and letters written on the face of it, but they don't make sense; P4P M2 T4 S22 WH1T C4M2S N2XT. Attached to the balloon is a little card that says:

A = 1
E = 2
I = 3
O = 4
U = 5

We stare at the balloon and the card for a moment.

"Ohhh," Rae exclaims as she pulls a pin from her hair. "Pop me to see what comes next!" She stabs the pin into the balloon.

A little note falls out, and I pick it up, unfold it, and read it out loud. "In order to find the next clue, you will have to go to the front desk and ask for something. To find out what to ask for, solve this riddle: I have cities, but no houses. I have mountains, but no trees. I have water, but no fish. What am I?"

I'm glad I've only had one glass of champagne, because apparently, we are going to need our thinking caps on tonight. I repeat the words and mull them over in my head. Then, I remember a few weeks ago, while Ben and I were visiting Drew, Hannah, and the kids, Gracie made Ben and me watch this cartoon with her. What were the odds?

"I know what it is!" I exclaim, and motion for them to follow me as I make a beeline for the front desk. The others don't hesitate and follow. When we make it to the front desk, I approach the young lady behind the counter and give her one of my brightest smiles. "Excuse me, um," I look at her name tag, "Gloria, would you by any chance have a map?"

Gloria beams and nods her head in delight. "Certainly, ma'am. Just a moment."

She bends behind the counter for just a second, and then pops up, holding a map of the hotel in her hands. She passes it over to us, and we open it, noting there is a route high-lighted. We thank Gloria and start to figure out where we are on the map. We follow the highlighted path and end up in a small room with a table set up in the middle of it. The table has a beautiful hand-painted silk table cloth, and on top of the table are twelve different desserts, a pitcher of water, and a dozen water glasses. Next to the pitcher sits a little locked black box, and next to that, tied to a little holder on the table, is another balloon.

Raeva pulls the pin back out of her hair and pops the balloon. Another note drops, and Mikaela picks it up and unfolds it. "One of these yummy desserts holds the key."

The key? To the box?

"Well, ladies, let's dig in," Hannah says as she grabs a fork.

"I call dibs on the crème brulee!" Rae says as she lunges toward her favorite dessert with gusto.

"I'll guess I'll go for this lava cake," Mik announces.

I myself am about to dig into a huge piece of triple chocolate cake when Hannah announces that she has the key. It's covered in frosting, though, so Mikaela pours some water in a glass and drops the key in it. We fish it back out, clean it off, and then open the box. Inside the box is yet another clue.

"A woman shoots her husband, then holds him underwater for five minutes. Next, she hangs him. Right after, they enjoy a lovely dinner. Explain."

The four of us look at each other before a giggling fit ensues.

"Nice lady," Hannah chuckles.

"Oh my God, I know what this means!"

We all look expectantly at Mikaela.

"Listen, when I was in school and had time for hobbies, I used to love to take pictures. Never digital, though. I was an old-fashioned girl—except when it came to clothes, of course," she says with a wink. "Anyway," she continues, "all of it can be explained. We need to find a picture or a darkroom or both. Hannah, does this resort have one?"

"Honestly? I am not sure. The resorts are Drew's territory."

"Wait," Rae says. "The map!"

Sure enough, when we unfold the map, we find that the resort does indeed have a darkroom. We head there immediately. The darkroom is located below ground level, so we take the elevator down and are relieved to find the room unlocked. But the red light outside is on, which means we can't go in. Fortunately, there is a balloon tied to the doorknob. We pop it, and once more, a note falls to the floor, but also four keys.

"A picture speaks a thousand words. But only one key works."

Each key has a keychain on it that reads a different direction. North, East, South, and West. Hmmm. Cryptic. We knock but get no response.

"Oh, screw it," I tell my friends. "I'm going in."

My friends reluctantly follow me into the darkroom, which is just that, dark. Besides the red glow that illuminates the room, it is devoid of brightness, but we notice there are several pictures hanging from a line. I step forward and inspect the images. On every picture, there is a terrace, and it looks to be the same terrace. In the middle of the terrace, tied to something is a balloon.

"I know where this is!" Hannah says excitedly. "It's the roof top terrace. There are four entrances, and I think one of these keys will open a door. Only thing is, I have no idea which. I say, if we want to win this thing, we need to split up."

"Yes, great idea," Mikaela chimes in. "There are four keys and four of us. We will split up, and whoever opens the door first and finds the balloon will call the others. Sound good?"

I am totally good with that. I really want to win the donation money for Ben's charity. Raeva divides the keys. She gives Hannah South, Mik West, me North, and she heads to the East. We all take the elevator to the top floor before splitting up.

On the top floor, there is a small stairwell that leads to the roof terrace. I head to my particular stairwell and climb up until I reach the door. I insert the key and squeal with glee when I attempt to turn the knob and it actually works.

I push the door open and step onto the terrace. When I do, I am mesmerized, my mouth falling open at the beauty before me. There are literally an ocean's worth of white lilies and candles spread on every surface. It is absolutely breathtaking, and I marvel at it a moment in silence.

Even the chilly December wind that brushes across my skin with its icy touch isn't a deterrent, and I move forward to investigate. I walk further onto the terrace and spot the balloon. I stride toward it with tunnel vision. I stop, because I realize that I have no pin. I look at the balloon and frown for a moment. A smile tugs at my lips when I realize I have something else I can use; a pen that I stuck in my purse after I wrote the donation check downstairs. I fish it out and pop the balloon, my face lighting up in victory.

Unlike with the other balloons, this time, there is a loud thud as something drops to the floor. I look down, pick it up, and stare at it. It is a small black heart, made from some type of stone. I'm turning it in my hand when I'm startled by a familiar voice behind me.

"My Angel, so resourceful."

I turn and see my gorgeous man sauntering toward me. He is wearing a three-piece black suit that is so perfect on him that I swear it has been sewed onto him. Ben always looks hot, but by God, when he wears a suit, he just blows me away. Every. Single. Time.

"Ben! You're finally here. You missed all the fun," I tell him regretfully.

"I have not missed a thing. Except maybe you," he tells me as he kisses the tip of my nose. "You look beautiful, Angel, but you must be cold." He shrugs out of his jacket and places it over my shoulders.

"What ya got there?" he asks as he nudges the heart clutched tightly in my hand.

"Oh this is—" I stop talking as the light bulb in my head finally goes on. Of course, a black heart.

Ben sees the recognition in my eyes because he lights up and cups my face. "Angel, what you're holding there so tightly in your beautiful hand is everything that I was, everything that I thought I would always be, and everything you changed with your love. For years, my heart has been black and cold as stone."

I look at him and shake my head softly because I know his heart is anything but cold, and I take my free hand and grip one of his in mine. I nod as he continues.

"I didn't think anyone would be able to love a man like me; broken, angry and cold. But since the very first time I laid eyes on you, I began to feel myself start to thaw. And, as time went on, I realized you had thawed it completely. I no longer prefer the darkness, because you are the light. You brightened my life by being the amazing person you are."

He looks down at his legs and then back into my eyes. "I have not felt whole since I lost my leg. But, Angel, you make me feel as if I have a thousand legs. You make me feel like, leg or no leg, the man I am now, with you, is more whole and complete and a better version of what I was even before my accident. I don't want to wake up another day without you next to me. I don't want to wake up another day without being able to call you mine—officially and legally. So, I am standing here before you, the man that you have made whole, asking you to please consider being mine forever. Give me a chance to brighten your life as you do mine. If you say yes, I promise that I will spend every waking moment of my life trying to make you happy, trying to make you smile, and most definitely loving you in every way you deserve, every single day for the rest of our lives."

Tears are streaming down my face as I watch Ben sink to one knee and present me with a box. "Jillian Baldwin, will you marry me?"

He opens the box to reveal the most beautiful ring I have ever seen, glittering up at me as it sits on a pillow of white satin. The center stone is a large, round black diamond with a white diamond halo surrounding it. The band itself is lined with little black diamonds and is stunning. It is so perfect for us. I am staring at the ring, sobbing and clutching on to the final clue—my little black stone heart. I'm overwhelmed and speechless and just keep looking from the ring back to Ben.

"Angel, you're kind of leaving me hanging here," he mumbles a little nervously.

I drop to my knees in front of him and cup his face in my free hand.

"There isn't anything I want more in this world than to spend the rest of my life with you. You already own me, Ben. We don't need a ring for that. But, yes, yes! I will marry you! Being your wife, being yours, nothing could make me happier!"

I lean in and our lips crash together, sealing our promise with a kiss. After a few seconds, he pulls back, grins broadly, and then lets out a roar. "She said yes!"

All the doors surrounding the terrace fly open, and the place starts to swarm with our friends and loved ones. I have barely made it back onto my feet when I nearly get tackled by Raeva. She is crying her eyes out. "I can't believe you're getting married," she sobs. "I am so happy. Congratulations."

"Hey, stop hogging the bride-to-be!" Mik jokes as she puts her arms around us both and squeezes tight.

"Show us the ring!" Hannah says excitedly as she joins us.

"Did you guys know about this?" I ask, although, I already know the answer.

"Guilty," Raeva admits.

"Yup, me too," Mikaela says

"I guess that makes me three." Hannah beams.

"Well, girls, thank you for helping Ben make tonight unforgettable," I say with a genuine smile.

We are congratulated by all our family and friends, and I'm completely surprised when I see my mom and dad appear in front of me. Apparently, Ben actually went and asked my dad for my hand in marriage, much to their delight, and he happily said yes. We eat, drink, and celebrate our new engagement. Just a few minutes before midnight, Ben takes me by the arm and leads me to the edge of the roof terrace. His arm snakes around my waist, and he pulls me close as we look upon the New York skyline. The view up here is breathtaking.

He leans down and looks into my eyes. "Were you surprised tonight?"

I smile. "I don't think I have ever been more surprised," I tell him with a smile.

"Good," he says, pleased. "I will continue to try and surprise you for the rest of our lives."

"I will continue to love that," I reply.

Ben kisses the top of my head. "On that note, I have one more surprise for you."

I turn to face him. "You're pregnant?"

Ben chuckles. "Not yet, Angel."

"Oh, that's disappointing," I say with a wink.

"I'm pretty sure we can practice making a baby a little later tonight, though, if you'd like."

Just the promise of seeing him naked has heat pooling between my thighs, and I bite my lip in anticipation. I know Ben has noticed because that cocky smirk on his face says it all. I catch his gaze and marvel for a moment at the beauty of his eyes. If eyes are truly the windows to the soul, then right now, his windows are wide open. He's completely bared himself to me, and I to him; this man who I will spend the rest of my life adoring. Behind us, people start the count down the time to midnight, but we continue to look in each other's eyes.

Ten... nine... eight... seven... six... five... four... three...

"I love you," he whispers as he leans in to take my lips.

...Two... "I love you, too."

...One...

HAPPY NEW YEAR!

. . .

Author Note:

Thank you so very much for reading Benjamin's story, The Ultimate Bid. If you want just a little more, Haylee and I wrote a short story about Jill and Ben's wedding, called Marrying Benjamin. You can download it here:
books2read.com/u/bMZrNX

Want even more of the Sapphires? You can read Drew and Hannah's story in a full-length, stand-alone, contemporary romance filled with lots of steam and has a nice happily-ever-after. Find out the seriously unique way Drew met Hannah and his struggle to make her his.
Keep turning the pages for a sneak peek!
You can grab the full story, The Auction Series, right here on any platform: http://bit.ly/AuctSer

CHAPTER
Seventeen

Five Months Later

I CLASP my hands nervously in front of me, turning my head to look at my brother standing beside me. It wasn't that long ago that our roles were reversed, and I was standing where he is now. How completely different it feels to know that my angel, my Jill, will be walking down this aisle any second to become my wife. No sooner than that thought crosses my mind, the traditional wedding march song starts, and my heart, already beating faster than normal, stampedes against my chest like a herd of wild horses.

I see the first glimmer of white as she steps through the arch of flowers at the end of the short aisle, breath stuck in my throat when she finally comes fully into view, and then gasp at how stunningly perfect she looks. I want so badly to look into her eyes, to see and have her see how much love exists right now, in this very moment between us, but her face his hidden behind a delicate lace veil.

"You're a lucky man, Benny." Drew whispers into my ear, his hand coming up to grip my shoulder.

"God damn right I am." I whisper back, still staring in awe at the vision walking toward me. My eyes sweep down the elegant dress she's wearing, and then back up to her face, where I can see her smiling, even through the lace, now that's she getting closer.

After what I know has only been a minute, possibly two, my bride-to-be finally comes to a stop beside me. She releases one hand from the bouquet of white lilies she's holding, and slides it into my waiting one as she looks over at me. "Fancy meeting you here."

I chuckle, unable to control the happiness coursing through me, smiling broadly at her in return. "I heard you were going to be here." I shrug, trying to be nonchalant, but fail miserably when I can't wipe the smile from my face. I lean toward her then and ever so softly whisper, "You look so beautiful my angel."

"Ladies and gentleman," the priest begins to speak, interrupting any other interaction between Jill and I, "thank you so much for being here to witness this blessed union of Jill Baldwin and Benjamin Michael Sapphire on this fifth day of May, two-thousand eighteen."

Jill's hand squeezes mine, her head turning slightly to look at me, her smile vibrant through the lace, and I know without a doubt that doing this; marrying her, is the absolute most right thing I've ever done in my life, and I squeeze her hand right back hoping it carries with it everything I'm feeling.

"Benjamin, Jill," the priest addresses us both, "I understand you have your own vows you would like to say to each other?"

I nod my head, Jill and I both answering yes in unison.

"Will you please turn and face each other and join your hands together?"

I watch as Jill passes her bouquet to Rae, who is standing to her left and then turns to face me, slipping both of her small hands into my larger ones.

"Benjamin, please proceed when you're ready."

I thought this would be so much harder to do when the time came. I thought finding the words to say, to describe how I feel about her, our love, our life together would be difficult. Standing here before her though, her fingers clasped in mine, her heart given completely to mine, I find they come as naturally as water flowing down a stream after a spring rain.

I clear my throat and begin to speak. "Jill, on this day, which will now be the happiest of all my days up until this point in my life, I take you to be my wife. I give you my heart as I give you my hands. The heart that is only whole again because of your love. I pledge my undying love, my devotion, my very soul to you as I join my life with yours. Wherever our journey leads, I will always be by your side, living, learning, loving, together. Forever. I love you so much."

"I love you too." She whispers in response, her hands clutching more tightly onto mine as I watch her lids blinking rapidly under her veil.

"Jill, please proceed with your vows when you're ready."

She nods her head and then looks straight at me. "Ben,

standing here in front of you and all the people we love so dearly, I promise to love you forever and am so honored to take you as my husband. I look forward to spending my days living with you, laughing with you, growing with you, and will cherish and carry your heart in mine for eternity. I started by calling you my boyfriend, and then my fiancé, and now, on this most perfect of days, I vow to love you forever as I get to call you my husband."

I want to sweep her up in my arms this very instant and crush my lips to hers, sealing our vows, and as I move forward to do just that, the priest grabs onto my arm to hold me back. "Let's exchange rings first, shall we?" He lets out a small laugh as I take a step back, nodding.

Drew taps me on the shoulder, placing Jill's ring into the palm of my hand when I turn to him. "Almost done," he smiles at me knowingly. I listen as the priest makes a speech about the importance of the rings, but can only focus on Jill, the rest of the world around me fading away. I watch as her lips lift into a smile and then as she mouths, *'pay attention'*, a soft giggle floating up under the lace.

"Ben, please place the ring you've selected for Jill on her left ring finger."

I take Jill's graceful hand in my calloused one, and place the band onto her slender finger and begin sliding it down its length as I speak. "Jill, I give you this ring to wear with love and joy. As this ring has no end, neither shall my love for you. I choose you to be my wife this day and forever more."

As I slide the ring completely on, she sniffles and then clasps her fingers with mine. "It's so beautiful Ben." She looks at me and then down at the ring, an eternity style, with black and white diamonds around the entire band. As soon as I saw it, I knew it would go perfectly with the engagement ring she already had.

"Jill, it's your turn to present your groom with the ring you've chosen."

I watch as Raeva hands her a ring, and then hold my hand out, her shaky fingers sliding the ring over my large finger. "Ben, I give you this ring as a symbol of my love and commitment for all the days of our lives. I choose you to my husband this day and forever more." She pushes the plain, quarter-inch, black platinum band all the way home and then looks up at me, a beaming smile on her face.

And finally, finally the words I've been waiting to hear. "It's my honor to now pronounce you husband and wife. Benjamin, you may kiss your bride."

I take a step forward, and using my fingers, lift the lace away from my angel's tear streaked face, then sweep her into my arms as I crush my lips against hers in a claiming kiss. Her arms wrap around my neck, her fingers latching onto my nape as she presses against me, kissing me back with equal fervor. After a moment, and to a chorus of cheers from our friends, we finally break apart, but remain connected, our hands still joined tightly.

"Ladies and Gentleman, it is with great pleasure that I present Mr. & Mrs. Benjamin Sapphire!"

IT FEELS LIKE A DREAM. The most wonderful of dreams. And I never want this moment to end. I look around at how amazing everything and everyone looks. My cheeks hurt from smiling so much, but I don't care because I don't think I'll ever be able to wipe this smile off my face. I am married to the man that is my entire universe, and I cannot imagine that there is a human being on this little planet made of dust and dirt, that is happier than I am, right here, right now.

The roof top looks amazing, and how fitting is it that we are getting married on the rooftop of a Sapphire Resort property; it's how we met after all.

The gown that Mikaela designed and made for me is fit for a queen. The dress has a bodice with amazing lace details and is tied with criss-crosses of silk ribbon up the back. The skirt looks like I am standing in waves of silk with a long train behind me. I look up at my husband, my chest tightening at the realization that he's officially and legally mine now.

"You ready, Mrs. Sapphire?"

A feeling of euphoria washes over me when I hear him call me that. "With you by my side, always Mr. Sapphire." I reply with a smile.

We make our way to the gorgeous table that has been set up for us. I have been so busy all day with preparations for the wedding, I have not eaten a single bite, and can't wait to sit down. We eat, drink, laugh and conversation flows freely while sharing this monumental time with some of our most favorite people. I'm eating with one hand, my other seemingly fused together with Ben's since the moment we said I do.

At some point, the band starts to play, and we're introduced for our first dance. We smile at each other and rise to our feet. Ben leads me to the dance floor and pulls me close against him, gently swaying me to the music. He leans down and kisses the tip of my nose.

"Are you happy?" I ask him.

"I am." He sighs contently. "But I'll be even happier when I can get you alone. I can't believe you made me sleep at Drew's last night." He gleams down at me. "One night away from you is one night too many."

He kisses me then. A gentle kiss, but one that's full of love and promises. He slides his lips from mine, moving them against my ear, his breath hot as he whispers, "And wife, no matter how perfect you look in this dress, I can not wait to peel it off of you."

"And I can't wait for you to peel it off of me." I admit breathily. I almost combust on the spot, desire coursing through my veins, every inch of my body feeling like it's on fire. I know this man practices what he preaches, and can't wait for him to get his hands on me. I glance over at our friends, who are all watching us with smiles on their faces.

"Are you thinking what I am thinking?" I ask as our eyes meet.

"Oh Angel, I fucking hope so."

WE MANAGED to stay for nearly another hour, and I think I can safely speak for us both that it was torture. As soon as we were able to escape, we headed straight to our waiting honeymoon suite. Butterflies danced in my belly, my desire for Ben so overwhelming, never having wanted him as much as I do right now. Is this what marriage does to someone?

The second we crossed the threshold into the room, our bodies fuse together, our lips crashing together. Tongues are dancing, hands are greedily exploring. Ben is powerful, intense, fierce. We are both totally consumed by our desire.

"Bedroom." He growls. We clumsily stumble our way through the living room, finally making our way into the bedroom. Ben pulls away and turns me around. He gently brushes my hair to the side, his breath hot against my neck as he whispers, "time to peel you out of this, Angel."

Agonizingly slow, he starts to undo the ribbon. His mouth caresses my shoulder, and when he gently bites, I nearly lose my mind. He whispers the dirtiest things as his fingers continue their quest to release me from this dress, heat pooling between my thighs. I let out a moan, and if I thought it would help, I would beg him to go faster.

He finally tugs at my gown, loose enough that it falls down my body until I'm standing in the pool of my dress wearing nothing but my stilettos and white panties. He whips me around to face him before pushing me down onto the bed. I bite my lip. The butterflies that were fluttering inside of my just a moment ago have flown away and have been replaced by fire burning in my belly.

Not taking his eyes off me once, Ben rids himself of his clothing and gets onto the bed, his eyes burning with a virile hunger. He removes his leg and prowls closer to me. He watches as my hand slides into my panties, a harsh breath sucked into his lungs as his eyes widen.

"I want to see." He tells me huskily as he reaches forward to rip the panties apart. He licks his lips as he watches me plunge two digits into my core. He pushes my legs further apart, his eyes glued to my center, then suddenly tugs my hand away, moving lightning fast toward my core. He takes my soaking fingers into his mouth and sucks without holding back. He throws my leg over his shoulder, his mouth connecting with my throbbing center, and begins lapping at my most intimate part, as if he's a parched man drinking from a well.

When he takes that bundle of nerves between his lips and sucks, I feel like I am slowly disintegrating with pleasure. I buck up off the bed, the stubble of his short beard rubbing against my thighs as his cheeks rise into a smile between my legs. He continues to lick, nibble and suck at me in earnest, the sweet pressure of my impending release building. And then he plunges two fingers inside of my walls, pumping them in a rapid pace, making beckoning motions as he exits. I explode, screaming his name, over and over, like a mantra as my orgasm overtakes me. My entire body is on total meltdown, and I swear it feels like every neuron in my brain has melted and is going to pour out of my ears any moment.

"Ben, please. I need you inside of me."

His eyes shine brightly at my words, the fiery look in his eyes making me feel like prey that just has been spotted by a predator. He grins and before I can even blink, he's on top of me, positioning himself at my entrance.

"Oh Angel, how I love to hear you beg for me." He tells me as he slides the head of his cock between my throbbing folds.

"Ben." I plead.

He smiles and then slams into me. Filling me completely.

I nearly cry from relief. I even welcome the slight sting. He pulls back out, slowly and then thrusts back into me. The pleasure is nearly indescribable. I beg for more as he continues to plunge into me, and when I feel another tsunami building inside of me, I beg him to come with me.

He bobs his head up and down, letting me know he's there, and then he lets out a growl as he slams into me a final time, his release exploding inside of me, my core clenching around his length as my nails rake down his back and I yell out his name.

"Holy fuck." I pant as I try to catch my breath.

"Amen to that." He replies.

After our heart rates have returned to a normal state, I curl into him, resting my head on his chest. "Who knew married sex is even better than engaged sex?"

"That was pretty fucking amazing." His voice vibrating under my cheek, before he suddenly rolls me over to hover over to grin salaciously down at me. "But I'm just getting started Mrs. Sapphire."

If you liked The Auction Series, and want a little bit more of the naughty, check out my Tempting Nights series. Each full-length book features a story about an escort from the elite Temptation Agency. Each book is a steamy, full length, stand-alone, and each one has a happily-ever-after.
The first book is called Tempting Secrets. You can check it out here:
https://geni.us/temptingsecrets

Afterword

If you made it this far in the book, I am thrilled, and so grateful that you liked the three books enough to read them in their entirety. Thank you, thank you, thank you!

If I could beg one more favor and ask you to leave a review if you're so inclined. It does not have to be long or wordy. A sentence or two describing your experience with the books is all it takes, but it makes such a big difference in getting the book seen by other readers.

You can find the link to the Auction Series here:
https://www.authormichellewindsor/books/

About the Author

Michelle Windsor is the author of over a dozen steamy, contemporary romances filled with alpha males and even stronger females.. She has achieved both Amazon and Barnes & Noble International Best Seller status, and was awarded Best Contemporary Romance Writer by Passionate Plume Ink in 2019. Her first book, The Winning Bid, was nominated for the Summit Indie Book Awards by Metamorph Publishing in 2017, and continues to be her best-selling book to date.

Michelle is married with three grown children, and lives north of Boston in the type of suburban neighborhood you read about in sweet romance books, (not hers)! When she's not working on another book, you can find her spending time with her husband, hanging out with her three sisters, or snuggled up with her three cats, yes three, watching a movie or reading a book.

You can find out more about Michelle, as well as links to all her books, on her webpage: www.authormichellewindsor.com

Also by Michelle Windsor

The Winning Bid:
https://geni.us/winningbid

The Final Bid:
https://geni.us/finalbid

The Ultimate Bid:
https://geni.us/ultimatebid

Losing Hope:
https://geni.us/losinghope

Love Notes:
https://geni.us/lovenotesbook

Catching Chase:
https://geni.us/catchingchase

Tempting Secrets:
https://geni.us/temptingsecrets

Tempting Tricks:
https://geni.us/temptingtricks

Tempting Justice:
https://geni.us/temptingjustice

Tempting Summer:

https://geni.us/temptingsummer

Tempting Nights Box Set Collection, Books 1 - 3

https://geni.us/temptingnightsboxset

Taking Flight:

https://geni.us/takingflight

Just One Christmas:

https://geni.us/justonechristmas